CW00557516

Bello:
hidden talent rediscovered!

Bello is a digital only imprint of Pan Macmillan,
established to breathe new life into previously published,
classic books.

At Bello we believe in the timeless power of the imagination,
of good story, narrative and entertainment and we want to use
digital technology to ensure that many more readers
can enjoy these books into the future.

We publish in ebook and Print on Demand formats
to bring these wonderful books to new audiences.

About Bello:

www.panmacmillan.com/imprints/bello

About the author:

www.panmacmillan.com/author/rcsherriff

R. C. Sherriff

On his return from the First World War, R. C. Sherriff settled in London, working as an insurance agent and writing plays in the evening. *Journey's End*, inspired by Sherriff's own experience of fighting, was his sixth play but the first to be given a professional production. It was an immediate, outstanding and phenomenal success. Thirty one separate productions ran concurrently around the world and it was translated into twenty six languages. Its success, however, was both a boon and a burden — while it allowed him to give up the day job and devote himself full-time to writing, it often overshadowed his later work or was used as the yardstick against which it was measured unfavourably.

Fortunately for Sherriff he was not only a playwright but also a novelist and a screenwriter. He wrote a best-selling novel, *A Fortnight In September* in 1931, and the screenplays for *The Invisible Man* (1933), *The Four Feathers* (1939) and classic films such as *Goodbye Mr Chips* (1939), for which he received an Oscar nomination, and *The Dambusters* (1955).

Although Sherriff was occupied as a playwright and screenwriter he did not lose his urge to write novels and he followed the success of his first novel with *The Hopkins Manuscript, Chedworth, Another Year* and others. Now, while *Journey's End* continues to define Sherriff's reputation, much of his work remains ripe for rediscovery.

R. C. Sherriff

ANOTHER YEAR

First published in 1948 by Heinemann

This edition published 2012 by Bello
an imprint of Pan Macmillan, a division of Macmillan Publishers Limited
Pan Macmillan, 20 New Wharf Road, London N1 9RR
Basingstoke and Oxford
Associated companies throughout the world

www.panmacmillan.com/imprints/bello
www.curtisbrown.co.uk

ISBN 978-1-4472-2101-2 EPUB
ISBN 978-1-4472-2100-5 POD

Copyright © R. C. Sherriff, 1948

The right of R. C. Sherriff to be identified as the
author of this work has been asserted in accordance
with the Copyright, Designs and Patents Act 1988.

Every effort has been made to contact the copyright holders of the material
reproduced in this book. If any have been inadvertently overlooked, the publisher
will be pleased to make restitution at the earliest opportunity.

You may not copy, store, distribute, transmit, reproduce or otherwise
make available this publication (or any part of it) in any form, or by any means
(electronic, digital, optical, mechanical, photocopying, recording or otherwise),
without the prior written permission of the publisher. Any person who does
any unauthorized act in relation to this publication may be liable to
criminal prosecution and civil claims for damages.

The Macmillan Group has no responsibility for the information provided by
any author websites whose address you obtain from this book ('author websites').
The inclusion of author website addresses in this book does not constitute
an endorsement by or association with us of such sites or the content,
products, advertising or other materials presented on such sites.

This book remains true to the original in every way. Some aspects may appear
out-of-date to modern-day readers. Bello makes no apology for this, as to retrospectively
change any content would be anachronistic and undermine the authenticity of the original.
Bello has no responsibility for the content of the material in this book. The opinions
expressed are those of the author and do not constitute an endorsement by,
or association with, us of the characterization and content.

A CIP catalogue record for this book is available from the British Library.

Visit www.panmacmillan.com to read more about all our books
and to buy them. You will also find features, author interviews and
news of any author events, and you can sign up for e-newsletters
so that you're always first to hear about our new releases.

PART ONE

Chapter One

Mr. Matthews had arranged to be called at seven that morning, but he was wide awake by five. With a long and strenuous day in front of him he tried to settle down for some more sleep, but after a while he gave it up and lay watching the moon go down behind the trees at the bottom of the Vicarage garden.

He thought of the village out there in the darkness, and he envied all the people in it. He envied them because they were content to go on living in Little Stanton until they died, and he wondered whether he had done a wise thing to surrender his security and happiness for the long thin chance of such a different kind of happiness.

His Bishop had doubted the wisdom of it. A Vicar who had gained such love and respect in his parish, he had said, should not become the unthinking slave of conscience. "I can't imagine Little Stanton without you," said the Bishop. "In fact, in many ways, you *are* Little Stanton."

Colonel Champion, the local Squire, had not gone so far as to say that. Only one man at a time could be Little Stanton—but the Colonel had spoken his mind when Mr. Matthews had announced his resignation. He had told him he was a downright fool to burn his boats and take a living in an East End slum at an age when sensible men were settling down to enjoy the fruits of a well-spent life. "You *know* you'll be a loss to this parish." said the Colonel—"how d'you know you'll be a gain to the one you're going to?"

What the Colonel really meant was that the cricket club was losing its only reliable Umpire and the Flower Show was losing in

Ruth Matthews, the Vicar's wife, an organiser who had made the Little Stanton Show the best in Dorset. Roger and Ruth Matthews had, in fact, a finger in every village pie and both well knew the sacrifice they were making.

Lying there in the darkness, he heard the owls come back from their night's hunting in Stanton Park and settle down in the hollow oak in the churchyard. He envied them because they too had no desire for wider fields and would go on living in Little Stanton until they died. His memory ran back across the years to the far-off day when he had made the resolution that he was only now fulfilling. He was nineteen—in his first year at Oxford, and he had come to London to see the boat race. He had stayed the week-end with an Uncle who was vicar of an East End parish, and he had made his resolution on the night before he left. It did not say much for his determination, he reflected, that he should have dallied for the best part of his lifetime.

His Uncle's Vicarage had stood in the cesspit of London, and young Roger Matthews had been appalled by what he saw. The old man, nearing eighty, was fighting a lonely battle against dirt and blasphemy and wretchedness, but the light of youth was in his eyes and the courage of youth was in his heart, and Roger had made his resolution on the last evening of his stay. He resolved to give up his plans for Colonial Service—go for the Church and give his life to the people of the slums.

It was a brave resolution, but it went astray. He became a clergyman, but he did not go to the slums. On the advice of his tutor he went as curate to a West Country town to gain experience in quiet surroundings before he began his harder task. "For five years," decided Roger—"and then the slums."

But in two years he was in love, and in three he was married. Ruth Desmond was the Vicar's daughter in nearby Little Stanton. She shared his resolution to work in the slums, and they began to make their plans. But her father's health declined: he wanted Roger to take his place, and Roger did not like refusing. "For five years," he said—"and then the slums."

But Little Stanton was a fascinating place, with meadows round it, and woods and streams, and the devil was hiding there, whispering every kind of temptation in Roger's ear. They made a host of friends; their daughter Rosemary was born, and there was always some compelling reason for postponing their departure. One thing led to another. A campaign was launched to restore the church, and they founded the Musical Society and the Flower Show to raise funds. But when the church was restored, the Flower Show and the Musical Society had flourished so well in Ruth's hands that they had to postpone their departure to look after them. Then there was the new cricket pavilion, the Boys' Club and the Natural History Society, all of which were Mr. Matthews' babies, and when a Roman Villa was discovered under a cornfield near the village, Mr. Matthews was appointed Secretary of the Excavation Committee, and it took a long time to dig the Villa up. It was fascinating work. Everything was fascinating in Little Stanton.

The original five years turned to ten, and ten to twenty. They never gave up the idea of working in the slums. They talked about it on summer evenings in the garden as the sun went down; they discussed it on moonlight walks in the Dorset lanes, but as the years went by and the ties of his pleasant parish grew ever stronger, Roger Matthews began to get a feeling that he never would go to that brawling slum of his youthful dream. But it was nice to go on talking about it because it eased his conscience.

Then one morning he woke up to face the fact that it was his fifty-seventh birthday. He looked out at the Vicarage garden and the sunlit trees in the distant park, and for the first time they gave him no happiness. It was now or never: in a few years he would be an old man, and while the fit of remorse was on him he wrote an advertisement to the *Church News*, announcing his desire to exchange his living for one in a poor neighbourhood of London.

He felt a good deal better when the advertisement was posted, and when no answer came he felt better still. He had shown his good faith. If no one desired to offer him a parish in the slums, none could blame him for staying where he was.

It was a shock when the letter had arrived from Mr. Todhunter, Vicar of St. Peter's, Woodbank. Mr. Todhunter wrote to say that he had just seen the advertisement and was willing, on account of his health, to exchange the parish of Woodbank for the country air of Little Stanton.

By that time Mr. Matthews had recovered from his attack of birthday remorse, and as he read the letter, Little Stanton seemed sweeter and more desirable than ever. But his challenge had been taken up. He had got to do something about it or brand himself for good as a backslider and hypocrite.

He knew nothing of London and had only vaguely heard of Woodbank, but a neighbouring Vicar told him that it was just the kind of parish for a man who wanted to work amongst the poor and under-privileged. The Bishop bore this out—with the reservation that a man so valued in his parish should think carefully before leaving it.

The Bishop's reservation gave Mr. Matthews an honourable opportunity to excuse himself and stay where he was, but when he discussed it with his wife she had said—"It's what you've always wanted in your heart, isn't it?—a difficult parish to test your faith. Of course you can refuse it, but if you do, I don't think you'll ever be really happy again in Little Stanton—and I don't think I would either. We should always be thinking of the might have beens."

Ruth had decided him, and with the decision made he was conscious of exhilaration and a self-respect that he had not felt for years. He knew then that he had never been really instrumental in bringing happiness to anyone in Little Stanton because happiness was woven into the fabric of that placid little place. In Woodbank he would be against stark misery and dirt, spiritual hunger and depravity. He would have his chance to prove what he was made of. The dying embers of his resolution glowed again, and he wrote to Mr. Todhunter agreeing to the exchange—promising to spend a night with him in Woodbank to arrange the details. He announced his decision to the parish and spent his evenings scheming and planning his new work in the slums with the ardour of a Crusader, and Ruth, he knew, was proud of his decision.

There were dark moments of doubt: there was one that morning as he lay watching the moon go down, waiting for the time to get up and dress and catch the early train to London. But as dawn came his doubts were gone. He no longer envied the placid people of Little Stanton who would drowse on in the village until they died: he no longer envied the owls in the hollow oak, and when Emily the housekeeper brought up his early cup of tea and said: "It's a dirty foggy morning, sir—pity it isn't better for your journey," he cared no more about the fog than Coeur de Lion cared about the rough sea in the Channel on the first day of his crusade to the Holy City. He was burning to be up and go. Before the sun went down that day he would see for the first time the town and people to whom he would give his best and final years.

It was in truth a dirty morning. A damp November mist lay over the stubble fields that fringed the rambling branch line to Yeovil Junction and the mist turned to a stagnant yellow fog as he reached the London outskirts. The train hung about in the suburbs and was an hour late at Waterloo. He had some coffee and a meat pie at the Buffet and set off to cross the city for the trains that went to Woodbank. He was a countryman by birth and temperament and the turmoil of London dazed him. He got into the wrong tube train and was half-way to Hampstead before he found out that he was going north instead of east. It was three o'clock before he arrived at Fenchurch Street, and a premature brown twilight lay over London as the train drew out on the last stage of his journey.

But the weather did not damp the ardour of his new adventure. He had the compartment to himself and from the window he could see the huddled houses and the maze of crowded streets. He could almost feel the warm breath of the seething humanity that surged in them, and he longed to be down there rubbing shoulders with them—understanding them and making friends. Here at last were the people he was pledged to work for. They would be different, he knew, from the humdrum West Country kind: different in manner and outlook and thought and speech, but the same at heart, and keener in desire.

Now and then he saw a church spire rising from the misty plain of roof-tops and he caught a glimpse of a cloistered house with trees around it that he guessed must be a Vicarage. He saw a clergyman standing at a street corner, talking and laughing with a group of boys, and his heart went out to him as a comrade in the days ahead.

There seemed to be a great many stations, so close together that the train only got up speed for a minute at a time. They were all alike—drab little chocolate-coloured stations badly lit and difficult to identify, for nobody called out the names of them as the train drew in. He began to worry in case he went past Woodbank in the gathering darkness, but he managed to spot the name of one of them, and from the map on the carriage wall he counted five ahead before his destination.

East London had been clear of fog, but it seemed to be coming up now from the river and the train began to crawl. It stopped for ten minutes outside the fifth station, and when it drew in he wondered whether he had counted them correctly. There was nothing to tell him that it was Woodbank and nobody in sight to help him. The guard was at the other end and the people who had got out were straggling away from him towards the exit. He took the chance, gathered up his bag and umbrella and clambered out.

"Is this Woodbank?" he enquired of the ticket collector at the gate.

The collector, whose head seemed permanently fixed through years of examining tickets in uncertain light, did not look up, but mumbled something that might have been "yes" or possibly "no".

"Can you tell me whether St. Peter's Vicarage is near the station?" asked Mr. Matthews.

The man shook his head, turned his back and went into a box. Mr. Matthews hesitated, thinking the collector was going to turn up a Directory to find out where the Vicarage was, but when he sat on a stool and began to eat a piece of cake out of a paper bag Mr. Matthews realised that the matter was closed, and went down the stone steps into an ice-cold subway that smelt of carbolic.

The fog was drifting up the side streets from the Thames and the lights were coming on in the gaunt brick buildings round the railway station. The High Street, with its tramlines and forlorn uncared-for shops, looked bleak and desolate, and stretched away in both directions as far as he could see. The river was hidden by the houses but he could hear the tugs hooting and he could see the cranes and derricks over the roof-tops against the tarnished relic of a sunset.

It was different from what he had expected. He had pictured narrow streets full of shouting children and men with hand-barrows selling fish and women in hair-curlers leaning out of windows. He had expected a glare of lights and a jostle of humanity, but except for a few dejected people waiting at a tram stop there was no one in sight. It was apparently Woodbank's early closing day, and the shops were dark and empty.

He looked around him, wondering which way to go. Down in Dorset, if you wanted to find the Vicarage in an unfamiliar town, the first person you met would tell you without hesitation. Up here in London people did not seem so well informed about their Vicarages. The ticket collector neither knew nor cared, and a little hunch-backed paper-seller outside the station had told him to ask a policeman. But there was no policeman in sight: it was getting darker and foggier and he felt dispirited and tired.

Normally he would have taken the way that looked as if it led towards the centre of the town, but the High Street gave no clue of going anywhere in either direction except into a murky darkness.

He turned to the right and set off at random, and presently saw some men at a street corner, leaning against the wall outside a public-house. They would be local men, he thought, and crossed over to them.

"I'm looking for St. Peter's Vicarage," he said: "I wonder whether you can help me?"

The men stopped talking and stared at him as if he had asked the way to the moon.

"There's no Vicarage round here," said one of them at last.—"Not round here there isn't."

Mr. Matthews hesitated. "This *is* Woodbank, isn't it?" he asked.

"It was when I got up this morning," said the man.

They all laughed at this, and Mr. Matthews felt it proper as the new Vicar, to join in. But when the laughter had subsided, and the men merely stared at him again, he said: "Thank you," and went on down the street.

He saw a man standing at the door of a half-shuttered pawn-shop: a pale, bulbous man in shirt-sleeves with a strip of shirt bulging out between the bottom of his tight waistcoat and the top of his trousers. He had a boil on his neck with a piece of plaster over it and one foot was bandaged up inside a carpet slipper that was slit to take the bandage. His big puffy face looked green and ghostly in the twilight.

"I wonder if you can tell me," asked Mr. Matthews, "the way to St. Peter's Vicarage?"

The man shook his head.

"Do you know anyone who might be able to help me?"

"No," said the man.

Woodbank High Street looked endless and more desolate than ever as he walked on. It looked as if it went on and on until it circled a fog-bound world.

He came to some boys playing at the mouth of a dark alley. They were hopping round some chalk squares on the pavement, and the game was a new one to Mr. Matthews. He wanted to find the Vicarage before it was completely dark, but after his rebuffs he thought he would break the ice with a friendly enquiry about the game before he asked the way. He got on well and easily with boys. In Little Stanton he knew them all as well as their parents knew them. He had christened most of them, and some had grown big enough to bowl him out at cricket on the green. But the pleasant days in Little Stanton were nearly over now. He had got to start again and get to know the Woodbank boys, and this seemed a good opportunity to begin.

"That's a new game to me," he said, "what d'you call it?"

They had not seen him coming in the dusk and the sound of his voice brought a sudden, startled silence. The boy who was hopping round the square stopped dead and stared, still standing on one leg like a stork. The silence was embarrassing, and Mr. Matthews wished he had chosen a more opportune time, in daylight, to make his friendly enquiry about the game.

"Is it your own invention?" he asked.—"How d'you score?"

There was still no answer. The boys looked wary and suspicious. Then a lanky boy with long black hair broke the silence. He was leaning against a lamp-post and he went on leaning.

"We can play what we like, can't we?" he growled.

"Of course you can," said Mr. Matthews, wishing more than ever that he hadn't started it. "It looked a good game and I just wondered what it was called, that's all."

"Everybody plays it," said the boy.—"Everybody knows what it's called."

Mr. Matthews saw his mistake. The game was evidently traditional in Woodbank. He could not have asked a sillier question if he had walked on to a village green and asked what a game of cricket was called.

"I come from the country," he explained. "I'm quite a stranger here. As a matter of fact I'm trying to find St. Peter's Vicarage. I wonder if any of you can tell me where it is?"

There was another silence, and then the ice broke with unexpected suddenness. Every boy began telling him loudly where the Vicarage was, but every boy, it seemed, had a different theory.

"That's it, down there—with the flag pole on it!" came a shrill voice.

"That's the Post Office, you twerp. Everybody knows that's the Post Office!"

"It's up by the tram depot!"

"It's down by the river—with a cross on top!"

"That's where they put the drowned men. They got one there now from under dad's barge—all blue and swelled up, dad said."

Some bigger boys came down the alley to see what the noise was about, and the argument grew strident and aggressive. One said the Vicarage was behind the goods yard.

"'Tisn't behind the goods yard!" shouted a fat boy with his stockings round his ankles.

"Bet you it is!"

"You're barmy!"

"Who's barmy?"

"You!—You're boss-eyed, too!"

There was a resounding slap and the fight was on. The fat boy caught his opponent's shirt and ripped it out of his trousers: there were yells of delight and shouts of encouragement; windows flew up and women shrieked out threats: the two boys toppled over and fought in the gutter, grunting and pummelling and wriggling like eels, and a policeman sailed out of the fog. There were shouts of warning and a sudden silence, and Mr. Matthews, dismayed by the disturbance he had unwittingly caused, thought it best to move quietly away.

"What's all this?" he heard the policeman say.

A chorus of shrill, excited voices answered. "It was him!—he started it!"

"Who?" demanded the policeman.

"Him in the black overcoat—there he goes!—over there!"

"Here!—You!" shouted the policeman. "Come here!"

Mr. Matthews felt cold and sick. He was a shy, retiring man who hated any kind of public scene, and nothing like this had ever happened in his life. Years ago, as an undergraduate at Oxford, he had once been involved in the breaking of a street lamp after an exuberant college dinner. He had been chased by a policeman and had escaped up a tree in the park, but that was fair sport and everybody had enjoyed it, including the policeman. But this was a very different thing—full of obscure, alarming possibilities. He was a stranger—quite unknown in Woodbank, and after what he had seen of these boys he put nothing past them. They would back up with one accord any wild accusation that any one of them might throw against him on the spur of the moment. Assault . . . attempted kidnapping . . . all manner of squalid complications raced through his mind as the policeman advanced upon him with the silent, expectant boys in the background. He had been a fool to walk away when he should have stood his ground and helped the policeman to stop the fight. That alone was enough to throw suspicion on him. He pictured a sordid police court with boy after boy coming forward to affirm the same fantastic charge . . . he caught a glimpse in the dusk of one of the boys who had fought in the gutter. His nose was bleeding . . . it was a revolting sight . . . like fruit juice trickling out of a suet pudding. He would probably be blamed for that as well. The policeman towered above him . . . a young man, big and powerful, with a hard, uncompromising face.

"What were you doing to these boys?" he demanded.

Mr. Matthews tried to make his voice sound calm. He loosened his woollen muffler to show the clerical collar beneath it.

"I'm the new Vicar of Woodbank," he said. "I asked if they could direct me to St. Peter's Vicarage and I'm afraid it led to a quite unnecessary argument. I assure you I did nothing to start the fight."

The policeman looked him slowly up and down and his eyes came to rest upon the small black bag he was carrying. Mr. Matthews had read of criminals disguising themselves as clergymen to help them in their evil work and he guessed what the policeman was thinking. But there was nothing remotely incriminating in the bag: a pair of blue pyjamas—a change of linen—a razor, and a detective novel . . . the detective novel, possibly—but that was too absurd! He was on the point of offering the bag for inspection when the policeman shot out a question full of new and alarming implications.

"I don't know of any new Vicar coming here," he said.—"Can they identify you at the Vicarage?"

Mr. Matthews was done. Nobody could identify him at the

Vicarage: nobody in Woodbank, for that matter, and hardly a soul in London could identify him personally as Mr. Matthews. He was a man of the West Country, and all his friends were there. The prospect of a night in a police cell loomed ahead. The new Vicar gaoled pending identification ... with vague and ugly rumours of a scene in the dark with some boys and a policeman! Whatever happened—however completely he was cleared, the rumours would stay and his career would be ended. The whole thing was a nightmare.

"As a matter of fact," he stammered—"I've only communicated with Mr. Todhunter by post. He wouldn't be able to identify me personally, but ..."

"Have you anything to show who you are?"

Mr. Matthews was in such confusion that it took him a space to remember the letter in his pocket. By mere chance he had taken it off his desk as he was leaving home that morning. With his trust in providence restored he fumbled for it and drew it out.

"Here's a letter from the retiring Vicar," he said, "asking me to spend the night at the Vicarage to discuss the exchange of our livings. ... Mr. Todhunter will identify the letter, I'm sure."

The policeman flashed his torch on it and returned it grudgingly. He seemed quite disappointed.

"All right," he said. "We have to be careful about strangers in this neighbourhood. I'd advise you to be more careful how you talk to people you don't know—specially these kids. They're up to anything."

The boys, who had waited hopefully for something dramatic to happen, took this as a warning and rapidly dispersed.

"I assure you," declared Mr. Matthews—"I had no sinister plans for stealing their pocket-money!"

His attempt at a friendly joke misfired. The man's face was like granite.

"I still don't know where the Vicarage is," he said, "I wonder if you can tell me?"

"It's in the old town," said the policeman. "You're going the wrong way. Go back past the Railway Station and take the third to the right by the Brewery. Keep straight down St. Peter's Lane till you see the railings."

"Thank you. Good night."

"Good night."

With a sigh of relief he went on his way, but he still had an uneasy feeling that he was under suspicion.

He had expected things to be rough and ready in Woodbank, but he was hardly prepared for a local policeman to warn him against the dangers of talking to his own parishioners.

He had wanted a 'difficult' parish. There did not seem much doubt that he had got it. He turned when he came to St. Peter's Lane, half expecting to see the policeman trailing him, but he was quite alone.

Chapter Two

St. Peter's Lane was old and narrow, with high brick walls on either side that turned the grey light of the evening into sudden darkness. Some big trees loomed beyond the walls, and Mr. Matthews, who had read up all he could find about the history of Woodbank, imagined they stood in the derelict gardens of the fine old houses that were built here in the days when the town had been a fashionable resort from London. Sheridan the playwright and Gibbon the historian had lived here for a time, and Mr. Matthews pictured them walking in these hidden gardens, planning their work on summer nights beneath those silent, fogbound trees. The houses, he guessed, had been pulled down by now, or converted into factories, for the old arched doors that led into the gardens were falling to pieces, and some had jagged holes in them that opened into black, mysterious spaces. This was evidently the "Old Town" that the policeman had spoken of, but there was no sign of any pride or interest in its past. It was a melancholy place, neglected and forgotten. As he went on the fog grew thicker and he could smell the damp odour of the river.

He came at last to the railings that enclosed the Vicarage. It was difficult to find the gate in the darkness, and still more difficult to open it, for it had sunk on its hinges and he had to lift it and push hard before it moved. The ironwork was thick and lumpy, as if it had been repainted many times with no attempt to remove the rust and old paint first.

A big chestnut tree stood close inside the garden, and the path was soft and slippery with fallen leaves. He was puzzled by the desolation and silence. The Vicarages in Dorset were busy, cheerful places, with people calling at all hours of the day and night, but the house ahead of him was like the home of a recluse ... ghostly and forbidding in the darkness. A dim light shone through the frosted panel of the door and he felt his way towards it, probing the uncertain path with his umbrella.

The door-bell, like the gate, was heavy and difficult, and he had to pull the rusty handle three times before he heard a slow, reluctant jangling in the distance. He was ready to be told that he had come to the wrong house, but the woman who opened the door expected him. "You're Mr. Matthews?" she said. "The Vicar is waiting for you."

There was a grandfather clock in the hall, some gloomy furniture, and a smell of boiled mutton. Boiled mutton in normal times offended him, but it was pleasant and reassuring now. He had begun to feel something uncanny and inhuman about the house, but the mutton must have come from a normal butcher's shop and the smell suggested that someone in the house was normal enough to cook it. He put his belongings on a chair beside the grandfather clock, and followed the woman down a twilit passage.

The study, like the rest of the house, was dark and gloomy, with heavy, tight-drawn curtains and a musty smell of carpets and old books, but the Vicar himself was a complete surprise. After what he had seen of the surroundings, Mr. Matthews was prepared to meet some frail and ghostly creature, sucked dry of life by the house he lived in, but Mr. Todhunter was so big and rosy and exuberant that it looked as if it was he who had sucked the vitality out of everything surrounding him. He was a huge man, with a magnificent head of sleek white hair, bright blue eyes and a glowing pink face. His shoulders were massive and his forearms bulged beneath his coat sleeves like a wrestler's. He was a bit too healthy-looking, thought Mr. Matthews, to be really healthy, and there was something about his exuberance that did not ring quite true. His hand was warm and clammy, like a poultice.

"Well—here we are at last!" he boomed. "Thought you had fallen in the river and got drowned!"

"I had a job to find the way," said Mr. Matthews—"the fog's getting bad outside." He did not mention his adventure with the boys and the policeman. He had a feeling that his host was the kind of man who would relate the story with relish to everyone he met.

"Well, you're here," said Mr. Todhunter—"and that's all that matters. What about some tea?"

Mr. Matthews said he would like some very much, and Mr. Todhunter made the light fittings rattle as he trod heavily across the room.

"Mrs. Burgin!" he shouted. "Tea! You must try a piece of Mrs. Burgin's cherry cake," he said. "It's excellent ... quite excellent!"

"Now then—make yourself at home!—After all, it's your Vicarage now—or very soon will be!" He laughed as though he were extremely glad that it very soon would be: he waved a fat hand towards a thin leather arm-chair and lowered himself with a grunt on to a sofa by the fire.

"Quite a journey from Little Stanton," he said.

"Quite a long one," replied Mr. Matthews, who felt that he had travelled from another world.

"Lovely place," mused Mr. Todhunter.—"... One of the loveliest in England, if you ask me. Years ago I went for a walking tour in Dorset and stayed a night at your little Inn there. I saw that old Vicarage of yours, and the Church, and I've never forgotten it. When I saw your advertisement in the *Church News* I was on it like a knife. If it isn't rude to ask, what d'you want to give it up for?"

Mr. Matthews was not prepared for such an abrupt question so early in the proceedings, and his host was quick to notice his hesitation. "Trouble?" he enquired.

The idea of "trouble" in Little Stanton made Mr. Matthews laugh.

"No," he answered.—"There's no trouble. I suppose one might call it a matter of conscience. I've been Vicar of Little Stanton for a long time, and in many ways I would be happy and content to stay there for the rest of my life. It's a charming place, as you say, with charming people, but I've been feeling for some while—and my wife has felt the same—that work under such easy conditions hardly justified one's vocation to the priesthood."

He paused, and Mr. Todhunter looked at him so blankly that he felt confused.

"I'm afraid that sounded rather pompous," he said, "I didn't really mean it that way. I don't pretend to be a born missionary or an inspired preacher or even to be giving up an easy life out of any lofty motive. I'm afraid it's a purely selfish motive if we come down to plain words. I'm getting along in years now, and I've spent my whole life in country parishes. I ought to have done what I'm doing now when I was a younger man, but I've still got my health and strength and I hope it's not too late. I want to make these final years a test of everything I have to give, by working in the London slums and doing my best for the people here. I'm afraid that sounds just as pompous as the first thing I said. I'm not good at explaining myself, but I'm sure you know what I mean."

Mr. Todhunter did not answer at once. He went on staring at his guest in blank surprise.

"You ... you mean," he said at last—"you mean that you are coming to Woodbank with the sole purpose of working among the people here?"

It was the turn of Mr. Matthews to look surprised. "I thought that was the usual purpose of men who work in the London slums," he answered.

Mr. Todhunter hesitated. There was a queer look in his eyes and Mr. Matthews had a feeling that his host was thinking quickly, to adjust himself to something that he had not expected.

"You seem surprised that I should want to work among these people," he said. "Is there any special reason why I shouldn't?"

Mr. Todhunter laughed. "Not at all!" he declared. "I ... I'm afraid I was rather misled by one of your letters when you mentioned that you were nearly sixty. One naturally associates the arduous kind of work that you anticipate with a younger man. I had assumed that you were coming to Woodbank for some personal reason ... to be near relatives in London—or to write a book, perhaps, in semi-retirement. But it's a fine thing," he went on hastily—"a very fine thing that you are doing!"

Mr. Todhunter was himself again—easy and exuberant, but there was something in his manner that filled Mr. Matthews with a vague dismay. His host was concealing something: what it was he could not guess, but of one thing he was certain: Todhunter was desperately anxious to get out of Woodbank: he had nearly said something that might have frightened his successor away: he had barely saved himself in time and was now working for all he was worth to cover up his mistake. . . .

"If more men of your age and experience would do what you are doing," he said, "the Church would be in a better position than it is to-day. The slums are *not* the sole preserves of younger men. Youth has vigour ... enthusiasm ... zeal ... but not the mature outlook and toleration that counts for more than anything in these poor districts. If it were not for my health ... my bronchial trouble ..."

The more the big man talked the more surely Mr. Matthews felt that some unwholesome mystery lay hidden in the background. The Vicarage was desolate. He knew by the rusty gate that few people ever came here: he had learned from his enquiries on the way that nobody even knew there was a Vicarage at all. . . .

"I came to Woodbank deliberately," he said, "because it was a poor, rough neighbourhood ... 'difficult' was the word my Bishop used when I consulted him. I am prepared for difficulties. . . . I expected them, but if there are any unusual problems, then I think it is only fair that I should know about them in advance. I admit that Woodbank is not quite the kind of place that I anticipated, but . . ."

Mr. Todhunter looked up with a start.

"In what way?" he asked quickly.

"I had expected the Church and the Vicarage to be more in the centre of the town . . . in closer contact with the people . . . it seems to be so remote."

Mr. Todhunter brightened up. The word "remote" appealed to him: he took it up eagerly and began to enlarge upon it.

"You're right!" he declared. . . . "It *is* remote!—that is exactly the problem you have just asked about!"

"It shouldn't be an insuperable problem."

"No"—said Mr. Todhunter rather vaguely.—"It shouldn't be. . . ." There was a knock at the door and the big man looked up with relief. "Ah!" he cried . . . "here's the tea!—Good!—put it down here, Mrs. Burgin."

He fell upon the tray with vigour. "Now then!" he said.—"Milk? . . . sugar? . . . Have a piece of Mrs. Burgin's famous cherry cake!"

He embarked upon a discussion of the weather—then topical affairs, with special reference to a recent earthquake in China. He had been born in China, he explained. His father had been a Missionary there, and on one occasion they had experienced an earthquake of severe proportions.

Mr. Matthews had been hungry when he arrived, but his appetite for tea had gone. The cherry cake in any case fell dismally below the glowing prediction of his host. It was heavy and sickly: the cherries seemed to have been forced to the top in a gluey mass by the sheer weight of the bottom of it, and it cloyed on his palate and stuck in his throat. Whenever Mr. Todhunter paused for breath he was conscious of the deep, suffocating silence that surrounded the dismal house, seeping into every corner of it—seeping into his own flesh and bones. He thought wistfully of the kind of Vicarage he had pictured here; throbbing with the life and movement of the crowded town: of children's voices beneath the windows as they played around the railings, and the rumble of traffic and the footsteps of passers-by, and the bell ringing to announce visitors with every kind of problem. There was silence, at night, in Little Stanton, but that was a clean country silence, broken by men returning from the Inn and the hooting of the owls. Here there was the stagnant silence of a tomb.

"Have some more cake?" said Mr. Todhunter. "Good, isn't it?"

"Excellent," replied Mr. Matthews—"but I won't have any more. I don't eat much cake."

He decided to try a lighter note to catch his host off guard and glean a little more about the mystery. "If there's a ghost in this Vicarage—or a devil in the Church," he said, "let's hear about it!"

Mr. Todhunter laughed heartily. "I can reassure you on that!" he said. "I've lived here seven years and I declare it free of ghosts of every shape and size—and the church, I guarantee, is innocent of devils!—As a matter of fact," he added with a touch of earnestness—"you will find a wonderfully devoted little circle round St. Peter's Church: mostly old people, of course, but very loyal. I have asked the two Churchwardens in to meet you this evening. They are typical of our little community here. You can talk to them and see for yourself."

"You describe the community as a 'little' one." said Mr. Matthews. "I understood this parish had eight thousand people in it?"

"Oh yes—quite that," said Mr. Todhunter rather vaguely.

"What is the average attendance at church on Sundays?"

Mr. Todhunter hesitated. "I would say, well . . . about thirty-five or forty."

"Thirty-five or forty out of eight thousand!" gasped Mr. Matthews.

"It isn't much," agreed Mr. Todhunter—"but it's very regular. Even in the worst weather we get over thirty."

At seven o'clock the two Churchwardens came in to meet their future Vicar. Mr. Cheesewright, the Vicar's Warden, was a nervous, disheveled little man who looked as if he had recently been run over. He practised in Woodbank as a dentist. Mr. Harper, the People's Warden, was a retired Income Tax official: tall and stout and firmly established in his own esteem. They talked a lot about the routine business of the church but never mentioned the condition of the parish. They spoke in high terms of the Parochial Church Council, especially of a Mrs. Bannister Paget, whom they described as a great woman: the life and soul of everything. They agreed to bring along the most ardent members of the Council, including Mrs. Bannister Paget, for an informal chat with Mr. Matthews on the evening he arrived to begin his duties, and they spoke in the most feeling terms of Mr. Todhunter and how sorry everybody was to lose him.

At eight o'clock Mr. Matthews had supper with his host. It was, as he had feared, the mutton he had smelt on his arrival—stewed with turnips and onions, with rather too much seasoning. There was a steamed jam pudding, flavoured with cinnamon, and a cup of luke-warm coffee. Despite his glossy appearance Mr. Todhunter was a teetotaler. They drank water throughout the meal, and Mr. Matthews would have given anything for a whisky and soda or a glass of sherry to relieve the weight of his increasing depression.

He tried to find out more about Woodbank: he asked about the history of its church and the work of the people and the social activities of the town, but Mr. Todhunter answered briefly, without interest, and turned the conversation back to anecdotes of China. Details of their coming exchange of Vicarages were discussed. To save expense they agreed to share the same furniture van, taking Mr. Todhunter's furniture early one morning and returning with Mr. Matthews' property in the afternoon. "By the way," said Mr. Todhunter, "I sent off a box of my books to-day—in advance, if you'd not mind putting them somewhere till I arrive."

Mr. Matthews said he would, but he had a feeling that Mr. Todhunter had sent them in advance to stake his claim and lessen the chance of Mr. Matthews altering his mind about coming to Woodbank.

Mr. Todhunter tried to persuade Mr. Matthews to exchange the curtains and carpets at the Little Stanton Vicarage for those at present in position at Woodbank. He argued that curtains and carpets never fitted properly in other houses, but Mr. Matthews knew that his wife would loathe the dank and musty stuff at

Woodbank and politely declined. Mr. Todhunter was offended: the conversation tailed off, and when Mr. Matthews made his long journey the excuse for an early retirement, his host looked pleased and said it was a wise thing to go to bed directly when one was tired.

He led his guest up the narrow, half-lit stairs.

"We haven't had a guest for quite a time," he said, "but Mrs. Burgin knows how to make people comfortable. Call out if you want anything. The lavatory is down there," he added, waving a plump hand along a passage steeped in darkness. "Good night."

Mr. Matthews closed the door with a sigh of relief. He had the detective novel in his bag, and he wanted to relax and read for half an hour before he tried to sleep.

But the room was not arranged for reading in. The only light, in a hard, frosted globe, hung close up against the ceiling above the dressing-table. He would have to move most of the furniture before he could get the solitary armchair under it to read by, and Mr. Todhunter would hear the commotion and come up to find out what was going on. So he decided to go straight to bed and lie there even if he could not sleep.

The bedroom was cold and the bed looked damp, but the air was stagnant, and he drew back the heavy curtains to open the window.

It was dark and foggy and uncannily quiet outside. The window looked out on to St. Peter's Lane, and he could see the chestnut tree, swollen by the fog, with a dense black pool of shadow under it. At the corner of the lane there was street lamp, and the tall railings that enclosed the Vicarage loomed against its eerie light. Mr. Matthews shivered. The house was more like a prison than a Vicarage, and he had a premonition that it would be his prison until the end of his days. He had a desperate longing to steal downstairs and take his hat and coat and escape from the deadly, doom-wrecked place while he still had time. But in his heart he knew that there was no escape. He had talked too much in Little Stanton to go back on it now: everybody knew that he had deliberately chosen a difficult parish: he would make himself a laughing-stock if he went back and said it was a bit too difficult and he wasn't going after all.

He had no inkling of the mysterious thing that lay between St. Peter's Church and the people of Woodbank. It was something strange and evil and insuperable. Todhunter was a cheerful, vigorous man who would have made friends with anybody under ordinary conditions, but Todhunter, after seven years, knew scarcely a soul outside the small "devoted" circle. Had it been some normal problem, Todhunter would have discussed it frankly and advised his successor on means to fight it. But Todhunter knew that the thing could not be fought: he knew that it was hopeless and kept silent in fear that his successor would refuse the task.

He looked down at the lifeless garden and knew that there was no way out for him. He could hardly confess failure and apply for a move within two years . . . two of the precious years he had set aside for the best work of his life. He wondered what two years in this ghostly house would do to his spirit and resolution. He drew the curtains and began to undress for bed.

He tried to induce sleep by going, in imagination, for a walk through the Dorset lanes, but every turning brought him back to Woodbank High Street, and a crowd of leering little boys who shouted: "It was him!—he started it!"

Now and then he heard a clock chime in the distance, and the mournful hooting of a tug on the fog-bound river.

Several times he tasted the unpleasant seasoning in the mutton stew, and it was nearly dawn before he fell into an uneasy sleep.

Chapter Three

Mr. Matthews had arranged to stay in Woodbank until the afternoon, so that Mr. Todhunter could show him the church and introduce him to the organist before he left, but soon after breakfast he began to smell the mutton stew again, and he made the fog an excuse to hurry away to catch an earlier train. He lunched at Waterloo and arrived back in Little Stanton in time for tea.

As he drew near home he began to wonder how he would break the dismal news of Woodbank to his wife. Ruth was all in favour of his plans to work in the slums, but she was a country woman born and bred, and her idea of a London slum was even more colourful and romantic than his had been. She was more interested in people than in church affairs and was looking forward eagerly to making friends with those in Woodbank. That, he feared, was going to be denied her. She loved a graceful home, and had made the Vicarage at Little Stanton a delight to live in, but in Woodbank she would have a gaunt, musty house that nothing in the world could beautify. She had made a garden at Little Stanton that strangers stopped their cars to see, but in Woodbank the garden was a dank, walled-in place like a prison yard. It was hard to think of Ruth in a place like Woodbank. About his daughter he had time enough to worry. Rosemary still had a year at boarding school and they could send her if necessary to spend the holidays with friends. But his wife's fate was bound to his: what happened to him must happen to her, and it worried him so much on the journey home that he almost forgot his own cruel disappointment.

She saw him coming down the footpath from the station and went to meet him. She was bursting for news and began asking a host of questions before they got back to the house.

Over tea he began gently by saying that Woodbank was "not quite what they had expected", but as Ruth had not the remotest idea what to expect, this only tantalised her and made her more enthusiastic, and he waited until they had started out for their evening walk before he told her the whole heart-breaking story.

"If I were ten years younger," he said—"I wouldn't mind, but when you're nearly sixty there isn't time to waste in a hopeless place like Woodbank. Even if I got out of it in a couple of years I would go with a stigma of failure, and I don't think I'd have the confidence and energy to start again. I've been a fool, Ruth—I ought to have seen the place for myself before I decided to go there. I've made a hopeless mess of things. I've wrecked everything we planned, and I'm awfully sorry."

When he had finished she walked along beside him in silence.

"Of course I'm not bound, even now, to go to Woodbank," he added. "I'm not Vicar there until I've been instituted and I could still tell Mr. Todhunter that I've changed my mind. But he's arranged everything to come here, and I can't see how it's possible to go back on it now."

Ruth was still silent, and it began to get on his nerves. "If you haven't anything to say," he said, "we might as well go home."

"I don't know what to say," she answered, "because I don't understand what on earth you're so worked up and disappointed about. It must have been the fog or that mutton stew that upset you. You wanted a difficult parish and you've got it, but you couldn't in reason expect it to be 'difficult' in exactly the way that suited your convenience. If it had been, then it wouldn't be difficult at all, and there'd be no point in going there. You surely didn't expect the people to hang the flags out and fall on their knees to thank you for coming to deliver them from evil?"

"But my dear," said Mr. Matthews—"I've *seen* the place!"

"You haven't seen anything," said Ruth—"except the fog and Mr. Todhunter—and if you ask me, Todhunter is at the bottom of all the trouble. The whole thing's as clear as daylight. He's made a mess of things in Woodbank. He's got up against those people or just failed to get their confidence and couldn't bring himself to tell you so. That's all there is to the 'mystery' you're making such a fuss about. Thinking there's a devil between those people and the church is just a lot of medieval rubbish. You talk about the whole thing as though it were a disaster when really it's a splendid stroke of luck. It's a thousand times better to follow a man who's been a failure than one who's been a success, because a successful man would have left nothing for you to work for. It's a wonderful chance for you, Roger, and I'm thrilled about it because it's going to prove what you can really do. All your life you've wanted something to fight against. Now you've got it beyond your wildest hopes, and you're wondering how you can get out of it!"

"And as for the Vicarage," she added, "I don't wonder it smells musty after what you've said about Mr. Todhunter, because he'd make any house smell musty. When we get there we'll open the windows and light the fires and get some fresh air blowing through it. And when we've got our own furniture in and our own curtains up, you won't know the place. As for the garden, we'll get busy directly we arrive, and there'll just be time to put it right by the spring. I'm even glad the garden's going to be 'difficult', because it'll show what we can do to that as well."

Mr. Matthews felt rather ashamed of himself, but a great deal better by the time they got home. Perhaps, after all, it was the fog and the mutton stew and Mr. Todhunter that had made things seem worse than they really were. He had a glass of sherry before dinner and felt even better, and during dinner he felt so well that he began making plans for bringing the parish of Woodbank back to life again.

"The Church Council is coming in to see us the night we arrive," he said. "I'll get a plan of campaign ready and make them see that I mean business. Todhunter told me they were devoted to the church, but as far as I can see he never gave them a chance to do anything to help the parish."

"Todhunter never gave you a chance," said Ruth, "so you can take it for granted he never gave anybody a chance."

"We'll make good use of the Church Hall," said Mr. Matthews.—"Todhunter says it hasn't been used for years, but we'll clean it up and have concerts and whist drives and dances. We'll get the young people keen . . . we'll show them the Church isn't the dull, anaemic affair they seem to think it is."

"We might have a Musical and Dramatic Society like we've got here," said Ruth.

"And a Debating Society," suggested Mr. Matthews.—"Once you make people see it isn't highbrow, they enjoy it. You remember the one I started at Wimborne?"

"Once you've set your mind to anything," said his wife, "you've always made a success of it, and you're going to make the biggest success of your life in Woodbank. It's going to be a great adventure and I'm thrilled about it."

Mr. Matthews, among other things, was Treasurer of the Cricket Club, President of the local British Legion, and a Governor of the Grammar School, and Mrs. Matthews had her own manifold activities to resign.

Their departure was marked, in consequence, by a spate of Special Meetings. Every Club and Society in the town had a meeting at which Mr. Matthews or his wife resigned their office, handed over official papers, and said good-bye. There were farewell speeches and tokens of regard. The Cricket Club gave Mr. Matthews an autographed bat and the Musical Society gave Mrs. Matthews an electric kettle: the schoolchildren gave them a framed photograph of the church, and the whole town combined to give them a clock and a cheque for fifty guineas. There were so many meetings and so many farewells that the pangs of parting were lessened by the quantity of them. It was easier to say goodbye to a multitude than to a few, and the Matthews had to say a personal good-bye to everybody except a retired general who had quarrelled with the Vicar over the Cricket Club.

They saw their daughter off to school, and gave their greenhouse carnations to the doctor. The day came when the furniture van arrived with Mr. Todhunter's belongings and took their own away. They went to stay their last two nights with friends, and on the Sunday evening before the day of their departure Mr. Matthews conducted his last service in St. Mary's Church.

There had been a heavy storm and there were snow drifts in the valleys, but some people walked five miles to be at Evensong that night. There were so many people that the verger had to bring some chairs across from the Village Hall, and Mr. Matthews looked pale and nervous when the moment came to say his farewell words.

"This is the last time," he said, "that I shall speak to you as Vicar of Little Stanton. I have been your Vicar for over twenty years and they have been the happiest of my life. No man could have worked in more beautiful surroundings or had such loyal friendship and support. It is because of that, I think—because there are so many things in Little Stanton which make a parish priest's life easy, that I have felt it right, while I still enjoy my health and strength, to undertake work of a different kind for Christ and His Church. You will, I know, give Mr. Todhunter, your new Vicar, a loyal welcome. He has laboured for many years in a parish that has given him little reward and he deserves the support and understanding that I know you will give him.

"For myself, I shall, like St. Paul, thank my God upon every remembrance of you. I know my failings, and I am grateful beyond words for your kindness and forbearance. My wife and I will value the many tokens of friendship that you have given us, but even more we shall treasure the remembrance of friends who have enriched our lives.

"I have one last request to make of you. I have no illusions about the work to which I am going. It will be more difficult, I think, than anything I have had to undertake before, but I shall be able to face the future with confidence if I know that I have the support of your prayers. Please pray that God's blessing may rest upon the parish of Woodbank and upon the work I am called to undertake there in His name."

It was still dark, and the snow remained when Mr. and Mrs. Matthews left their neighbour's house next morning to catch the early train to London. They were hoping to get away without any more good-byes, but the two boys who delivered the papers in the village were waiting outside the gate.

"We've got to pick up the papers at the station," said one of them. "So we thought we'd carry your bags along. Mr. Matthews."

They talked about the football match the boys were playing that afternoon. "Write and tell us how you get on," said Mr. Matthews. "I hope you'll often write and tell us what you're doing—and about the cricket in the summer, too."

"You must come down and see us sometimes," said the boys.

"We shall," said Mr. Matthews. "We'll come down quite often. We'll come for the school sports and the Flower Show for certain."

They looked out of the window as the train moved off. The winter sun was rising, and they saw the two boys, with the bundles of newspapers around them, waving good-bye. Then the train ran round the bend and the woods concealed them. It was the last they saw of Little Stanton that morning—the last they ever saw, for they never went back.

Chapter Four

Mr. Matthews had wanted to get rid of Mrs. Burgin, the lugubrious housekeeper at the Woodbank Vicarage, partly because she was lugubrious, and partly because, whenever he looked at her, he would be reminded of his melancholy evening with Mr. Todhunter, and he wanted to wipe the slate clean of those unhappy first impressions and begin afresh. There was always, too, the risk of her making a cherry cake, which might appear without warning at a tea-party.

He had written accordingly to Mr. Todhunter, suggesting it might be better if they brought Emily, their own housekeeper, to Woodbank, and that Mr. Todhunter should take Mrs. Burgin with him to Little Stanton.

But Mr. Todhunter, still smarting under Mr. Matthews' refusal to exchange carpets, got his own back. He replied tartly that it would be most inconsiderate to expect a woman of Mrs. Burgin's age to surrender a host of friends and begin a new life in a strange place. He threw in a mild threat at the end by suggesting that it would create an extremely bad impression in Woodbank if the new Vicar began by dismissing from his service a woman who had proved herself a loyal and devoted member of St. Peter's Church.

The letter had left Mr. Matthews in no doubt that, while Mr. Todhunter wanted to get rid of Mrs. Burgin himself, he was equally determined that Mr. Matthews should have her, and would leave no stone unturned to see that he did.

Ruth thought it was probably for the best. "Emily would never be happy at Woodbank," she said.—"And I shall need somebody like Mrs. Burgin who knows where all the meters and pipes are in the Vicarage, and where to shop and get a plumber and a good laundry, and a dozen other things. If she turns out impossible we can always get rid of her later on."

But Mrs. Burgin turned out quite differently from what Mr. Matthews had anticipated. The van had arrived ahead of them and Mrs. Burgin had brought some friends named Mr. and Mrs. Goatley to help get the furniture into place. Mr. Goatley had worked for a London furnisher and was invaluable. He saw the way to lay the carpets and suggested how the curtains could be lengthened inexpensively to fit the windows. He pointed out that half a house well furnished was better than a whole house half-furnished, and on his advice they locked up and discarded two bedrooms and a small breakfast-room.

It was a fine breezy day and Mrs. Matthews had all the doors and windows open, and very soon the Vicarage smelt fresher than Mr. Matthews had dared to hope. "It was all that musty furniture of his," said Mrs. Burgin, "that made it smell so bad," and as the afternoon went on it dawned upon the Matthews that Mrs. Burgin, whom they had imagined to be hand in glove with Mr. Todhunter, was actually glad to get rid of him and completely on their side. "He was a good-natured, cheerful gentleman," she said—"but so untidy, and he never seemed to care. It's nice to have a lady in the house and your furniture looks so fresh and clean." She painted a terrifying picture of conditions in the Vicarage when she had first arrived as Mr. Todhunter's housekeeper five years ago. Slugs as big as babies in the scullery sink, she said—coming up the waste pipe as bold as brass. She spoke in the highest terms of what she had done to put things right, and Mrs. Matthews congratulated her, with certain private reservations when she found a cockroach in the pantry cupboard.

By tea-time the house was well enough arranged to spend the night in. The Matthews asked Mr. Goatley and his wife to come in next day to help clear up and hang the pictures, and went out for a first look at the garden while Mrs. Burgin made the tea.

Some steep steps, with old-fashioned maroon-coloured balustrades, led down into the garden from the dining-room. It was a small garden for so big a house, though spacious enough, they imagined, for one so near to London, and its limitations were deepened by the high brick walls that closed it in. There was a tired old lawn with grey patches in it, and a bare place like a shadow, beneath a fir tree, where the acid of the fallen needles had destroyed the grass. Beside the walls ran border beds with the drooping relics of uncared for dahlias, and near the house stood a gnarled old walnut tree with a walnut on it and a carpet of sodden leaves beneath.

It was a melancholy, neglected place, but there were signs that someone, at some distant time, had cared for it. There was a small sunken rockery and the relics of a tiny lily pond to its brim in fallen leaves and a sundial that would tell the time again if the rank trees overhead were pruned.

Ruth looked around her. A glimmer of sunset lit the eastern wall, but the garden was already in semi-darkness. "It'll always be dark," she said—"but I don't see why we shouldn't make a very nice garden here. We can read up and find out what flowers will grow without much sun. There's still time to get some crocuses and tulips in—and I'd say a bed of lilies of the valley would do quite well. We'll need a sack of lime to sweeten the soil, and a load of stable manure to put some heart into it."

"Mr. Goatley is the kind of man who'd know where to get some stable manure," said Mr. Matthews. "We'll ask him in the morning."

"Things aren't nearly so bad as they might have been," said Ruth, as they walked back to the house: "We can make quite a charming garden here—and the house is a good, solid one, even if it isn't pretty. As for Mrs. Burgin, I think she's wonderful. I believe we're going to be surprised in Woodbank, Roger. I think we're going to be really happy here after all."

The lights were on in the library and the curtains drawn and the fire made up, and Mr. Matthews looked round him at a room transformed. It was hard to link these pleasant, warm surroundings with the cheerless place where he had spent that miserable evening with Mr. Todhunter.

"I think you're right," he said. "Things are going to turn out much better than I expected."

"I felt it all along," said Ruth.—"Todhunter was at the bottom of everything. He didn't care and he didn't try. He let the parish rot as he let the house and garden rot. I'm glad you've got the Church Council coming in this evening. You can give them a good pep talk and get things going right away."

Mrs. Burgin brought in the tea. To Mr. Matthews' relief there was no cherry cake, but some very passable home-made rock buns and a jam roll.

"There'll be time to get down to the shops before they close," said Mrs. Burgin, "if I go now I'll be back before the people come."

She proposed an omelette for supper and herrings for breakfast, and when tea was over Ruth went upstairs to unpack and Mr. Matthews sat down to read over the notes for his meeting with the Church Council.

He staked a great deal on this meeting. He knew the value of first impressions and he wanted the Council to see from the start that he meant business. His plans were ambitious for a parish that had stagnated for so many years, but a hard impact produced the best rebound and he decided to launch the whole grand scheme at his meeting that night.

He heard Mrs. Burgin come back with the herrings, and as the time for the meeting drew near he began to feel nervous. He wondered what his new friends were going to be like. He wanted to appear before them cool and collected so he went upstairs to wash and brush his hair to calm himself down.

Ruth was changing into a dark blue dress that she kept for formal occasions.

"You mustn't expect too much at the first meeting," she said. "Todhunter never gave them anything to do so they're bound to be a bit rusty and slow to respond. But they will when they've got over their surprise and realise you mean to do things."

They went downstairs to await their guests, and promptly at six o'clock the gate squeaked and the first members of the Council arrived. A few minutes later it squeaked again and the second lot arrived. Mr. Matthews waited out of sight in the study with Ruth until the Council had settled down in the drawing-room. Then Mrs. Burgin looked in and said: "They're here, sir," and Mr. Matthews said: "Thank you, Mrs. Burgin," and went across the passage with his wife to meet them.

There were eleven people there: seven women and four men including Mr. Cheesewright and Mr. Harper, the Churchwardens. The two other men were plump and spectacled and dressed sedately in dark blue suits. They brought their wives forward and introduced them, but when the two ladies moved back amongst the others, Mr. Matthews could not have picked them out again because they were all so much alike. They were a nondescript, ordinary-looking lot. They were not the kind of people who would set the Thames on fire, but they looked earnest and dependable and he had a feeling they would support him and work with him.

"We're all here except Mrs. Bannister Paget," said Mr. Harper. "She asked me to tell you that she would be a little late and I think we ought to wait for her."

Mr. Matthews remembered that Mrs. Bannister Paget had been mentioned to him as a great lady and a great supporter of the Church, and he agreed that they should wait. There was a little small talk: they discussed the recent fall of snow and decided, upon comparison, that it had been somewhat less severe in Woodbank than in Little Stanton. Mr. Harper said that his sister lived in Beaminster, not far from Mr. Matthews' old parish. She was married to a Colonel Watson who was a very successful turkey breeder. Mr. Matthews said that turkeys, although delicate, did well in Dorset, and that a farmer in his parish made quite a business of them. Mr. Harper ventured the opinion that Colonel Watson probably knew the farmer through their mutual interest in turkeys, and for a little while they discussed the likelihood of this.

At a quarter past six Mr. Matthews began to get impatient. There was a lot to do and he wanted to get on with it. At twenty past he told Mr. Harper that they had better start without Mrs. Bannister Paget, but Mr. Harper seemed quite astonished by the suggestion. "I think we had better wait," he whispered, "we really couldn't start without her."

It was half-past six before Mrs. Bannister Paget arrived, and she came in with an air about her that convinced Mr. Matthews that her late arrival had been deliberately staged. She was a big woman—tall and masculine, with a thin aquiline nose and arrogant, pale grey eyes. She was clad in what at first sight appeared to be quite a number of separate dresses of varying shades of purple that showed round and between and above and below each other. Her apologies were brief and formal, and she moved without question to an arm-chair by the fire which the others, by mutual accord, appeared to have reserved for her.

Mr. Matthews waited until she had unloosened some of her little purple capes: he then said a few polite words about his pleasure in being the new Vicar of Woodbank, and got down to business.

"As you are aware," he said, "I am a stranger here. I have a lot to learn about this parish, but I'm offering you my plans at once, so that you can think them over and advise me.

"There are eight thousand people in Woodbank, and only forty of them come to Church. That's a sad state of affairs, but with your help I shall begin at once and do my best to put things right. I understand there are two separate districts in Woodbank; the 'old town' and the new one that has grown up around it in the past few generations. The problem is—how can we get at these new people and attract them to St. Peter's Church?

"Mr. Todhunter told me that there are no social clubs connected with our church. I think that's what we need, because a healthy social life around a church is bound, in the end, to bring health to the church itself."

He paused for comment, but as his listeners seemed anxious for him to go on, he plunged at once into the details of his plan.

It was to be a "three year plan", he said, based on a new club with headquarters in the Church Hall that had not been used for many years. It was not to be called a "Church Club", because that would frighten people away. He would prefer to call it the "Woodbank Club"; that would cover every kind of activity to suit all tastes and ages. There would be Dances and Whist Drives: Badminton and Concerts: Billiards and a Dramatic Society: Debating and Quiz teams—each to have its own committee and organising secretary and each to have the use of the Hall one night a week.

He went into details of membership and finance and organisation and he produced the draft of a pamphlet describing the club, which he proposed to have printed and distributed in the parish. He had worked it all out very carefully, but he made it clear to his listeners that the whole plan was open to a great deal of improvement and he invited discussion and criticism before he had it published. He laid stress on the younger generation: he wanted to encourage them and give them responsibility. He proposed no subscription for the first year. "The people of Little Stanton," he said, "gave me a cheque for fifty guineas when I left. I would like to donate this to start a foundation fund: if we can raise another fifty guineas we shall have enough to cover the first year's expenses—and then, when people see that the Club is worth supporting, we can decide upon a yearly subscription."

He stopped, and glanced around him. In his enthusiasm he had talked for half an hour, and he hoped that he had not overdone it. His audience was very quiet. Whether they were thrilled beyond words, or stunned with surprise, or merely anxious to get home to supper he could not tell—but they had listened with attention and he felt that on the whole he had put the plan over fairly well.

"I call it a 'three year plan'," he added—"because we cannot hope to see immediate results. We are bound to have our failures and set-backs. In some quarters we may find prejudice against the church in Woodbank, and we must be ready for opposition and hostility. It means hard work and patience, but if we work together and put our hearts into it, I'm sure we shall succeed."

There was a long silence. One or two people moved uneasily in their chairs, and then with one accord they all began to look at Mrs. Bannister Paget as if it were unseemly to speak before she had spoken.

Mrs. Bannister Paget had sat through the Vicar's speech without a movement: upright in her chair, her hands upon her lap, her eyes upon him in a fixed, unblinking stare.

"I don't quite understand you," she said. "I don't exactly understand who you are talking about."

Mr. Matthews looked at her blankly. The remark was so strange that he wondered whether he had heard aright. Possibly, he thought, it was meant as a kind of dry joke, but when he looked around him no one was smiling, and there was no humour in her face. But he was conscious of a sudden relaxation among the others: a furtive nodding of heads and exchange of glances. Now that Mrs. Bannister Paget had spoken, they all, it seemed, knew where they were and how they stood.

"I am speaking," said Mr. Matthews, "of the people in this parish who are at present outside the life of the Church. I thought I had made that clear. I'm sorry if I didn't."

Mrs. Bannister Paget neither moved nor blinked.

"It is a pity," she said—"a very great pity that you did not explore and understand this parish before you wasted your time and ours. We have known Woodbank all our lives and you have known it for one afternoon."

This time a timid murmur of approval ran round the room.

"If the things you have just suggested were desirable or possible," she continued, "then why do you think we have not carried them out ourselves?—because we had not the courage?—or the intelligence?—or sufficient faith in our church?"

"I made no reflection," began Mr. Matthews, "on the ..." She stopped him with a petulant flutter of her hand and went on in a louder voice. Two little patches of colour rose up and flushed her cheeks. Her eyes never blinked or left his face.

"I will tell you why," she said—"it is because your suggestions are so puerile that they never dawned upon us. The doors of our church are always open—wide open to these people you are talking about. They are free to come and worship if they choose: but they do not choose, and on that account we do not want them.

"You propose to lure them to our church with a vulgar programme of entertainment. You expect this Council to perform the antics of cheapjacks and showmen to entice them. If that is your way of filling St. Peter's Church, then you are insulting and debasing religion.

"But I prefer," she said in a calmer voice—"I prefer to think that you conceived these foolish plans hastily, without proper reflection or knowledge of this parish. Your predecessor, Mr. Todhunter, was a very great and good man. If he had considered these undignified devices necessary he would have put them into practice himself. But he did not. He conducted the services at St. Peter's Church with dignity and decorum, and we consider it your duty to follow his example and do the same."

Mr. Matthews listened incredulously. He looked round at the other members of the Council, but none of them had anything to say. Some looked sheepish and uncomfortable: others had suddenly taken on the appearance of small-sized Mrs. Bannister Pagets.

She stood up to go and Mr. Matthews wished that he had got up first.

"I'm sorry," he said. "I counted a great deal on your help. But I came here to do my best in a disgraceful parish, and I shall carry on with my plans because I think they're right."

Mrs. Bannister Paget buttoned the last of her purple capes and picked up her gloves.

"What you do in your spare time is not our concern," she said, "but I understand your plans depend upon the use of the Church Hall?"

"Naturally they do—and I shall use it."

"In that," she answered, "I am afraid you will be disappointed. The Church Hall is controlled by this Council. and we shall vote unanimously against its use for such unseemly exhibitions."

Mr. Harper opened the door for her and she went out. Mr. Cheesewright ran down the passage and opened the front door for her and she went out of that as well. The Council followed: the gate squeaked and they were gone.

Mr. Matthews went back to the drawing-room. The air was heavy with the odour of stale lavender from Mrs. Bannister Paget's purple silk. He opened the windows and drew the curtains over them.

"Well," he said—"that's that. I suppose I asked for it. I ought not to have gone so bull-headed at them. I ought to have gone quietly and persuaded them by degrees."

"No matter how you did it," said Ruth, "you would have had that woman dead against you. She wasn't defending the dignity of St. Peter's Church at all. She was defending something else—and she was frightened."

"*She* was frightened?—but my dear Ruth!"

"Of course she was. Nobody would have been as rude as that if they weren't frightened."

"But why should anybody be frightened of a social club?"

"She was frightened because you were threatening to pull down and destroy her own snug little world. Don't you see? ... she's cock-of-the-roost of that 'devoted little circle round the church'. She looks upon St. Peter's Church as her own private monopoly: a comfortable little club complete with a docile Vicar to run about at her beck and call. Nobody has ever disputed her possession of it before—and suddenly you come along and threaten to fill her exclusive little church with a crowd of nasty people from the new town who might even refuse to run about and do what she tells them. It's enough to frighten anybody!"

He sat down by the fire. "It's going to be difficult," he said. "I never dreamed that anything like this would happen. She's got the whole Church Council in her pocket. They're all against us."

"I'm sure they are," said Ruth—"and probably the organist and the verger and everybody else as well. In the garden you've got the onion maggot and the turnip maggot. In the Church you've got the Bannister Paget maggot that eats into the heart of it and sucks the life out of it—and Bishops wonder what's wrong with the Church and why so many decent, ordinary people keep away."

"What are we going to do about it?"

"I don't know," replied Ruth. "I'm not sure what we can do."

Mrs. Burgin came in to say that dinner was ready.

"I owe you an apology, Roger," said Ruth as they went into the dining-room. "You were right and I was wrong. There *is* a devil between the Church and the Woodbank people after all!"

Chapter Five

St. Peter's Church was beside the river, with a boat yard on one side of it and a warehouse on the other. On the opposite side of the river stood a tall brick flour mill with a smudge of flour around its lower windows and a cluster of barges against its wharf. The church was at a corner where the lane from the Vicarage came down to the shore, and there was only the narrow, cobbled towing path between the churchyard and the river.

Mr. Matthews came down the lane on the morning after his arrival at the Vicarage, and thought what a fine position the church must have had in the days when Woodbank was a village and open meadows fringed the Thames. It stood on a gentle rise with a wide sweep of the river before it, and from the tower there must have been long, uninterrupted views across the marshes to the estuary, with the spires of the city to the west, and the wooded slopes of Kent in the southern distance.

But now the churchyard was a solitary green clearing in a jungle of chimney-stacks and cranes—squeezed and jostled by massive concrete buildings that looked as if they had done their best to break the church from its ancient anchorage, and revenged themselves for their failure by darkening its windows and making it look as unwanted and as out of place as possible.

The scenes around him were new and interesting to Mr. Matthews. He watched the tugs with their long strings of barges swaying among the hidden eddies of the tide, and he admired the skill of the men who steered the big, ungainly vessels straight to their mooring places against the wharves when the tugs let go of them in midstream. He watched the cranes lift sacks of flour and swing them through the doors of the mill as lightly as if they had been sacks of feathers.

When he turned from the busy scene and entered the churchyard and walked up the flagged path between the ancient tombs and lolling grave-stones, he had the illusion of stepping from a roaring factory into the quiet shade of a country village. For a few yards the yews surrounded him and the illusion was complete, and then the farther end of the churchyard came to view and he saw a yard full of half-dismantled tram-cars, and the illusion ended.

The verger was waiting for him in the porch, and they went into the church.

It was an old foundation—reputedly Norman in its origin, but the interior had been refashioned and rebuilt during Woodbank's palmy days in the solid, prosperous Georgian way. It still had its three-decker pulpit, and there was some stained glass of an earlier period, but the austere grey walls were smothered with ugly, obtrusive tablets and memorials of the Regency period, in highly polished, dead white marble that made them look like toilet fittings. But it was a good church—better than he had expected—although it smelt as if the river fog made too much use of it.

The verger was an elderly man with a bad cold in his head. He said he had risen from his sick bed to meet the new Vicar that morning, so Mr. Matthews confined himself to a brief discussion on routine and said he would come back in the afternoon and see the church alone.

As he was leaving he told the verger he would like to see the Church Hall. He had made up his mind to challenge Mrs. Bannister Paget's threat to deprive him of it, and he told the old man to give him the keys and go home to nurse his cold.

But the verger seemed very much disturbed by this and began to make excuses.

44

"I don't think you can, sir," he said. "It's all closed up and hasn't been used for years."

"I know," replied Mr. Matthews. "But it's going to be opened up again now, because I'm planning to use it quite a lot."

This statement seemed to hit the verger like a bombshell. He stared at the Vicar in astonishment and dismay.

"I really don't think we can get in, sir," he mumbled—"the locks and keys . . . they're . . . they're all rusty and . . . and won't turn."

So Mrs. Bannister Paget has been at him already, thought the Vicar. "Give me the keys and I'll see what I can do," he said.

But the verger was determined not to give up the keys. He gripped them as if his life depended on them and when Mr. Matthews persisted, he looked as if he were going to cry. At last he gave in and muttered miserably, "I better come with you, sir. . . . I think I better."

Mr. Matthews felt fairly sure that the verger had received some kind of orders to keep him out of the Church Hall. He was sorry for the old man, but a firm hand from the start was his only chance.

St. Peter's Hall was opposite the tram depot: an ugly building of the Queen Victoria Jubilee period, of pale red brick with a steep slate roof. But it was big and solid, and looked a very adequate place for the club that Mr. Matthews had in mind.

There was a padlock and heavy chain round the tall iron gates and the gravelled path to the doors of the hall was covered in moss and weeds.

"I don't have the key to the main door," said the verger—"there's a side entrance round here."

"Where's the key to the main door?" asked Mr. Matthews—but the old man, who was deaf on occasions, did not answer. He led the Vicar down a narrow side path almost blocked by the neglected laurels.

The side door opened into a passage with a row of small rooms leading off it. They were empty and dusty but in good condition.

"Dressing-rooms!" said Mr. Matthews—"you've got a real stage here, then?"

"Oh yes, sir, there's a real stage, with a curtain and footlights and everything."

Mr. Matthews had not expected this, and visions of a Musical and Dramatic Club grew bright and rosy. He was more determined than ever to get the Hall as he followed the verger up the steps on to the stage.

The stage was good, with deep wings and a heavy drop-curtain. "This is excellent!" he exclaimed: "the very thing I want!—Let's have the curtain up for a look at the Hall."

But the old man did not share the Vicar's enthusiasm. He looked the picture of dejection and dismay.

"I don't think we can, sir. It hasn't been up for years."

"Never mind!" said Mr. Matthews. "Have a try!"

The verger fumbled with the cords and pulleys, and presently the curtain went up slowly and creakily.

It revealed a spacious auditorium that would seat, thought Mr. Matthews, a good three hundred people, but he was astonished to see the whole place stacked and littered with a mass of furniture and junk that looked as if it had come from some kind of an office. There were old tables and desks and chairs—bundles of old books and dusty files—vast heaps of papers done up in red tape and a stack of black japanned deed-boxes painted with people's names. There was so much of it that it blocked the windows and filled the air with a heavy odour of camphor and musty leather.

"What on earth's all this?" he asked.

The verger hesitated. "Mrs. Bannister Paget had it put here," he said. "It came from the lawyer's office—Paget, Bannister and Paget. They were lawyers in Woodbank for hundreds of years, but when Mr. Richard died—that was Mrs. Bannister Paget's husband—there was nobody to carry on, and the firm ended. It was very sad after all those years, sir, and Mrs. Bannister Paget had everything put in here, because some of the papers might be needed, she said."

"How long has it been here?"

"About fifteen years, sir."

"But why is it in the Church Hall?—why not a furniture depository?"

The old man looked pained. "It didn't seem right to put such precious, private things in a depository," he said.

"And presumably Mrs. Bannister Paget has the key to the main door?"

The verger looked dreamily at the litter of untidy rubbish. "Mrs. Bannister Paget said the papers were very private and not for prying eyes," he said. "She told me never to let anybody in."

"But the hall belongs to the church!" said Mr. Matthews.

"In a manner of speaking, sir," replied the verger—"one might say it does—but Mrs. Bannister Paget's father built it and gave it to the church. They were a fine family, sir—so good and generous—and Mrs. Bannister Paget is the last of them. She's wonderful to the church, sir, and we couldn't do without her. It only seems right to let her husband's things be in the hall."

Mr. Matthews went back to lunch and told his wife about it.

"Whether I've a right to use the hall over the heads of the Council I don't know," he said, "but I do know that woman has no earthly right to use it as a free depository for all that old junk of hers, and I'm going to tell her so."

"I'd be careful," said Ruth. "I wouldn't if I were you—at least, not yet."

"But she's kept a perfectly good public hall locked up and full of her own rubbish for fifteen years! I've never heard of such a thing!"

"I know," said Ruth—"but I'd wait till you definitely want the hall before you do anything. It'll look like a bit of cheap revenge if you do it now, and you'll put them all against you more than ever. I've got a feeling there's a big fight ahead with Mrs. Bannister Paget. At present she's got all the big guns and there's no point in running into them till you're ready."

They spent the afternoon unpacking books and hanging the pictures. Mr. Goatley came in to help, and promised to get them a load of stable manure from the Brewery. At four o'clock Mr. Matthews went off to meet Mr. Watson the organist, who was a teacher at the local school and also the choirmaster.

Mr. Watson was a languid young man with a thin pale face and a lot of dry, dusty black hair. He was off-hand and insolent. He gave Mr. Matthews to understand that he was paying St. Peter's Church a considerable compliment in playing the organ and running the choir. He had high qualifications, he said: he had studied music in Germany and should really be filling a considerably higher post, although he left in doubt the reason why he wasn't. He made a few complaints about the dirtiness and scarcity of choirboys and the poor quality of the organ, and went home.

"Well," said Mr. Matthews over dinner. "I've met them all now: the charlady—the verger—the organist—the sides-men—the churchwardens and the council, and if I'm not very mistaken, Mrs. Bannister Paget has got the whole roaring lot of them in her pocket. There isn't one of them who'd lift a finger until she gives the word."

"We're orphans in the storm," said Ruth—"two against the world."

After dinner they sat down to talk things over.

"It's going to be a hard job," said Mr. Matthews.

"With the Council dead against me I'm tied up like a trussed chicken."

"There's only one thing for it," said Ruth. "You must turn them out and get a new Council that'll back you up."

"And how, my dear, does one do that when one's an orphan in the storm and trussed up like a chicken?"

"It may not be so difficult," she answered. "That woman's got the Council in her pocket—and people like the verger and the organist—but that's about all. We know that only forty people come to church, so that's about the strength of her party. But there are eight thousand people in Woodbank. There must be a few among those eight thousand who keep away from church because of this gang that runs it, and if you go about it the right way you can get them on your side. Suppose you only got one in a hundred—that's eighty—and eighty is double the number she's got."

Mr. Matthews began to brighten up. He saw the idea and

wondered why he had not thought of it himself. "Ruth" he said, "you've got something—a sort of putsch—a coup d'état!"

"It's not that," said Ruth, "because it's perfectly democratic and legal. There may be no need to have a war against this woman at all. As far as she and her satellites are concerned, you will be a model Vicar. You will conduct the services at St. Peter's Church with dignity and decorum, like the good Mr. Todhunter. That's a normal thing to do in any case—but meanwhile you go to work in the parish, building up your own party—younger people—fresh ideas—new blood. Then at Easter next year comes the re-election of the Church Council. The new people put up their own candidates with a two to one majority in their favour. Out goes the old gang and in comes a new Council that backs you to the hilt."

"Wonderful!" exclaimed Mr. Matthews.—"But it sounds a bit too wonderful: there must be a snag somewhere."

"Don't you think you can get one in a hundred of these people behind you?"

"If I can't—then I'm no good. In the name of reason I ought to get one in a hundred."

"The only snag that I can see," said Ruth, "is the Bannister Paget gang getting wind of what you're doing and running their own campaign to raise their numbers. I don't think they could do much in any case. They're out of touch with the parish. They live in a world of their own—and I don't imagine any of the outside people would back them up."

"You don't think it's shabby and underhand—going round behind their backs?—hatching a kind of plot?"

"They've treated you rough," she said. "You've got a right to treat them rough—and it's for the good of the parish, anyway."

Mr. Matthews got up and began to walk about the room.

"I'll begin to-morrow!" he said. "I'd begin to-night if it wasn't so late. I'll call on every man and woman in the parish!—I'll get a hundred supporters or burst!—You said Woodbank was going to be a great adventure, Ruth. You never said a truer thing!"

Chapter Six

Mr. Matthews went into the town next morning to buy a local directory. It gave him a list of names and addresses and a street map of the area, and he began to work out his house-to-house campaign.

On a large-scale map, Woodbank looked like the skeleton of a flat fish, with the High Street as a backbone and the side streets coming in like ribs. The bend of the river gave the fish its belly and the railway formed its back. The builders of the town had tried to cover up what they had done by giving the streets the names of flowers—beginning with Aster Avenue and finishing with Zinnia Drive.

He decided to begin with Marigold Road on the eastern boundary of the parish and work westward to Primrose Street on the other side. There were forty streets with about fifty houses in each ... two thousand houses averaging four people to a house. He reckoned that if he visited ten houses every afternoon and ten each evening, he would cover the parish in about three months. He hoped, as he went along, to make friends whom he would revisit, and he set aside a day a week for this, with tea at the Vicarage on Sunday afternoons for his most ardent supporters. He aimed at a hundred supporters to give him a clear majority over any additions that Mrs. Bannister might scrape together when she got wind of what he was doing.

He spent the morning copying out the names of the people in Marigold Road, and after lunch he was ready to start.

"Go easy at first," said Ruth. "I don't expect many of them have seen a clergyman at close quarters since they were christened."

"I don't expect they have," he said. "I'll just begin by making myself known, that's all."

"Good luck!" she called out as the gate squeaked behind him.

It was a fine clear day in early February. The air was keen and springlike and Mr. Matthews felt the zest of adventure as he walked briskly down the High Street to Marigold Road.

It was a long, dreary road of small, red brick houses all of which appeared to have more chimneys than rooms. He was lucky with the weather, but not so lucky with the children. He had hoped they would all be in school at that hour of the afternoon, but for some reason it was a holiday, and Marigold Road was swarming with them. It was soon apparent that a clergyman was a novelty in this part of the world. The children stopped their games and hushed their voices when they saw him coming, and he began to wish that he had planned to start his visiting at the first house in the road instead of the one at the farther end, for as he went along the children fell in behind and followed him. By the time he was half-way down the road there were a dozen children at his heels and two cats running along in front.

No. I was the home, according to his notes, of Mr. Abel Wainwright, and when he entered the gate the children crowded round in growing excitement.

"Somebody's dead," said a little girl in a blue frock.

As he rang the bell Mr. Matthews saw the pale, scared face of a woman peering at him between the front room curtains. It moved away, and presently the door opened and the woman stood staring at him with terror in her eyes.

"Mrs. Wainwright?" he enquired.

"Yes?" she said in a strangled voice.—"Yes? . . . what's happened?"

Mr. Matthews was rather put out by her distressed appearance, but he collected himself and gave her a reassuring smile.

"I'm the new Vicar of St. Peter's Church," he said. "My name is Matthews and I just wanted to say 'how d'you do', and tell you that I'm here to be of service to you if you ever need me. I shall be at home at the Vicarage every evening from five till six, and I shall always be pleased to see you if you care to come in for a chat. That was all I wanted to say, and I hope I haven't disturbed you."

Mrs. Wainwright went on staring, then she put her hand to her eyes with a moan of relief, and he thought she was going to faint.

"Oh . . ." she gasped. . . . ". . . It isn't my husband then?"

"Your husband?" enquired Mr. Matthews. . . . "I . . . I haven't met your husband. Is . . . is he ill? . . . in hospital?"

"Oh no!" cried Mrs. Wainwright.—"Not if you haven't come to say so!—But he's working right on top of the paper mill chimney to-day and it's terrible up there at his age . . . with his giddy turns. He won't tell them about his giddy turns for fear of losing his work . . . and . . . and it's so dangerous and . . ." she nearly sobbed . . . "and I thought they'd sent you round to say he'd had a horrible accident."

"I'm very glad I didn't come with any news like that!" said Mr. Matthews, feeling that she couldn't have looked worse if he had. There were beads of perspiration on her forehead, and her face was deathly pale.

"I've got a bad heart," she murmured.—"And you gave me such a terrible turn . . . you shouldn't do it!—it isn't right, and I can't stand it!"—she began to cry as she closed the door and left him on the step.

Mr. Matthews departed, distressed but relieved. He was touched by Mrs. Wainwright's anxiety for her husband, but very glad she had not died on the doorstep. It would have been a bad start if the first person he had visited had fallen dead at the sight of him.

The children were standing round the gate in an awed, respectful silence. "Has Mr. Wainwright fallen down the chimney?" asked a little boy.

Mr. Matthews reassured him. As far as he knew, he said, Mr. Wainwright was still at the top of the chimney. The children lost interest on hearing this. They seemed to take him for a fraud. They went off to their games again, and Mr. Matthews felt quite lonely as he followed one of the cats into the next gate.

No. 3 Marigold Road was occupied, according to his list, by Mr. Hubert Hobbs, and Mr. Hobbs himself came to the door in answer to the second knock. The cat went straight in, and Mr. Hobbs kicked it out again. He was a burly man in an open, collarless shirt and carpet-slippers, with braces dangling down behind him. He blinked at Mr. Matthews with bleary, blood-shot eyes, and when the Vicar had made his speech of introduction he sighed and nodded wearily.

"I was asleep . . ." he said. "I'm on night duty at the Post Office."

"I'm sorry," replied Mr. Matthews. "I must apologise for disturbing you."

"It's hard enough to get off anyway," said Mr. Hobbs. "What with the baker and everybody else. With all these kids about as well, it's something cruel."

"It must be," agreed Mr. Matthews—"and I'm very sorry I disturbed you. I'll call again another time."

Mr. Hobbs nodded and watched the Vicar out of the gate with a blood-shot eye around the edge of the door.

Mrs. Alice Richards lived at No. 5. She was a withered little woman with beady eyes and a shock of untidy grey hair. She was hostile and suspicious, and listened to the first part of Mr. Matthews' speech with the chain still up on the door. But when he got to the point where he offered his services, her manner changed: she brightened up and took the chain off and asked him into a foetid little sitting-room and made him sit down.

"You're just the gentleman I want!" she said—"they'd *have* to listen to a clergyman. They couldn't help themselves."

The people who would have to listen turned out to be the Gas Company, who had misread Mrs. Richards' meter and cheated her out of fourteen shillings.

"It's the Inspector," she said—"and it was deliberate. He's had his knife in me ever since I reported him last year. I never use the stove except for breakfast because I always light the range, and he swindles me because my eyes are bad. I went straight down and reported him, but they don't listen because I'm poor and haven't got anybody to stand up for me. But they'd *have* to listen to a clergyman!"

She took him into the scullery to see the meter. There were the usual meaningless rows of red and black figures, showing through little slots, and Mr. Matthews said he thought they ought to make them easier to understand.

"*I* understand them all right!" retorted Mrs. Richards—"I understand them a darn sight too well for their liking!"

"Then I think you should go to the Company," said Mr. Matthews, "and ask for the Secretary. . . ."

"I've done it!" she shouted, working herself up into a fury—"Time and again . . . and they keep me waiting and don't see me. But they wouldn't dare treat a clergyman like that!—You can take all the bills with you so as you'll know what you're talking about."

Mr. Matthews started to explain that it was unwise for a Vicar to interfere in disputes of a purely business nature, and to his dismay she began to abuse him.

"You're all the same!" she cried: "Humbug and pious words!—You come here saying you want to help, and when a poor woman's in trouble you start a lot of excuses! What d'you do it for if you don't mean a word you say?"

In the end Mr. Matthews said he would do what he could. No use ever came of a Vicar interfering in the commercial disputes of his parishioners, and he had seen enough of Mrs. Richards to feel fairly sure the Gas Company was in the right, but the atmosphere in the room was appalling and he either had to surrender or suffocate.

"The Gas Company's in Chalfont Street," she said—"And don't you move until they've knocked that 14s. off!"

"I'm very busy now," he said, "I'll do the best I can." And Mrs. Richards closed the door, muttering that people never wanted to help anybody who was old and poor.

When Mr. Matthews reached the street again he saw that he now had a competitor, for an Indian in a seedy blue turban and a brown overcoat was canvassing the houses opposite with an armful of rugs, and it looked as if there was going to be a door-to-door race up the street.

But he soon outstripped the Indian, for there was no answer at No. 7 and No. 9. Mrs. Wright at No. 11 told him she couldn't wait because her iron was hot and Mr. Podmore at No. 13 was rude. Outside No. 15 he looked back with envy at the Indian, who was still in animated discussion at No. 6, not only with the lady of the house, but with the lady next door as well, across the fence. Mr. Matthews sighed and went on. He wished that Marigold Road was as interested in God as it was in rugs.

At No. 15 he met Mr. James H. Wilson, whose name was engraved upon a brass plate on the door. Mr. Wilson was a jovial man with plastered black hair and two bright red patches on his cheeks like a wooden soldier. When Mr. Matthews offered his services, Mr. Wilson, who was an Insurance Agent, offered his in return and advocated a pedal cycle policy. Mr. Matthews said he had ridden a bicycle for forty years without serious accident, but on this Mr. Wilson looked grave and told him he had cheated fate too long. "The laws of average are against you," he said—"with all these motors on the road and a man of your age ... you can't depend on your sight and hearing like you used to. If you lost a leg you wouldn't say 'no' to a pound a week for life, would you?—the premium is ten shillings a year with £500 on a fatal accident if you die within a month. It's worth doing, Mr. Matthews. I wouldn't say so if it wasn't."

Mr. Matthews accepted the proposal form and said he would consider it—but what he was really considering was Mr. Wilson himself, who was the first alert and likely person he had met that afternoon.

"You're one of the men I'm looking for in Woodbank," he said: "I'm going to organise a social club, and I want the help of a few keen people with the right spirit and plenty of friends—it's a job worth doing. . . ."

He told Mr. Wilson his plans and Mr. Wilson listened good-naturedly with occasional glances at the clock.

"It's a good idea," he said when it was over. "I'm too busy for that kind of thing myself—but you go ahead. I'm not against the Church, mind you—I always say it's a fine thing for people, but Sundays are my busy days because it's the only time I'm certain of catching people at home."

He saw Mr. Matthews to the door and said he would drop in at the Vicarage one evening and pick up the pedal cycle proposal form when Mr. Matthews had had the time to fill it in.

"The Regal Insurance Company is first-class," he called out down the path. "If you have a bad tumble, they pay up and don't argue."

By four o'clock Mr. Matthews had called at twice the number of houses he had allowed for in one afternoon. The news of what he was doing appeared to outstrip his own progress down Marigold Road, for as he went on the element of surprise was lacking. Children answered the doors and said their mothers were out, although in most cases he clearly saw the mothers looking at him between the window curtains. "They think I'm after money," he thought as he went out of the last gate and turned into the High Street on his way back to the Vicarage. "It's a mistake to go from door to door . . . to-morrow I'll make quick, surprise calls, here and there in different streets, and see if that works better."

Chapter Seven

But the quick surprise calls worked no better than the methodical house-to-house ones. Some days he tried one way and some days the other. He gave up thinking of them as "house-to-house" and called them "door-to-door", for that was about all it ever came to.

"It's disappointing," he said: "I'm up against a brick wall and I'm not getting anywhere."

"You can't cure years of prejudice in a week," said Ruth.

"I don't think it *is* prejudice," he answered. "People have got to feel something to be prejudiced, but these don't feel anything. They just don't care, one way or another. I thought some of them would be prejudiced against Mrs. Bannister Paget and her gang for freezing them out of the church—but I don't believe any of them have ever heard of Mrs. Bannister Paget. If I told them I wanted to throw her out of the Church Council they'd probably say: 'Why throw her out if she wants to stay?'"

He began looking through the note-book in which he kept a record of every visit. It was depressing reading.

"Most of them imagine I'm after money," he said. "When I say I'm not, they seem to think I'm playing some kind of confidence trick. They can't believe anybody would take the trouble to call unless they wanted to sell something. If I had something to fish out of a bag and show them, like these fellows with furniture polish and shirt buttons, I might get somewhere. It's something solid and visible that sets the ball rolling."

"What about that pamphlet you wrote about the club?" said Ruth. "Make it interesting and attractive to look at and have it printed and sell it to them at sixpence a time—the sixpence to go into a foundation fund. Once they've put some money into it they'll be interested and want something in return. As long as you go about saying you don't want any money they think there's something fishy about it."

Mr. Matthews thought it was an idea worth trying, so he laid off his visiting and re-wrote the pamphlet. He designed a picture for the front page, showing people acting a drama and playing badminton and dancing, and titled it with the one sentence—"WHAT ARE YOU INTERESTED IN?" He had 500 copies printed. It cost him most of the money the people had given him when he left Little Stanton, but it looked attractive, and he began his new campaign refreshed and hopeful.

It certainly worked better than the old one. People were interested to see what he had got and quite a number paid their sixpence. He followed this up with a form of membership to fill in and the free use of his fountain pen.

Most of them fought shy of the fountain pen. They said they would fill up the form when they had talked it over with somebody who was always out at the moment, but would be in later on.

But Mr. Matthews soon discovered that clubs were not born from pamphlets carried by lonely strangers from door to door. When barely a dozen forms came back he began return calls on those who had seemed most interested. But he found that an epidemic of second thoughts had now set in. Some said they hadn't got the time: others that they belonged to a club outside the parish and saw no reason for another one, while one man bluntly expressed what the others were no doubt thinking when he said the whole thing was a sprat to catch a mackerel. "After all," he declared "it's a church club, isn't it?—whatever you like to call it. You aren't running it because you're mad about seeing us dancing and playing cards. You're doing it because you're the Vicar here and it's your job to get people into church any way you can."

"There are worse things than going to church," retorted Mr. Matthews.

"There are better things, too," said the man—"when you've been cooped up in a flour mill all the week."

But Mr. Matthews kept at it, and finally collected seventeen completed forms of membership. In the space marked: "What branch of the club are you specially interested in?" nine said Whist Drives, three said Dances, two were for Drama and one for Debating, while two expressed a willingness for anything that came along.

It was not encouraging, but seventeen were enough to justify a preliminary meeting. "We can appoint some of them as organising secretaries for the various activities," he said. "That'll spur them on to rope their friends in."

He sent out post-cards calling a meeting at the Vicarage for eight o'clock one evening, adding at the bottom—"bring your friends," and Mrs. Matthews and Mrs. Burgin spent the afternoon cutting sandwiches and preparing cakes and coffee for thirty, to be on the safe side.

By eight o'clock eleven people had arrived. They looked incredulously at the fine array of apparently free food, and when Mrs. Matthews invited them to help themselves they fell upon it as if they half suspected it to be a mirage that would melt away before it was inside them. Mr. Matthews listened anxiously for the bell, but by eight-thirty no one else had come, and he began the meeting to save his furniture and carpets from being eaten.

He had been watching the future leaders of the club attentively, and was not very much impressed. There was a gaunt young man with wild eyes who had talked incessantly, waving his sandwiches to drive home his points. There was a lady with cropped grey hair who sat languidly on the sofa, smoking cigarettes from a long green cigarette-holder. There was a stout lady in a light blue dress who laughed so uproariously at feeble jokes that Mr. Matthews dreaded what might happen to her if somebody made a good one. There was a plump man in pince-nez who was being the life and soul of the party and a few quiet, lonely ones who stood timidly around hoping that somebody would speak to them.

He made a few introductory remarks, and threw the meeting open to discussion. The young man with the wild eyes jumped up. He advocated a Woodbank Symphony Orchestra and offered to conduct it. The lady with the long green cigarette-holder said she had taught elocution in Newcastle and offered to do the same in Woodbank. A nervous young man with a stammer, who had not said a word, suddenly stood up and made a twenty-minute speech on the pleasures of debating, and the plump man in pince-nez said he'd like to dance.

Mr. Matthews listened with an ebbing heart. In the end he proposed the wild-eyed young man as Organising Secretary of the Musical Society and the lady with the cigarette-holder as Chairman of the Drama Committee. They both made long speeches of acceptance, but both were astonished and openly disgusted when they were told there were no musicians or actors to organise at present, and it was up to them to find some. The lady in the bright blue dress was appointed Secretary of Whist Drives, and asked if anybody would like to have a game right away. The young man with the stammer proposed himself as Secretary of the Debating Society and the meeting terminated. They hovered for a little while around the crumbs on the empty plates, and then dispersed into the night.

"I hate being ungenerous," said Mr. Matthews—"but they aren't at all the people we're looking for. In fact they're utterly, hopelessly wrong. I bungled the whole thing: I ought to have met them, individually, before I called the meeting; as it was, I had to propose some of them as organising secretaries."

"I don't think any of them are likely to have wide circles of friends," said Ruth.

"If their friends are anything like they are, I hope they haven't," he answered—"and as for attracting new people, I'm afraid they'll frighten them away."

Sitting in his silent study when Ruth had gone to bed, he understood more clearly Mr. Todhunter's earnest desire to nurse his bronchitis in Little Stanton.

Little Stanton ... with its woods and meadows and friendly people ... what miles away it seemed that night.

Chapter Eight

One day a crocus bloomed in the Vicarage garden, but next morning the milkman left a bottle on it, and that ended the spring in Woodbank.

Summer came, and Mr. Matthews reached the last roads of his parish. He now went visiting in a straw hat: the flies became a bigger nuisance than the children, but otherwise things were very much the same. He had given up hope of gathering a steady stream of supporters as he went along, and now pinned everything on finding one super-supporter: one vigorous, influential man with a wide circle of friends who would join him and go forward with him in a grand crusade. But the super-supporter failed to appear, and the blight still lay on Woodbank like a sodden blanket.

He conducted every service at St. Peter's Church with scrupulous regard, but no one ever came to the weekday services. He rang the bell and donned his surplice and read the lesson to himself in the empty church with the stagnant silence broken now and then by the hooting of the tugboats and the rattle of the cranes.

Sunday was, of course, the day of Mrs. Bannister Paget and her friends. At Matins she appeared in purple: at Evensong in black. There were thirty-nine of them and their numbers never varied. None ever seemed too ill to stay away or well enough to risk a Sunday off. They sat in the same places and wore the same clothes and looked so exactly the same every Sunday that it seemed as if time had ceased its onward progress and was now revolving in little cycles, coming back to the same place once a week like a gramophone record with a flaw that continually forces back the same small fragment of sound.

He gave great care to the preparation of his sermons, hoping by steady persuasion to bring a new feeling into his congregation, but he never saw a glimmer of response in their placid, cow-like eyes. If he had read a page of football results with a sing-song intonation it would have served as well as anything he said.

Mrs. Bannister Paget was polite and formal, unbending a little to say a word about the weather before departing. He never knew if she was aware of his attempts to start the club. She never gave any sign of it, but he felt fairly sure she knew all about it—including his abject failure. He was carrying out his duties like a model Vicar: so far as she was concerned he was following in the footsteps of Mr. Todhunter, and she had got him where she wanted him.

Life was lonely at the Vicarage. They rarely entertained, but one evening Mr. Matthews invited Mr. Cheesewright, the Churchwarden, to bring his wife to dinner. He liked the shy, sandy-haired little dentist, who more than once had gone out of his way to be friendly when none of the Church Council were about. He felt that Mr. Cheesewright was secretly on his side, and he wanted to get him alone and have a talk with him.

Mr. Cheesewright was pleased and flattered by the invitation, but during dinner he was nervous and ill at ease. So long as the conversation was not about the parish he was happy, but every time Mr. Matthews tried to talk about Woodbank, the little man would glance furtively at his wife, or at Mrs. Burgin, the housekeeper, if she happened to be in the room, as though he suspected her as a possible agent of the Bannister Paget party and was frightened of committing himself.

But after dinner, alone with the Vicar in the study and mellowed by a glass of port, he became easier, and presently approached the affairs of Woodbank on his own initiative.

"There's something I've wanted to tell you, Mr. Matthews," he said, "ever since that unhappy meeting on the night you came here.

I've wanted to tell you how ashamed I was of myself and the whole council—because I think your plans were splendid, and deserved the support of all of us."

"Then why on earth didn't you get up and say so!" exclaimed Mr. Matthews.

Mr. Cheesewright's eyes roved unhappily round the room.

"You'll despise me when I tell you," he said. "And I deserve to be despised. My life is not a happy one, you see. My work is hard and I'm not very strong. Long hours of standing exhaust me rather, and my wife is impatient sometimes because I am not more successful. I understand her feelings. She deserves a better life than I can give her in a place like Woodbank, but of course it means hard words and unhappiness. Sometimes I wonder how I can find the strength to carry on, and the Church is the only thing I have to help me. To me the Church means peace and consolation—but if I had stood up and said what was in my mind that night it would not have meant peace any longer: it would have meant strife and bitterness and feuds that would have gone on for years—and I would not have had the strength to face it. That's why I kept silent, Mr. Matthews, and I'm glad I've had this chance to explain, even if you despise me for it."

"If I despised you," said Mr. Matthews, "I would have to despise myself—because in your place I would have done the same. Peace in ourselves is too precious a thing to throw away on the long chance of another kind of victory: peace in ourselves is a victory of its own."

Mr. Cheesewright looked gratefully at the Vicar—but his nervousness came back when Mr. Matthews threw a leading question at him—

"What do you think about Mrs. Bannister Paget?" he asked.

"I think," said Mr. Cheesewright, "that she is a very lonely, unhappy woman. She is the last of the old gentry that used to dominate Woodbank, and she lives with her memories in a world that none of us can understand or share. In her own way she loves St. Peter's Church: it is all that she has, and if it were taken away from her, she would have nothing."

"The last thing I want to do is to take it away from her," said Mr. Matthews. "I only want her to share it with others. Can't we make her see what a happier town she would live in if more people shared St. Peter's Church?"

Mr. Cheesewright shook his head.

"She sees things in a strange way," he said. "She believes it is better that God shall be worshipped by a devoted few than by a crowd who have to be persuaded. Persuasion to worship, in her mind, is an insult to Christianity. That is why she was against your club. To wheedle people into church by means of dances and whist drives and concerts is to her a thing of sacrilege."

"Even if the people who come by way of dances and concerts are ultimately faithful?"

"She is old," said Mr. Cheesewright. "She has her creed, and I do not think it can be altered."

There was nothing to be gained by talking any more about Mrs. Bannister Paget and Mr. Matthews dropped the subject. "You've worked here as a dentist for many years," he said, "and you know a lot of people. Why is it that I can't raise a glimmer of response in them? I've done my best. I've tried every way, but they just don't seem to care. I'm afraid it's something in my manner that's wrong, and I want you to tell me honestly, as a friend, what it is."

Mr. Cheesewright smiled rather sadly. "No," he said. "It's not your fault. It's the fault of the men who built this town ... what we call 'the new town'. It's such a dreary, hopeless place. There's nowhere for people to go except the pictures and the pubs and the dog-racing. They hardly know the meaning of the open air. There ought to be a promenade beside the river, or some gardens for them—but there's nothing. There's a little recreation ground behind the station that was given to the town by Mrs. Bannister Paget's grandfather, but he put such a big memorial on it to commemorate his gift that it left no room for the people to sit down. When you wonder why people do not come to church, you must ask yourself what there is to thank God for in Woodbank."

The clock struck nine, and Mr. Cheesewright rose to go. "It's been a wonderful evening for me, Mr. Matthews," he said—"a memorable evening—and I wish I could be of more help to you. But I'm afraid there's so little to be done. To change these people you would have to change the town, and it's too late for anybody to do that now."

It was not until his guest was on the point of leaving that Mr. Matthews got some really useful information. He told Mr. Cheesewright about the Boys' Club he had organised in Little Stanton. "Even if it's too late to do anything about the older people," he said, "I could do something for these boys if I could find some way of getting to know them."

He explained the kind of club he would like to organise for the older boys in Woodbank. Mr. Cheesewright listened patiently, and shook his head again with a gentle smile.

"You will never do anything with the boys in Woodbank," he said, "so long as Joe Briggs is proprietor of 'The Fighting Cocks'. Joe Briggs was Heavyweight Boxing Champion of London at one time: the boys hero-worship him, and he's got them in the palm of his dirty hand. He runs what he calls a 'Boxing Club' but he degrades the boys who go there. He makes them drunk—fighting drunk—and offers them big prize-money. He's clever, and keeps on the right side of the police—but there's dreadful stories told of those drunk lads, fighting till they half kill each other. When Mr. Todhunter was Vicar he thought it was his duty to interfere—but it wasn't his duty, and he shouldn't have done it."

"What happened?" asked Mr. Matthews.

Mr. Cheesewright did not answer. The fate of Mr. Todhunter appeared to be too painful for words. He fumbled with his hat and looked at the door.

"I want to know because it's my business to know," said Mr. Matthews.

"It's *not* your business!" burst out Mr. Cheesewright with unexpected spirit. "It's the business of the Magistrates and the Police!"

"What happened to Mr. Todhunter?" persisted the Vicar.

"He was badly hurt. No one knows how badly, because he stayed behind the closed doors of this house till he was well again. They say his nose was broken and his arm was dislocated—but he tried to hush it up for the sake of the church. What hurt him more were the horrible, obscene things written on the garden wall. He had them wiped off every morning but they were written up again, night after night, and it was terrible for all of us who had the good name of St. Peter's Church at heart. For the sake of yourself, and of all of us, Mr. Matthews—leave Joe Briggs alone. It isn't your business. You would only bring more insults on the Church and harm to yourself."

Mr. Matthews walked down to the gate with his guests to see them off. It was a warm summer night and the twilight lingered around the cranes and derricks on the river side. He heard the half-hour strike from the Town Hall as he watched his guests go down St. Peter's Lane. The public-houses closed at ten in Woodbank and it was barely a five minutes' walk to "The Fighting Cocks".

He went back to the house and took his hat and walking-stick from the hall and called out to his wife that he was going for a stroll before he settled down to work.

Chapter Nine

As he drew near the bottom of St. Peter's Lane, Mr. Matthews saw the bright lights of "The Fighting Cocks" ahead of him, and he was nearly at the swing doors of the public bar before he began to wonder what he was going to do when he got inside.

The news of Joe Briggs and his "Boxing Club" had come like a stream of light to a man who had groped for months in darkness.

There had always been something about the Woodbank boys that he had not understood. He had met a few insipid youths on his parish calls, but the type he wanted to meet—the type that had formed the backbone of his club in Little Stanton—had eluded him. He knew they went to the football on Saturdays and the dog-racing on Thursdays, but what they did with the rest of their spare time was a mystery until Mr. Cheesewright had enlightened him.

He was exhilarated by the discovery. He strode down St. Peter's Lane like a Crusader, burning to come to grips at last with one of the evil things of Woodbank, but he eased up a little when he got within a few yards of the public-house, and decided to walk by and calm down before he joined battle with the iniquitous Joe Briggs.

He went as far as the High Street and stood there for a while, wondering what he was going to say to Joe Briggs when he got inside. He also wondered what Joe Briggs was going to say to him. A full moon was rising, and he thought how much nicer it would be to go for a long, quiet moonlight walk instead. He could hear voices in the public bar and a loud piano, and he began to wonder whether it really was a matter for a Vicar of the Church to interfere in. To see a Magistrate and get some legal action going might be better, and the more he thought about Mr. Todhunter's broken nose the more inclined he felt towards the idea of leaving it to the Magistrate.

The Town Hall clock chimed out the three-quarter-hour. In a little while "The Fighting Cocks" would close. He knew that it was now or never. If he left it until another day he would have thought up a dozen new reasons for shirking the job. He stopped thinking about it, braced himself and walked back and pushed open the swing doors.

There were not many people in the public bar. An automatic piano was playing away by itself in a corner, two bargees in blue jerseys were drinking beer at the counter and a few men and women were sitting round tables in the alcoves by the walls. It was a gaudy, ugly place, with a lot of hard bright lights and brass fittings, but it looked clean and respectable enough. Mr. Matthews strolled across to the bar and said "Good evening" to the two bargees. They looked him up and down in some surprise, murmured "Good evening" and went on with their conversation. The people at the tables stopped talking and nudged one another, but when Mr. Matthews behaved quite normally they settled down again and took no further notice of him.

The barmaid was pushing some bottles about on a shelf behind the bar when Mr. Matthews entered, and she looked quite startled when she turned round and saw a clergyman at her elbow. She was a youngish woman with gay blobs of rouge and bright yellow hair that was coming up a mousey colour at the roots. A long wave in front was trained to fall languorously over one eye in imitation of Veronica Lake, the film star, serving a double purpose in concealing a slight squint.

Mr. Matthews ordered a glass of beer and she served him without comment. He mentioned that the night was warm for May, and she said it was indeed. He told her he was the new Vicar of St. Peter's Church, and she said "Oh, yes?" and moved away to serve the bargees with another round of beer. She was guarded and, it seemed, a little puzzled—but no more so, thought Mr. Matthews, than any barmaid would naturally be on the sudden appearance of a clergyman.

Left by himself he began to feel an anti-climax. There was no sign of Joe Briggs or any boys. The place looked so normal and ordinary that he began to wonder whether Mr. Cheesewright's dramatic story was a wild exaggeration of some isolated incident—distorted and enlarged, no doubt, by prejudice and rumour. He had keyed himself for something so breath-taking that he felt quite disappointed and let down.

When the barmaid was free again he said:

"I believe Mr. Briggs is proprietor here?—I'd like to meet him if he's free."

"He's not here," she said—and moved away to serve some new arrivals.

There was nothing to be done about it. The whole thing had fizzled out. He stood there alone beside the bar, and the longer he stood there the more conspicuous he felt. The new arrivals were having a good stare at him now, and he decided to go. But just as he was on the point of leaving, things began to happen. They happened so quickly and so startlingly that they quite took his breath away.

First the automatic piano stopped, and in the sudden silence he was aware of a confused, mysterious murmur from beyond a closed door at the far end of the bar. Then the door flew violently open by a kick from the other side and two men appeared, red in the face and laughing uproariously. They were carrying empty glasses and seemed well primed with drink. They left the door wide open behind them as they crossed to the bar, and Mr. Matthews could see down a long, dark passage into a brightly lighted room. The sounds that had been muffled were now loud and riotous. There was cheering and roars of laughter, and one hoarse, bellowing voice that came between the cheering. There was a silence—the thud of a falling body and another burst of cheers and laughter.

Mr. Matthews acted smartly. He put down his half finished glass of beer and walked towards the door before anyone had time to close it. The barmaid also acted smartly. She had evidently been watching him out of the corner of her eye, and he had scarcely turned before she called out harshly:

"You can't go in there! It's private."

"Boxing, isn't it?" called back Mr. Matthews in an innocent, eager voice. "I like boxing!" And before she could do anything to stop him he was through the door and in the passage.

The passage was narrow and roughly timbered—evidently a covered way across a yard—and when he was half down it somebody slammed the door ahead of him, leaving him in pitch darkness. He groped forward and fumbled for the door and pushed it open.

He found himself in a big room, built, no doubt, as a training gymnasium for professional boxers, well fitted with gymnastic apparatus and bars and punching balls, with seats in a double tier around the walls.

There was a dazzle of light and a reek of tobacco smoke and beer. The seats were packed, and as he looked around him Mr. Matthews knew that he was at last among the boys of Woodbank who had eluded him so long. There must have been a hundred of them. There was a scattering of older men, but mostly they were boys around the age of seventeen and twenty.

He was prepared for anything to happen when he stepped into the room, and he wondered afterwards at his courage in doing it. His entry, however, fell quite flat. The whole assembly was too intent upon the scene in front of it to notice him.

The fight in progress was the strangest he had ever seen. There was something sublime in it, and something ridiculous: something repulsive, yet something that impelled and fascinated him. The two boys were tall and finely built and fearless. They were stripped to the waist, fighting barefooted in old flannel trousers tied up with string. They were tuzzle-haired and scarlet in the face—streaming with sweat and completely drunk. Both were having difficulty in keeping a balance as they swung murderous, scythe-like blows at one another, and their drunken efforts to knock each other out accounted for the cheers and laughter that he had heard from the public bar.

"Five pounds the winner and drinks on the house!" came a bellow from the midst of the tobacco smoke, and Mr. Matthews saw a man who could only be Joe Briggs himself. He was in harmony with the scene: an outlandish caricature of an old-time pugilist gone to seed: bullet-headed, broken-nosed, hugely fat, with two little gleaming eyes as black and as hard as buttons. He stood in front of the crowd, squatting forward with his hands on his knees, bawling at the fighting boys. The boys would sway and stare at him between their futile blows, then brush their hair out of their eyes and try again.

One was dark and the other fair. Physically they were splendidly matched, and Mr. Matthews, who admired good boxing, could see that both had been well taught. Despite their far gone condition, both now and then squared up by instinct and aimed a blow that any boxer would be proud of, but the force of these efforts sent them staggering out of control across the room.

Presently the fair boy, more by chance than by design, connected with a sickening blow low down in the stomach of his opponent. The crowd yelled: the dark boy doubled up in agony and Joe Briggs fairly danced with joy.

"Come on, Pete!" he yelled. "Where's your guts?—at him, boy!"

The excited spectators now raised a shout that sounded like: "All in!"—"All in!" It filled the room, and Joe Briggs gave a sign to the seconds crouching in the corners.

They darted forward—wrenched the gloves off the drunken boys and left them with bare fists.

Mr. Matthews, to his secret shame on later and sedate reflection, was hypnotised and carried away by what followed. The reason why he was in the room: the things that would happen when he was discovered: everything was forgotten in a primitive, overwhelming instinct of admiration for courage and endurance. The dark boy straightened himself from the pain of the foul blow and charged his opponent like a bull. His blows connected now. A powerful, bare-fisted right caught his opponent in the mouth and a left swing gashed his cheek below the eye. The force of it sent him reeling into the arms of the spectators, who eagerly thrust him back into the ring. Blood ran from his mouth and oozed from his gashed cheek: he threw himself on his opponent and caught him a second blow in the stomach—but the dark boy, who seemed beyond pain now, led back. Both swayed precariously, but both held their ground, and for a full minute they lashed and pounded furiously at each other's faces. The yells of the spectators were deafening. Mr. Matthews thought of the crowds at a Roman Carnival in a fight to death of Gladiators, with Joe Briggs in the role of a bloated, intoxicated Nero.

Reason came back to him, and he felt ashamed. The moment had come, he knew, to intervene. He thought enviously of men like Gary Cooper and Spencer Tracy whom he admired so much in the films. If he had been Spencer Tracy or Gary Cooper, playing a fighting parson in a picture, the moment had now come to step forward and deal Joe Briggs a mighty blow that would send the camera swinging at top speed after him as he whistled through the clouds of cigarette smoke. But Mr. Matthews was neither a Tracy nor a Cooper. He was, unhappily, a middle-aged parson, thinking about the broken nose his predecessor had received for interfering in the affairs of Mr. Briggs and "The Fighting Cocks". He remained unheroically in the dark corner by the door, telling himself, to ease his conscience, that interference at such a moment would in any case do more harm than good. It would turn every boy, in his present mood, against him, the fighters, probably, more than any. He would cut a ridiculous figure in front of the boys whom he wanted, by some means, to win over in the end, and, truth to tell, he was feeling the old primitive instinct surging back again. He had less and less desire to intervene, and more and more desire to throw concealment to the winds and shout "Bravo, Pete!—Get at him, boy!" for the boy called Pete had taken another foul blow below the belt and was standing up to it and fighting back with a cleanness and a courage that filled him with admiration.

The fight was near its end. With battered faces and swollen, half-closed eyes—with blood-smeared bodies and heaving chests, it was incredible that they could still go on. Then Pete drew back: he passed a hand across his eyes, gathered himself and landed a final, smashing blow to the chin of his opponent. The fair boy went down like a log and the crowd roared. Joe Briggs lunged forward, lifted Pete's arm as a symbol of victory and bawled for silence.

"Okay, boys!" he shouted: "Next Wednesday you'll see young Billy Jackson get his own back on Big Jim Scott. A fight to the knockout!—no points and no punches pulled!—Now get out and go quiet."

Mr. Matthews stood back against the wall as the spectators jostled out in a babbling crowd. Most of them had empty tankards in their hands: some were drunk and none took so much as a glance at the Vicar through the haze of the tobacco smoke.

Joe Briggs was busy with the two exhausted fighters. Pete already had a tankard in his hand and was trying to get his battered lips around it. The other's face was grotesquely swollen and bleeding badly, but he had come round, and he too was trying to drink from a tankard held by a supporter.

"Good fight," said Joe. "And see you get your own back next week, Tony. Double entrance money and a seven pound stake."

He hustled the fighters and their seconds into a dressing-room and shut the door on them. Despite a lot of domineering bluster he seemed nervous, and anxious to get the place clear as quick as possible. He blew out his cheeks, looked round the room and saw the solitary figure standing by the window. He stared, and blinked—and stared again as if he thought his eyes were playing tricks.

"Good evening," said Mr. Matthews.

Joe Briggs still stared, and the Vicar began the introduction he had used a thousand times in the past few months at a thousand houses in his parish. It seemed a little out of place in the warm reek of sweat and smoke, but by force of habit he said:

"I'm the new Vicar of St. Peter's Church. My name is Matthews."

Joe Briggs went on staring.

"I came to see you because I'm told you're an old heavyweight champion, and you're the man I want."

Joe Briggs looked puzzled. "You want me to knock somebody out for you?" he asked.

Mr. Matthews laughed. "There are lots of people I'd like to see knocked out in Woodbank," he said. "But it wasn't about them I came."

Joe Briggs did not seem to know what to make of it.

"Well," he said at last—"What *did* you come for?"

"I'm an old boxing man myself," said Mr. Matthews. "I boxed lightweight for my college. I never did anything to write home about, but I love the game. It's the finest sport on earth and I'd like every boy in Woodbank to enjoy it. I would like to organise a Boxing Club in a Hall we've got, down by the river, and I thought if you could spare the time you would come along and lend a hand as Instructor."

The possibility of reforming Joe Briggs by appealing to his vanity had occurred to him on the spur of the moment, and it looked as if he had a sporting chance of pulling it off. There was a gleam of pleasure in the little buttons that passed with Joe for eyes: he fidgeted in a queer child-like way and licked his lips as if the idea appealed to him. Then the slow, fuddled brain began to work. He looked the Vicar up and down, and apparently decided that there was a catch in it somewhere.

"Any boy who wants to box can come here," he said. "They all do, for that matter—them with guts do. We don't want no other club."

"There are boys who might not be able to come here," said the Vicar.

"Why not?" demanded Joe.

"Well . . ." began Mr. Matthews—"in some cases parents might not . . ."

"Parents don't come into it," snapped Joe. "We don't want kids who're tied to apron strings—and we don't want no choir boy cissies, neither."

Mr. Matthews wished he had not mentioned parents, and Joe began to look truculent and suspicious.

"It's a matter we would have to talk over ..." began the Vicar—"there're lots of things to ..."

"Sure," broke in Joe. "There's lots of things—and some are yours and some are mine. Your job's praying and mine's boxing. If you stick to your job I'll stick to mine."

"I can't pray all the time," said Mr. Matthews. "There are other jobs—and one of them is to take an interest in the boys here ... to see they grow up into healthy men and good citizens."

Joe's face mottled up in scarlet patches and his little eyes gleamed with malice.

"Now see here," he said: "there was a fellow named Todhunter in your line of business. He was like you. He didn't know where his job stopped and mine began. He came round interfering one night, and if you want to know what happened to him, go and ask him. If you want to start a club, go and do it—but don't come sucking round me. I carry on my business according to the law. A fellow's got the right to run his own gymnasium if he's got a licence. If you don't believe it, go and ask the Police."

"I don't know anything about laws and licences," said Mr. Matthews, "but I know a good deal about the rules of boxing. I saw two boys fighting here to-night ... fighting, I said ... not boxing. They looked straightforward, decent boys to me, and I've never seen a better display of courage. But they were drunk and you made them drunk. If you encourage them to go on living as they're living now, they'll be physical wrecks before they're twenty, and you know it."

"Get out of here," said Joe, without raising his voice. "Get out and stay out."

"I'll get out and stay out," he answered—"on one condition. You've got these boys in the palm of your hand. If I had a tenth part of the influence you've got over them, I would be a proud and happy man. Influence with boys of this kind is the most responsible and important thing a man can have. If you use it for the good you'll never regret it, but if you go on degrading them as you did to-night you degrade yourself, and sooner or later these boys will know it, and you'll get what you deserve."

He turned away and walked to the door. He felt better now—he even felt a bit like Spencer Tracy. He had a feeling that his words had gone home, for Joe Briggs stood there, strangely silent.

He turned the handle, but the door refused to open: he pulled harder, but it still refused to move, and suddenly the truth dawned on him. They had set a trap. An accomplice had locked him in, and he was alone with a heavyweight champion whom he had bitterly insulted. He knew now why Joe Briggs had taken those last scalding words so quietly and amiably. He had time to play with. He was going to get his own back at leisure in the locked gymnasium, and Mr. Matthews did not feel like Spencer Tracy any longer. He felt more like a little boy who had thrown a stone and broken a window and run away to find himself in a cul-de-sac. Visions of Mr. Todhunter's broken nose enveloped him: he could almost feel the sudden agonising pain of it. He wondered whether Ruth still kept the shilling first aid box in the bathroom cupboard, and he wondered how far a shilling's worth of lint and plaster would go by the time Joe Briggs had finished with him. . . .

"Open this door," he said. But his mouth was dry and the words were thin and rasping.

Joe did not move. He stood in the middle of the room with his hands in his pockets—a towering, menacing ape of a man with the light behind him.

"Open this door!" demanded Mr. Matthews. "If you don't you'll regret it!"

"Try the other knob," said Joe.

He had not seen the small brass knob above the wooden handle. He turned it and the door moved easily.

"That scared the eyelids off you!" said Joe, and a burst of uproarious laughter followed Mr. Matthews down the passage.

The moon was shining in a starlit sky when the doors of "The Fighting Cocks" swung to behind him. He turned down St. Peter's Lane and three boys passed him, arm-in-arm, singing lustily. They stopped singing when they saw a clergyman's white collar gleaming in the moonlight: there was a short embarrassed silence, then one of them struck up: "O God, our help in ages past", and the others laughed and joined in. They only knew two lines of it, but they sang them again with gusto as the darkness of the high-walled lane closed round the Vicar.

Chapter Ten

When Rosemary came back from school for the Easter holidays, her parents had planned a series of excursions to London.

They took her to some matinées and the latest pictures, and the British Museum and the Tate Gallery and the Houses of Parliament. They took her round the West-End shops and the Tower of London and the Zoo. They gave her the most varied entertainment they could devise, partly to compensate her for having to spend her holidays in Woodbank, but chiefly to find out what she was interested in, so that they could plan a career for her when she left school.

But when it was all over they had to admit that the only things their daughter had been really interested in were the lacrosse rackets in a sports shop and the jazz band in a place where they had lunch. Art and Music and History and Drama were to Rosemary like water on a duck's back. It worried Mr. Matthews, because she was due to leave school at the end of the Summer term, and the prospect of her living at Woodbank Vicarage with nothing to do filled him with alarm.

"Fair" appeared rather too monotonously against the various subjects listed in her school reports—with "excellent" against General Behaviour. Mr. Matthews would have preferred it the other way round.

"Lacking in self-confidence", was the Head Mistress's comment under General Remarks.—"Shy, and reluctant to assert herself, but obedient and painstaking."

"In other words," said Mr. Matthews—"a country parson's daughter with a vengeance."

All this was strange in the face of other things, for Rosemary in the past few years had developed into a girl of unusual beauty. It was a shy, elusive beauty that made people turn in the streets to look at her. In a bus or tea-shop she drew so many eyes that it quite embarrassed the Vicar and his wife, and the only one who seemed unconscious of it was Rosemary herself.

"She'll grow out of her shyness," said Ruth. "It's better, really—at seventeen. If she were too flighty, goodness knows what would happen."

"What she needs is companionship," said Roger. "Young people of her own age: boys to dance with and take her out."

There were none quite suitable in Woodbank to take her out, so when the summer holidays came round they took her to a lively hotel at Brighton where there was companionship in plenty for her.

When she came down to dinner on the first night in a pale blue dress she was a sensation. Every young man wanted to dance with her, but all of them, her parents noted with regret, gallantly surrendered her to someone else after the first dance or two, and went into the bar for stimulant.

"She's marvellous to look at," said a boy in Mr. Matthews' hearing, "but she just doesn't have a thing to say for herself. She's the dumbest cluck I ever met. She just doesn't tick." And Mr. Matthews, from his seat behind a fern, was obliged to admit in his own mind that the boy had hit the nail on the head. Rosemary, despite the glory of her outward charm, was unhappily a dumb cluck.

Her school fees were heavy, but they decided to send her back for another year in the hope that something would suddenly happen inside her to make her tick.

They saw her off to school again in September. She looked so lovely that a young porter who carried her bags refused to take the tip she offered him. Mr. Matthews, who witnessed this unique incident, resolved to let Rosemary do all tipping in the future, but he went home puzzled and disturbed. He wondered how a girl so beautiful could be so quiet and shy. He wondered how the world would treat her if she were alone.

Winter returned to the lonely Vicarage. Woodbank lit its fires and drew its curtains and remained unmoved by the Vicar's efforts to put some life into it, and the Matthews were driven back upon their own resources to pass the long dark evenings. They took up dominoes and chess: they played two-handed whist and read their library books aloud to one another until the monotony began to get too much for them. Arguments blew up over trivial things, and one night they had the first big quarrel of their lives. Mr. Matthews wanted to have dinner an hour later to make the second part of the evenings shorter and Mrs. Matthews said it wasn't fair on Mrs. Burgin, who liked to get the kitchen cleared by nine. They quarrelled violently, and Mr. Matthews slammed the door and wandered up and down St. Peter's Lane in the fog and darkness.

Ruth had gone to bed when he came back, and he went up to her.

"If we go on like this much longer," he said, "we shall turn into a couple of raving lunatics. The people here don't want us, and that's all there is to it."

"Sometimes I think that too," said Ruth—"and then the other night I dreamed that something happened. I don't know what it was, but suddenly everything changed and everything was wonderful. I don't think dreams are much to go on, but there it is. . . . I did dream it."

"I could go to the Bishop to-morrow and ask for a move," he said, "but it would be a confession of failure. I couldn't in reason ask for another difficult, worth-while job after the mess I've made of this one. They would just write me off as too old, and give me a country village to while away the last few years. I hate admitting failure, but I can't go on like this—concealing it. You've always advised me well, Ruth. I've never needed it so desperately as I do to-night. Think about it while I go down and lock up and turn the lights out."

He pottered about downstairs to give her time to think. He poked out the fire and collected the cards that lay where they had been left when the quarrel started.

Ruth was sitting up in bed when he went back.

"If you ask to be moved," she said—"with so little done in Woodbank—then I think it'll mean exactly what you say. They'd turn you out to grass in some harmless place where nothing you do will matter very much one way or another. But if you stay on here, there's always the possible chance that something worth-while *might* happen. Why not give it another year?—if nothing's happened in a year from now—that ends it."

"Right," said Mr. Matthews. "Another year." And he went to bed with a feeling that they had scored some kind of victory.

He started next morning on a new set of plans and schemes, and one of the things he decided to do was to take an allotment. It would be easier, he thought, to talk to people and get to know them if he worked beside them with a fork and spade. In his old sports shirt and flannel trousers they might forget he was the Vicar and treat him like one of themselves. "Even if they don't," he said, "the vegetables I grow will come in very handy."

He set off with Ruth to see the vacant plots. They went down St. Peter's Lane and along the High Street and down a drab side road that tapered off on to the allotments beside the waterworks.

Spring was on its way again. It was a fine sunlit evening, and when the plot was chosen, Ruth proposed a walk.

"We've never explored the river bank on the other side of the waterworks," she said. "There might be a path around it to save us going through the town."

A man at work on a near-by allotment told them there was a quicker way.

"You see that piece of waste land over there," he said, "with the big trees round it?—You can climb through the fence and go across it and come right out on the river bank."

Mr. Matthews had explored most ways in Woodbank in his wanderings round the parish, but this was new to him, and when they reached the fence he saw ahead of him a wild, neglected field, covered in brambles and tall weeds, with some fine old elms around it and its far side open to the river.

"There's a hole in the fence along there!" shouted the man across the allotments. "It's private—but nobody's going to stop you!"

"Thank you!" called back Mr. Matthews.

"I really don't think," he said to Ruth, "that Vicars ought to crawl through holes in private fences."

"You've done worse things in Woodbank than crawl through holes," said Ruth—"come on—let's go."

They scrambled in and picked their way through the long rank grass.

"I thought I knew every corner of Woodbank," said Mr. Matthews. "I never realised there was any open land like this. Look how these elms close it in. You can hardly see a single house or chimney. When the leaves are out you could stand here and imagine you were miles away in the country."

"Look at that clump of trees," said Ruth. "It's almost a wood."

A dozen saplings were clustered round the rotting trunk of a fallen elm. They were young and fresh, with a delicate haze of spring in them that moved against the sunlit sky.

They went in between the trees, and sat on the fallen trunk. "We could bring a picnic lunch out here, and imagine we were in the woods at Little Stanton," said Mr. Matthews. "In the summer we could sit here and forget the chimney-pots and the tram-lines, and see green leaves and wild grass for a whole afternoon. There's something about this place that's—fascinating."

Ruth got up and began to explore the brambles. "Look!" she called out—"Come over here! Am I seeing things or are these primroses?"

He went over and pushed the grass aside. "They're primroses all right," he said—"fine ones, too . . . primroses in Woodbank, ten minutes from the High Street!"

There were about two acres of the land, roughly square, with a narrow frontage to the Thames. At one end an old brick and timber building faced the river, with steps up to a wooden balcony surrounding some upper rooms.

"It's an old boat-house," said Mr. Matthews—"You can see the slipway for the boats. Let's have a look upstairs."

They found the upstairs door unlocked, and went into a big room where some relics of furniture remained. There was a long deal table and some chairs, and over the fireplace a board engraved "GRASSHOPPERS ROWING CLUB. Founded 1895". Beneath were the names of the Club Captains, beginning in 1895 and ending in 1902.

"I wonder who the Grasshoppers were—and what happened to them," said Mr. Matthews. "Whoever they were, they had a grand club house."

A door at the back led into a small kitchen. Another opened into a changing-room, with rows of pegs and lockers, and an old hand pump that had once fed a line of wash-basins and a shower.

They went out and stood on the balcony. "I wonder why it's been deserted all these years," said Ruth.

Mr. Matthews looked around him. The sun was setting behind the trees, and he saw the trees like sentinels around the last green land that Woodbank would ever have.

"If I were a rich man ..." he began ...

"You'd buy it," finished Ruth.

"I'd buy it ... no matter what it cost. I'd have tennis courts and a bowling green: I'd lay sands along the riverbank for the children and a swimming-pool and a gymnasium for the boys. I'd leave that little wood and keep it as a wild corner for primroses and bluebells in the spring ... I would make something here that would shake the blight from this God-forsaken town."

He looked down at the river. There was a new romance in it with the lights gleaming through the dusk from the buildings on the farther shore. There was beauty in it. He saw the small wood where they had sat on the fallen tree, peaceful and mysterious in the twilight. The wild grass round it reminded him of the downlands of the west country; of his years of happiness and the dreams of the great things he would do one day to make life happier for other people. From a distance—from another world—came the sounds of Woodbank: the rattle of the derrick chains and the hooting of the tugs and the restless murmur of the traffic in the High Street, but near at hand, from the wood below them, a thrush was singing.

"It's what I've wanted all these years. It's the last chance and the last hope for this forsaken town. If I don't get it—and someone builds a factory here, it'll slam the door for good and all, and Woodbank will go on being a dark, forsaken place till the end of time."

"It's big," said Ruth. "It would cost an awful lot."

"I don't care what it costs. All my life I've waited for a chance like this to do something lasting and worth while. I've groped about and made false starts because I never really knew what I was looking for. But it's here at last, and I'm going to have it, Ruth."

The offices of Stoddart and Jupp, Estate Agents, were opposite the Railway Station, and they caught Mr. Jupp as he was locking up his office for the night.

Mr. Jupp had had an overdose of Mr. Matthews, who had called on numerous occasions to interest him in his various schemes, and when he saw the Vicar coming he looked at his watch to show that he had no time to spare.

"It's all right," called out Mr. Matthews—"it's not the church to-day!"

Mr. Jupp looked suspicious, but he unlocked the door and switched on the light and took them into a room behind the office.

"It's about a piece of land," said Mr. Matthews, "beside the river—with an old boat-house on it."

Mr. Jupp's face fell. His hopes of a small business deal departed.

"You want it for a school treat or something?" he enquired.

"No. I want to buy it."

Mr. Jupp laughed.

"So do I," he said—"so does the Claremont Timber Company and the Collins Wharf. Plenty of people want to buy it."

"Then why isn't it sold?"

"I thought everybody knew," said Mr. Jupp. . . . "It's ancient history now. It belongs to an old lady named Ponsonby. Her father was a big man here at one time. He owned a lot of land and built that boat-house for a Rowing Club he started. When he died the club died with him, and his daughter got that piece of land. But she was one of the old die-hard gentry of Woodbank. She hated the wharves and factories because it made the place impossible to live in. She moved out and vowed she would never sell that land to any of them. She was cutting off her nose to spite her face, because she could have got a handsome price for it. I've sent her good offers time and again but she doesn't even answer. Between ourselves, she's a bit cracked. It's a mania with her and you can't budge her."

"Was she interested in the church?" asked Mr. Matthews.

"All the old people were," said the Estate Agent. "It was everything to her."

"Then if you told her the Vicar wants it as an open space for the people here?"

Mr. Jupp laughed again. "She hated the new people like poison," he said. "She hated them worse than the factories."

"You could ask her."

"It wouldn't be any good. I know that old woman. I know how her mind works. She wouldn't listen to you."

Mr. Matthews held his ground. The Estate Agent looked at his watch—but the more he looked at his watch, the more the Vicar held his ground. Finally, to get rid of him, he promised to write. "But she won't answer," he said. "I can tell you that now. She never does."

Mr. Matthews waited a month: he waited on tenterhooks—fuming at the delay. But even while he fumed and waited, he wondered what on earth he would do if he got a favourable reply. His balance at the bank was £97 and he had nothing else except his books and furniture. He had jogged along comfortably enough on his salary, and money had meant little to him. Now it meant everything. He thought about it night and day, and wondered feverishly what he could do about it. He searched his library for hidden treasures in his first editions. He picked some out and sent them to a bookseller who offered £3 for one of them and sent the others back.

"If only I were a rich man!" he said—"rolling in money!"

"If you had a million," answered Ruth, "it wouldn't make any difference if the old lady's cracked and refuses to sell."

"Money can do almost anything," said Mr. Matthews—"you might even mend cracked people with it."

Every day he rang up Mr. Jupp and got the same reply. "We shan't hear now," said Mr. Jupp. "I never thought we would in any case."

Finally Mr. Matthews took things into his own hands and went down to Hove to see Miss Ponsonby and have it out with her.

She was a frigid, unlovable old woman, and for the first time since he came to Woodbank Mr. Matthews found it useful to be a clergyman. Had he been anything else, he felt, she would have slammed the door on him.

She entered into a long tirade against the desecration of Woodbank. Mr. Matthews was prepared for this, and she was rather annoyed when he joined in and outdid her with his own denunciation of the wharves and factories. It was not the people's fault, he pleaded: the people were the wretched pawns of the big business man. They were suffering as she had suffered, but, unlike her, they had no means to move away from it. "What a wonderful way," he said, "of showing these grasping factory owners what we think of them! If we build a playground where they hoped to build a factory, what a lesson for them!—What a nemesis to their unscrupulous ambitions!" He had a poor hand, but he played his trumps for all they were worth. Miss Ponsonby was profoundly suspicious, and asked a lot of searching questions. In the end she gave in. "Very well," she said—"I trust you as a man of God. I would trust no one else. I will sell the land for £500 on strict condition that it remains exactly as it is. You may cut the grass and repair the fence and make a garden—but not one stone or brick must ever be built upon it."

Mr. Matthews returned to Woodbank, walking on air. "It's mine!" he said—"I've got it!'

"How much?" asked Ruth.

"£500"

"I hate to pour cold water," she said—"but where's the £500?"

"I don't need it," replied Mr. Matthews, who had been reading up a book on land tenure. "You can always raise a mortgage on good land, and it's easily worth £500. The interest would be about 4 per cent: £20 a year. I can manage that. . . . I'll get some evening work—I'll address envelopes—I'll do anything—and I'll put a little aside every year to pay off the capital."

He went to see Mr. Jupp, and Mr. Jupp sat back and laughed.

"I'm afraid you don't understand these things," he said. "Nobody would loan £500 on a piece of land that must never be built on. What would be the good of it to them?"

Mr. Matthews went down to Hove again. He had to listen to another and completely similar tirade from Miss Ponsonby about the Woodbank wharves and factories, with an additional tirade against himself for pretending he had the money when he hadn't.

But finally she said she would let the land to him at £40 a year, and Mr. Matthews could buy it when he had scraped £500 together. The rent was to be payable £10 a quarter with orders to quit at three months' notice if she thought better of it.

She was not quite so cracked as Mr. Jupp made out, but Mr. Matthews went back to Woodbank an exhausted, happy man. If he spent the rest of his life achieving it, he would leave wild primroses to Woodbank when he died.

Chapter Eleven

The agreement was signed, and at midsummer Mr. Matthews was free to enter upon the land.

The tenancy was precarious. Miss Ponsonby could turn him off whenever she wanted to and Mr. Jupp the Estate Agent said that if things had been left in his hands he could have got the land at half the price. "Considering you aren't allowed to do anything but walk about on it," he said, "you haven't got much for your money."

But Mr. Matthews was not worrying about what Mr. Jupp might have done. He was more concerned about what he did himself and the proper way to do it. He wanted to get some volunteers without stirring up the same lot of people who had made such a fiasco of his earlier plans. If he called a public meeting, the lady with the green cigarette-holder would turn up again and want to start a school of elocution in the boat-house, and lots of people would offer to run the whole thing if Mr. Matthews merely found the money and the labour. He meant to get the right people this time and decided to start quietly with Ruth as his only helper until good volunteers began to come along as the thing developed.

He began with a measuring tape and a roll of drawing-paper and spent the first week making a scale plan of the land. He bought a scythe and a sickle to cut the grass, and a wheelbarrow to cart away the old tin cans and dump them in the river. He got some tools to dig the garden beds and brooms to clean the boat-house. They got the stove working and made tea, and sat out on the balcony on the summer evenings watching the busy traffic on the Thames. By July they had sickled off the grass and rooted up the weeds and thrown the rubbish in the river. "It looks bigger with the grass cut," said Mr. Matthews. "The more I see of it the more I think what a wonderful place we can make of it ... if only that old woman doesn't change her mind and turn us off. Every time I see the postman coming I imagine he's got a letter telling us to quit. If only we had £500 to buy the land and make us free!"

"£500 isn't going to drop from heaven," said Ruth. "Even to oblige a clergyman. We'll have to set to and earn it somehow."

Mr. Matthews knocked off his evening glass of sherry and saved £2 a month, and Ruth knocked off her magazines and saved ten shillings. He got a spare-time job working on research for a man who was writing an Ecclesiastical History. He received £1 a week for this and Ruth worked at home on embroidery for a West End firm and averaged £3 a month. "We'll soon be putting by £10 a month," said Mr. Matthews. "In five years—if all goes well—we shall have the money, and the land will be ours."

But one day Mr. Matthews had to have some teeth out, and the new ones cost him £15. It put him back six weeks, he reckoned, but Vicars must have teeth to smile with in a place like Woodbank. They economised in clothes. Ruth did their own laundry and Mr. Matthews made his collars last three days. They economised on lights and turned them out whenever they left a room, but groping out of his dark study one night into the deeper darkness of the passage Mr. Matthews hit the open door and broke his spectacles. "I saved a ha'porth of light," he said—"and lost £2 on glasses." There were unexpected things to buy in tools and cleaning stuff for the boat-house and they seemed to work so hard to save so little. Sometimes £500 looked hopeless when Mr. Matthews thought of it as 120,000 pennies—the laundry bills on his collars for two hundred years.

But by the first of August £12 was saved, and paid into the bank to earn some interest on the capital. It was a red letter day on that account, and for another reason—because that evening something else occurred in the thread of small events that were guiding Mr. Matthews to an unexpected destiny.

He had gone off by himself that evening after dinner, in an old sports shirt and sweater, to finish digging a flower border round the boat-house before dark, and he was coming home along St. Peter's Lane in the twilight.

As he drew near the Vicarage he heard an odd sound—a kind of drowsy humming that might have been the wind in the trees if the night had not been still and overcast. The high walls of the lane increased the darkness, and it took him some moments to locate the sound. He traced it to a shadow on the ground that merged, as he drew nearer, into a prostrate figure sprawled across the path with its back against the railings of the Vicarage garden.

A closer view revealed a youth of about eighteen, very much the worse for drink. A battered felt hat was lolling on the back of his head: a clump of dark hair hung over one eye and he was happily beating time to his drowsy song with his fists upon the pavement.

"Hallo," said Mr. Matthews. "What're you doing here?"

The boy looked up—blinked sleepily, and gave Mr. Matthews a dazed but friendly smile.

"Goin' home," he murmured.

"You won't get home very fast at this rate," said Mr. Matthews.

"Not . . . not'd thish rate," agreed the boy.

"Where d'you live?"

The boy pondered. "'Ushed to live in Foush . . . foush. . . ."

"Fuschia Street?"

"Fuschia Street!—You got it!"

"That's a long way away—the other side of the town."

"Doeshn't matter"—assured the boy—"'Cos I don't live there now—not for weeksh and weeksh—"

"Where d'you live now?"

"Dunno," said the boy—"Wanna—wanna go sleep . . . goo night." And he closed his eyes.

"If you go to sleep here you'll have the police after you," said Mr. Matthews.

"Don't mind police."

"Anyway—it's going to rain. If you sit here all night you'll catch pneumonia."

"Won't," said the boy—"won't catch anything. . . ." His head dropped forward on his chest and he began to snore.

Mr. Matthews wondered what to do. The boy looked big: too big in any case to carry. If he went into a drunken stupor there would be no hope of moving him, and Mr. Matthews kicked him smartly on the sole of the foot.

"Come on!" he shouted. "Wake up!—this is my house—come inside."

"All right where I am," said the boy.

"You're not all right, and you can't lie here in the rain. Come on!—I'll give you a hand."

He got round behind and took hold of the boy beneath the arms. He gave a lug but nothing happened.

"Come on!" he said again. "These are my railings and I don't want you lying up against them!"

This time the boy opened his eyes and looked up in polite concern. "Well—if—if they're *your* railings," he said—"thatsh different—*quite* different!" and he began to make an effort to get up.

It was a hard struggle. The Vicar hoisted from behind and the boy heaved himself by one of the railings. At last he was on his feet, and Mr. Matthews wished he had opened the gate before he had started. The gate was difficult enough at any time: with a reeling young giant to hold up as well it was impossible. So he propped the boy carefully against the railings while he opened the gate, then steered him through.

"Now we're all right!" he said—but he spoke too soon, for his guest fell over a tree root and the business of getting him up began all over again. But he was good-humoured and quite resourceful considering his condition, and used the chestnut tree to help.

Mr. Matthews propped him against the porch while he opened the front door. He was glad that Mrs. Burgin and his wife were not about to see the precarious journey down the passage, and luckily the study door was open. He got his guest to the sofa without knocking anything down and lowered him on to it by a dexterous piece of navigation.

The boy sprawled out with a sigh of content. "Apologise," he murmured, and with another smile he closed his eyes. This time, instead of a snore, there was a loud, convulsive hiccough, and Mr. Matthews acted quickly.

Ruth was reading in the drawing-room, and jumped up in dismay at her husband's dishevelled appearance. "Roger!—what on earth have you been doing?" she cried.

"I've got a boy in the study. He was lying on the path outside. He's drunk, and I rather think he's going to be sick. Could you get me a basin or something as quick as you can?"

Ruth hurried away, and came back from the kitchen with a big enamel bowl. "Shall I come and help?" she asked.

"Better leave it to me," he said. "You might get some strong coffee ready."

He arrived in the nick of time. He managed to get his guest forward and the basin in position. The boy was copiously sick, and the odour of stale beer and whisky filled the study. "Good!" said Mr. Matthews—"feel better?"

"Fine . . ." said the boy. ". . . apologise."

"I've got some coffee coming. Just sit back and take it easy."

The boy lay back on the sofa and looked his rescuer up and down for the first time. His eye ran slowly over the old tweed coat and open sports shirt, and Mr. Matthews was glad he was dressed that way. A formal Vicar might have embarrassed his involuntary guest, and the less he had to worry him the better. He was lying back quite comfortably now, as if nothing had happened. He finished his scrutiny and began to chuckle as if there were something amusing about the grey-haired man in front of him. "Uncle Dick!" he murmured.

Who Uncle Dick was Mr. Matthews did not know. He was more interested in the boy. He was looking at him for the first time in the full light of the room, and the face was vaguely familiar. He had seen him somewhere in Woodbank, but could not recollect where. Then he noticed a long scar above the boy's right eye, and a badly healed gash between the lip and chin, and he remembered. It was the boy called Pete who was fighting at the public-house when he had gone there to see Joe Briggs—Pete, who had taken the foul blows and fought back and won. He saw the scene again ... the glare of lights and the reek of sweat ... the dazed, blood-spattered boys and the sadistic button eyes of Joe. ...

Pete laughed. "Good old Uncle Dick!" he murmured.

"I'm not Uncle Dick."

"You *are* Uncle Dick ... good old Uncle Dick!"

"All right," said Mr. Matthews—"I'm Uncle Dick, and you're Pete, aren't you?"

The boy looked vaguely surprised. "How d'you know I'm Pete?"

"I saw you boxing one night at 'The Fighting Cocks'."

Pete leaned forward with a gleam of interest. "You know Joe Briggs?" he asked.

"Yes," said Mr. Matthews with conviction. "I know Joe Briggs."

The boy stretched out his hand with an elaborate flourish: "Shake!" he said. "Any friend of Joe Briggs is a friend of mine!"

He gripped the Vicar's hand and pressed it till he winced. "Joe's a swell guy!" he murmured, "... swell guy."

Mr. Matthews did not think it quite the time to argue whether Joe was swell or not. Had he done so it would have made no difference, for it was Pete's last effort. He dropped the Vicar's hand, lay back with a tired sigh, and fell into a blissful sleep.

Presently there was a knock at the door. "Here's the coffee," called out Ruth.

"Just a minute," said Mr. Matthews. He pushed the enamel basin under the sofa and opened the windows. The rain had started; it rustled like sand in the dry summer leaves of the chestnut tree and a cool clean breath of air came in. When the room smelt better he went over to the door and opened it. "All right," he said—"come in. He's gone to sleep. We'd better leave him as he is."

Ruth put the coffee on the table and looked down at Pete. His shirt was open at the throat and his tie half round his neck. A clump of dark, unruly hair lay across his eyes. She saw a smear of dirt on his face and bent down to examine it.

"Did he hurt himself?" she asked.

"I don't think so. Those are old scars on his face. He's one of the boys I saw fighting at the public-house that night."

Ruth watched him for a while. "He looks a nice boy," she said.

"I think he is," said Mr. Matthews. "He didn't bluster or swear when I made him get up. He even apologised for being sick."

"D'you know where he lives?"

"He doesn't know himself."

"Mrs. Burgin might help. She knows a lot of people round here."

"Ask her to come in," said Mr. Matthews.

When Mrs. Burgin arrived she took one look and nearly fainted.

"It's Pete Brown," she whispered—"drunk on your sofa, sir!—it's horrible!"

"What do you know about him?" asked the Vicar.

"He's a terrible boy, sir. He drinks and fights and bets. He's always in trouble, sir—he's no good."

"D'you know where he lives?"

"With his mother at Harper's Mews, over the stables at the back of the Laundry. She's a nice woman and it's cruel on her to have a son like that. His father was a fine man too—a Sergeant killed in the war. She works in the laundry, and Pete's at the brewery, but he never does a thing to help her—he drinks something terrible. They were going to send him to the reform school once, but they let him off for his mother's sake. They ought to have sent him . . . it might have saved him from prison."

"Has he been to prison?"

"Not yet, sir—but he will. It's a short step from drinking and gambling to thieving and murdering."

"He doesn't look like a murderer yet," said Mr. Matthews. "All right, Mrs. Burgin. I'll take care of him."

Mrs. Burgin was horrified. "But you can't keep him here, sir!—I wouldn't sleep in the house with him downstairs!—You must call the police!"

They calmed her down and told her to go to bed and lock her door if she felt like it. "You might get the thermos flask," he said to Ruth. "We'll keep the coffee hot."

She got the flask and poured the coffee into it. "I'll sit up with you if you like," she said.

"It's all right," he answered. "You go to bed. I'll do some work until he wakes up."

When Ruth had gone he took the basin upstairs and washed it out and dried it and brought it back in case it was wanted again. Then he turned on his desk light and began to prepare some notes for his Sunday services.

It was difficult to compose a sermon for Mrs. Bannister Paget and her friends that night. He thought of Pete's mother waiting in her lonely room above the Mews. The Mews were not far away. He thought of walking round to tell her that Pete was with him and would be all right. But Pete might wake up while he had gone and wonder where he was and prowl about the house. If he were as bad as Mrs. Burgin made out it was hardly fair to leave her and Ruth in the house alone.

He had another shot at the sermon, but gave it up and threw the scrappy notes aside. He closed the window and drew the curtains and sat down in the arm-chair to wait.

The light from the desk lamp threw a half shadow across the boy, concealing the scars of his fighting and the flush of his hectic night. In the shadows, relaxed in sleep, he did not look at all like the monster that Mrs. Burgin had locked her door against. There was something likeable and disarming about him. It was a pity, thought Mr. Matthews, that the only Woodbank boy who had ever come into his study was there because he could not walk straight enough to go anywhere else. He thought of the things he would like to do if by some miracle Pete had come that night of his own free will and said: "I want to get clear of this Joe Briggs fellow and his gang. . . . I want to do something better than unload barrels at the brewery. . . . I want you to lend me a hand to find a way out of it into something better and more worth while."

Up in the bedroom cupboard were two old rucksacks that he and Ruth had used in the days when they used to go walking in the Highlands. He would give one to Pete and send him home to pack it. He would take him on a walking tour in Cumberland and stay at the Inn at the foot of Kirkstone Pass. There would be no sermons or lectures or earnest talks about temperance and being a good boy. If Pete could fight clean in the foetid atmosphere of "The Fighting Cocks" his spirit would break through in triumph to the wooded crags of Cumberland. They would climb the hills and fish the rivers and explore the woods. They would return fast friends, and Pete might even call him "Uncle Dick" without having to be drunk to do it.

But Pete was not in the Vicarage of his own free will. He would wake up sober, wretched and humiliated . . . appalled at the ridicule his friends would load upon him if they heard where his helplessness had landed him, for if Joe Briggs had not taught them to laugh at and despise the parson, then Joe Briggs was not the man he seemed to be. An instinct for straight fighting would tell the boy that the parson had caught him off his guard and won on points: it would tell him to sit there with his aching head and listen while the parson enjoyed the fruits of victory and got his sermon off his chest.

He stirred in his sleep and Mr. Matthews sat up tensely, waiting for him to open his eyes and look around him. But he settled down again with a sigh and breathed more peacefully.

Mr. Matthews sat on for a while, thinking what a grand scene Spencer Tracy would play with the boy in one of those pictures in which Spencer Tracy was a fighting parson. He would put his hand on the boy's shoulder and talk magnificently—and the boy would look up, fighting his tears, and say: "I'm with you, sir . . . you've shown me something I never understood before . . . we'll fight it out together."

He sighed, and wished that he could be one of those film stars for half an hour and work a miracle. But he could hardly practise being a film star at the expense of a boy who was feeling sick and in his power. He got up and went over to his desk and took a sheet of notepaper. He tore off the Vicarage address and wrote:—

Dear Pete,

You looked so comfortable, I didn't wake you. I'm going to bed but I've left the front door open. You'll find some coffee in the flask and your home is at Harper's Mews behind the Laundry. I'm telling you this because you said you'd forgotten and you might not remember when you wake up!

Good luck and God bless you.

"Uncle Dick"

He put the note on a corner of the desk and stood the thermos flask on it. He left the light, and the front door on the latch, and went up to his room.

He lay listening for a long time. The rain had stopped, and it was very quiet. He thought of Pete's mother, listening in her room above the Mews, and the hours went by and the dawn began to come. It was past four when he heard a slight sound downstairs, and the furtive closing of a door. He got out of bed and went to the window and saw Pete walk down the path and out of the gate and along St. Peter's Lane. He put on his dressing-gown and went down to the study. The light had been turned off, but the coffee stood untouched and his note lay there beside it. He locked the front door and went back to bed. After a while he slept a little, and dreamed of taking Pete climbing in the hills of Cumberland.

PART TWO

Chapter Twelve

When he went out next morning, Mr. Matthews found Pete's hat in the garden under the chestnut tree where Pete had fallen down. It was a very old hat with a strong smell of brilliantine, and a dog-racing programme folded up in the lining.

"I don't imagine he'll miss it," said Ruth. "It couldn't have held together much longer anyway."

"It looks the kind of hat a fellow gets attached to," said Mr. Matthews. "He wouldn't have kept it so long if he wasn't fond of it. I'll wrap it up and post it back to him."

"Or take it back yourself," she suggested. "You'd like to see him again, wouldn't you?"

"Yes," he said—"but I couldn't use his hat in that way. It would look as if I were taking advantage of it to claim some thanks for getting him out of the rain last night."

"All right," said Ruth. "Do it your own way. You're always complaining that you never get a chance of meeting these Woodbank boys, and when you find one lying on the door-step you throw the chance away. You tip-toe up to bed and wonder how you can return his hat without being found out. You'll never meet any of them at that rate," and she picked up her bag and went off shopping.

Mr. Matthews walked up and down the garden. He was angry with Ruth. He had expected her to applaud the tactful way he had saved Pete from embarrassment. He went in and found a piece of brown paper and tied up the hat and addressed it to "Mr. P. Brown, Harper's Mews, Woodbank." He took it down to the Post Office, but when he got there he brought it back again. The more he thought about what Ruth had said the more upset he felt. He had let the boy go without trying to make friends, and thrown away a golden opportunity. But he could not bring himself to return the hat in the way that Ruth suggested. Pete was no doubt wondering who the odd fish was who had sneaked off to bed and left him to find his own way out. He would look a still odder fish if he now revealed himself dramatically as the Vicar, and returned the hat with a flourish of trumpets.

He walked up and down the garden again, trying to think of some means of returning it that would appeal to Pete's sense of humour and make a friend of him. Finally he decided to leave it over the week-end and hope for a good idea. Possible an amusing note inside the parcel would do the trick—if he could think of anything amusing enough by Monday morning.

He tried to forget about it, and settled down to write his sermon. He told himself he was being ridiculous about a drunk boy and a worn-out hat, but when he went to bed he could not sleep for thinking what a heaven-sent chance he had lost.

Next day was Sunday, and he preached as usual to Mrs. Bannister Paget and her friends. But thoughts of Pete upset his sermon. His mind was not on it: he stumbled and hesitated, and once or twice Mrs. Bannister Paget looked up and raised her eyebrows in surprise and disapproval. At Evensong the futility of it all began to boil up inside him, and on the way home with Ruth that night he boiled right over.

"I hate the sight of that insufferable gang of hypocrites," he said—"and I despise myself for preaching to them. I believe that boy was sent to me the other night to test me: to prove whether or not I was fit to do my proper work in Woodbank. I missed the chance—and here I am, back again, preaching to that appalling woman in her purple dress. I'm no good here and I've no right to stay."

"It's a pity you sent the hat by post instead of taking it yourself," said Ruth.

"As a matter of fact," he confessed, "I didn't post it. I couldn't make up my mind."

"If Providence sent the boy to test you," she said, "maybe the hat was left behind to give you a second chance if you missed the first. Providence takes a lot of trouble when it wants to help you."

"I'll take it back to-morrow," he declared.—"I'll go round at five o'clock and catch him when he comes home from the brewery."

With his mind made up he was happy again, but he never took the hat back after all.

He was trimming the garden hedge before dinner that night, thinking what he would say to Pete next day, when Pete himself appeared, walking slowly up the lane. He was bareheaded—looking vaguely to and fro. He stopped short of the Vicarage and peered through the railings of a neighbouring house, and Mr. Matthews did not have to be a Sherlock Holmes to know what he was looking for. The sight of the Vicar would, he thought, send the boy in the opposite direction, so he waited under cover of the hedge to catch him when he was too near to get away.

Pete came on, rubbing his chin, trying to piece together his misty recollections. He got to the Vicarage and saw the chestnut tree and looked more alert. The tree apparently stirred a hazy memory, for he searched up and down the path and began to peer through the railings. Then he saw the Vicar behind the hedge, and stiffened up self-consciously and began to walk away.

Mr. Matthews saw his quarry disappearing for a second time and acted swiftly. He dropped the hedging shears and ran to the gate and called after the retreating boy. . . .

"Looking for your hat?"

Pete jumped. He turned round and pretended to see the Vicar for the first time. Vicars were clearly creatures to be avoided in his world, and he looked embarrassed.

"Yes," he said. "Have you seen one?"

"A brown felt hat?"

"That's it."

"It's in the house. Will you come in and get it?"

Pete looked wary. It sounded too much like the spider and the fly business. He went red and fidgeted, but stayed where he was.

"It's in my study," said Mr. Matthews. "I'll go and get it for you if you like."

The shot came off, and Pete looked slightly reassured.

"That's all right," he said—"I'll come and get it."

He followed the Vicar down the garden path and along the passage to the study. The boy, guessed Mr. Matthews, had never deliberately walked into a Vicarage in his life. He had probably not spoken to a clergyman since he was a child at school, and Mr. Matthews racked his brains for something to say to set him at his ease. He was desperately anxious to hold the boy now that he had got him, but he was not good at small talk, and "Nice evening," was all he could think of as they entered the house. "Yes," mumbled Pete as they walked down the passage. "Quite nice."

The hat was on the mantelpiece, wrapped up in its parcel.

"As a matter of fact," said Mr. Matthews—"I've done it up. I was going to post it back to you."

"Thanks," said Pete. He turned the parcel over and looked perplexed. "How did you know where to send it?" Then his eyes began to rove around the room in dawning horror. They took in the couch, and the table beside it, and the desk lamp, and the arm-chair, and for a critical moment Mr. Matthews thought he was going to turn and make a bolt for it. But he stood his ground and stared at the Vicar in astonishment.

"Was . . . was this where . . . where I . . .?"

"This is it," said Mr. Matthews. "Don't you remember me? . . . Uncle Dick?"

Pete stared blankly at the Vicar in his sedate black Sunday suit.

"Who's Uncle Dick?" he asked.

"I don't know! . . . but that's what you called me!"

Pete's eyes were popping out of his head. "You!" he gasped.—"It . . . it . . . it was *you* that evening?"

"I found you outside. You'd had a gay evening and . . . well . . . I think you'd have done the same for me."

The boy stiffened and squared his shoulders. His pride was telling him to be defiant. He towered above the Vicar with a "Fighting

Cocks" look in his face—then suddenly he coloured up and lowered his head.

"I'm sorry I gave you all that trouble," he said.

"No trouble at all," declared Mr. Matthews—"to tell you the truth I quite enjoyed it. It's rather dull being Vicar in a place like this. It took me back to my days at College and made me feel quite young again."

Pete did not know what to make of this. He looked at the Vicar suspiciously—then for the first time he smiled. His sober smile, thought Mr. Matthews, was quite as charming as his drunk one.

"You don't mean *you* ever got like that!" he said.

"Between ourselves," said Mr. Matthews—"I was chased on one occasion by a policeman and escaped up a tree in the park."

Pete laughed. "Well," he said—"thanks awfully for what you did—and thanks for my hat. I'll be getting along, sir. Good night."

"Have a glass of beer before you go," said Mr. Matthews quickly.

Pete went back into his shell. "Not now, thanks," he answered.

Mr. Matthews opened a cupboard. "I'm having one myself," he replied. "I've just been preaching. It's thirsty work on a warm night."

He did not like beer on an empty stomach, but he poured himself a glass. "I wish you would," he said. "I shan't drink it all."

Pete relaxed a bit. "Well," he said—"if you're having one—all right . . . thanks."

He poured Pete a glass.

"Well, here's luck."

Pete mumbled something and politely sipped his beer. Silence fell, and they both stood fidgeting with the glasses in their hands. For the life of him Mr. Matthews could not think of anything to say. There was something cheap about bringing up Pete's hectic evening and joking about it again: he could not talk about "The Fighting Cocks" or Joe Briggs, and there was no other common touch between them. The weather was inept and the church inopportune. He had no notion of what Pete's interests were beyond fighting and drinking and betting on the dogs. Probably there were none. He saw the boy getting restless and ill at ease: in a minute he would finish his beer and go. He saw Pete, for the second time, on the point of moving away into a world that was closed to him. This time it would probably be for good, and he searched desperately for something that would start an easy conversation. He thought of inviting Pete to sit down and make himself at home, but Pete would take that as a prelude to a lecture, and escape at speed.

In after-days—when he thought back upon the strange events that sprang from his meeting and friendship with Pete, Mr. Matthews gave first credit to the oar that hung upon the study wall.

At Oxford he had rowed in his College second boat. The crew had not been a specially good one, but with a bit of luck they had made five bumps and gone head of the second division. By custom they had received their oars as trophies of victory with the blades artistically inscribed with the College crest and a record of the crew and the Colleges defeated. For twenty years the oar had decorated the study wall at Little Stanton, but it seemed out of place in the gloomy atmosphere of the Woodbank Vicarage and Mr. Matthews had consigned it to the box-room. It was Mr. Goatley who insisted upon hanging it in the study. "It's a fine souvenir," he said. "It'll look well over the fireplace and brighten up the room." And over the fireplace the oar had gone.

If Pete had not glanced up and seen it as he put his empty glass down, he would have said "thank you" and gone for good. But Pete glanced up and saw the oar and it caught his interest.

"I won that rowing in my College boat," said Mr. Matthews. "If you make five bumps, or go head of the river, they let you keep your oar as a souvenir."

"What do you call a bump?" asked Pete.

"At Oxford the river's too narrow to row races abreast," said Mr. Matthews. "So you start one behind the other and race after each other. If you catch the boat ahead, you bump it, and next night you start ahead of it and race for the next. It sounds rather silly—but it's tremendously exciting when you do it."

Pete went closer and looked at the dark blue blade.

"What are all those names on it?" he asked.

"Those are the crew with their rowing weights. We were a light crew that year. I rowed No. 7 at ten stone ten, and the heaviest man was only twelve three. . . ."

"I'm thirteen nine," said Pete proudly.

"They'd put you in the middle of the boat. You'd make a good oarsman. You're the right build for rowing"—and a sudden possibility went racing through his head.

"Have you ever rowed?" he asked.

"No," said Pete—"they do have some kind of race on the river—up by the tannery. I've never seen it, though."

"It's a grand sport," said Mr. Matthews. "It needs so many things—skill and strength and watermanship and guts: team-work above all. To be in a boat with seven other men rowing perfectly together—it kind of sings to you—it's the finest feeling I've ever known in my life. And when you beat another crew in the last few yards of a mile race—you feel like kings!"

Pete did not answer. He was looking at the leather binding on the oar. "I guess you do," he said at last.

"I've got a piece of land by the river," said Mr. Matthews, "there's a boat-house on it, with an old four-oared racing boat inside that belonged to a rowing club that used to be there once. How about getting a few fellows together and cleaning up the boat and trying it out? If you get along all right you could fix up some races with the clubs at Putney and have some good fun."

He saw the wary look come back in Pete's face and guessed what he was thinking.

"It wouldn't be a church club—I wouldn't interfere myself: you'd run it on your own."

"I wasn't thinking so much of that," said Pete slowly—"I don't think I'd have the time."

"What time d'you leave your job?"

"Five o'clock."

"You could be down at the boat-house by half-past. You could practice for an hour and be off by seven. Why not walk over to-morrow night and have a look round?—I don't even know whether the old boat will float yet, but we could soon find out.

There's a changing-room there—with showers and everything. It's a fine place really—I've got a feeling you'd like it."

Pete hesitated. He was thinking hard. He glanced once more at the oar on the wall, with its coloured crest and the names in gold.

"All right," he said at last—"I'll walk over. I don't promise I can do it, though."

"To-morrow?—about five o'clock?"

"Okay."

Chapter Thirteen

Mr. Matthews put on his sports shirt and grey flannels and went down to the boat-house in good time to have a look at the four-oared boat before Pete arrived. He had seen it under an old tarpaulin and paid no attention to it before. He pulled the cover off with some misgivings, for the boat could not have been in the water for years, and everything depended on whether it would float. From what he could see through the dust and cobwebs it looked all right, and he sorted out some oars from a pile of odd ones in a corner. The equipment was good enough, and everything now rested upon Pete.

He had been elated by his success with the boy on the previous night, but he did not feel too confident about seeing him again. A lot might have happened since Pete had left the Vicarage. He might have got drunk again at "The Fighting Cocks" and forgotten all about it—or he might have told his friends and been laughed out of getting mixed up with the Vicar. But he hoped devoutly that the boy would come. He had a feeling that Pete was the leader of a gang. If he could win him, he might win them all.

He heard five o'clock striking in the town and went on to the balcony to watch for Pete across the allotments. He reckoned it would take him about ten minutes to get there.

He thought of the Club they might build up if Pete got keen and brought the other boys along. He could rub up his memories of rowing and coach them into a polished crew and take them to race in the Thames Regattas. He thought of the pleasure of working with them and the friendships he might make with them: the summer evenings teaching them to row, and suppers in the club-room in the winter. They could fry sausages over the oil stove and bake potatoes and have a sing-song afterwards, and billiards, possibly, if he could get a table. He built castles in the air, and pictured the day when they might have a waiting list of boys who would count it an honour to belong.

Everything depended on Pete, but at ten past five Pete had not come. At twenty-past there was still no sign of him, and at half-past it began to rain. It rained so hard that Mr. Matthews could scarcely see the gate that Pete would come by. He went into the boat-house and watched out of the window for another ten minutes. He watched the puddles growing on the dismal path, but Pete still did not come. He waited a little longer, then gave it up and went into the kitchen, where he had prepared some tea. He turned out the stove and put the plate of biscuits away. He was disappointed but not much surprised. He had thought all along that it would not come to anything. He put on his mackintosh and locked the door and started sadly home.

He was half-way across the allotments when he heard a shout. He stopped and turned round, and the world lit up again, for there was Pete coming from a different direction down a lane beside the trees. He had his old worn-out hat on the back of his head, and he waved and came through the pouring rain with his coat wide open as if the sun were shining.

"Sorry," he said—"I got held up. Am I too late?—Have you got to go?"

"Not at all!" said Mr. Matthews. "I've plenty of time. I was afraid the rain had put you off."

"I don't mind the rain," said Pete. "A lorry came in. I had to help unload it."

They walked back together across the allotments. Pete seemed rather ill at ease, and looked around him as if he were afraid of being seen in such unusual company.

"Let's have a look at the boat before we do anything else," said Mr. Matthews.

He pushed back the rusty doors of the lower boat-house and they went inside.

"There's no light laid on," he said. "I'll get an oil lamp in the town to-morrow."

The boat lay on an upper rack in the darkness at the farther end. It was an old, heavy-built clinker boat, coated with the dust of years. The riggers were painted black and red and a small flag of the same colours was painted on the bows.

"What would these colours be?' asked Pete.

"I imagine they're the Grasshoppers Rowing Club that used to row here years ago. What d'you think of the boat?"

"You know more about it than I do," said the boy.

"From what I can see it's sound enough," said Mr. Matthews—"built by Sims of Putney—one of the best boat-builders on the river. It's bound to leak a bit until the wood swells, but I don't see any reason why we can't use it."

"Is it yours?" asked Pete.

"Well," said the Vicar—"I rented the land, and the boat-house with it. Nobody said anything about what was *inside* the boat-house and I don't suppose anybody knew there was a boat here—so why raise the point?"

Pete laughed. "That isn't the way for a clergyman to talk!" he said.

"If you could find a couple of boys and bring them along to-morrow," suggested Mr. Matthews. "We'll lift the boat down and have a good look inside it."

Pete was intrigued: he began peering up inside the boat and feeling the riggers.

"Let's get it down now," he said.

"Not by ourselves," replied Mr. Matthews, who did not want to start the enterprise with a double rupture. "We need at least four fellows . . . one at each rigger."

"Come on!" said Pete.—"We can do it all right. You just take the pointed end. I'll do the rest."

Mr. Matthews looked at the heavy boat with grave misgivings, but he did not want Pete to think he was a weakling. He tried to argue, but Pete insisted, so he found some tressels and offered up an urgent prayer for his blood-vessels.

"All ready?" asked Pete.

"Yes. Easy does it."

Pete put his powerful arms beneath the boat and gripped the gunwhales and heaved. But it was heavier than he had bargained for. He raised it a few inches, went scarlet in the face and let it down again.

"Half a mo," he said—and pulled off his coat and rolled up his sleeves.

"Don't go and strain yourself," said Mr. Matthews. "Why not wait till we get some help to-morrow?"

"We don't want any help," said Pete. . . . "Come on!"

He got under the boat and gripped hold once more. "Now!" he shouted—"Up she goes!"

The veins stood out from the boy's arms like whipcord and the boat rose slowly from the shelf. Mr. Matthews did his manful best with the bows. His heart began to pound: he felt sick and dizzy, but by good fortune the boat came safely down on the tressels. Pete had taken at least three-quarters of the weight: the strain must have been immense, but he looked none the worse for it. If anything he looked better.

"Good," he said, "well done!" and Mr. Matthews smiled wanly and pretended to examine the interior of the boat while he waited for the expected heart attack.

"There's a stretcher loose here," he said when he felt sufficiently recovered—"and these heel blocks are badly worn, but we can do all that ourselves."

"Look!" cried Pete—"the seats slide up and down!"

"They always do in racing boats. They give you a longer reach and a stronger leg drive."

"Well! . . . I never knew that!" The boy was fascinated by the sliding seats. He pushed them up and down their rusty rollers like a child with a new toy.

"If we grease the runners and oil the bearings," said Mr. Matthews—"and varnish the hull to stop the leaks—we'll have the boat in running order in a week or two."

"We'll want oars."

"There're plenty up here. They're mostly odd ones—but I've sorted out a set of four."

It was a motley collection, discarded years ago as out of shape, or sprung, or broken, but Pete took one and handled it tenderly. "If we win some races," he asked—"can we keep our oars and have them painted like that one in your study—and hang 'em up in our rooms?"

"Of course," said Mr. Matthews—"if you win, you'll deserve it."

Pete stood the oar back against the wall ... loath to leave it. He was thinking of it on his bedroom wall, painted with some names in gold. "Come along upstairs and see the rest of the place," said Mr. Matthews.

He showed Pete the club-room and the kitchen, and the changing-room with its lockers and cupboards and showers.—"It's a fine place," he said ... "built by an old chap with lots of money who was keen on rowing. When he died, the club died with him—and here we are ... it's all ours."

Pete was silent. He walked about, probing into corners. "The pump doesn't work," he said at last.

"Lots of things want seeing to," replied the Vicar. "But we can do it all ourselves. What d'you say?—shall we try and make a go of it?"

He watched Pete anxiously. The boy was slow to make up his mind and he guessed the things that troubled him. He wondered what Joe Briggs would say if one of his best fighters went flirting with the Vicar. . . .

"What about a cup of tea?" he said.

Pete said he'd like it and Mr. Matthews got the biscuits out again and Pete ate the lot while the Vicar got the kettle boiling.

They took the tea into the club-room and sat down to talk.

"We'd only need five boys to start with," said Mr. Matthews—"four to row and one to steer. We can't go straight out and row that four-oared boat: we'll need a pair first—what they call a "tubbing pair'. It's steadier to learn in. When the crew gets going we'll look round and find some other crews to race against. Then later on, when more fellows join, we'll get an eight-oared boat and enter for the big Thames Regattas."

"How many fellows have you got so far?" asked Pete.

"Well . . ." said Mr. Matthews rather lamely—"I haven't got any yet, except you. You see, I'm not in very close touch with the boys round here. I was rather depending on you for that."

Pete looked relieved at this. Lurking suspicions of a choir boys' club were set at rest. "I reckon I could get 'em," he answered.

"Good!" said Mr. Matthews—"what about bringing some down to-morrow evening and get the boat repaired?

"I'll see what I can do."

The rain had stopped and the sky was shining between the trees as they went down the boat-house steps. Pete lingered by the lower doors and peered in at the boat upon its tressels. "Shall we lift it back where it came from?" he asked.

"Good gracious, no!" cried Mr. Matthews, with an ache in his chest at the thought of it. "We'll need it where it is to work on to-morrow."

"I can easily do it," said Pete.

"You might," retorted Mr. Matthews. "But I'm sixty next March."

Pete grinned—"Okay. You're the boss!" He paused and looked the Vicar up and down with interest. "You don't look sixty," he said.

They walked across the allotments and down the road that took them to the High Street. There was a glow of light from the setting sun and the streets smelt fresh and clean from the shower of rain . . . fresher than they had ever smelt before in Woodbank.

"See you to-morrow about half-past five," said Mr. Matthews.

"Okay," said Pete.

"Good luck."

"Good luck to the club," said the boy, and Mr. Matthews walked home on air. Pete had said he didn't look sixty. He didn't feel it either. He felt younger than he had felt for years . . . like a boy on the edge of a great adventure.

Chapter Fourteen

Mr. Matthews got up early next morning and went to Putney to find a pair-oared tubbing boat. He hired one for £1 a month and arranged for two watermen to row it down to Woodbank on the ebb tide. He took a bus to London and bought some books about rowing and went to a sporting outfitter about club colours and rowing vests.

He studied the rowing books on his way back and spent the afternoon in Woodbank buying varnish and brushes and bolts and screws to put the boat in order. He packed everything in his rucksack and got down to the boat-house in time to make himself a cup of tea before the boys arrived. It was a fine August evening and the first of the geraniums he had planted that summer were in bloom. They threw a bright splash of colour round the boat-house and gave a happy augury to the days ahead. He wished that Ruth was there to enjoy it, but Ruth had insisted upon keeping in the background where the rowing was concerned. He might persuade the boys to swallow a Vicar, she said, but it wasn't fair to expect them to swallow a Vicar's wife as well.

He sat on the balcony in the sunshine, drinking his tea and admiring the geraniums and studying his rowing books. He had not been near the church all day and he wondered what Mrs. Bannister Paget would think if she knew what he was doing. He did not care very much what she thought. He was on top of the world, and the text-books, with their rowing illustrations, brought back happy memories of Oxford.

He had been wondering all day what kind of boys Pete would bring along with him that evening. If they were strapping fellows like Pete himself they would have a splendid crew. If they were fighters like Pete so much the better, for boxing taught the quickness and balance that rowing needed. Pete, he felt sure, would bring big fellows with him, and he began to conjure rosy visions of a crew of giants that would sweep the board at the Thames Regattas and bring a blaze of glory to the fledgeling club.

By the time he had finished his cup of tea he had won every race on the river and got his crew selected to represent England in the Olympic Games, but he came down to earth when he saw Pete coming, for there were only two boys with him instead of four.

When Pete arrived and introduced his friends, the Vicar had another disappointment. In a glance he knew that the best coaching in the world would never make good oarsmen of them. Their names were Dick Potter and Tom Gibson. Dick was a small peaky boy with round shoulders and spectacles as thick as glass marbles and Tom was a lanky red-haired youth who looked all arms and legs. He had no body to speak of, but enormous feet. Tom might do at a pinch but Dick was too small for anything, and Mr. Matthews was angry with Pete, who ought to have known better.

He did his best to conceal his disappointment. He gave them a hearty welcome and took them up to the club-room for some tea. They polished off the remainder of his biscuits, then took their coats off and carried the boat out on to the grass and set it up on tressels and began to work on it.

Tom said nothing all the evening except an occasional "Okay". He had a cold and sniffed a lot and breathed noisily through one nostril as he sand-papered the boat. Mr. Matthews had a feeling that Pete had bullied him into coming against his will, for now and then he heaved a long despondent sigh.

But Dick, the small boy, was bubbling with enthusiasm and bursting with advice. His uncle, he said, once rowed for a club on the River Lea and Dick claimed this as giving him an exclusive knowledge of the art. In a few minutes he was telling Pete and Tom, and Mr. Matthews into the bargain, all about rowing and how it should be done. Mr. Matthews could not get a word in edgeways and began to feel he had wasted his money on the text-books and his time in reading them. He admired Dick's enthusiasm but wished he was half as talkative and twice as large. He was troubled, and when he got the chance took Pete aside.

"You know, Pete . . ." he said—"these two boys are good sound chaps, but we're not going to win races unless we've got power in the boat. We've got to have big, tough fellows to beat the crews we shall race against."

"Tom's tough all right," said Pete.

"I'm sure he's tough, but he's not quite the right shape—if you know what I mean. And Dick's too small to take a long enough stroke. He wouldn't be able to keep time—and time is everything in rowing."

Pete looked angry and sullen. He did not like his friends being criticised. "If you can get better fellows," he said, "then why not get 'em?"

"I told you, Pete, I'm not in touch with the boys and you are. We might make do with Tom—but couldn't you find a couple of big fellows like yourself to balance up the crew?—we only need two."

Pete thought about it. "I don't know," he said. "I might get Tony Jensen and Jack Hughes—but it isn't easy and they might not like it."

"Do your best," said Mr. Matthews.

"But Dick's okay!" Pete suddenly flared out. "He can't help being small—but he's got more guts than six of most of 'em. He's clever, too. He draws and writes as good as any stuff you see in books. Everybody likes him, and I don't know why you don't!"

"But I do!" declared the Vicar. "I can see he's a good chap. It's just his size I'm thinking of." He was thinking, too, of the queer and unexpected friendship that aroused Pete's angry defence of the small bespectacled boy who "drew and wrote". It gave him a new idea of Pete.

"Dick might cox the boat," he said. "But he looks a bit short-sighted. You need sharp eyes with all these tugs about."

"He could see a tug," said Pete.

"There's other things like tree trunks in the river here—even dead dogs. They're on you in no time when the tide's running."

"He's got another pair of spectacles for watching the dog-racing," said Pete. "If he could see a running dog he could see a dead one."

"Not in the river," said Mr. Matthews.

But Pete had an answer for anything where his friends were in question. "The dogs go up and down on the tide for weeks," he said. "They get ripe and float high."

"All right," agreed the Vicar. "I'll talk to him about steering the boat, and you see if you can get those two big fellows to row in it."

The watermen came down on the tide with the tubbing pair. The boys helped to carry it ashore and Mr. Matthews asked one of the watermen to give a professional opinion of the four-oared boat. He soon wished that he hadn't—for when the man had walked round it once or twice, and squinted down it from the bows, he straightened up and shook his head.

"It's warped," he said. "Bow-side gunwhale's down a good two inches."

"What can we do about it?" asked the Vicar.

"Precious little," replied the waterman. "You might raise the bow-side riggers to compensate, but you'll always row lopsided. I'll bring some tools along to-morrow to see what I can do—but I don't promise anything. She's been lying too long on a lopsided rack."

The waterman threw a damper over the evening, and Mr. Matthews knew that his stock had fallen with the boys. He had told them the boat was all right and the boys had taken his word for it until the professional had shown him up. They went on scraping and cleaning the boat, but the heart had gone out of them.

"If it's lopsided, what's the good?" said Pete.

"These old professionals are always pessimistic," answered Mr. Matthews. "He'll put it right ... you wait and see"—but Pete looked at Dick and shrugged his shoulders as much as to say: "How can we trust this fellow any more?"

They worked until twilight, and Mr. Matthews went home feeling that the bottom had fallen out of it. He had called out: "See you to-morrow, Pete!"—and Pete had said "Maybe" and slouched off with his friends without saying good night or waiting for him to go with them. He was a moody, difficult fellow, and Mr. Matthews was disappointed in him.

He was oppressed by other things besides Pete that night. In one day he had spent as much as he had earned in a month: £2 for the brushes and varnish—£1 for the rowing books—10s. for the watermen, and more when the man came down to repair the boat next day. He was committed to buying club colours for the boys and £1 a month for the tubbing pair. His bank account was down to zero and in a month £10 was needed for the rent. They needed oil lamps for the boat-house and a raft to launch the boats from at low tide. Goodness knows what a raft would cost. . . £10 at the least.

He would have to draw the money they had scraped together so arduously to buy the land. Buying was out of the question now. It would be a desperate hand-to-mouth business merely to meet the rent and all the unforeseen expenses that were crowding on him.

He was tired when he got home. It had been an exhausting day, and he missed his glass of sherry. But the sherry had disappeared in his economy campaign.

He worked till three in the morning, translating Latin excerpts about early English bishops from worm-eaten books that smelt of sickness and decay. He hated it, but it earned him an extra £1 a week. He reckoned it would take him ten weeks working half the night to get the money to buy the raft, and Pete had gone home in a sulk because the boat was lopsided.

He worked until his eyes gave out, and the dawn was coming behind the factory chimneys when he drew the curtains to go to bed. It was worth it—however hard it was ... worth it because it was his last chance of doing anything that might endure.

Chapter Fifteen

Next evening Pete redeemed himself and brought down Tony Jensen and Jack Hughes to join the club, and the sight of them made Mr. Matthews forget all about his money troubles and arduous night, for Jack and Tony were the answer to a rowing coach's prayer.

Jack worked with Pete at the brewery, and he looked like an Ancient Briton. He was dark and swarthy and immensely broad and solid, with long, powerful arms like a gorilla's. He had a broken nose and a battered face that looked as if it had taken plenty at "The Fighting Cocks", and given plenty in return. He did not say much, but he chewed gum and spat long distances with no effort at all. Pete confided to Mr. Matthews that Jack could bend iron bars. Mr. Matthews was pleased to hear it, but hoped he wouldn't bend the boat too much when he began to row in it.

Tony was as different from Jack as day from night. He turned out to be the boy whom Pete was fighting when Mr. Matthews had gone to see Joe Briggs at the public-house. His father was a Norwegian sailor who had settled in Woodbank and married an English wife, and Tony was a towering fellow—magnificently built—with the physique of a natural oarsman. His hair was like a straw thatch, and he looked like a Viking.

The arrival of these two set Mr. Matthews' mind at rest about the horse-power of his boat. The power was there in plenty if he could harness it to the delicate balance and timing of good oarsmanship. He had the makings of a first-class crew and congratulated Pete on his good work.

"They're Okay," said Pete. "They'll row till they bust."

The waterman arrived to trim the boat, and when he had finished he pronounced it as good as new. "I've fitted leather washers under the bow-side riggers," he said, "and lowered stroke side to compensate. You won't have to row lop-sided after all."

Mr. Matthews gave the man five shillings and announced the good news to the boys. It cheered them up and they set to work in high spirits, scraping the boat for its coat of varnish. The wind was blowing and the sky was clear. They took off their coats and worked in the evening sunlight, whistling and singing and asking Mr. Matthews all manner of questions about boats and rowing. He had studied his text-books all the afternoon and managed to answer pretty well. He threw in some good stories about his own rowing days and they got on famously together. In his old grey flannels he did not look like a Vicar, and they soon forgot he was one. They called him "coach" and he was happier than he had ever been in Woodbank . . . happier than ever in his life. The boys began to sing "Pack up your troubles in your old Kit Bag" and he joined in with fervour.

But Pete soon got tired of sandpapering the boat and wanted to get it out on the water for a row. "Come on!" he said. "Let's see what it feels like. We can dry it off and varnish it to-morrow."

Pete's sudden impulse jolted the Vicar back to earth again. He had not yet told the boys what hours of patient practice lay ahead in the tubbing pair before they could row a lighter craft without disaster. He had planned to break it gently, but Pete had forced his hand and put him in a quandary.

"We can't take it out before it's varnished," he said. "It would leak like a sieve."

"What's it matter?" said Pete. "We can take a tin with us and bale it out."

Mr. Matthews looked down at the river. The wind was blowing a gale, coming in from the west on the tail of the ebbing tide—pushing up long angry rollers and flecking them with foam.

It was the kind of water that would try a veteran crew. For Pete and his friends it was impossible.

"Come on!" said Pete. "What are we waiting for?"

Mr. Matthews hesitated. He was up against it. If he told Pete it was dangerous, Pete would want to do it all the more. If he told him straight that they wouldn't be fit to row in the racing boat for at least a month, Pete would pack up, as he had nearly done the night before, and go home in disgust. And Pete was the keystone. If Pete went, the others would go with him.

There was a narrow strip of comparatively calm water in the shelter of the bank. It was against his better judgment, but he had got to do something to save disrupting the club.

"I tell you what we might do," he said. "If we took the four out to-night we'd damage it and take weeks to put it right again, but I'll take you and Tony for a practice trip in the pair."

Pete was disappointed, but he seemed to think it was better than nothing, and Mr. Matthews took the two boys up to the club-room and sat them on boxes and showed them the motions of rowing. He began to talk to them about the principles of oarsmanship, hoping to interest them and postpone the outing until a calmer evening, but Pete soon got bored with theories. He was burning to start work on the river. "Come on!" he said. "Let's cut the cackle and get the boat out."

It was difficult to launch the boat from the shelving shore without a raft, and the others had to wade up to their knees to hold it steady for the crew to embark.

Pete and Tony, getting into a boat for the first time, were like a couple of bulls in a china shop. The others clung on while Mr. Matthews showed the two boys how to adjust their stretchers and get their oars through the tholes. Tony nearly fell in when he reached out to fix his oar, and Mr. Matthews wished he had the strength of mind to call the whole thing off. It was a crazy enterprise, but he stepped in and took the rudder lines and told them to shove out.

The boat floated calmly on the smooth water in the shelter of the shore.

"Now," said Mr. Matthews. "Remember what I've been telling you in the club-room. Take it easy. Don't strain at it. Come forward: ready: paddle!"

But Pete and Tony had no intention of taking it easy. It was clear from the start that it was to be a trial of strength as bloodthirsty as any that the two had ever had in the ring at "The Fighting Cocks". Both were determined to pull the boat round against the other, and as neither had ever been in a rowing-boat before, it ended as it was bound to end. When Mr. Matthews said "paddle", Pete gave a mighty lug that took the water square and nearly lifted the boat out of the water. Tony tried the same thing but his blade sliced in diagonally. The tide bore it down and the handle caught him in the chest and knocked him off his seat into the bows. . . .

"Steady!" shouted Mr. Matthews—"Easy does it, boys—don't fight it!"

He might as well have shouted at the gale to take it easy. The light of victory was in Pete's eyes. He had drawn first blood, and took another tremendous stroke while Tony vainly struggled to heave himself out of the bows.

"Easy!" shouted Mr. Matthews. "Stop rowing, Pete!" But Pete's second stroke had driven the boat out of the calm shore water into the fringe of the storm, and the first wave struck the bows and swung the boat round like a straw. Mr. Matthews tugged a rudder line, but the boat was running down the ebb tide with no resistance to grip the rudder.

The boys on the bank enjoyed it all enormously. They shouted: "Go it, Pete!" and "Atta boy, Tony!" as the boat got up speed on the swell of the tide. They saw no danger in it, but Mr. Matthews felt the sickness of disaster. The boat was broadside to the storm, buffeted by the waves—racing helplessly towards a tug and a line of heavy barges that were ploughing painfully up against the tide.

Tony had clambered back on to his seat and the boys began

aiming fierce but futile strokes at the water—missing it when they found a hollow between two waves—shooting up showers of spray when they hit a crest.

The tug hooted and the wind howled, but all Mr. Matthews could do was to shout to Pete and Tony, "Stop rowing!—Listen to me!—Easy all!" If he could stop them and let Pete row alone there was a bare chance of swinging the bows into the wind and steering the boat back to the shore. But Tony was getting his own back and had no intention of giving way to Pete.

The tug hooted again, but the tubbing pair raced on towards it. The skipper swung the tug to starboard and Mr. Matthews and his boys shot by within six feet of it. "What the bloody hell are you doing!" yelled the skipper—then he turned and bawled out "Watch it, Mike!"

Mike was at the rudder of the leading barge. The nose had swung away with the sudden change in the tug's direction and the tubbing boat was plunging straight towards the evil, sloping prow that would crush a small boat like an eggshell and suck it to its doom. But Mike was cool. He seized a pole and caught the boat amidships, thrusting it clear in the nick of time and swinging it nose-end down the river.

The peril was over, but the change in the boat's direction revealed to the unhappy Vicar a new and still worse one ahead. They were swirling down the middle of the river, and the Railway Bridge, with its three sharp concrete buttresses, was racing up to meet them. They were heading straight for the centre buttress, but this time there was no resourceful skipper to swing to starboard and no obliging bargee with a pole. Mr. Matthews saw the desolate, storm-lashed river beyond the bridge, with the black wharves rising sheer from the water on either side. If they hit the buttress—and it seemed inevitable—nothing could save them.

A man's whole life is supposed to flash through his brain when he is on the point of drowning, but Mr. Matthews did not have this far-reaching experience. He only had one fixed, gruesome recollection ... of a small boy's voice calling in the darkness on

126

the night he had first come to Woodbank ... "that's the place where they put the drowned men: they got one there now—all blue and swelled up." He saw himself on a shelf beneath a sheet ... all blue and swelled up. "Both boys!—Row!" he yelled.—"Row hard!" The boat had swung broadside to the tide again. If the boys could take one stroke together they might still clear the buttress.

But Tony caught another crab and fell back in the bows. Pete's oar was wrenched through the rowlock and out of his hand, and he sat watching it helplessly as it raced along on the tide a few yards out of reach. The sinister shadow of the bridge loomed over them and they hit the buttress with a splintering crash.

They hit it squarely, and were saved from breaking in two by a balk of rope around the buttress that took some of the shock. But the full weight of the tide was on them now: the boat was pressed against the buttress like an insect to the windscreen of a racing car, and the river was boiling up against them, sucking down the stroke side gunwale.

"If we go over—cling to the boat!" shouted Mr. Matthews. Pete leant forward, panting from the futile efforts. The sweat was dripping off his chin and his hair was tangled by the wind. He looked at the Vicar and broke into a broad grin. "Poor old Uncle Dick!" he murmured.

Mr. Matthews wondered what strange process in the boy's mind had brought back the memory of "Uncle Dick" at such a parlous moment. An hour ago he would have been very happy for Pete to call him Uncle Dick—but now he would rather have been plain Mr. Matthews on dry land than Uncle Dick on the verge of dissolution. He smiled wanly back, and said "Good luck!—Hang on!"

Neither Pete nor Tony seemed very much disturbed by their predicament. Tony's yellow hair was standing up on end, but that was a permanent feature. It stood up all the time, whatever happened, and was not caused by fright. Mr. Matthews caught the boy's eye peering at him over Pete's shoulder. He looked slightly bewildered, but when the Vicar gave him a smile he got a broad, encouraging one back. "If I'm going to drown," he thought, "I'm not going to drown in such bad company after all."

"What do we do now?" asked Pete.

"Trim the boat away from the tide," said Mr. Matthews—"and sit tight."

They moved gingerly across the boat, nearer to the buttress, until the stroke side gunwale rose sufficiently to stop the water coming in.

"We might ease ourselves off the buttress," said the Vicar—"but we'd be worse off than ever, pelting down the river with only one oar. The next bridge would finish us."

A train thundered overhead—flecking them with quick squares of darkness. A signal rattled up, and they were alone again.

"Can you swim?" asked Mr. Matthews.

"A bit," said Pete. "Not enough to make any difference though."

Tony said he could swim a bit.

"Can you?" Pete asked the Vicar.

"Not much."

"D'you suppose we'll have to?" enquired Tony.

"Depends what happens," said Mr. Matthews. "The tide will fall another six feet yet. If we can fall with it, we may be all right: if we get wedged, we'll turn over. If we do—hang on to the boat and go with it . . . wherever it goes."

"Look!" shouted Pete.

Mr. Matthews looked, and saw a gladsome sight. Some men had appeared on a wharf some distance above the bridge. They were shouting something, but the words were blown away on the wind. Then a ferry boat emerged from behind the stern of a moored barge and dropped down on the tide toward them. Two old and dirty men in blue jerseys were rowing it: the boat was old and battered, but to Mr. Matthews it was a vision of enchantment.

The men pulled out to mid-stream—eased off and dropped down until they were beneath the bridge and level with the shipwrecked Vicar and his boys. They began to row harder, keeping their boat stationary against the tide while they examined the position of the tubbing boat and considered what to do.

Finally the stroke man called to Tony:

"You with the yellow hair!—crawl up in the bows—keep flat—don't stand up."

Tony did as he was told: the watermen rowed harder, gaining slowly against the tide until they were a few yards above the tubbing pair.

"When we drop down on you, catch hold and keep hold!" called the man.

They eased off a little: their boat came back until its stern was within a yard of Tony in the bows—

"Now,"—shouted the man.—"Catch hold!"

Tony reached out and gripped the stern of the ferry boat.—"Hang on!" bawled the men—and they put their backs into it, strained against their stretchers and rowed for all they were worth.

Luckily for all of them Tony was big and heavy. A smaller boy would have been dragged out into the river, but Tony clung on like a limpet to the stern of the ferry boat and presently the tubbing pair began to move.

"Lie down, you others!" yelled the stroke man—"out of the wind!" There was a sudden jar and a hair-raising lurch as the tubbing boat dropped from its pinned-up place against the buttress. It heeled over and shipped a lot of water, levelled up and straightened out behind the rescue boat.

"Keep where you are!" shouted the men.—"Keep low!"

They took a slanting course across the river to the calm water in the shelter of the shore, and Mr. Matthews and the boys, still lying flat, were towed back ignominiously to the place where they started from.

"You're lucky," said the stroke man of the ferry boat. "Another minute and you'd have been sucked under—without a dog's chance."

He helped the chilled, bedraggled Vicar to land. The shore was slimy and strewn with rotten wood and oil scum from the falling tide: it smelt of tar and dead fish but for Mr. Matthews it was the sweetest bit of solid England his feet had ever trodden on. He gave the watermen twelve shillings and his grateful thanks. The lives of Pete and Tony and himself were under-valued, he thought, at four shillings each, but it was all he had.

"You're shivering," said Pete.

"I'm all right," he answered—"bit wet, that's all."

The excitement over, reaction had come and he knew that he had caught a chill. His teeth were chattering, and he felt sick and tired. A pain was throbbing in his back from the shock of hitting the buttress.

"Come along with Tony and me," said Pete. "We'll give you something to warm you up."

Mr. Matthews said he would go home for a hot bath and dry clothes, but the boys took him to a little wharfside inn called "The King's Head". Pete got him a large whisky-and-soda and insisted on paying for it himself.—"It was my fault," he said—"so drinks are on me."

There was a deep bay-window in "The King's Head" parlour, with a long view down the Thames, and in the distance they could see the buttress of the bridge. It was pleasant, resting comfortably in the alcove, talking over their perilous adventure and miraculous escape. The mutual danger had drawn them together and they talked more easily than they had done before. Pete was overwhelmingly generous and told Mr. Matthews he had saved their lives, and Mr. Matthews said: "Nonsense!—we saved ourselves because you fellows kept your heads."

"I guess we were a couple of clumsy goops who thought we knew how to row and didn't," said Pete. "I was scared like hell when we hit the bridge."

"You didn't show it," said the Vicar.

"It wasn't the bridge I minded," returned Pete. "It was you. I was scared like hell in case you started to pray."

Mr. Matthews did not quite know how to take this, but he

thought it was a compliment. The whisky had warmed him up, but there was a dull pain in his back when he got up to walk home with the boys.

Chapter Sixteen

Mr. Matthews woke up next morning with such acute lumbago that he could barely crawl through his morning work. His back felt like a board and he went to bed in the afternoon with a hot water-bottle. Ruth wanted him to stay there but he said he would have to go down to the Club. If he stayed away the boys would follow his example and the Club would fall to pieces. So he rubbed some embrocation in and hobbled off.

When he got there he was well repaid, for the mishap in the storm, alarming though it had been, had done more to establish the Club than any amount of coaxing and persuasion.

The boys now saw that rowing was a tough game with a spice of danger and adventure in it, and Pete and Tony owed the river a grudge for making fools of them. They set to work with a firm determination to master the craft of oarsmanship and beat the river at any tricks it had in store for them.

Mr. Matthews rigged up a rowing machine in the changing-room for stormy nights, and when it was calm he coached the boys in the pair-oared tub with Dick behind him with the rudder lines, learning how to steer.

He taught them that rowing was not a battle of brute strength to get the better of one another, and showed them how to work together as a team. He taught them balance and control, and how to swing forward with resting muscles and row the blade in clean and square with a spring of the back and legs. They stuck to it patiently and one day Mr. Matthews said they were ready for their first venture in the racing boat.

He put on his old College blazer and rode his bicycle along the bumpy towing-path, coaching through a megaphone. They were over-anxious and the boat plunged and rolled. They tried to steady it by rowing harder, which made it worse. Mr. Matthews shouted: "Take it easy!—don't fight it!" but the boat went on plunging and rolling, and Pete, who was rowing at stroke, lost his temper and began to swear. He shouted abuse at the skipper of a passing tug for sending up a wash. The skipper ignored Pete and shouted abuse at Mr. Matthews on the bank, and Mr. Matthews ignored the skipper and shouted at Pete to shut up and pay attention to what he was doing.

They came back with bleeding knuckles and frayed tempers and looked at Mr. Matthews as though he was the cause of it. He told them it was bound to be uncomfortable at first. He gave them some boracic ointment to rub on their lacerated bottoms and went home painfully to put some on his own. The two-mile ride along the bumpy towing-path had paid him out and he felt his lumbago coming back again.

All the week the boat went badly. He began to lose faith in his power to coach and wondered how long the boys would stand it. Their hands were blistered and their rowing shorts were stained with blood from raw places that were rubbed and broken freshly every night. Pete developed a boil that must have given him agony, and Mr. Matthews suggested a few days off to let it heal. But Pete cut a hole in the seat of the boat to fit the boil and went on rowing.

One evening the boat rolled worse than ever and Mr. Matthews nearly gave up hope. They turned at the railway bridge and there was a slight wind against them and the river was as smooth as glass. "Sit back at the finish of the stroke and keep your knees down," said Mr. Matthews through his megaphone—"don't hurry it." He had said the same thing a hundred times without result but this time something happened and it worked a miracle.

At the first stroke the four blades came out clean and square. The boat moved off on an even keel and the boys, for the first time, recovered easily. They swung forward and took the second stroke as cleanly as the first; they gathered speed and a rhythm

133

fell like a charm upon the wrenched and tortured boat. Mr. Matthews could hardly believe his eyes and nearly rode into the river. The boys reached out with a new confidence, unleashing their long frustrated power, and Pete, at stroke, rose to it like a hound on scent. The muscles rippled across his powerful shoulders and the heart of the Vicar leapt to see the old boat rise to it and send the water sizzling past its bows. He wanted to shout: "Bravo!—Well done!" but he kept quiet lest his voice dispelled the charm.

"How was that?" he called out when they easied.

Pete looked across the river with a gleam of triumph. 'Okay," he said. "Grand."

They were jubilant and he was very proud of them. "Now you know what rowing really feels like," he said. "It was worth all the trouble—all the sore places and blisters and broken knuckles."

The boys said it was, and sang and whistled in the changing-room.

"It's time we had a race against somebody," said Pete—and Mr. Matthews said he would look round for a crew to challenge.

He led a double life that autumn. He was Vicar of St. Peter's Church and he was coach of the Rowing Club and be kept the two lives carefully apart. He preached to Mrs. Bannister Paget and her satellites on Sundays but the futility of it no longer irked him. He spoke with his lips to them and with his heart to the boys whom he would see again next evening at the Club.

He had promised Pete that it was not going to be a "Church Club" and he kept his word. He never talked about the church and he never went to the boat-house in clerical attire. He changed into his ancient College blazer and grey flannels before he went there, and as the days went by and the restraint between them died away, they treated him as one of them, and called him "coach" and never thought of him as Vicar.

The boys, in their own way, led a double life as well. They never mentioned Joe Briggs or "The Fighting Cocks" and Mr. Matthews never asked them questions. He knew they still went to "The Fighting Cocks" most nights after rowing because they turned up some evenings with gashed faces and bruised eyes. They never explained these souvenirs and the Vicar pretended not to notice. He did not mind the fighting, but it troubled him when they came down to the boat-house bleary-eyed and sullen from an all-night drinking bout. The boat went badly those evenings and everybody got bad-tempered.

He enjoyed the autumn evenings coaching them from the towing-path as the mists crept up the river and the sun went down: he enjoyed lighting the lamps in the changing-room while they put the boat away, and while they took their shower and dressed he sat on a wooden bench beside the lockers, talking over their evening practice and planning the work to come. He treasured those brief hours of companionship but knew that he only held them by a slender thread. When they said good night and hurried across the allotment path in the gathering darkness and went through the gate that led back to the town he knew they were returning to their other life in which he was forgotten. He would go into the changing-room and hang up their carelessly thrown down rowing clothes and turn out the lights and go back to the Vicarage alone. They occupied his thoughts all day, but he was only in theirs between the sounding of the factory hooters and the setting sun. An unguarded word attacking their loyalty to Joe Briggs and "The Fighting Cocks" would blow the Club to pieces, and he played for time, hoping that the thread would strengthen as their feeling for it grew stronger.

The day must come when Pete and his friends would have to make their final choice between the Rowing Club and their old ways of life. It came when their first race was arranged, for a race meant serious training . . . a rigid discipline of training to which the smoke and drink and late hours at "The Fighting Cocks" were poison. They could not have it both ways any longer. They enjoyed the rowing and wanted to prove their mettle in a race, but the Vicar knew the malignant influence of Joe Briggs and could picture the scorn and ridicule that Joe would pour on them if they dared to leave him for the Vicar's "choir boy" Rowing Club.

They were glad to hear about the race, and said they'd knock the hell out of their opponents, who came from a London Technical School and called themselves "The Tigers".

"When's it to be?" asked Pete.

"In three weeks," said Mr. Matthews. "That means we must register the Club with the Rowing Association and settle on the colours we're going to row in. We ought to elect a Captain and Secretary as well. Until we do that we're not officially a Club at all, so we'll have to have a proper meeting."

"Come on," said Pete—"let's have one now."

They christened themselves "The Mudlarks" because of the mess they got into when they carried the boat through the low tide slime to the water's edge. Mr. Matthews proposed Pete as Captain and Tony as Vice, and Pete proposed Dick the cox as Secretary because Dick had neat handwriting. Mr. Matthews then produced some sample Club colours that the outfitters had sent him. They settled on battleship grey, to be edged around their shorts and vests, and blue striped caps with white crossed oars on them.

Mr. Matthews said a few words about racing tactics, but made no mention of strict training. They had a good outing on the river and came in full of the frightful beating they were going to give "The Tigers".

Mr. Matthews went into the changing-room and sat down on the bench beside the lockers. He tried to look as calm as usual but he knew the time had come.

"Well," he said. "I went to see your opponents practising this afternoon. They're big fellows with more experience than us. We've got to go all out and get racing fit."

"We're fit all right," said Pete from underneath the shower.

"Your rowing muscles are all right," said Mr. Matthews. "It's a matter of staying-power now . . . getting in top condition. From Monday it means full training . . . four golden rules . . . no smoking: no drinking between meals: regular food and bed at ten for a good night's sleep."

He expected it to be a bombshell but he had no idea how they would take it. Vaguely he expected a furious argument which he hoped to win by a commonsense appeal to their team spirit, but the bombshell went off like a damp squib. Tony said: "Hurrah!" and Tom said: "Atta boy!" and the others merely laughed. It quite upset him and made him forget all the good points he had thought of to support his argument. They took it as a joke and went on whistling and singing.

"I'm serious about it," he said. "Every crew goes into strict training before a race. You can't win unless you do."

Tom stopped whistling and Jack stopped chewing gum and Tony looked up in astonishment with one leg in his trousers. Silence fell and Pete came out from underneath the shower.

"Whose idea is that?" he said.

"I'm telling you as your coach."

Pete looked at Mr. Matthews as if he had never seen him before. He went over to the mirror and began to comb the water out of his hair. "That's a lot of silly bunk," he said.

"If you think it's bunk," replied the Vicar, "go and ask the men you're racing against. They're training in the way I'm asking you to train because they're going all out to win."

"They can do what they like and we'll do what we like," said Pete.

"Even if I tell you as coach that you've got to train in the proper way?"

"You can tell us as God Almighty if you like," said Pete. "It's a lot of bloody silly balls. Why not tell us to put on night-shirts and sing in your choir and done with it?"

He turned his back and began to rub himself down. The others laughed and Mr. Matthews got up and went over to the door.

"I've put a lot of time into this Club," he said. "I've given up my evenings to coach you because I thought you were keen and meant to win. But I'm not going to waste any more time on a crew that doesn't train."

He shut the door behind him and went out on the balcony. He was trembling with anger at Pete's insolence and groping desperately in his mind for the right thing to do. He could not go back to the changing-room. If he went home the Club would end and he would never see the boys again. It was growing dark and the lights were showing along the wharves on the north side of the river and over in the allotments an old man was placidly scraping his spade. He shouldered it and picked up a cauliflower and started quietly home. Mr. Matthews envied him: he wished he had taken an allotment and gone in for cauliflowers instead of mixing himself up with boys who were beyond his power to control.

Behind the closed doors of the changing-room there was an ominous silence with now and then a murmur of sullen voices. After a while the door opened and the boys came out, and his heart fell when he saw them carrying their rowing clothes and towels. They had never taken them home before and it meant the Club was over. They looked shamefaced rather than angry, and kept their eyes from him as they crossed the balcony and went down the steps.

"Five o'clock to-morrow?" said Mr. Matthews. "We'll practice a few starts and paddle over the course."

"There isn't going to be any to-morrow," said Pete.

"What shall I tell The Tigers?"

"Tell 'em to go on training till they spew up all the milk they drink."

The others laughed, and turned along the path that led back to the town.

"Pete," called Mr. Matthews.

Pete slung his towel across his shoulder and went on.

"Pete!"

The boy turned sullenly. "What is it?" he said.

"Just a minute. Come up here a minute."

Pete hesitated. "I'll catch you up," he called to his friends, and slowly came back up the steps. "What d'you want?—I'm in a hurry."

Mr. Matthews waited until Pete was on the balcony, and the other boys had moved away.

"If I put over those training rules too bluntly," he said, "I'm sorry, Pete—but you don't honestly believe I'm wrong about it, do you?"

"I don't care if it's right or wrong!" shouted Pete in a burst of pent-up fury. "If you'd told us straight out from the start we'd have given you a straight answer! You let us muck about down here all these weeks and then start talking about a lot of damn silly rules we can't keep!"

"You can't—or won't?"

"We can't!"

Pete towered above him like an outraged giant, but he saw the boy's hand trembling as it gripped the soiled grey flannels that had been cut down for rowing shorts. He saw the dried patch of blood on them and thought of the evenings when Pete had rowed with a festering boil and gone through agony rather than give up.

"You wouldn't say 'can't' without reason," he said.

"If I said you'd got to give up your church to coach us—wouldn't *you* say 'can't'?"

"That's different. The Church is my job. I'm not asking you to give up yours."

"You're asking me to give up boxing!"

"But your job's at the Brewery."

"And where's that getting me!" demanded Pete. "£3 a week for an eight-hour day rolling barrels!—I make £5 in ten minutes at 'The Fighting Cocks'—with another fiver in side-bets if I win!"

"And you don't train for it?"

"We don't have to train!"

Mr. Matthews pulled out his pipe and began to fill it. He sat down and turned a chair for Pete, but the boy ignored it and stood glaring across the river.

"I'm in a difficult spot with you, Pete," he said. "I'm a parson, and if I say too much you'll tell me I'm preaching. But I'll say what I've got to say and get it over."

He lit his pipe. The clock was striking seven in the town and it was nearly dark. The light of the match glowed on his face. Pete looked at him, then turned his head away.

"If you decide on the boxing," he said—"then that's your affair.

It's up to you to choose. I believe you'd do well as a boxer if you had a proper chance. But you'll never get a chance at 'The Fighting Cocks'. It's a dirty, wretched business down there, and you know it."

"You've got to take things as they are," said Pete. "There's dirty business everywhere. I wouldn't mind betting there's some in that church of yours."

"There is," said Mr. Matthews with a spirit that made Pete turn and look at him. "I don't mind telling you. In some ways it's as dirty as 'The Fighting Cocks'."

"And you go on with it," said Pete—"same as I go on—because you earn your money there."

"I go on with it because it's the only way to fight it. As long as you go on at 'The Fighting Cocks' you help to keep it dirty."

Pete moved impatiently and prepared to go.

"Well—that's how it is," he said. "I'm sorry. It's been good fun down here but you've made me choose and I've got to earn the money."

Mr. Matthews got up. "I'll turn the lamps out," he said. "We'll walk back to the town together."

He went into the changing-room. By force of habit he glanced around the floor and under the benches to collect the boys' rowing clothes and hang them up to air. It was a forlorn, deserted place without them. He turned out the oil lamps on the mantelpiece and the light of the rising moon came through the trees.

Pete was waiting on the path outside. "You can get some other fellows and start again," he said—"fellows that aren't tied like we are. There's plenty round about."

They shut the gate and took the path across the allotments.

"I don't think I shall start again," said Mr. Matthews. "I'll take one of these plots and grow potatoes."

"You'll start again all right," said Pete. "You're keen on this rowing. You'll soon make some other fellows keen."

"It wasn't only the rowing," said Mr. Matthews. "It was what we might have done if we had worked together. When we made you Captain to-night it didn't seem much to be Captain of four boys and two old boats. But I was thinking of the day when you'd be Captain of a Club with a dozen boats rowing at the Thames Regattas all the way to Oxford. I was thinking of a Club that we could open every night of the year—with football and cricket and other things as well—and the kind of boxing that's really in your heart. It's been my ambition ever since I found that piece of land. I wanted to see you Captain because you're a leader and you could have done a grand thing for the boys round here. When we settled on those colours for the Club tonight it didn't mean much then—just grey and blue—but I was thinking of a day when boys for miles around would count themselves lucky and proud to wear them."

It was easier to talk to Pete walking along in the darkness. He let himself go and talked as he would never have dared to talk in the daylight. He told Pete all his hopes and secret dreams. Pete listened and said nothing till they came to the corner where they went their different ways.

"You believe all this?" he asked—"You believe it could be done?"

"If you believe it, Pete, I know it could be done. We wouldn't make any money out of it, but we'd make other things we'd never regret. Things we'd remember all our lives."

Pete stood in silence, thinking.

"First of all," he said at last—"we'd have to beat those Tiger fellows—to show we meant it."

"That would be the first thing."

He hitched his rowing clothes under his arm. "Okay," he said. "We'll beat 'em."

"And you'll train for it?"

"You needn't worry."

"Five o'clock to-morrow, then. We'll practice starts and paddle over the course."

"Okay."

What Pete said to Joe Briggs at "The Fighting Cocks' the Vicar never knew and never asked, but proof that he trained, and made the others train, was soon apparent in the crew. Jack lost the bloodshot edges round his eyes and the brown cigarette stains round his fingers, and Pete lost the blowsy look around his jowls. Tom's perpetual catarrh cleared up, and Tony, who had been too fat, lost his stomach and got firmer every day. By the end of the first week they could row a hard three minutes and sit up fresh when it was over.

Mr. Matthews arranged a nightly training supper at "The King's Head" Inn, where the boys got better food than they could get at home. It was a quiet old place on the river side with the flavour of the tideway in it, and the landlord, who had once been a professional sculler, knew the kind of training food to give them. He used to come and yarn with them when the meal was over, and he told them useful things about the mysteries of the eddies and how to steer their course when they raced The Tigers. They made him the first Honorary Member of the Club and promised to send him one of the blue and grey Club ties when they arrived from the outfitters. At eight o'clock they went for a training walk along the river bank and home to bed.

If Mr. Matthews needed any confirmation that Pete had kept his word he got it on the day before the race when he left a note for Pete at Harper's Mews and met Pete's mother for the first time.

She was, as Mrs. Burgin had once said, a nice woman, with a friendly smile. She told Mr. Matthews that she had wanted to meet him for a long time to thank him for what he had done for Pete. The rooms she lived in with her son were overshadowed by the laundry where she spent her working hours. They were small and dark but neat and clean.

"He's a different boy," she said—"and I don't know how you've done it. I never believed he was really bad . . . it was just the place, and the people he got in with, and sometimes it nearly broke my heart. I've never seen him so keen on anything before. He's in bed at ten and up at seven training with a skipping rope in the yard. He looks so well and I'm so grateful to you . . . I'll never be able to tell you how grateful I am."

She took him into Pete's bedroom and showed him two big rivets that Pete had fastened in the wall. "He says you're going to let them keep their oars if they win," she told him—"he's measured the wall and says it'll just fit in along there above his bed."

He looked round the small bare room. A book about rowing lay on the table by the bed and the skipping rope hung on a hook behind the door. He went back to the Vicarage with a deeper gratitude than even Pete's mother was feeling, because his gratitude was to God for giving him the chance he had prayed for in the lonely nights of defeat and disillusion.

When he got home he found that another woman had been thinking of him that day, for on the hall-stand lay a small blue crested envelope. He opened it and read:—

> "Elm Lodge",
> Woodbank.
> *5th October.*

Dear Mr. Matthews,

I shall be obliged if you will kindly make it convenient to call on me at *3.30* to-morrow afternoon. There is a matter that I wish to discuss with you.

> Yours very truly,
> Catherine Bannister Paget

Chapter Seventeen

Elm Lodge, where Mrs. Bannister Paget lived, was the last of the big Woodbank houses to remain in private hands. It lay behind its tall brick garden wall, shrouded by its ancient trees—a sad old bastion against the tides of time.

In Woodbank's palmy days a number of these spacious houses had set themselves among the pleasant groves behind the church, and the names of their first occupants had read like a page of history. There were famous statesmen and men renowned in literature: illustrious soldiers and a sprinkling of exiled dukes and kings. Two young lawyers named Bannister and Paget had also come to found a legal firm that became a byword in Woodbank for the best part of two hundred years.

As time went on the statesmen and the exiled kings retired before the increasing flow of sewage down the Thames and went to live above the smell at Isleworth. But the Bannisters and Pagets took root and grew. They dominated the commerce and society of the town and plastered the walls of St. Peter's Church with memorials to their dead. They took so many front places in the churchyard that when the Thames encroached and carried a corner of it away, two Pagets were found sticking out and a tomb full of Bannisters went down the river to the sea. They put up Jubilee Memorials in the town with Queen Victoria briefly mentioned as an "also ran": they gave an organ to the church and a drinking trough to the horses. The Bannisters married the Pagets and the Pagets married the Bannisters, and they grew extremely rich by leaving their money to each other.

Towards the end of the century the supply of Bannisters ran out and the Pagets had joined the name to theirs in token of remembrance.

Mr. Matthews had gleaned all this from the dusty shelves of the Bannister Memorial Library in the Town Hall. He was interested in local history and the exploits of the Bannisters and Pagets had intrigued him.

With the turn of the century the Pagets, too, had shown increasing signs of giving out. Richard and Catherine Bannister Paget were the last of them, and their only child had died in infancy. When old Mr. Richard passed away, the firm passed with him, and his widow retired behind the tall brick walls of the family home to live in the solitude of her dreams and memories.

Mr. Matthews had never been to the house alone. Once or twice he had gone with Ruth to a formal tea-party and had always been relieved to get away. He did not know why Mrs. Bannister Paget had asked him to go and see her but he had a fairly good idea. The church organ had been wheezing badly at recent services and on the previous Sunday had nearly given out. She had mentioned the question of repairs and he had already written for an estimate.

But there were more important things in his mind that afternoon as he approached the gloomy house. He had long been waiting for an opportunity to see the old lady by herself and was glad the chance had come.

It was nearly two years since she had declared herself against him on the night of his arrival, but nothing had since occurred to bring the war to open conflict. He had carried out his duties to the church like a model Vicar: nothing in his Boys' Club threatened her authority, and of late he had felt that she had shown an increasing willingness to be conciliatory. Time had helped him to understand her tragic loneliness—even to understand her fierce determination to fight for the only sanctuary that remained to her, and he was resolved that afternoon to make friends with her and end the feud.

He was going to invite her to be an Honorary Patron of his Rowing Club and get her to unveil something or give away the prizes after the pair-oared race with which he planned to close the season. If he could persuade the boys to be polite to her, the old and the new might come together in a double victory, and he went through the tall iron gates and along the drive between the melancholy elms with a firm determination to achieve it.

An elderly manservant answered the door and led him down a twilit passage to the drawing-room.

The old lady was sitting in a high-backed chair beside the fire with a piece of tapestry on her lap and a work-basket full of drab-coloured skeins of wool beside her. The firelight flickered on a musty collection of Bannisters and Pagets around the walls and through the long windows he could see the lawns and trees, darkened by the high brick walls and autumn sky. An old bent man in a gardener's green apron was raking leaves and a wisp of smoke was rising from a bonfire by the garden gate.

She looked up when the Vicar was announced, invited him to be seated and bent her eyes upon her work again.

"We've seen the last of the summer, I'm afraid," he said. "We shall be getting our overcoats out in a day or two."

She raised her eyes, and they seemed to look at him from an infinite distance. "Yes," she said, "autumn has returned."

It was the first time he had ever seen her by herself. She looked smaller and frailer and far less formidable than when she sailed into church on Sunday mornings at the head of her fawning little satellites, and as he watched her sitting there, fingering her tapestry, his prejudice died away and he felt a yearning pity for her. He thought of her lonely hours in this desolate room, with the ghosts of her family and the cry of the rooks at sunset and the owls at night, and the distant rattle of the cranes and derricks that had spelt the end of almost everything that had been her life. He had the impulse to ask her at once to be the Honorary Patron of his Club and give the prizes away ... to plead with her and bully her if need be into something that could easily bring a new lease of happiness to her days.

But he decided to wait until they had talked a little of other things. He was on the point of telling her about the cleaning of the organ when he realised that she herself was speaking. Her head was bent over her needlework and her voice was at first so low that he could scarcely hear what she was saying:

"I beg your pardon?" he said.

She raised her head and looked at him.

"I said, Mr. Matthews, that I have been Chairman of our Church Council for many years. I have had many duties to carry out in the interests of our church. Some have been pleasant—some difficult—but none, I am afraid, so unhappy and distasteful as this.'

She laid her work down with a sigh, and her eyes moved away from him. She spoke slowly and deliberately as if her words had been carefully meditated.

"For some time, Mr. Matthews, we have felt that your heart is no longer with us in St. Peter's Church. We have detected a lack of devotion to our congregation and a lack of sincerity in the manner of your service. It has grown so evident in the past few weeks that we have been forced into an action which all of us deeply regret. We had a long, informal meeting of the Council yesterday. Every Member was present and we were unanimous in our decision to ask you whether—in all circumstances—you feel it right to continue as Vicar of Woodbank?"

Mr. Matthews was dumbfounded. The bluntness and deliberation of it left him speechless.

"We think it only right," she went on, "that you should have proper time to make your formal reply. We propose to hold a Meeting at eight o'clock on Friday week. I feel sure you will then give the correct and only answer in the circumstances."

Mr. Matthews had got his breath back. One part of him still floundered in a mist of unreality—the other was as calm and as deliberate as the woman in the high-backed chair.

"I can give you my reply at once," he said. "I have not the slightest intention of resigning."

"Even in the face of a unanimous opinion from the Council?"

"You can tell the Council I'm amazed at their behaviour in discussing this behind my back."

She gave a little hitch to the shawl around her shoulders and looked into the fire.

"I shall not take that as a final answer," she said. "You are not at present in a condition to give our verdict proper thought."

"You can take it now as definite and final," replied the Vicar. "If you have your meeting I shall be delighted to come and tell the Council exactly what I think of them, and I shall give them a flat refusal to resign."

She was silent for a while. Her eyes moved from the fire to the garden window. The bent old gardener was trundling a barrow of dead leaves across the lawn.

She sighed again, and moved her hand across her forehead.

"Very well," she said. "If that is your final answer, then you force me to say what I hoped would be unnecessary. I hoped you would have had the feeling to understand, but since you have not—then I must tell you.

"You came to this parish with plans that we considered undignified and unworthy of our church. Despite our disapproval you pursued these plans and they failed completely, as we knew they would.

"Out of revenge for your failure you proceeded to drag the dignity of St. Peter's Church to an even lower level. You associated yourself with a drunken and dissolute section of the boys of this parish. If it had been your purpose to guide them into the ways of our church, then we should have approved, although we should have known it to be futile. But you made no effort—no attempt to do so. I am told that you have never, on one single occasion, mentioned the church to them. On the contrary you have gone out of your way to dissociate yourself with the church as though you were ashamed of it—even to the point of discarding your clerical clothes and going every night to a low public-house on the water front and drinking with them. Frankly, Mr. Matthews—it has amazed and disgusted us."

"And that is the real reason why you ask me to resign?" he asked.

"What other course could any Council take?" she answered. "Any Council with the good name of its church at heart?" ...

"You feel no shame?" she went on when he did not answer—"No regrets for the indignities you have brought upon us?"

"On the contrary," said the Vicar. "I'm glad—immensely glad that you've brought this into the open on your own account. I suggest you report the whole thing to the Bishop of this Diocese, and I'll give him, in the presence of the Council, a full report of all that I have done, and all that you have done to obstruct me. The Bishop has the welfare of these boys at heart. I shall bring some of the boys themselves to tell their own stories, and we shall hear what the Bishop has to say."

Her face was deadly pale and he saw her hands trembling as they moved to and fro along the arms of her chair. All pity for her was gone. He knew by those trembling hands that he had beaten her, and he was glad.

"We have no intention of parading this sordid affair before the Bishop," she said.

"I didn't for the moment expect you would," he answered, "because you know what the result would be."

She was silent, and he rose to go.

"I shall carry on my duties at St. Peter's Church," he said—"and I shall carry on my Club with everything I have to give."

"You refuse to resign . . . and you refuse to give up your degrading association with these boys?"

"I do most certainly."

She raised her head and looked at him. The cold light from the window fell across her face and he saw in it a hatred and a malevolence that shocked him.

"In that case," she said, "I shall take immediate steps to see that you no longer have the means to disgrace us. The lady who allows you to use the land beside the river is a dear friend of mine and I know the terms on which she let it to you. It was to be a recreation ground for the people and nothing more. I shall tell her that you have broken the agreement and are using her land to encourage the very boys who drove her out of Woodbank by their rudeness and blasphemy. She will turn you off at once, and I shall urge her to take full legal action against you—not only for wilfully breaking the terms of your agreement, but also for taking a boat and oars that do not belong to you. That is a common, wilful theft and we shall see whether you enjoy yourself before a Judge and Jury as much as you say that you would have enjoyed yourself before the Bishop. It will end your Club, and your career as well, as a Vicar of the Church. I am deeply sorry, but you have forced me to it. I am determined that the good name of St. Peter's Church shall be upheld in the character and behaviour of the Vicar who serves it."

Ruth was in the garden when he got back to the Vicarage, and he told her what had happened.

"I can't believe it," she said. "I can't believe that any woman could be so mean."

"If you'd seen her face you'd have believed it," he answered. "It was horrible . . . diabolical. She's a religious maniac."

"I don't think religion was in her mind at all," said Ruth. "It's just plain, downright, jealousy. She's dominated the Vicars here for years, and they've always given in to her for the sake of peace. She hates you because you don't run after her like the others did. She hates your Club because she knows you're more interested in those boys than you are in her. That's why she's out to smash it."

"She's out for more than that," he said. "She's out to ruin me and hound me out of Woodbank."

Ruth laughed. "Nobody would take you into the Courts on a thing like that. It's too ridiculous!"

"She'll do everything on God's earth to ruin me. I've never seen such venom in a human face and I hope I never shall again. A clever barrister could probably prove I *stole* that boat and those oars. In the eyes of the law I suppose I did. I was a fool not to ask permission."

"If you had you would have been refused—you know that."

"I know. That's what they'll say, and I couldn't deny it. Whatever happens they'd make me look a criminal I'd *have* to leave this town."

Ruth stood up from the flower-bed she was weeding and wiped her hands. "Well," she said. "You've got to decide whether you're going to give in or fight it out."

"I'd rather go to prison than give in."

"Then here's what I'd do. The rent on the land falls due next week. I'd send Miss Ponsonby £20 for six months right away and tell her you're paying two quarters in advance to save trouble. Directly the cheque's paid through it's legal, and the land is safe until the spring. That gives a breathing space and time to decide what to do next. But write the cheque and post it off to-night before that old woman has time to start her mischief."

"I'd send her a year's rent if I had it," he said. "But there's only £12 in the bank. I've had to spend so much on the Club these past few weeks ... all kinds of odds and ends ... it's eaten into our reserves and we're up against a money crisis in the bargain."

"Then you'll just have to sell those silver candlesticks and done with it," said Ruth.

The candlesticks had been a wedding present. They were antiques, and they reckoned them worth about £20.

"They stand there on the sideboard doing nothing," she said—"so why not make them do a useful job?—Take them up to Marshalls in Piccadilly first thing to-morrow and get the money into the bank before the cheque comes through."

"That still doesn't put me right about using the boat ... and the land for a Boys' Club."

"Never mind," said Ruth. "Let's do one thing at a time."

He went in and wrote the cheque and posted it on his way down to the Club.

The boys rounded off a perfect day for Mr. Matthews by losing their race against the Tigers by three lengths. The water was rough and they started badly. They raced all the way but were up against a more experienced crew.

It was the last evening of summer-time. A cold wind was blowing down the river and it began to rain as Mr. Matthews waited in the twilight to help the boys in with their boat. He watched them paddling home in the misty twilight and there was something pathetic about the new club colours they had put on for the first time that night. They had looked so bright and clean when they had set out in them, determined to cover them with glory on their first appearance. As they returned in defeat the blue and grey trimmings were sodden by the rain into a dirty-coloured purple that looked like strips from Mrs. Bannister Paget's purple dress.

The bottom had fallen out of everything, and he almost hoped that the boys would throw the whole thing up in disgust. It would save him a world of trouble and anxiety if they did. . . .

He took the blade of Pete's oar and drew the boat into the raft. "Hard luck," he said. "You rowed a fine race."

"It wasn't hard luck," said Pete. "We rowed a lousy race and deserved it. Go and tell those Tiger fellows we'll race 'em again any time they like and beat the stuffing out of 'em."

They had been so sure of winning that they had planned a victory supper in the club that night. It was a victory celebration nevertheless, for the victory over adversity was more heartening to the troubled Vicar than any that might have been won against the Tigers, and he felt ashamed that he had wished, even for a moment, that the boys might solve his problems by throwing up the Club.

Dick the cox had brought down some sausages and jam tarts and potatoes and Pete produced six bottles of beer and a special bottle of sherry that he gave to Mr. Matthews as a consolation prize.

He opened the sherry while the boys were changing and they drank some while Dick got the supper cooking on the oil stove. The sherry was rather sweet and sticky but it took away the evil flavour of the woman he had seen that afternoon. They got a log fire blazing from some wood cut from the fallen elm, and by the time they sat down to supper Mr. Matthews was ready to fight the world for the survival of his Club.

He liked the way the boys had taken their defeat. It had stung them to a fierce determination to get their own back and they were full of new plans for the winter. They would row on Saturday afternoons, they said—and open the Club three nights a week to practise on the rowing machine and rig up a gymnasium. On moonlight nights, Pete said, they'd get the boat out and fix a light on it and take a long row up to Hammersmith, have supper there and row back on the changing tide. "It's mileage we want," he said, "sticking together and keeping at it."

They drank the rest of the sherry to the future glory of the Mudlarks and drew their chairs around the fire. They were out of strict training now, and lit their first cigarettes while Mr. Matthews filled his pipe. It was raining hard outside: a steady downpour that increased the comfort of the room. The lights from over the river were blurred against the windows that were lashed by gusts of rain.

"Look——" said Pete. "There's something we've been wanting to know about. Who pays for all this?"

It took the Vicar by surprise, and he was not sure what to say.

"Who pays for what?" he asked.

"Well—everything . . . the whole caboodle . . . the raft down there and the new oars we rowed with to-day and the new club colours . . ."

". . . and the paint and varnish," put in Tony.

". . . and the oil for the stove and the coal for the boiler," said Dick.

"It doesn't cost much," said Mr. Matthews.

"It comes out of your pocket?"

"Well . . . yes—I suppose it does."

There was a silence.

"That's where we reckoned it came from," said Pete.

"It's worth it," said the Vicar. "I enjoy it and get my money's worth."

"If you're a millionaire—then that's okay with us," Pete answered. "But I never reckoned you made a lot out of that church of yours."

They began asking him about the land and how much he paid

for it, and who it belonged to. It was clear that they had talked about it among themselves a good deal more than Mr. Matthews had realised. They led him on, and finally he told them everything, from the evening he had first seen the boat-house with his wife down to that afternoon when he had called on Mrs. Bannister Paget, and what she had said to him.

"You mean," said Dick, "she threatened to break up the Club and get you into trouble for using that boat?"

"That's what she said," replied the Vicar—"and she'll do it if she can."

"The old bitch," said Pete.

"I've told you all about it," said Mr. Matthews, "because you're keen on the Club and you ought to know how we stand. But I'm not going to drag you into all these troubles. I started it and it's my affair."

"If it's our Club it's our affair," said Pete. "The first thing to do is to break her windows and show her what she's in for if she starts arsing about."

"For God's sake no!" cried Mr. Matthews. "That's the worst thing to do. It'd give her exactly what she wants! She'd prove we were a lot of hooligans and get us out of here in five minutes!"

Dick the cox was sitting on the floor, nursing his knees—his eyes upon the fire. "If we got £500," he said—"we could buy the place and do what we wanted with it?"

"That's part of the agreement," said the Vicar—"but it's a lot of money . . . an awful lot."

At ten o'clock the party broke up, and the boys went into the changing-room to get their coats. They were away so long that Mr. Matthews wondered what they were doing, and presently Pete came back and gave him a handful of coppers and a few pieces of silver.

"Look," he said—"there's seven and ninepence. 'Tisn't much—but it's a start anyway. From now on we're all going to pay five bob a month—and if they send you to prison about that boat, we'll break that old bitch's windows and come with you."

Chapter Eighteen

Next morning Mr. Matthews took the candlesticks to London. He could not get them into his suitcase, so Ruth did them up in a brown paper parcel. He felt unhappy with it on the bus because it had a sinister shape and the conductor kept on looking at it. They were not quite so antique as he had hoped, and he only got £12 for them, but it was enough to cover the cheque he had written, and he got the money into the bank that afternoon before it closed.

He received an acknowledgement from Miss Ponsonby, and when the cheque was safely through the bank he breathed again. He had stolen a march on Mrs. Bannister Paget by getting six months' rent accepted before she had had time to stir up trouble, and he felt a good deal happier.

He arrived at the boat-house on Saturday afternoon to find Dick the cox waiting for him with an interesting scheme. In his spare time Dick had written a play, and he wanted to produce it in the club-house in aid of the Vicar's fund to buy the land.

"We could get a hundred seats into this big room," he said.—"We could charge two bob a seat and make £10, with a bit extra on the programmes. But there's a lot more to it than that. I know a man who knows a play agent in London, and he's promised to get him down to see the show. If the play's a hit the agent would get it produced in London, and I'm going to give half of everything I earn to your fund. We might make enough to buy the land and get new boats and paint the boat-house and tell that old woman to go to hell!"

Mr. Matthews thought it was an excellent idea. He did not

reckon too much on the London production, but £10, with possibly another £2 on the programmes, would come in very handy and help to pay for the raft. What appealed to him most was the good fun it would provide for the winter evenings. It would keep the boys together and introduce more people to the club, and he told Dick to go ahead and promised to help in any way he could.

Dick was so gratified by the encouragement that he offered Mr. Matthews the part of Julius Caesar. "It's a big part," he said—"with lots of funny situations and good lines—and you'd look exactly like Julius Caesar when you were dressed up."

Mr. Matthews said it would be unwise for him to appear as a Roman Emperor in the winter because of his lumbago, and Dick suggested as an alternative the part of Oliver Cromwell, who could wear any amount of underclothes and still look all right outside, but Mr. Matthews said he had never acted in his life and would only let the show down if he tried, so they arranged that he should take the tickets at the door instead.

"I'll go right ahead and get the people together," said Dick, "and start rehearsals."

On Sunday Mr. Matthews took the usual services at St. Peter's Church. After his stormy scene with Mrs. Bannister Paget he wondered what would happen, and whether the whole congregation would stay away in protest. He had read about people doing that when they disapproved of their Vicar, but they all turned up as usual, and everything was exactly as it always was except that nobody stayed to talk to him when the services were over.

On the following Sunday the same thing happened. Mrs. Bannister Paget and her friends sat frigidly through each service, coming and going without a word. There was not a smile; not a glimmer of recognition that a fellow human being was speaking to them from the pulpit, and Mr. Matthews went home, perplexed and worried. Two weeks had passed, and nothing had come from Miss Ponsonby to suggest that his enemy had carried out her threat to expose what he was doing at the boat-house. He knew she would never make a tame surrender and leave him with the victory, and he wondered what was in the wind.

On succeeding Sundays the atmosphere grew steadily more nerve-wracking. The evil woman sat through every service with unblinking, venomous eyes that never left his face. They hypnotised him like the eyes of a poisonous snake, waiting its time to strike and kill, and when each service ended, she rose and left the church as if she had glutted herself upon his misery and suspense.

He was a man to whom warm friendships and human gentleness were the breath of life. Hatred was something he had never experienced, and he felt it seeping into him like a foul infection. When he pictured the weeks and months ahead, with the same torment every Sunday, he knew that she would defeat him unless he took some steps to end it: she would defeat him by driving him from his parish into a mad-house, and one evening he resolved upon a desperate measure to break the intolerable strain.

He sat down and wrote a long letter of confession to Miss Ponsonby, explaining everything he had done. He admitted that he had broken the agreement of his tenancy. He confessed that he had used the boat and oars, and appealed to her generosity and understanding. He told her how the boys had changed since they had had the chance of using the boat-house on her land, and invited her to come and see for herself how different they were from the days when she had known them. He finished up by inviting her to become the Honorary Patron of their Club, and offering to buy the boat and oars on monthly instalments. Ruth thought it was a good letter with a sporting chance of winning her over.

He waited in suspense, then got an answer quite different from what he had expected. It came from Miss Ponsonby's niece, saying that her aunt was ill and unable to attend to business for some little while. It was a friendly, understanding letter ending with the suggestion that Mr. Matthews should carry on until her aunt was well enough to make her own decision. "For my own part," said the niece: "I think your club sounds fine, but of course it is for my aunt to say the final word."

The letter took a great load off Mr. Matthews' mind. Nobody, he thought, could now accuse him of stealing the boat after such a frank confession and offer to buy it. He saw now why Mrs. Bannister Paget was fighting a war of nerves instead of going ahead with the drastic measures she had threatened. She had no doubt written her mischievous letter and could do no more until her friend's recovery. He did not wish Miss Ponsonby any harm, but he hoped that she would remain unwell for as long as possible—not so ill, of course, as to suffer any pain, but ill enough to keep her from listening to his enemy's accusations. The whole business was certain to boil up again sooner or later, but he had got a reprieve and made up his mind to forget his troubles and enjoy the coming production of Dick's play.

Dick had given him the play to read with an eager request for a frank and honest criticism, but after reading it very carefully Mr. Matthews did not quite know what to say or what to do.

The length of it was staggering. For sheer massive endeavour it compared with Tolstoy's *War and Peace* and Gibbon's *Decline and Fall of the Roman Empire*, but while Gibbon and Tolstoy had modestly confined themselves to Imperial Rome and Napoleonic Europe, Dick's play (which was called "Upsey Daisy"), began with Adam and Eve and ended with the coronation of King George the Fifteenth—a mythical British Monarch of the future, who was to be crowned, apparently, in Wembley Stadium to give more people a chance of looking on.

Ruth had produced plays in Little Stanton and knew more about them than Mr. Matthews did. He consulted her concerning the production difficulties and alarming length of the drama and she confirmed his fears. In its existing form, she said, it would play without stopping for about three days.

The scenes, too, presented problems, opening, as they did, with Adam and Eve in "a vast primeval forest that must reveal that the world has only recently begun", and closing with Wembley Stadium—"thronged with peers, etc., in ermine robes and tweed caps."

Dick had assured Mr. Matthews that the cost of production would not exceed £2, but there were twenty scenes, each outdoing its predecessor in scope and grandeur, and Mr. Matthews could not see how the average cost could be kept at 2S. a scene. Considering the funds at their disposal, said Ruth—and the size of the stage—it would be like building the *Queen Mary* for £2 and launching it in a bath tub.

The main theme of the play was a parody on history, showing how modern invention would have influenced famous episodes of the past. Telephones and radios and aeroplanes were all mixed up with Julius Caesar, Henry the Eighth and Bloody Mary. Some of it, Ruth thought, was quite funny, while other parts were in rather doubtful taste, such as the scene in which Bloody Mary got into trouble with the fuel authorities for burning too many martyrs in restricted hours. But they admired Dick's enormous industry, and the amount of history he must have read.

Dick, however, was equal to everything, for he had the rare gift of inspiring people to a fever pitch of enthusiasm without the least idea of what they were being enthusiastic about. When Mr. Matthews turned up at the first rehearsal he found the club-room crowded with young men and girls whom he had never seen before—all talking at once and all predicting a tremendous success for something which none of them had read. Some thought it was an opera and some a pageant, while others, it seemed, had brought light shoes under the impression that it was to be a dance.

Dick approached his task in a practical, realistic way. He announced that there were twenty-seven parts in the play: seven big and twenty small, with an unlimited selection of non-speaking parts in riots, battles and coronations. Anyone, he said, who would guarantee to sell ten tickets could have one of the big parts and those who could sell five could have a small one. You could walk on in full costume in the front ranks of the crowd if you sold one ticket or guaranteed two candles for the footlights, or you could be at the back of the crowd, in costume down to the waist, for the loan of a chair for the auditorium. The parts were then put up for auction. A lively girl named Elsie, with freckles and rabbity teeth, secured the lead on a guarantee to sell fifteen tickets in the front row at 3s. each and Pete got the thunder in the wings for a candle. Bill and Tony secured the role of Napoleon's white horse on a promise to supply the jam tins for the footlights and a fat girl named Ada became Bloody Mary at the knockdown figure of a chair. It was not, thought Mr. Matthews, the most aesthetic way to cast a drama, but it was a very sensible one. Elsie, for instance, was assured of a resounding success as leading lady with fifteen friends in the front row, while those in the crowd scenes could hardly expect more than the light of the candles they supplied.

The first rehearsals were such dire confusion that Mr. Matthews was in despair, but the fires of enthusiasm burned unquenched and there was much surprising talent. Among the boys were plumber's mates and carpenter's apprentices, painters and mechanics, and between them they wrought miracles.

The sliding doors of the changing-room were removed and a raised stage built with a drop-curtain, wings and footlight gulley, and the painters produced remarkable effects with ingeniously designed back-cloths. The Houses of Parliament could be converted in a few seconds into the Marble Arch by turning them upside down, and the River Thames became the Niagara Falls by the simple expedient of turning it sideways. A girl from a music shop borrowed a gramophone and saved much trouble and expense by producing the battles, riots and thunderstorms on records, and a boy who worked for an upholsterer made the wigs by pilfering the contents of a horsehair sofa. Everybody supplied their own costumes and everybody enjoyed it, and Mr. Matthews forgot his troubles and felt like a schoolboy on holiday.

Ruth helped Dick to cut the play to manageable proportions and became stage manager and wardrobe mistress, while Mr. Matthews was in charge of tickets, programmes and labelling the chairs with numbers. Their daughter Rosemary had just returned from her final term at school. She was, unfortunately, as shy as ever, with vague ideas of going to an art school, and her parents were glad to find her something useful to do in helping to paint the scenery.

One day Dick asked Mr. Matthews whether he would let Rosemary act a small part in the play.

"She's awfully pretty," said Dick—"and she'd look stunning as the Quaker Girl."

Mr. Matthews talked it over with Ruth when they got home. They thought it would do Rosemary a lot of good to act a part. It would give her self-confidence and something interesting to think about, but Rosemary was so painfully shy that they feared she would get stage fright and forget her lines and let the show down.

But Ruth said everybody would forget their lines more or less. The sweep of the drama would carry all the lame ducks before it, so Rosemary was cast to play the Quaker Girl who had to save King Charles the Second from the Roundheads by hiding him in a secret cupboard. They were afraid that Rosemary, in her confusion, would forget where the secret cupboard was, but Ruth coached her in her lines and made a charming costume for her.

By Christmas the rehearsals were going well enough to fix a production date in the second week of January, and one evening Dick told Mr. Matthews that his friend had persuaded the play agent to come and see the show.

"The whole thing's going fine," said Dick. "It'll be terrific if the agent likes it and puts it on in London. We'll make a fortune, and you won't have to worry about that old woman any more."

Mr. Matthews said that would be wonderful—but his main concern was about the £10 they hoped to make on the tickets. It would not in any case be £10 now, for there had been a lot of odds and ends to pay for, and he had put his hand in his pocket more times than he liked to think about. But he had a plan to make things up on the souvenir programmes. He designed an attractive cover and had 200 printed; they cost £4, but by selling them at 2s. each to the cast and audience he hoped to clear a useful little profit.

There was a turbulent dress-rehearsal: a desperate last-minute cutting, and the great evening was upon them with a sprinkling of snow that gave the boat-house a fairy-like appearance with the coloured lanterns strung along the balcony to herald the occasion. Tug-boat skippers looked in wonder at the festive sight as their craft went down the river on the ebbing tide. "Woodbank's bucking up," they said. "There hasn't been a coloured light in that old town for years."

Knowing what the makeshift dressing-room would be like, Ruth arranged for Rosemary to change into her Quaker dress at the Vicarage and walk down with them to the boat-house in her overcoat. They went through the powdery snow beneath the stars, and as the icy wind blew round them Mr. Matthews was glad he was not a bare-legged Roman Emperor.

He retained but the haziest recollection of that fantastic, tumultuous night. He vaguely remembered taking the tickets at the door and fumbling about among the disordered chairs to seat the audience. He had a jumbled memory of a blare of music from the gramophone and a bedlam in the dressing-room: of helping a harassed Charles the Second into his too tight breeches and a grotesquely padded Henry the Eighth into his beard, with Dick yelling: "Hurry!—Hurry up, everybody!—we're late!—it's ten past eight!"

He remembered the soft snow flecking the windows when the lamps went down, and the lights from the distant wharves shining across the river into the darkened, silent room. He remembered the aching delay before the curtain rose, and a fevered argument behind it, but from the moment it went up upon a group of Romans in a forum the show was a great and riotous success. There was a short silence as the audience absorbed the scene, then shouts of glee as they recognised their friends. There were cries of "Look at Bert!"—"That's Harry, Maggie!"—"Look at his hairy legs!"

Somebody shouted: "Order!—give 'em a chance!" and silence was restored sufficiently for the actors to begin. But the enthusiasm broke all bounds at the end of the scene, and the murder of Julius Casear had an encore.

Dick was everywhere—prompting, bullying and applauding, but his main concern was about the play agent. He had told Mr. Matthews that professionals did not like to sit too near the stage, and the two seats—the only ones with arms to them—had been reserved in the middle of the third row. But they were empty when the curtain rose, and at the first interval they were still unoccupied. Dick was despondent, but he told Mr. Matthews to keep on watching for the important guest. "I'm certain he won't let us down," he said.

The play agent did not let them down. During the second act—about nine o'clock, a tall, bald man with a face like a jackdaw came slowly up the boat-house steps with a short, foreign-looking friend. Mr. Matthews showed them to their seats and tip-toed round to give Dick the satisfactory news. Dick had seen them come, through a crack in the wings, and was urging the cast to greater efforts. "He's here!" he whispered—"The agent's here!—it's now or never, boys!" And as the word went round, everything—including most of the lines of the play—was forgotten in a loyal endeavour to back up Dick and get his work accepted.

Rosemary's scene came near the end, and Mr. and Mrs. Matthews were very pleased with her. She looked enchanting when the curtain rose and there was a spontaneous murmur of admiration from the audience. Ruth had coached her carefully in her lines and she spoke them pleasantly and clearly. She was shy and nervous, but this added rather than detracted from her charm, and there was a round of genuine applause when the curtain fell.

Dick kept urging Mr. Matthews to go round into the auditorium and watch the agent's face, and come back and tell him how he was reacting—specially when the Henry the Eighth scene was on, because Dick reckoned that to be the best in the show. Mr. Matthews did as he was asked—but what the orderly, professional mind of the agent was making of the unholy muddle he dared not contemplate. On his first observation the agent was cleaning his finger-nails with a corner of his souvenir programme: on the second he was looking at the ceiling and on the third he was looking at his watch. His swarthy little companion appeared to be asleep, and Mr. Matthews wished the agent was, too.

The show began to pall upon the audience towards the end, so they cut out the discovery of America and finished promptly at eleven o'clock. The sudden and unexpected ending revived the enthusiasm and there were great scenes at the finish. Dick was called forward and he made a speech and handed the £10 ticket money to Mr. Matthews. Mr. Matthews made a short speech in return and the thing was over.

Short as the speeches were, however, they appeared to have been too much for the agent and his friend, for when Dick pushed through the crowd to find them, they were nowhere to be seen.

Dick was crestfallen, but he tried to reassure himself. "Naturally he'll want to think it over," he said. "He'll probably write. It's a good sign, really. If he hadn't liked it I think he'd have said so at once, don't you?"

Mr. Matthews said he thought he would have done, but he had caught a glimpse of the agent's face as the final curtain fell, and was fairly sure they would never see or hear from him again.

Chapter Nineteen

It was midnight when they got back to the Vicarage. Ruth took Rosemary straight to bed and Mr. Matthews went into his study to smoke a pipe and settle down before he followed them. It was bitterly cold outside, and he poked the embers of the fire and drew his arm-chair close to it.

After the high spirits and excitement at the boat-house his study seemed very quiet and desolate. The show had filled his time and thoughts for weeks and it was hard to adjust himself to the sudden emptiness that it had left behind. It had given him a holiday from his troubles, but the fall of the curtain on the last scene of the play had marked the end of his holiday and the return of all the nagging problems that had temporarily been forgotten.

He began to worry about the endless money difficulties again. Far from a profit, the play had been a loss, but he had not had the heart to tell Dick that the ticket money had been more than swallowed up. To make things worse there was the disaster over the souvenir programmes. He had banked on selling them at 2s. each to clear a useful profit of about £5, but he had unwisely left them on a window-sill in the boat-house, and in the general excitement a girl had picked them up and given them away for nothing. When every penny meant so much the programme disaster had been the last straw. In his desk lay the unpaid bills for the raft and oars, and a miserable bank balance of £3 was all that stood between precarious solvency and final debacle. There were no more silver candlesticks to sell, and no way out this time.

He began to think of the evil woman in her dark house behind the trees, nursing her hatred and biding her time to ruin him. She had threatened legal action if he refused to give up his Club and he knew that she meant it. She was wealthy: she could afford the best lawyers in the country, and he wondered where he would find the money to defend himself.

He thought of all the damning evidence a clever barrister might trump up against him to blacken his character and seal his doom.

"There are two indictments against the accused"—the barrister would say: "Firstly, having signed a binding agreement to use a certain piece of land for no other purpose than a public recreation ground, he did, knowingly and deliberately, break that agreement and form a private boat-club. Secondly, knowing full well that the contents of the boat-house were not his property, he did, wilfully and deliberately, appropriate for his own use a certain boat and oars. . . ."

Ruth had ridiculed the idea of such an action but Ruth had too much blind trust in the goodness of human nature. The judge was not likely to be a sentimentalist. "You are not here," he would tell the jury, "to be swayed by the story of a poor clergyman, trying to help the boys of his parish. You are here to decide whether or not this man took this boat, knowing it to be the property of another person. If you decide that he did, then that is a theft, and the accused must pay the penalty. . . ."

He wondered how long the judge would give him. He wondered who would look after Ruth and Rosemary while he was in prison and what would become of him when he came out again, disgraced and ruined. He worked himself up to such a pitch of nerves and despondency that when he heard the faint sound of a distant car somewhere down in Woodbank High Street he could almost persuade himself that it was a police car on its way to arrest him and take him off to prison.

He turned out the desk lamp to go to bed, and as he groped through the darkness towards the passage he was aware that the car was no longer in the distance. It was coming steadily nearer, and it was in St. Peter's Lane.

Cars rarely came along St. Peter's Lane, even in the daytime. At midnight they were unheard of, and in his high-strung state the sound of its steady approach disturbed him. He stood in the darkness, listening to it come nearer and nearer. He went to the window and peered between the curtains, and the sight that met his eyes had the macabre unreality of a nightmare.

The faint glow of the street lamp threw an eerie light across the snow, and into the illumination crept a sinister black car. It came to a halt outside the Vicarage and the man at the wheel was in the dark blue uniform of a policeman.

The man got out. He opened the door of the saloon, and two plain-clothes men emerged. They spoke a word to the driver and entered the Vicarage gate.

Mr. Matthews let the curtain fall and stood in the darkness of his study. He felt sick and faint. It had happened more suddenly and horribly than his worst imaginings. Behind that deadly mask of silence his enemy had been at her evil work . . . accumulating evidence: consulting legal advisers: building up an overwhelming case against him . . . bullying the sick and helpless Miss Ponsonby into final action. . . .

He listened to the muffled footsteps coming up the path, and the mutter of low voices. It was inhuman of them to come at such an hour, but the stern arm of the law was impervious to time.

"The accused was permitted a few moments with his family before he was taken away"—he had read that in his morning paper about a cashier arrested for defalcation. . . .

He went into the dim-lit hall and waited. The detectives were apparently having difficulty in finding the bell, for after their footsteps halted in the porch there was an agonising silence.

At last he heard the creak of the rusty handle, then the thin jangling of the bell, and he walked down the passage like a man to execution.

The two men were standing back from the door as if they expected him to make a dash for liberty. They stood in dark silhouette against the glimmer of the street lamp: one tall and thin, the other short and sturdy: the collars of their great-coats muffled up against the cold.

"Mr. Matthews?" asked the tall thin man.

"Yes?" said the Vicar. "I am Mr. Matthews."

"My name is Palmer. I'm a play agent. Sorry to disturb you at this late hour, Mr. Matthews, but we came down to see that show of yours to-night and wondered if we could have a word with you."

Mr. Matthews stared. For a moment he could not believe it, and then the incredulous relief of it ran like a warm spirit through his chilled and stiffened limbs. From the depths of despair his hopes went surging to the skies. A hard-headed business man like Mr. Palmer would scarcely call at such an hour unless he were deeply interested in Dick's play, and his thoughts began to riot over the dazzling possibilities of it. A West End production: a fortune of money and the purchase of the land: the defeat and confusion of the villainous Mrs. Bannister Paget and a glorious future for his club. He felt like throwing his arms round Mr. Palmer's long thin neck and kissing him in sheer relief and joy.

"Of course!" he said—"It's perfectly all right!—come in, please!"

He took them to his study and pulled the couch up to the ashy fire. "I'm afraid it's rather cold in here," he said: "I was just on the point of turning in . . . but there's no hurry!—none at all!—I'm delighted you came. . . . I'm afraid you didn't see the play under very good conditions, but I expect you're accustomed to making allowances for amateurs. The boy who wrote it is really clever and tremendously keen . . . he'll do anything you suggest for improving it."

The play agent seemed rather confused by the Vicar's bubbling enthusiasm. He glanced at his companion and said:

"It's not that. It's not about the play."

"Not about the play?"

"No. There's nothing to be done with that, I'm afraid. It was something else," and he looked towards his swarthy little friend again. "This is Mr. Benfleet," he said: "It's his business. You'd better go ahead and explain it, George."

Mr. Benfleet, so far, had not said a word. He was an alert, vigorous man with keen black eyes and glossy hair. He did not seem in any desperate hurry to begin. He smiled to himself, as if some secret thought amused him, and pulled out a leather cigar-case, embossed in gold.

"Cigar?" he said.

"I'll smoke a pipe, if you don't mind," said the puzzled Vicar—"but go ahead yourself, please."

Mr. Benfleet bit the end off a long cigar and spat the remnant into the grate with a neat little "plick" from his pursed up lips. He pulled out a gold lighter and a rich aroma began to fill the study.

"I'm over here from the Coast," he said.

"The Coast?" queried Mr. Matthews.

Mr. Benfieet smiled. "It's the name we have for California . . . Hollywood, to be exact. I'm what they call a Talent Scout . . . for Paragon Pictures. Maybe you've heard of them?"

Mr. Matthews certainly had. He went every Thursday with Ruth to the near-by Odeon and knew the flamboyant Eagle with outstretched wings that heralded a Paragon film.

"Of course," he said—"I know them well."

Mr. Benfleet shot a quick, inquiring glance at him.

"You like pictures?" he inquired—"You approve of them?"

"Definitely," said the Vicar, wondering what it was all about. "I go regularly. In a place like Woodbank they're a great help to all of us."

Mr. Benfleet seemed relieved. "Fine!" he said—"I'm glad about that. Some parsons don't—but I'm glad you do." He paused, and gently puffed a rich blue ring of cigar smoke into the room—so rich and blue that it made the light-fittings look cheap as it floated majestically past them on its way to the ceiling.

"We're making a big picture this summer," he proceeded—"based on a thing called the 'Children's Crusade'. Did you ever hear of it, Mr. Matthews?—it's something that really happened. It's historic."

"You mean the tragic thing that happened in France when the crusades of Coeur de Lion were going on?"

"Sure," said Mr. Benfleet. "And I'm glad you think it's tragic. In Hollywood we reckon it's great ... can't think why nobody's ever made a picture of it before ... thousands of kids, all ages from ten to seventeen—inspired by the Crusaders to march on the Holy City by themselves—no help from anybody—no grown-ups ... just kids. Hundreds died on the way, hundreds got kidnapped and taken by pirates and sold into slavery. Just ten of 'em got through to the Holy City, Mr. Matthews ... ten out of all those thousands ... ten heroic kids. ..."

"I didn't know that any actually got there," said Mr. Matthews.

"Ten do in our picture," retorted Mr. Benfleet rather sharply.

Mr. Matthews did not argue the point. He sat there wondering what a big motion-picture of the "Children's Crusade" had got to do with a Vicar in the East End of London. ...

"The leader of this kids' crusade—in our picture," explained Mr. Benfleet—"has got to be a young peasant girl. A lovely seventeen-year-old peasant girl—with a sort of enchanting, poignant innocence, if you know what I mean. It's hard to explain: you *can't* explain. You just have to wait until you *see* the kid with your own eyes and *feel* the simplicity and loveliness inside her—"

He made another smoke ring and watched it dreamily as it floated slowly away.

"It's no use looking for a kid like that in Hollywood," he said—"they aren't simple, and by the time they're good enough actresses to make you think they are, they're too old. We've got to find a girl who's as fragile as an angel and as brave as a saint: she must have beauty and sincerity and honesty and innocence. If she hasn't, the whole damn thing does down the drain.

"I've searched all England, Mr. Matthews. I've been to amateur shows at girls' colleges: I've sat through beauty contests. ... I've walked the streets, watching out for her. Last night Jim Palmer told me about this show of yours: it was a chance in a thousand, like all the rest—but when that show was over to-night, I knew my search was over, too. ..."

He paused, and flicked his cigar ash into Mr. Matthews' tobacco jar.

"I've found the girl at last," he said. "It's your daughter."

The Vicar looked up in astonishment. He glanced at both men sharply and suspiciously, wondering whether his boys had planned the whole fantastic visit as a practical joke.

Mr. Benfleet laughed. "I guessed it would be a bit of a surprise," he said.

An explanation dawned upon the Vicar.

"But that wasn't my daughter playing the leading part," he stammered. "That was a girl named . . ."

Mr. Benfleet laughed again. "The kid with the rabbit's teeth?—No, not her!—I mean the one who played the Quaker Girl in the white collar and grey dress. That was your daughter, wasn't it?"

"Yes," said Mr. Matthews in bewilderment. "That was my daughter . . . but . . . I'm afraid there's some mistake. Rosemary has never acted in her life before. She's only eighteen, and . . . and she's so shy and inexperienced that we . . . we seriously doubted whether . . ."

Mr. Benfleet slapped his knee in delight. "Swell!" he cried—"You've said the very thing I hoped for!—Eighteen!—Never acted!—Shy!—The one thing that scared me was the chance that she was really older than she looked, and *could* act, and just put on that simplicity stuff out of cleverness. She's it!—Mr. Matthews!—She's the girl we want! The girl in twenty million!"

Mr. Matthews could not think of any adequate reply. He sat there looking blankly at the brisk little man on the sofa. Rosemary a film star!—Rosemary whom a boy once called a "dumb cluck" . . . Rosemary who "didn't tick". It was fantastic and impossible. . . .

"Films are funny things," the Talent Scout was saying—"most parts need an actress who can act down to her fingertips—then once in a while there comes along a part like this one in the 'Children's Crusade' that needs a girl who doesn't know what acting means!—an unknown kid who sort of rises from the earth to lead those children to the Holy City—or maybe comes down from Heaven to lead them. Of course," he added with a sharp return to business—"the last word doesn't rest with me. The studio has to make the final decision. I want you to let your daughter come to London to-morrow—to the Paragon Offices—St. James' Square—say eleven o'clock. I'll take her along to make some tests and fly them off to Hollywood, and have word back within a week. Maybe they'll say she's wrong—but I'll stake my reputation that she'll be a world-famous star before next Christmas."

Chapter Twenty

It was one o'clock when Mr. Palmer and Mr. Benfleet left the Vicarage. Mr. Matthews watched them drive away, and he saw Ruth looking over the banisters in her dressing-gown when he turned to go back to his study.

"What is it?" she whispered. "What's happened?"

"I'll turn the lights out and come and tell you," he said.

She was standing by the bedroom door when he went up to her. She looked pale and drawn, and he guessed what she was thinking.

"It's all right," he said—"it wasn't the police."

She gave a sigh of relief. "I heard the bell and I saw the car outside, and the driver looked like a policeman. What was it all about?"

"It was a man from Paragon Pictures. He wants Rosemary to go to Hollywood."

He made her get back into bed and he told her what had happened. After her first surprise she took it more calmly than he had expected, but Ruth had a way of being calm about miraculous things. "What did you say?" she asked him.

"I said I'd have to talk to you about it and ring them up in the morning."

"What did they look like?" she asked.

"You saw them at the show."

"I'm wondering if they're genuine. It might be some kind of a trick to get Rosemary to take lessons in film acting at a guinea a lesson, or something. People are up to all kinds of games like that."

"I thought the same thing at first," he said. "But here's his card—'George Benfleet, Casting Office, Paragon Pictures,

Hollywood': a big company like Paragon wouldn't play tricks like that. It's genuine all right, but it's incredible, isn't it? ..."

Ruth took the card and read it, and put it down beside her on the bed.

"It's incredible to us," she said—"but from their point of view I suppose it's reasonable. You remember 'The Song of Bernadette'?: there was a young girl in that who had never been in pictures before, and because she was so simple and genuine the picture was really beautiful. I suppose the 'Children's Crusade' would be the same kind of picture and Rosemary is rather like that girl in 'The Song of Bernadette' when you come to think of it."

"Then you agree to it?"

Ruth was silent. "I don't know," she said at last. "It's difficult. . . . I don't know what to think: Rosemary is so young. For good or for bad it would change her whole life. It's not like acting a part in an amateur play and going home and taking up one's ordinary work again. If I thought Rosemary were a born actress I'd say 'Yes' at once—but I don't think she *is* an actress—and I don't think she ever will be. She might be a tremendous success in this one picture because, as Mr. Benfleet says, she suits the part and wouldn't have to act."

"But she might be hopeless in anything else they tried her in."

"That's what I'm afraid of. She might never come near success again. But after the thrill and glamour and excitement of that one great experience, she would never be quite normal again. It wouldn't be in human nature for her to understand, and come back and lead the life of an ordinary English girl once more. She would always be trying to repeat it, and she would be angry and bitter and full of resentment and self-pity if she failed. It's happened to many girls in Hollywood . . . it might ruin her whole ife."

Mr. Matthews began to wander about the room.

"If we don't say anything about it," he said, "there's no need for her ever to know what's happened to-night. We only have to tell the film people we disapprove, and she'll be none the wiser. It would save her all the unhappiness and misery of failure."

"*If* she failed," said Ruth. "That's the difficult part. How do we know that she would fail?—How do we know that a good director might not discover something in Rosemary that we've never suspected, and make her a great film star?—Parents aren't always the best judges of their children. It may be that the very things we see against her would turn out in the end to be the things that make her a great success. I don't think we *can* say 'No'. I don't think we've got the right to. I think we've got to let her make the test to-morrow. After all, nothing might come of it. The people in Hollywood may decide against her."

"If they don't," he said—"if they accept her, there's no drawing back. It would break her heart and she'd never forgive us."

"I realise that," said Ruth. "But we must go on with it now. If they accept her, then we can only hope and trust that she'll be successful. If she's not . . . then it'll be for us to do our best to help her."

Chapter Twenty One

Next morning Mr. Matthews rang up the London office of Paragon Pictures and asked for Mr. Benfleet. He half expected to find they had never heard of Mr. Benfleet and the whole thing was a practical joke, but the girl at the other end knew all about it and said: "Oh, yes, Mr. Matthews. Hold on please, I'll give you his office." And in a few seconds he was through.

"I've discussed the matter with my wife," he said. "We are quite agreeable to the tests being made."

"Swell!" said Mr. Benfleet. "Send her right along."

It was a raw, cold morning, and he walked with Ruth and Rosemary through a slush of melting snow to the corner of the High Street and saw them on to the bus for London. Then he walked back alone to gather up the threads of the day's routine as best he could.

But his mind was too confused to think of anything else. He went into his study, where the smell of Mr. Benfleet's cigar still lingered, and drew his chair up to the fire.

By all the laws of reason he knew that he ought to be thrilled by Rosemary's wonderful opportunity. A right-thinking father, he told himself, should set aside his personal feelings for his daughter's sake, but he was troubled by something that had nothing directly to do with Rosemary's future. It had kept him awake all night and he had to go on thinking about it.

If the film tests were successful Rosemary could not go to Hollywood alone. Ruth would have to go with her and take care of her, and make a proper home for her to return to every night after her day's work was done. That was obvious: Ruth would have to go, and he would have to carry on in Woodbank alone. If he were sure of Ruth's return he would gladly face the days without her, but he had a feeling that she never would return: that the last years of his life would pass in a desolate loneliness hard even to contemplate.

If Rosemary became the famous star that Mr. Benfleet had predicted, then it would be more necessary than ever for Ruth to stay with her and help her to keep a level head and live a sensible life. However strongly Ruth might feel the urge to return to him in Woodbank, her duty would be with Rosemary in Hollywood and his to accept it.

He thought of their long years of happiness together: of her tireless help and her sense of humour that had turned so many difficulties into journeys of adventure: he thought of her warm companionship and steadfast faith in him, and he wondered how he could face the years ahead without her.

They would try and persuade him, he supposed, to give up his work in Woodbank and live with them in Hollywood. In that case he would be no more than his daughter's pensioner: living uselessly in a foreign land among people with whom there would be no common interests—tolerated because he happened to be the father of a star. If he refused to leave his work in Woodbank, then Ruth, in America, would never be happy in the knowledge of his loneliness.

The stagnant silence of the Vicarage was a grim foretaste of the days ahead: the stale smell of Mr. Benfleet's overnight cigar symbolised the end of his family life and all his happiness. He wandered sadly from room to room, all touched by the gentle hand of his wife who would soon be leaving him. He thought of his lonely meals, with Mrs. Burgin trying in a clumsy way to comfort him—arranging clumsy vases of flowers where Ruth had once arranged them. He walked down to the church to conduct the usual week-day service. As usual, on week-days, no one came, and for the first time in his days at Woodbank he was glad to have the church alone.

It was nearly dark when Ruth and Rosemary got back from London. They had had a long and tiring day, but full of interest and excitement.

Mr. Benfleet had driven them in his big black car to a studio in the North of London. They had dressed up Rosemary as a kind of peasant girl and done her hair and given her a few lines to learn. They had taken a lot of scenes at different angles and fussed about with the lights, and Mr. Benfleet had seemed very pleased, and taken them to lunch at the Savoy hotel, where they had lobster thermidor and ice-cream. Then he had driven them to another studio for a lot of "still" pictures, and back to the office for a talk with the publicity manager, who wrote down a lot about Rosemary's childhood and school days, and asked Ruth a lot of questions as well.

Ruth seemed to have lost her doubts and fears: she was full of enthusiasm about the kindness everybody had shown, and Mr. Matthews tried to be enthusiastic with them. But in it all he tasted the bitter loneliness of the days to come ... already his wife and daughter were together, and he was out of it.

When Rosemary had gone to bed, he felt the time had come to have a heart to heart talk with Ruth about their own future, but Ruth said the best thing to do was to forget all about it until they heard something definite.

"For all we know the whole thing'll fizzle out," she said: "Rosemary certainly looked lovely when they'd dressed her up, but honestly, Roger, I don't think she'll ever make a screen star, and I think those hard-headed men in Hollywood will realise it when they see the tests. We'll just be wasting time if we talk about it any more."

So they pretended to forget about it, and tried to get back to their normal routine. Mr. Matthews went down to the boat-house and helped to clear up the litter of the show. Three boys who had acted in the show came down and said they would like to join the Club and Mr. Matthews began to buck up again and think about an Eight next summer in place of a Four.

At the end of two weeks, when no word came from Mr. Benfleet about the tests, he began to think it had fizzled out as Ruth had predicted. He knew it was wrong to feel relieved when it meant such disappointment for Rosemary, but when Ruth herself admitted that she would be glad if it never came to anything he felt much happier and almost normal again.

"Mr. Benfleet said we would hear within a week," said Ruth, "but it's over a fortnight now. I don't think anything'll happen, and I think it's a blessing in disguise."

But one morning a few days later the phone rang, and Mrs. Burgin came in to say that Paragon Pictures wanted to speak to Mr. Matthews.

It was Mr. Benfleet, and he sounded jubilant.

"It's okay," he said. "I've just had a cable from the Coast. They've seen the tests and they're crazy about her. They want her in Hollywood as quick as we can get her there, so I'll come right along and fix things up. It's great, isn't it?"

Mr. Matthews was making a feeble effort to agree that it was "great" when he heard a click and Mr. Benfleet had gone.

An hour later the Talent Scout appeared in person in his big black car. He came in the squeaky gate and up the path with a jaunty step—full of pep and gusto. He was pleased because his own judgment had been confirmed by the great men in Hollywood. It was a feather in his cap, and he said so.

"I knew from the moment I saw her that she was right," he said: "I'm not the fellow to make mistakes when it comes to spotting stars."

He read a long cable to them. There were three full pages of it, and Mr. Matthews thought it must have cost a good £10. Most of it was Greek to him . . . technical jargon about terms and options and starting dates, but Mr. Benfleet translated it into simple English.

They offered Rosemary a guarantee of sixteen weeks at $500 a week to make a smaller picture to try her out before the big one. They then had an option for twenty weeks at $1000 a week in which Rosemary would star in "The Childrens' Crusade", followed by an option at $2000 a week for a year.

"It's quite usual to try a new girl out in a small picture first," said Mr. Benfleet—"it's good for her and good for us, because she gets experience and we check up on her before we start the big thing.

"And here's some news for you and the wife," he went on. "They want you both to go over with your daughter as guests of the studio—all expenses paid—while she makes her first picture and settles down. We know you wouldn't like her to go alone, and it'll be a grand holiday for you in the sunlight—away from all this snow and slush."

Mr. Matthews had hoped from the start that Ruth's fare would be paid, but he never dreamed they would include him.

"Did you say *me* as well?" he asked.

"Sure," said Mr. Benfleet. "We can't leave dad behind!"

"It's extraordinarily generous," said Mr. Matthews. "There's nothing I'd enjoy more. But I'm afraid . . . at the moment . . . there are special reasons why I couldn't possibly leave the parish. . . ."

He told Mr. Benfleet about the Boys' Club, and how necessary it was to be at hand to see it safely through its early stages. He told him about his troubles with the Church Council and how he would have to be near at hand to watch developments and deal with them as they arose—but all the time his dutiful side was talking, the romantic side was shouting what a fool he was to deny himself a glorious adventure.

He hardly expected an American Film Executive to understand the problems of an obscure clergyman, but Mr. Benfleet listened sympathetically, and his advice was forceful and convincing.

"I see your point about the Boys' Club," he said. "A man gets keen on things like that, and I'd feel the same if it was mine, but don't you think it'd be the making of those kids if you put them on their mettle and let 'em run it on their own for a few months? Why not pick out the best of 'em and put him in charge, and I'm ready to lay you'll be surprised how well they get along.

"And as for those people in your church—they always say in

Hollywood that the best way for an actor to get the respect of the studios is to pack his bags and clear out and say he's sick of the sight of them. In a few weeks he gets big offers to go back, but if he'd hung about waiting for a job they'd have turned their backs on him. What happens in Hollywood happens everywhere, because it's human nature.

"You say these people in the church don't want you. Okay then: pack your bag and go, and let 'em find out what a good man they've lost. When you come back in four months' time, you'll find they'll be eating out of your hand."

Mr. Matthews could not quite see Mrs. Bannister Paget eating out of his hand, but he saw what Mr. Benfleet meant.

"Look at it another way," said Mr. Benfleet. "Suppose you say 'No: I can't go.' To-morrow you go out and get run over by a bus and go to hospital for four months. They've *got* to do without you then—and when you come out of hospital you'd find everything had gone on just as if you'd been there all the time—and you'd say, 'Why didn't I take that swell trip to Hollywood instead of being run over?'"

"There's another thing," put in Ruth. "I wouldn't dream of going without you, Roger—and if I don't go, Rosemary can't. It's the thing that's worried me all the time: I knew we couldn't both afford to go and I knew I couldn't leave you here alone. Now this wonderful offer clears up everything."

"Swell!" exclaimed Mr. Benfleet as if Ruth had settled it—"the *Queen Mary* sails next Tuesday. That gives you a comfortable six days to get ready."

"Six days!" gasped the Vicar. "But ... but I couldn't!—I shall have a hundred things to do!—I must arrange for a deputy to take my place ... I must pack, and arrange my personal affairs ... and most important of all—I must see the Bishop and get leave of absence. If the Bishop disapproved, I'm ... I'm afraid it would be very difficult. ..."

Mr. Benfleet stuck out his chin and strutted up and down like a dictator.

"Where is this Bishop?" he demanded. "I'll fix the Bishop for you!"

"Oh, no!" cried Mr. Matthews in alarm—"That's something I would have to do myself!"—he had a vision of Mr. Benfleet striding into the Episcopal Palace blowing smoke rings and saying: "Now see here, Bishop—"

"If I wrote to him at once," said Mr. Matthews, "explaining the urgency and asking for an appointment . . ."

"What's the matter with the phone?" broke in Mr. Benfleet. "Aren't Bishops on the phone?"

Mr. Matthews was a tidy man who liked official things to pass through proper channels. An interview with the Bishop was an affair to be arranged by an orderly exchange of letters, but Mr. Benfleet was overwhelming when he meant business. He stood over Mr. Matthews while he searched for the number, shuffling with impatience and looking at his watch.

The Vicar finally made contact with the Bishop's chaplain, who went away and returned with the surprising and gratifying news that the Bishop would see Mr. Matthews at twelve o'clock on the following morning.

For the next three days Mr. Matthews felt like an actor in a trick motion-picture that is geared to make everybody and everything move at twice the normal speed.

He began with the conviction that he could not possibly be ready in time, but he had not reckoned with the magic powers of an American Film Company in full cry. To Paragon Pictures it was all in the day's work to pack up a Vicar and his wife and daughter and shoot them off to Hollywood in less than a week. Mr. Benfleet said they had once got an actress off in six hours, complete with a new wardrobe, new eyebrows and a pet monkey. Their whole machinery was geared for speed—by-passing difficulties, crushing down red tape and swallowing fussy officials up like gnats. Every department was governed by a specialist who was master of his craft, and their creed was never to take "no" for an answer.

At nine o'clock on the morning after Mr. Benfleet's visit, a man named Mr. Ekelberger turned up in a big blue car. Mr. Ekelberger was in charge of Passports, Visas and Travelling Permits, and he whisked Mr. Matthews off to the American Consulate with Ruth and Rosemary.

A lot of people were sitting round in a waiting-room, but a word from Mr. Ekelberger took the Matthews sailing past the bogged-down applicants, straight into the private office of a Vice-Consul. In five minutes they were out again, with Passports stamped and Visas signed—speeding on their way to the Paragon Offices. Even the traffic lights turned green at the sight of Mr. Ekelberger's car, and the lift in the big building in St. James' Square went shooting up without anybody apparently doing anything to start it.

At the Paragon Offices Mr. Ekelberger disappeared out of Mr. Matthews' life as abruptly as he had entered it and a man named Mr. Fergus McCulloch took over. Mr. McCulloch was a lawyer in charge of Contracts. A twenty-page document appeared from nowhere, and Mr. Matthews had to sign it as Rosemary's parent on account of her age. Mr. McCulloch was so efficient that he helped the Vicar on with his spectacles, and a special girl stood by to blot the signature. In a few minutes the Matthews were off again in charge of a Mr. Peasmarsh, the Transportation Manager.

Mr. Peasmarsh's office was decorated with framed pictures of Ocean Liners and Aeroplanes and racks of timetables and travel pamphlets, and Mr. Peasmarsh was so breezy that he almost blew the Vicar's hat off. He filled in numerous forms for their accommodation on the *Queen Mary* and showed them a wonderful coloured plan of the redoubtable ship, pointing out where their cabins were, and a short cut to the sea. While this was going on Mr. Benfleet came in to say that a special appointment had just been arranged for Rosemary to go at once to "Maria Teresa" the famous dressmakers, who would see that Rosemary had a proper wardrobe for her journey. "And you," said Mr. Benfleet to Mr. Matthews, "can go off and see that Bishop. If you have any trouble, just ring me up and I'll come along."

The impression of a speeded up motion-picture abruptly ended when Mr. Matthews walked into the cloistered calmness of the Bishop's Palace and sat down to await the critical interview. The events of the morning had whetted his appetite for the thrills of Hollywood. He was burning to go now, and he began to think how terrible it would be if the Bishop refused to let him. The Bishop might have heard about his trouble with the Church Council and say that, in all the circumstances, it was his duty to stay in the parish. He could not think what he would do if that were to happen, and while he waited he prayed that things would be all right.

The Bishop was a sturdy man with a ruddy, humorous face and a touch of side-whiskers that made him look like John Bull. He listened with a twinkle in his eye while the Vicar blurted out his story, and when it was over he lit his pipe and gave Mr. Matthews a broad smile that put new hope into him.

"Well," he said—"You're making Church history, Mr. Matthews—I imagine you're the first Vicar of the Church of England to apply for leave to go to Hollywood. How long do you want to go for?"

"Four months," said Mr. Matthews—"allowing ten days for travelling each way, I would be back in my parish for certain by the middle of May."

"Lucky man!" said the Bishop—"I wouldn't mind the trip myself. Have you any plans for a deputy to take your place?"

"I really haven't had time to think of that," replied Mr. Matthews. "You see, it's all been so sudden."

The Bishop glanced through some papers on his desk. "There's a man named Montagu," he said—"Curate of St. Paul's at Wanfleet ... he's not getting on with his Vicar and wants a move. He can take your place while you're away."

Mr. Matthews left the Bishop's Palace with a joyous glow of freedom in his heart: he was over the last hurdle with the great adventure clear ahead. He sat inside the bus on the homeward journey, looking out at the murky twilight of the winter afternoon and the grey slush in the gutters, thinking of orange groves and cowboys galloping down sun-drenched canyons, whooping and waving their wide-brimmed hats: he thought of the big white studios rising against palm trees and warm blue skies, and tango bands and Gary Cooper and Katherine Hepburn and trees dangling with juicy grape-fruit, and he wondered at the strangeness of it all, and why a man so little worthy of it should be granted the boon of such a great adventure.

Thursday and Friday were tempestuously busy, with more visits to the Paragon Offices and journeys round London getting cabin trunks and razor blades and six new collars and a comfortable tweed cap for sitting in a deck-chair on the *Queen Mary*. Mr. Matthews still wondered how he could possibly be ready in time, until, at six o'clock on the Friday night, he found himself in Mr. Benfleet's office, receiving a bulky package containing copies of the contract, a letter of credit for his expenses on the journey, the passports and the travel tickets.

"Well," said Mr. Benfleet—"That's that. You're okay now. Your time's your own until you catch the seven o'clock boat train from Waterloo on Monday evening."

It was hard to believe that everything was settled with two days in hand. There must be, thought the exhausted Vicar, hundreds of forgotten things. All the way home he tried to think of them, but he could think of nothing but the final packing of their bags.

"We'll take it as a kind of week-end holiday," said Ruth. "It'll be rather fun, just pottering round the garden and doing normal things as if nothing had happened and nothing was ever going to happen."

Mr. Montagu, the deputy Vicar, came in for a talk that evening. He was a tall, ascetic-looking young man with a pale face and a blue chin. He was off-hand about his temporary duties in Woodbank, and rather half-hearted about the whole thing, but having quarrelled with his Vicar in Wanfleet he was glad to fill in time until a new appointment came along.

Mr. Matthews did not tell him about his difficulties with Mrs. Bannister Paget and the Church Council. He saw no point in bringing a deputy into a thing like that. On the whole he did not like Mr. Montagu very much, but he had a feeling that the bored young man would stand no nonsense from Mrs. Bannister Paget and that Mr. Benfleet's prediction might come true. The Church Council might get so sick of Mr. Montagu that they would welcome their old Vicar back and patch up their differences. Mr. Montagu was a bachelor, and it was arranged that Mrs. Burgin should look after him at the Vicarage until the Matthews returned.

On the Saturday afternoon he went down to the Boat Club and told the boys that he was going away. He got out his bicycle and coached them from the bank for the last time, and when he thought of all the happy evenings they had spent together he felt very sad at leaving.

They made tea in the club-room and talked about the winter programme they would carry on with while he was in America, and afterwards Pete walked back to the town with him alone.

"I'm leaving you in charge, Pete," he said. "Keep the old Four together and take those new fellows out in the tub pair and teach them how to row. With those boys we've got seven now: if you can find one more we'll get an eight-oared boat next summer and row in the Thames Regattas."

"There's a big fellow named Watson at the Tannery," said Pete. "I talked to him last night. I think he'll join."

"Fine!" said the Vicar. "Keep the club evenings going once a week. Get them all down and go for a run and keep fit. Next year we'll try and get a billiard table and a piano."

They came to the corner of the High Street where they always went their separate ways.

"I envy you that trip," said Pete. "I'd give a lot to see America."

"I'd give a lot to have you come, Pete."

"What time d'you leave?"

"Half-past five on Monday night—to catch the boat train from Waterloo at seven."

"Gee!" said Pete. "I envy you!"

For the first time in their days of friendship he thrust his hand out and took the Vicar's and shook it. "We're going to miss you, down there at the boat-house," he said.

He walked away along the misty High Street where the dirty snow still clogged the gutters and the lights were beginning to come on in the dingy shops. Mr. Matthews watched the tall boy cross the road and disappear in the twilight, then he turned and went back to the Vicarage to complete his packing and get his cabin trunk strapped up.

On Sunday, at evensong, he announced the news to Mrs. Bannister Paget and her satellites. It took them completely by surprise. Mrs. Bannister Paget stared at him incredulously and fussed with her musty little cape to regain her composure. He cut the announcement as short as possible, told them the name of his deputy and closed the service.

Following his custom since they had begun their campaign of ignoring him, he went straight to the vestry to wait until they had gone. He heard their footsteps shuffling in the aisle, a murmur of voices, and silence. When he was ready to go, the church was empty except for the verger turning out the lights. The old man was too deaf to have heard what had happened, and Mr. Matthews said "good night" and left the church.

It was a clear winter evening, and he walked along the riverside a little way, watching the tide moving in towards the rising moon, thinking of all the strange things he would see and experience before he saw the moon rise over the Thames again. The last lights went from the windows of the church. He heard the verger close the door and he saw the old man move away like a small grey ghost among the tombstones.

The day of departure dawned with a drizzling rain. Rosemary's new clothes arrived by special messenger and Rosemary spent the morning trying them on and running about the house in them. It got on Mr. Matthews' nerves because he wanted to pack the things and strap the bags. At lunch-time Mr. Benfleet rang up to ask if everything was okay. Mr. Matthews said yes it was, and Mr. Benfleet said, "Swell!—see you at Waterloo."

The time passed very slowly after lunch. It was impossible to settle down to read a book or have a nap with so much ahead of them that evening. They walked round the garden and Ruth showed Mrs. Burgin where they had set some daffodils and grape hyacinths that autumn, and Mrs. Burgin promised to keep the cats off them, and write and tell them when the first daffodil came out.

At three o'clock Mr. Matthews decided to tie some extra labels on the luggage in case the stick-on ones came off: then Ruth and Rosemary went upstairs to dress, and Mr. Matthews put his overcoat and umbrella and new hat in the hall to save a scramble when the taxi came. He found a small edition of *Treasure Island* and slipped it into his overcoat pocket to read in the train.

There was something unreal about sitting by the library fire at tea with the familiar sounds of the river coming to them through the growing darkness. It was so ordinary and humdrum: so like a hundred other afternoons, and when Mr. Matthews looked out at the bare branches of the chestnut tree he found it hard to believe that presently a taxi would come, and when they travelled in it down St. Peter's Lane they would be covering the first few yards of a journey that would not cease until the Pacific Ocean gleamed before them half the world away.

The feeling of unreality remained as the taxi drove along the twilit High Street. Mr. Matthews looked down the long, lamplit side roads as they went by them, and thought of all the hours he had spent in them, knocking at doors and going away. He saw the place where he had spoken to the boys on the evening of his first arrival, and where the policeman had come after him and questioned him. It was remote and dreamlike now: something that might have happened in another world.

When they got to Woodbank Railway Station they were surprised to see Pete and Tony waiting outside with half a dozen of the girls and young men who had acted in the play. They had come to give the Matthews a send-off, and they got hold of a luggage truck and ran the truck and bags up the long slope to the platform.

When the train came in, Pete and Tony heaved the cabin trunk into the luggage van and Dick and the boy who had been Charles the Second in the play found an empty compartment and put the bags in. The guard blew his whistle and waved his flag.

"Take care of the Club, Pete," called out Mr. Matthews. "Keep the flag flying!"

"Okay!" shouted Pete. "Give my love to Hedy Lamarr!"

"Send me Clark Gable's autograph!" shouted Maisie.

"Don't get lost on the *Queen Mary*!" called out Dick.

He waved to them out of the window until the little drab-clothed group was lost in the twilight. The train went thudding across the iron railway bridge and he thought of the stormy evening when he had been wedged against the buttress in the tub pair with Pete and Tony. He looked along the river and caught a last glimpse of the boat-house among the trees.

PART THREE

Chapter Twenty Two

They went to Southampton on the evening train because the *Queen Mary* was sailing early with the morning tide. The passengers were to go aboard after breakfast and the Paragon people had arranged for the Matthews to spend the night at the railway hotel beside the docks.

Mr. Matthews did not like hotels in big towns, but when he went up to his bedroom on the top floor and drew back the curtain he was thrilled by the scene beneath him. The *Queen Mary* lay at a berth quite close to them, brilliantly lit by flood-lights from the quay. All along beside it swarmed a crowd of tiny men like dwarfs around the prostrate Gulliver, and the sea beyond was gleaming and sparkling in the light of a clear half moon.

"This is wonderful!" said Mr. Matthews. "Let's get dinner over and come back here!"

They hurried through dinner and went up in the lift again and settled down at the bedroom window to watch the scene beneath them. The ship was so vast that it seemed much closer than it really was: so close that Mr. Matthews felt as if he could almost lean out of the window and knock his pipe out against the nearest funnel. Now and then a group of men would come along the quay, show their papers and go aboard, and the Matthews took guesses at what each man's job was on the ship. The first they saw arrive were a bunch of swarthy, thick-set men in blue jerseys, with kit-bags slung across their shoulders. Mr. Matthews thought they were too dirty to be sailors and too muscular for waiters: he guessed they were stokers and the guess seemed right when smoke began to drift out of one of the funnels soon after their arrival. A fat man in a bulky overcoat came next, with a leather bag and a brown paper parcel ... possibly the chef, they thought, or the man who played the trombone in the orchestra. Then came an officer with gold braid on his shoulders. The policeman at the gangway saluted him: he did not even have to show his papers, and they wondered if he was the Captain. Ruth thought there would have been more fuss if it had been the Captain. He might be the purser or the doctor. An incongruous, unseaworthy little man arrived in a bowler hat, and strutted up the gangway as if the ship belonged to him. Mr. Matthews did not think he could amount to very much: perhaps a shipping clerk going to check the stores. "They'll turn him off before we sail," said Ruth—"he'd never cross the Atlantic in a bowler hat."

At ten o'clock the staff began arriving in a steady stream, coming out of the darkness into the flood-lights round the ship and disappearing up the gangway. There were girls who looked like stewardesses: boys who probably worked the lifts: a big fat woman who arrived by herself with a small black bag, whom they put down as the hospital nurse: big men and small men ... tall girls and short ones—all going aboard as casually as people to their offices—so many that Mr. Matthews began to wonder how there could be any room left for the passengers in the morning.

And while the staff went streaming on—and far into the night—three big cranes heaved nets of cabin trunks and heaps of bags across the gunwales and down the hold. It went on for so long that Mr. Matthews could not imagine how the ship could go on floating with such a load inside, and just when he began to think the hold must burst they calmly slung aboard a dozen motor-cars. And the strange part was that after hours of ceaseless loading the ship did not appear to be an inch deeper in the water than before it all began. It was uncanny and frightening to think of a ship with such a vast dead-weight inside her, plunging on a dark night through the giant seas of mid-Atlantic.

They were closing the window to go to bed when a small covered van appeared. It drove into the pool of light close to the ship, and some men began unloading mysterious oblong boxes with such care that there must have been something very valuable inside them. Mr. Matthews said it was probably bullion or bar gold or secret diplomatic papers, but suddenly a flap dropped down from the ship's side near the water line, and a man in a white apron and a tall cook's cap popped out like a cuckoo from a clock and took the boxes in. The cook would scarcely be in charge of the bullion, and the boxes no doubt contained the caviare that Mr. Benfleet had told them would be served at the Gala Dinner on the night before they berthed in New York Harbour.

A clock in the town struck midnight. "Come on!" said Ruth. "If we don't go to bed we'll oversleep and miss the boat to-morrow."

It was hard to tear oneself away from the fascinating scene, and when Mr. Matthews was at last in his pyjamas and ready for bed, he took one final look and had to call Ruth back again.

"Come here!" he said. "Look what's happening now!"

A huge pipe had been uncurled across the quay and fastened to the ship's side. A pump began to throb, and they saw the pipe swell up like a giant snake taking a gulp of food.

"Water," said Mr. Matthews. "Look at the size of the pipe! Fancy all that water going in after all those thousands of trunks and motor-cars! . . . We're bound to sink: I can't see how we can avoid it!"

"Somebody's checking it all," said Ruth. "They must know what they're doing."

At two o'clock Mr. Matthews got up to see whether the *Queen Mary* had sunk yet. Most of the flood-lights were out. Everything was quiet, and the great ship lay in darkness, digesting its vast meal of trunks and motor-cars, with a solitary policeman standing by the gangway.

While they were having breakfast a man named Mr. Selkirk was announced. Mr. Selkirk was the Southampton representative of Paragon Pictures and had come to see them safely on to the ship. He knew all the ropes and took charge of the luggage and saw them through the formalities of embarkation and gave Mr. Matthews a telegram from Mr. Benfleet wishing him *bon voyage*.

Embarking on the *Queen Mary* was more like getting off a ship than going on to one, for the quayside, with its chains and cables and smell of tar, had more kinship with the sea than the luxurious vestibule they entered when they crossed the gangway. There were big arm-chairs and flowers and attractive lights, and the whole place was so solid under-foot that it seemed impossible for it to be afloat. It was crowded with passengers talking to friends who had come to see them off, and some of the ship's officers were standing round, greeting old friends among the seasoned travellers.

Mr. Selkirk did not seem to know any of the officers, but he pointed out the Staff Captain and showed the Matthews the shop where they could buy ash-trays with a picture of the *Queen Mary* inside them. He was very attentive, and when he had shown them where their cabins were he offered to take them for a tour of the ship. This worried Mr. Matthews, because he wanted to explore everything quietly on his own when the ship had sailed, but Mr. Selkirk insisted upon taking them down to the dining-room to reserve a table. "You've got to be smart about that," he said—"or you'll find yourselves pushed away into a corner."

The head dining-room steward was in the lobby with a plan of the room spread out on a tressel table, and when he had checked their names he took them into the dining-room to select a place.

It was the biggest and loveliest room they had ever seen, with flowers and lamps on every table, and spotless linen and gleaming silver. There was a buffet table all ready prepared for lunch, with lobsters and chickens and galantines of ham and tongue, and a complete boar's head covered in dark brown jelly with an orange in its mouth.

Mr. Selkirk pointed out the gallery where the orchestra would play, and a huge chart of the Atlantic painted on the wall that would show, by a small coloured light, exactly where they were all through the journey.

He suggested a position at the far end of the room near the

Captain's table, so that they could watch the Captain come in and out, but Mr. Matthews decided on a modest table near the door in case they hit an iceberg during dinner.

Mr. Selkirk then began to look for a deck-chair steward named "Johnny" because it was important, he said, to pick a good place on the sunny side of the promenade before the rush, but Mr. Matthews begged him not to go to any further trouble. He was burning to be free, to wander about quietly with Ruth and Rosemary, and watch all the intriguing things that were building up to the climax of departure. He was glad when somebody blew a bugle and a voice called: "All ashore!—all visitors ashore!" He thanked Mr. Selkirk for everything he had done and hurried off to his cabin to unstrap his bag and get his tweed cap out and go and watch the ship cast off.

He need not, in fact, have been in such a hurry, for a good deal of time went by before they saw the gangway pulled on to the quay and the cables fall and splash into the water. Even then the great ship only moved by inches. They peered down its precipitous side from the promenade deck—watching the strip of water widen very slowly between the dock and ship—then they hurried round to watch the little tugs churning and straining on the other side to get the ship away. It seemed to be such a business that Mr. Matthews began to wonder whether the vast load of cabin trunks and drinking water and motor-cars had not been too much for the ship after all. He wondered whether they were stuck in the mud, and the tugs would simply pull them out to sink in deeper water.

But gradually they lost the ungainly helplessness of the quayside. The ponderous giant became a graceful ship that brushed the fussy tugs aside, and in a little while they were gliding serenely down the Solent with the grey fringes of England fading in the winter mist.

Soon after lunch they anchored off Cherbourg to take aboard some travellers from France and some crates of celery. Ruth and Rosemary went down to their cabins to unpack, but although his legs were beginning to ache, Mr. Matthews went on walking round. There were so many things to see and so much to think about that it was impossible to sit down with his book and read.

They hung about for a long time at Cherbourg, waiting for the tide, and the short winter day was nearly over when the anchor rattled up and the ship swung slowly round to head at last towards the sunset and the open sea.

They moved as smoothly and as easily as if the setting sun were towing them, but when darkness fell and the decks became deserted, Mr. Matthews began to feel an unexpected sadness creeping over him. Deep down inside him he was frightened by the vast emptiness ahead and the steadily increasing depths beneath them. Small things that had meant little in the daylight began to take upon themselves a new significance. At lunch he had noticed a short length of rope dangling beneath his chair, with a clasp to fasten it to a ring set in the floor. The tables were permanently screwed down, and a little silver fence ran round the buffet table to keep the galantines of ham and tongue from sliding off in stormy weather. Even the tooth-glass in his cabin stood in a cradle of its own and a wooden ledge was fitted round his bed to keep him there in emergency. It awed and humbled him to dwell upon the immeasurable power of an ocean that could make such things essential in a ship as big as a cathedral.

He tried to shake off his forebodings by going down to dress for dinner. He was sharing a big double cabin with Ruth, and Rosemary had a smaller, single one that communicated by way of a luxurious bathroom. Nothing could have looked safer and more comfortable. The curtains were drawn across the port-holes, and his wife and daughter were there in charming evening frocks—and yet the very comfort and luxury of it all disturbed him. He would have been happier if it were simpler and more like a ship than a grand hotel. A ship, he felt, should concentrate upon its task of weathering hurricanes and leave the winter gardens and glamorous cocktail bars for the safety of dry land.

They took a turn round the promenade deck before going down to dinner. It was ablaze with lights, and a lot of people in immaculate evening dress were strolling round. Everybody seemed happy: some were quite hilarious—but to Mr. Matthews, in his mood of undefined anxiety, there were too many diamonds and cigars. He had a feeling that in some way they would pay for it. One ear caught snatches of society gossip and talk of politics and stock markets, but the other heard the mutter of the wind through the inky darkness beyond the windows. Now and then a port-hole light would glint upon an angry wave that would throw back an eerie greenish glow. The great ship brushed the waves aside, glorying in its size and strength, but the waves drew back into the darkness—undefeated—waiting their time to lash back in revenge when the ship was at their mercy a thousand miles from land. He saw the cigars and the pearls and the portly stomachs and thought of the *Titanic* and the last days of Pompeii.

Some passengers were standing with one of the ship's officers, peering out into the darkness. He heard the officer say: "Bishop Rock. ... Scilly Isles" and saw the gleam of a distant lighthouse and some tiny pinpoints of scattered light that marked the last small outpost of his homeland.

The sight of those tiny lights increased his sadness and filled him with an overwhelming passion of remorse.

He knew, too late, what a ghastly mistake he had made in coming on this hairbrained luxury adventure. His duty was in his parish: he should have had the courage and strength of mind to stay there and let Ruth and Rosemary come alone. He had deserted Pete, who had stood so loyally by him: he had left the boys at a critical hour to waste his time in Hollywood. He got a whiff of perfume from a woman in blue velvet and a puff of cigar smoke from a millionaire and longed with all his heart for the earthy scent of the land around the boat-house by the river. Ruth seemed to guess his thoughts, and took his arm and said: "Come on—let's go and have some dinner." ...

No one could feel downhearted in the magic of that dining-room. The gaiety and beauty and proud achievement of it swept everything aside. Myriads of little lamps glowed on the tables: the stewards in their smart uniforms looked alert and keen: there were flowers and lovely dresses, a chink of glasses and soft, romantic music that made the dark Atlantic seem a thousand leagues away.

The head-steward showed them to their table as if they were the only people on the ship who mattered, and they liked their young table-steward the moment they set eyes on him. He had a broad smile, clean finger-nails and a rosy, polished face. When he saw his people struggling with the unfamiliar menu, he did not stand by, flurrying them into ill-considered orders. He left them alone, and came back with a dish of plump black olives and celery, and radishes and pickled gherkins, all snugly nested in a little bed of ice.

The menu was so interesting that Mr. Matthews decided to smuggle it away to read in bed. There was a picture of the *Queen Mary* on the front page and then the "Chef's suggestions" —artistically spaced out with margins round them. On page three came a riot of dishes for those who did not like the Chef's suggestions—from Whitstable Oysters and Salmi of Pheasant to sago pudding and gooseberry fool. Many of these dishes were quite new to them, such as tomali, antipasto and chili con carn. Mr. Matthews thought it best to play for safety on the first night out, but decided to have a go at the antipasto when he felt more confident.

They ordered Minestrone and Scallops Mornay, Aylesbury Duckling with new peas, and Strawberry Ice-cream and Coffee, and when the waiter had gone, a magnificent old man with a gold chain round his neck appeared with the wine list. He was tall and stout, with side-whiskers and a port wine face, and he made one think of Feudal Castles and Ducal Mansions. Mr. Matthews felt that he must have cost the Cunard Company a lot of money, but he was worth every bit of it, because of the feeling of security he gave. It was impossible to think of that mellowed symbol of eternal England taking to the boats in a night-shirt or clinging to a spar. The stability of him would hold the ship sate in a hurricane and his face would melt an iceberg.

Paragon Pictures had given Mr. Matthews a generous Letter of Credit with instructions to use it for "anything he required". Was wine, he wondered, a "requirement" in the true and honest sense of the word? He did not want to take a mean advantage of Paragon's trust in him, but he had hardly tasted wine since he had given up his glass of sherry a year ago, and the spirit of that dining-room cried out for a bottle of good claret. He consulted Ruth, and Ruth said: "Certainly I'd have it. Paragon Pictures aren't going to miss the price of a bottle of claret. In fact, I don't think they'd respect you if you didn't splash about a bit."

So Mr. Matthews had a splash: a medium splash with a bottle half-way down the price list.

They had selections from "The Merry Widow" with their soup: a prelude from "Traviata" with the Aylesbury Duckling and a lovely medley of old-time waltzes with the Coffee and Ice-cream.

Mr. Matthews sat back in his chair, no longer troubled by the little piece of rope beneath it. He sipped the claret and looked around him, breathing in the sheer enchantment of the scene. The evening frocks were lovely, and some of the women even lovelier. Here and there a gleam of gold braid revealed where one of the ship's officers was sitting: bronzed, dependable-looking men they were, and they made him feel proud of England and glad that a lot of Americans were on board to see them. Far beneath, the giant propellers throbbed—thrusting them on and on—nearer and nearer to the sun and palms of Hollywood:—Hollywood!—Clark Gable!—Ginger Rogers!—glamour ... mystery and adventure. ... He could not imagine why he had felt so depressed up there on the promenade deck. His boys would be all the better for a few months on their own. They'd think a lot more of him, too, when he came back full of genuine Wild West yarns and glamorous first-hand stories about Hollywood: he might even be able to tell them he had actually talked to Hedy Lamarr and Ginger Rogers and Gary Cooper and Wallace Beery. In the eyes of those boys he'd never be a futile old suburban parson any more. And as for Mrs.

Bannister Paget and her seedy little satellites—to blazes with them and good riddance!

"A little brandy, sir?" enquired the wine-steward. The old man looked fruitier and more serene than ever in the glow of the delicious vintage claret. . . .

"What about you, Ruth?" asked Mr. Matthews.

"Perhaps I will," said Ruth—"to celebrate."

After dinner they sat in the lounge to watch the dancing. It had already got round that Rosemary was a sensational Hollywood discovery, and a handsome young officer of the ship came up and asked her for a dance.

"How different she is!" said Ruth. "Do you remember that miserable holiday at Brighton—and the boy who said she was a 'dumb cluck'?"

She was so lovely and radiant that Mr. Matthews could hardly think of her as the demure little parson's daughter seeing the sights of London. She was talking away vivaciously to the young officer, and he was listening, fascinated. He might well be fascinated to hear the yearning dream of a million girls from the lips of one to whom the dream had come miraculously true.

Mr. Matthews slept like a top, without a murmur from the duckling and ice-cream. When he awoke the daylight was coming through a chink between the port-hole curtains, and he guessed it must be nearly eight o'clock. The ship was steady and they were going at full speed, for the purr of the engines was deeper and fuller than when he had gone to bed. His tooth-glass tinkled now and then in its little metal storm-guard, and sometimes the ceiling creaked a bit, like a new boot. It was restful, lying there in a comfortable bed, with no hurry to get up. He heard the sound of something being pushed under the cabin door and got out of bed to find a compact little morning paper, printed on the ship. There was news by radio from England and a programme of the day's events on board: lifeboat drill at twelve o'clock: a picture in the lounge at five and "Bingo" (whatever that might be) in the smoking-room at three. Watches were to be retarded by one hour at midnight and the swimming-bath was now available.

Half the paper, he thought, must have been printed previous to sailing, for it contained things like crossword puzzles and jokes which could hardly have been thought up during the night—but the rest was up-to-the minute news, even to a stop press column with a cup-tie result, a tram strike and a murder in Liverpool. It gave him a comforting feeling of proximity to home.

At half-past eight the cabin steward brought a tray of tea and biscuits. He was a cheerful man with iron-grey hair and a look of the sea about him. He said it was a fine day, but when Mr. Matthews got up and drew back the port-hole curtains, he saw that the sea was not so calm as the steadiness of the ship had suggested. There were heavy, scudding clouds, and the Atlantic was running in long dark grey swells that sometimes sent a dash of spray across the porthole. He searched for other ships, and was surprised to see an empty, desolate horizon.

After breakfast Johnnie the deck-chair steward fixed them up in a sheltered alcove on the south side near the stern. Johnnie was cheerful. He said the glass was rising and they were going to have a good crossing. Mr. Matthews sat down, intending only to test the chair, but Johnnie immediately wrapped his legs up in a blanket, so neatly and firmly that Mr. Matthews could not, in courtesy, shake it off to go and get his book. He had to stay there for half an hour, and wait until Johnnie had gone away.

The day passed swiftly. They explored the ship from stem to stern and wondered what had happened to all the motor-cars. They had a look at the swimming-pool and took a ride on the automatic hobby-horse in the gym. They played a game of deck quoits and went to boat drill, where everybody looked solemn for a few minutes and put on cork jackets. Mr. Matthews had a good look at the people who would be in his lifeboat if they sank, but he did not think he would have much to talk to them about after the first few days adrift. They wandered round the arcade of shops and

Mr. Matthews bought two *Queen Mary* ashtrays: one for himself and one to send to Pete. Ruth had a wave and Mr. Matthews had a hair-cut, and before tea they took books out of the library. Then they went to the picture in the lounge and played Bingo, and Mr. Matthews chalked up another bottle of claret against the Film Company.

The second day dawned in dismal rain. It was cold and damp on the promenade and they felt an anti-climax. They wished they had not explored everything so thoroughly on the first day and had kept a little of the ship in hand. They spent a good deal of the time wrapped up in their deck-chairs reading, or standing in the stern watching the propellers, and the cardboard boxes and the cabbage leaves that the cooks threw overboard.

At lunch-time on the third day out the light on the big chart in the dining-room showed them to be in mid-Atlantic. It was another dark and wintry afternoon, but now the wind was rising, and towards evening Mr. Matthews felt his premonitions of disaster creeping back. They had not seen another ship all day, and even the gulls that had followed them from land had left them. They were a thousand miles from land in all directions, and the vast surrounding ocean was frightening in its desolation. As darkness came his restlessness increased: they were nearing the iceberg zone and he could not sit easily in the lounge, closed in behind the curtains, not knowing what was happening outside. He wished he could go up on to the bridge and help to keep a look-out. Then suddenly something happened that sent his heart into his throat. From above—from out of the inky winter night—came a great mournful cry from the siren. For one aching moment he waited for the three short blasts and the final long one that would be the awful summons to the lifeboats, but there was only that long, solitary one—followed in a minute by another. "Fog," said a man in the arm-chair next to him.

At dinner he noticed that the Captain was not in his accustomed place. He had no appetite and decided against a bottle of wine.

He wanted to be alert in case of disaster, and he wished the people round him would not talk so loud. If the siren changed its note and called them to the boats, nobody would hear it in that senseless babble. He looked up at the chart of the Atlantic on the wall, and saw that the light that marked their position was terribly far from land.

He lay in bed, listening to that ominous siren crying in the fog like a lost soul. He could not sleep, and the minutes passed like hours. They seemed to be running slower and slower, and towards midnight he could feel no vibration from the engines at all, even when he pressed his ear against the pillow. He wondered whether they had broken down and were drifting helplessly towards the ice-fields.

But towards dawn the siren began to sound at longer intervals: it sounded, he thought, more cheerful, and then it stopped for good. To his joy and relief he heard his tooth-glass tinkling again: the vibration was returning and the engines were once more gathering their power. He felt hungry then—and wished he had had a better dinner. He slept, and woke to see the sunlight shining through the curtains, and life began again.

On the fourth day came the routine preparations for the journey's end. Cabin trunks were strapped and taken on to the promenade deck in readiness for the Customs men; the bureau was open for the exchange of money into dollars, and as they drew nearer to America it seemed to Mr. Matthews that there were more Americans on board than when they started.

That night came the Gala Dinner, and the chef outdid himself with a menu that included some wonderful American dishes and Russian caviare. There were Christmas crackers on the table, and Mr. Matthews got a Turkish fez with a golden tassel. Ruth got a sailor's hat and Rosemary had a poked bonnet that made her look like one of the Brontë sisters. As a grand finale a page boy pulled a string that released from the ceiling a glorious cascade of rainbow-coloured balloons. Everybody cheered, and the orchestra played "Auld Lang Syne", and people began punching the balloons about, and Mr. Matthews punched a big blue one that sailed across the room and came down on the Captain's dinner.

Afterwards there was a farewell dance, and all the young men wanted to dance with Rosemary. The doctor came and asked Ruth for a waltz, then Mr. Matthews danced with her till bed-time. They took a last walk round the promenade deck and the sea was calm beneath a clear full moon.

"How strange it is," said Mr. Matthews, "to see that moon and think it's the same one that was rising over the Thames on the night I left the church for the last time a week ago. What ages it seems—and what a wonderful trip it's been."

"A second honeymoon," said Ruth.

They slept soundly and securely that night, and when they awoke the ship was moving very slowly.

"Are we there?" Mr. Matthews asked the steward when he came in with their morning tea.

"Almost, sir," said the steward. "We're just coming up to the Nantucket Lightship."

Mr. Matthews jumped out of bed and put his overcoat over his pyjamas and hurried up on deck. The sun was rising, and the sea was like a sheet of glass. His ideas about America had led him to expect the Nantucket Lightship to be the biggest in the world. He had pictured some vast kind of marine skyscraper and was surprised to see, instead, an old-fashioned, tubby little ship, rising at both ends like the kind one made for children out of paper. It lay there, pinkish brown in the light of the rising sun.

Chapter Twenty Three

On the tug that brought the Customs and Immigration Officers came Mr. Chester Page, from the New York office of Paragon Pictures. He came to welcome the Matthews to America, and he sat with them in the lounge while they waited their turn to go before the Immigration Officer.

Among other things he broke the exciting news that Norman Walter was to be the leading man in Rosemary's first picture. Norman Walter was one of Rosemary's favourite screen actors and she was thrilled about it. Mr. Matthews was pleased because Norman Walter played the quiet, dependable kind of characters that he admired. He was rather like a younger Gary Cooper, though not so tall.

Ruth asked whether they could have a copy of the screen play so that Rosemary could learn her part on the journey out to Hollywood, but Mr. Page said he had no copy in New York. "they'll fix it all up when you get there," he assured them—"they'll give her lots of time to learn the words."

Rosemary asked—with bated breath—whether Norman Walter would marry her in the picture. Mr. Page said he did not know for certain, but he guessed so.

He then sprang a rather unpleasant surprise. Mr. Matthews had been looking forward to a few days in New York to see the sights before they took the long four-day train journey to Hollywood, but Mr. Page said the Studio wanted Rosemary without fail before the end of the week. "But that'll be okay," he said. "You can have three days in New York and fly out to the Coast on the night plane, Friday."

Mr. Matthews did not answer this at once. He had never flown in his life, and was not sure whether it would agree with him. "The fact is," he said—"we were very much looking forward to the interesting journey across America in the train."

"In that case," said Mr. Page, "why not leave New York for the journey home? We'll be ashore by eleven and fix you up for the day at the Biltmore Hotel. That's right over the Grand Central Station, handy for the train. You can just relax till lunch-time, and I'll send one of the boys to take you a drive around the city in the afternoon. He'll have you back at the Biltmore in good time for the Chicago train that leaves at half-past six. You don't have to worry about a thing: we'll check your bags right on to the train and get the tickets."

Mr. Matthews said that sounded very nice. It would be a hustle, but he was prepared for hustle in America. In any case he had by now such perfect faith in Paragon Pictures that he was certain everything would be all right.

During the last hours of the journey something rather sad had happened to the *Queen Mary*. On the previous night she had been the grandest ship in the world, with the Gala Dinner a climax to five days of triumph. She had carried 2000 people 3000 miles through angry winter seas without the breaking of a teacup, yet now, upon this morning of arrival, she had suddenly shed her grandeur and was like a bleak seaside hotel closing for the winter. The lounge, on the previous evening, had been a scene of magic beauty with lovely dresses and romantic music, but now it was like a waiting-room in a railway station, with ugly tressel-tables lined with humdrum clerks and Immigration Officers making blue pencil ticks on endless forms. The promenade deck was an untidy dump of trunks and bags, with Customs Officers rummaging amongst them, and the staff was surreptitiously preparing for the homeward journey.

The passengers, too, had changed. They had lost all interest in the ship, and were wandering aimlessly about in hats and overcoats, fretting to get ashore.

As he went down the gangway Mr. Matthews thought how

ungrateful they all were—walking off without a word of thanks. It was as if the ship were dying, with its life-blood flowing out on to the seething dockside. He thought of the Captain, up there on the bridge, unthanked and forgotten, and the stokers and engineers and cooks and seamen who had never been seen at all.

Mr. Page soon got them through the turmoil on the quay and into a taxi for the Biltmore. They went down a squalid dockland way called East Fifty Second Street: it looked and smelt like Woodbank, but with surprising suddenness they turned into Broadway, where the electric signs were alight outside the cinemas although it was only eleven in the morning. They turned into Madison Avenue, with buildings that soared into the sky. Mr. Matthews peered out of the taxi window, but he saw no more of the world above him than a beetle in a trench. The hotel was a bewildering medley of revolving doors and resplendent porters and bustling bell-boys. They were pushed into what appeared to be a small and comfortable sitting-room. Somebody slammed the doors, and before Mr. Matthews realised it was an elevator they were on the twenty-seventh floor and in a pleasant suite of rooms. Mr. Matthews looked fearfully out of the window at what appeared to be a line of matchboxes running down the street and a jostle of tiny mice on the pavements. He drew away with a weakness in his shins, very glad they were not flying out to Hollywood.

"Now," said Mr. Page—"just relax and take it easy. Have a good lunch and the boy'll be around at two to take you for a run around the city. You don't have to worry about a thing."

It was strangely quiet and peaceful in that sitting-room in the sky. Mr. Matthews wrote to Pete, telling him all about the journey and hoping the Club was going well. He wrote to the Bishop, because the Bishop deserved a letter for making so little fuss about his leaving. He also wrote to Mr. Cheesewright, because he knew that the Churchwarden would be proud of a letter from America and show it to the Church Council. The notepaper had a picture of the Hotel on it, and he put a cross against one of the top windows and wrote "our room" against it to show how high they were.

At twelve they rang "Room Service" (as Mr. Page had suggested) and ordered lunch for one o'clock. Then they took the elevator down to the lounge and bought some stamps with a portrait of President Munroe on them and posted their letters. Then they took a walk along Fifth Avenue to see the shops. The shops were interesting, but it was far more interesting to look straight up at the thousands and thousands of windows that grew smaller and smaller and closer together as they stretched up into the sky. The slow-moving clouds gave an impression that the skyscrapers were swaying forward, until one half expected them to topple over and fall across the street.

At two o'clock a cheerful young man with a snub nose and round blue eyes turned up to take them for a drive around the City. He told them to call him Ben and took them along Park Avenue and across the City to Greenwich Village, where he said the Artists lived. He pointed out the Woolworth Building and the Rockefeller Centre, which left the Matthews quite humbled with admiration, not only because the buildings were so vast and tall, but because they carried a matchless grace with them as well. But Ben was not interested in showing them the buildings: he was impatient to get them up to Central Park to see the squirrels. "They're cute," he kept on saying. "You'll be tickled to death."

The squirrels, however, were a dismal disappointment. Mr. Matthews expected to see the biggest squirrels in the world, but they turned out to be dusty, flyblown little things . . . more flyblown even than those in Regents Park at home. But Ben stopped his car for quite a while to enable his guests to observe them. Mr. Matthews evinced sufficient interest to accord with courtesy without enough to lead the young man on to show them any more. But Ben seemed convinced that his guests were the kind of people who would revel in these rustic scenes, and he stopped again to allow them to watch a fat baby feed an even fatter pigeon. The Matthews again expressed delight, but they yearned to be back among those fascinating streets where policemen wore revolvers and swung their truncheons about like the cops in films.

Ben said his grandmother came from Kent in England, and when Ruth told him that her grandmother had also come from Kent the young man was delighted, and said it just showed how small the world was. "I guess it's swell in Kent," he said.

There was time for tea before they went to catch the train, and after so many meals in crowded rooms it was a pleasant change to kick one's shoes off and put one's feet up on a chair. It grew dark much quicker in New York than it did at home, and they watched the lights flicking on in the countless windows of the city. The lower rooms got dark before the higher ones, and the lights began down there, flicking on in twos and threes, upwards and upwards until at last they mingled with the early stars.

At six o'clock Mr. Page rang up to say he was in the lobby ready to take them to the train, and a private door led them from the hotel straight into a vaulted passage that took them into the main hall of the Grand Central Station.

Nobody had mentioned Grand Central Station as one of the sights of New York, but to Mr. Matthews it was the most wonderful thing he saw on that eventful day. It was more like a cathedral than a railway station, magnificently built in polished stone that looked like marble. The floors were so clean and highly polished that one could almost see one's face in them, and the vaulted roof was painted blue, with stars in it that twinkled. At one end a marble staircase, vastly wide, led up to the street; at the other a balcony overlooked the hall with a big American Flag in the middle of it, floodlit and fluttering in an artificial breeze.

Every corner of the great edifice was brightly lit, and yet there were no ugly, glaring lights: every corner of the United States could be reached from here and yet there was nothing to suggest a train within a mile. That was the most remarkable thing of all: no sign or vestige of a train: no trace of smoke or whiff of oil—no waving flags or whistles.

At a London terminus one always saw the trains through railings or steel gates, with the engines staring through like animals in cages, and it took Mr. Matthews some time to notice the cool and spacious passageways that led down to the platforms.

The only drawback to the grandeur of the place was that it made the passengers look so shabby. Tweed overcoats and trilby hats and baggy modern trousers were out of keeping with its cool and spacious elegance. To harmonise with such surroundings all passengers should wear white flowing gowns with wreaths of flowers and jewelled sandals like Athenians, and certain New World habits should be set aside as well, thought Mr. Matthews, for in his short progress across the hall he collected a pellet of chewing gum on both his heels.

Over the passageways that led to the trains there were names that fired the spirit of adventure: there were trains that evening to Washington, and some intriguing places that he had never heard of before, like Poughkeepsie and Utica and Schenectady. He wondered what those quaint-named places looked like—far away out there, under the rising moon. Their train to Chicago appeared to be a very important one, for a red carpet led down to the platform, and beside each carriage stood a Negro porter in a spotless white jacket and big black shiny boots.

"I've got you a drawing-room in the observation car," said Mr. Page, "with a small roomette beside it. A drawing-room's a bit of a squeeze for three, so we took the extra space. You'll have the same accommodation on *The Chief* from Chicago to Los Angeles."

The drawing-room was, in fact, a neat little metal cabin with steel grey walls. Two broad seats faced each other by the window and a narrow couch was along the inner side. There was a wardrobe for coats and a private lavatory through a narrow door in a corner with a bundle of clean hand-towels and a piece of unused soap in a paper packet.

"I'd order your dinner in here to-night," said Mr. Page. "The dining car's away up the train, and I guess you're tired. If you like chicken, try it fried. They do it swell on this train—and the salad's good."

He bade them a pleasant journey and they thanked him for all he had done for them.

"Our people will meet you in Chicago," he said, "and see you across to the Hollywood train. You don't have to worry about a thing."

Chapter Twenty Four

At first the train moved underground, with nothing outside but coloured lights and tunnel walls and signals. The carriages were air-conditioned, and sealed off so effectually from the outside world that an engine went by as if it were running on rubber wheels, and when the tunnel ended there were none of the transition sounds one heard in normal trains: they only knew they were in the open night when they saw the stars, and the full moon rising.

All that evening they ran beside the Hudson river, lovely and mysterious in the light of the moon. Along the far bank a dark cliff rose and fell from time to time, sprinkled with the lights of houses that sometimes gathered in clusters to mark a little town. There were islands with banks of trees and scattered huts, and narrow piers on wooden stilts that jutted out into the river. Ferry boats glowed like fireflies, and a flock of night birds followed them, close to the water near the shore.

They ordered dinner, and a waiter put a table up and brought a complete half of a young chicken for each of them, and a salad in a wooden bowl with a wooden spoon to serve it. They went into the observation car while the porter made their beds. There were windows all round it and chairs along the walls, and a revolving bookcase full of magazines. Rosemary got a Film Fan publication and found an article about Norman Walter. There was a full-page portrait of the handsome young actor, and she sat gazing at it, thinking how wonderful it was going to be in a few days, when she would actually be talking to him—perhaps having lunch with him ... even being kissed by him in the picture. Ruth found an article by a chef who had cooked at the White House. She was interested in the recipes he gave and made a note of some of them to try when she got home. Mr. Matthews read an article about British Policy in India. It was not very complimentary, and rather unfair, he thought, but it was interesting to find out what the Americans thought about England in private.

The porter came in to say the beds were ready, and they found their rooms astonishingly transformed. The beds had been concealed in the compartment walls and were much roomier than they had expected. All kinds of useful gadgets had been revealed, like hooks to hang one's watch on and nets to hold night necessities, and small, phosphorescent blue dots on the light switches to show you where they were in the dark. The sheets looked so inviting that they went to bed without delay. Ruth and Rosemary had the drawing-room and Mr. Matthews the roomette next door.

He got into his pyjamas and lay watching the Hudson River in the moonlight—picturing the homes behind the lights on the far bank, and wondering what the people were doing in them. He thought of the first colonists paddling up the river and camping in the perilous woods where now the pleasant houses lay. To meet America for the first time under the light of a full moon was a rare experience.

He had never passed a night in a train before, and when the gentle motion of it lulled him off to sleep, he slept much deeper than he had thought possible. He woke up thinking he had dozed for half an hour, but it was almost light and the river had gone, and they were running through a boundless farm land.

Soon after breakfast they were in Chicago, and a man from Paragon Pictures met them and got them into a taxi and drove them down a sordid street to the Sante Fé Station, where *The Chief* was waiting to take them to Los Angeles.

The things that Mr. Matthews had read about Chicago had prepared him for blood-curdling events. He half expected the roar of tommy guns in the station lobby, with gangsters mowing down police, but there seemed to be no gangsters about that morning. None of the people looked as if they had ever been chased or shot at, and the only policeman in sight was fat and amiable, and sharing an orange with a little girl. He remarked upon this unexpected tranquillity to the Paragon man, who laughed and said he had lived in Chicago for twenty years and never seen a gangster or heard a gun fired. "It's a big city," he said, "and the rough stuff happens down the other end." Mr. Matthews could not resist a feeling that Chicago had let him down. They saw fine buildings in the distance but the streets they passed through were as dull as Woodbank.

The Chief had a big illuminated profile of an Indian Chief attached to the observation platform. Their rooms were like those in the New York train and there was time to lay in a store of oranges and shelled walnuts in cellophane bags before they left.

"You're all set for Hollywood now," said the Paragon man. "There's no more changing till you get to Los Angeles the evening after to-morrow."

On the outskirts of Chicago they passed some big enclosures full of cattle that would soon depart in little tins to every corner of the world. They ran through vast prairies where the cattle roamed, and at sunset they saw the Mississippi. They were now in the America that Mr. Matthews knew from his reading of Mark Twain. They saw boys like Huck Finn sitting on gates in wide-brimmed hats and dungarees, and a coloured man like Jim the nigger dozing on the veranda of a tumbledown old shack.

During the night the train began to climb. It laboured heavily and their ears began to crack, and when they pulled the curtains in the morning the scene had completely changed. They had taken a wide sweep to the south. The sparse green prairies were behind them and they were in the desert: all tumbled boulders and scrubby bushes, with strange dome-shaped hills in the distance like hunched-up human shoulders—pink and gleaming in the sun.

When they went down the corridor to get their breakfast and crossed the open platforms between the cars they were startled by the gust of hot dry air that greeted them. In New York their drawing-room had been warmer than the outside night, but conditions had slowly reversed themselves, and they were now in cold storage for their journey across the desert.

In February the heat of the desert was no greater than an August afternoon at home. When breakfast was over they sat outside on the observation platform, basking in the sun—thinking of the fog and slush in Woodbank and watching some strange little animals that sat in rows on their hind legs like begging dogs, staring at the train.

The country grew more desolate. There were native Indian villages of ramshackle mud huts and dark thin men with long black hair and bulky women in shapeless cotton frocks nursing dark-brown babies. Mongrel dogs prowled round, and the cattle were nearly as thin as the bleached skeletons of the dead ones that lay in the aching heat among the rocks. Sometimes it seemed as if they were in a land untouched by white men, then suddenly a tarred modern road would swing out of nowhere and run along beside the railway, with signs against it—"EAT AT JOE'S PLACE. CHICKEN DINNER. 2 MILE".

At sundown they came to Albukerque, and the train stopped long enough for passengers to stretch their legs and see the Museum of Indian relics that adjoined the station. Some old and dirty Indian women were selling souvenirs, and Ruth bought a silver brooch of native workmanship to send to Mrs. Burgin, and Mr. Matthews bought an ash-tray shaped like a Mexican hat.

The quick tropic twilight came while they waited for the engine to refuel, and when the sun went down the stars came out and the air grew keen, and they saw the luminous blue sky and knew the magic of the desert night.

When the train moved on the desolation was more awesome in

the darkness. In the dining-car the lamps were lit and the curtains drawn. They had sliced turkey, with a green salad and fresh figs and ice-cream, and it seemed miraculous to have such delicacies in such a stricken wilderness. Mr. Matthews lay in bed in the darkness so that he could better see the desert in the moonlight. Eerie-looking cactuses raised distorted arms like witches, and sometimes, far away, he saw a tiny, lonely light.

The last day opened with a stop to take a second engine on the front and one at the back to push. They began a panting, grinding climb that went on for miles, twisting and turning through ravines so steep that even with three engines they groaned along at walking pace. The more they climbed the more relieved Mr. Matthews felt about the engine at the back. If the train broke in two, with nothing behind their helpless carriages to stop them, they would run all the way back to Chicago unless they took a precipice on the way. They could hear the engines panting, even through the sealed windows of the air-conditioned car. Fierce crags rose sheer on either side, with dark birds hovering over them like vampires: there were deep red furrows down the mountains where the floods roared when the rare storms came, and Mr. Matthews' ears began to crack alarmingly, and his head felt like a pumpkin.

By lunch time they had reached the summit of Cajon Pass, and stopped to take away the extra engines. The hardest stretch was over, and the train ran easily, almost free wheeling down to the Pacific Coast. Mr. Matthews' ears began popping back again, but for days his head felt swollen and buzzed inside.

It was California now, and slowly the colour came back into the cheeks of the land. They saw a genuine cowboy in a wide-brimmed hat with a knotted scarf around his neck—exactly like a cowboy in a film, riding a frisky little horse that was galloping away to nowhere in particular. They saw broad fields of maize: and then a neat plantation with irrigation channels down it, and trees with lush green leaves and yellow fruit. "Oranges!" Ruth suddenly exclaimed:—"look at them—thousands of oranges!—even on the ground!"

The ones on the ground astonished Mr. Matthews most: he had never thought of oranges lying about as windfalls. "What a waste," he murmured—"what a terrible waste!"

The orange groves were soon surrounding them on every side: thousands of neat bushy trees like regiments on parade. Sometimes there were lemons and sometimes grape-fruit. There were notices beside the road, "ORANGE JUICE. AS MUCH AS YOU CAN DRINK. 5 CENTS".

The towns grew bigger and more prosperous, with tree-lined avenues and shady bungalows and trim gardens full of flowers. They passed a college where boys were playing football, grotesque with their padded shoulders and crash-helmets and tight knee-breeches. The porter came in to brush them down and take their luggage. "Los Angeles in ten minutes," he said.

Chapter Twenty Five

Mr. Matthews had imagined Hollywood as a kind of super-Monte Carlo with esplanades along the Pacific Ocean lined with the mansions of the film stars and monster luxury hotels. He found instead that Hollywood was merely a suburb of the mighty city of Los Angeles, and rather an ordinary, shabby little suburb at that.

Its fame as the great Film City of the world now rested on its memories, for most of the big studios had long since outgrown its narrow confines and moved into the wider spaces of the surrounding plain. It was no longer fashionable to live in Hollywood itself, for the stars had moved westward into the cooler districts nearer to the ocean—at Beverly Hills and Westwood and Santa Monica.

But thousands of sightseers came to Hollywood every summer, and its name had stuck to every American film, wherever it was made, as surely as the name of Cheddar sticks to every cheese that traces its ancestry to a forgotten English village.

Mr. Matthews discovered these things later on, when he had the leisure to think and look around him, for during the half-hour following his arrival he was too bewildered and distracted to think of anything at all.

The train had scarcely stopped before an enormous man clambered up the steps and lumbered in to meet them. He was so big that he could hardly squeeze into their small compartment.

"Well!" he cried—"here we are at last!—fine!—swell!—have a good trip?—You did?—well, that's great!"—and he shook them all by the hand and patted them on the shoulders as if this were the supreme moment of his life.

Mr. Matthews had never seen such a remarkable man. He towered above six feet and was immensely broad, although the cut of his jacket made it impossible to tell where nature ended and the shoulder pads began. His face was round and fat like an enormous cherub. He wore a mustard-coloured jacket with a huge check pattern in it like hundreds of lit-up windows in a skyscraper. His tie was like a strip of ornate wallpaper: his sweater bright green: his trousers white with a black pin-stripe in them and his socks were yellow. His shoes were half white canvas and half brown leather and he wore a ring with a stone in it that looked like a blue glass eye.

His name was Len Cogweiler, from the publicity department of Paragon Films, and when the greetings were exhausted he steered the Matthews along the corridor and waved towards a group of men with cameras waiting beside the train.

"Some of my boys," he said.—"Okay!—let's do the shooting!"

The photographers all had different-shaped cameras and some had little sticks with flash-bulbs on them. First of all Mr. Cogweiler posed the Matthews in a group: Ruth and Rosemary were told to laugh and Mr. Matthews had to hold his hat up in the air as if acknowledging applause. Then Rosemary was taken alone on the observation platform, waving a handkerchief and laughing—then Mr. and Mrs. Matthews had to walk along arm-in-arm like Darby and Joan, and Mr. Cogweiler liked this so much that he took them twice. Finally Mr. Cogweiler himself was taken—shaking hands with each of them in turn. The photographers worked away like demons—sometimes squatting on their haunches—sometimes on tiptoe with cameras above their heads, and they took it in turns to blow their flash-bulbs off.

Some passengers and coloured porters gathered round to watch in mild amusement, and Mr. Matthews had never felt such an abject fool in all his life—specially when he had to laugh and hold his hat up in the air and remain transfixed in that idiotic pose while one of the men adjusted a misfired flashlight bulb. By the time it was over be disliked Mr. Cogweiler more than any man he had ever met. At first he tried a feeble protest, but Mr. Cogweiler ignored it. He swept it aside and appeared to have no regard whatever for the Vicar's dignity and feelings: he mesmerised him with his overpowering personality and put him through his antics like a poor browbeaten circus animal.

Worse things soon threatened the unhappy Vicar, for when the camera men had finished Mr. Cogweiler announced that he was going to "take care" of the Matthews for the rest of the day. Ten minutes of Mr. Cogweiler had reduced the Vicar to a pulp—an hour, he felt, would finish him, and he had a yearning impulse to run away down the rail tracks and escape—even if it meant a slow death in the desert.

But a remarkable transformation now came over Mr. Cogweiler. The difference between Cogweiler the publicity man and Cogweiler the host was the difference between a Jekyll and a Hyde. In his work he was ruthless: he would push a victim over a precipice if it made a story for his Press Department, but in private—as the guide, philosopher and friend of newcomers to Hollywood—he was a delightful man with a boyish enthusiasm that was quite disarming.

When the camera men had gone he mopped his brow, relaxed and smiled. He seemed to grow smaller: even his check coat appeared to lose a little of its bite. "I guess you quiet folks from England find it hard to take that stuff," he said. "But it's just one of those things out here. You've got to go through it, but it's over now and it won't happen again. If you come along to my car I'll drive you out to a nice little house we've taken for you in Beverly Hills."

At first it was a network of squalid streets and jangling tram-cars. There were a lot of dark-skinned Mexicans about, and Chinese and negroes, and a good many shops with "Chop Suey" written over them, and Chinese signs beneath.

"We've got all kinds out here in Los Angeles," said Mr. Cogweiler. "It's a big city—the tenth biggest in the world with close on two million people in it. From the centre here you can drive twenty miles in any direction and still be in the city. It's well spread out because it's in the earthquake belt. That's why you don't see many tall buildings. Small wood-framed ones take the shaking best."

"Do you have many earthquakes?" enquired the Vicar.

"Two or three a week," said Mr. Cogweiler. "But you don't have to worry. You don't even feel most of 'em—just a window shaking, or a cup chinking on the dresser, maybe."

They soon got clear of what Mr. Cogweiler called "downtown Los Angeles". They lost the tram-lines and the ugly brown brick stores and apartment houses and drove into a cleaner, fresher district of smaller buildings painted white and cream, generously spaced with little squares of lawn around them. They turned into a street so wide that three cars moved abreast in both directions. "Sunset Boulevarde," said Mr. Cogweiler. "It goes right on through Hollywood and Beverly Hills until it hits the ocean at Santa Monica twenty miles away."

The name well suited the boulevarde at this hour of the evening, for straight ahead the sun was setting: a golden, cloudless sun that left a luminous, treacle-coloured sky behind it. The shops and private houses were mixed together in a rather haphazard way, with empty spaces of long rank grass at most of the corners. There were "drive in" restaurants where people took their cars right up to a café, and girls in smart uniforms brought hot food and sandwiches on little trays that fitted outside the car windows. There were lots of cafés and eating-houses advertising "charcoal-grilled steaks" and "barbeque" and "chicken dinner", and Mr. Cogweiler said that half the population of Los Angeles ate most of their food away from their homes.

The shops were arranged quite differently from those in England. There were no separate butchers or fishmongers or dairies or grocers or fruiterers, because all these things were sold in the big covered "markets". The rest of the things you needed were mainly in the "Corner Drug Stores" that sold books and newspapers and soft drinks and cigettes besides the normal goods one bought at chemists. The only individual shops seemed to be dry cleaners, beauty salons, jewellers and those that sold clothing and cut flowers.

They passed through Hollywood, which looked no different from the other shopping districts except for bigger restaurants and a few tall hotels. Mr. Cogweiler pointed out a piece of waste land where Charlie Chaplin made his early pictures, and a tumbledown old place where Douglas Fairbanks began his climb to fame. He showed them where the old Keystone Comedies were made in the open streets, and a dark, foreign-looking cemetery where they buried Rudolf Valentino. The old film colony was as deep beneath the new business town of Hollywood as the remains of Roman London were beneath the Banks and Insurance Offices of the modern city.

"We got you a little house on Maple Drive in Beverly Hills," said Mr. Cogweiler. "Because we guessed you'd rather have your own place than a suite in a hotel. It's nicer for quiet folks accustomed to their own ways, and you can always dine out when you want to."

He gave them some useful homely hints that came rather unexpectedly from such a hard-boiled film man. "Take it easy at first," he said—"Don't try long walks or climbing the hills until you get used to the climate, because the air's thin and you'll get over-tired. You'll find yourselves getting sleepy, too—so relax when you feel like it, and always put a woolly on at sundown, because it's cold at night—even in the summer. Eat lots of salad and you'll be okay."

It was nearly dark when the car turned down a wide quiet road lined with palm trees. "Beverly Hills," said Mr. Cogweiler—"Where the stars live."

He pointed out the houses of people whose names were known the whole world over. "That's where Wallace Beery lives," he said. "Ronald Colman's up there behind those trees, and Mary Pickford's on that ridge with David Selznick the producer next door. Here's Hedy Lamarr's and that's Herbert Marshall's. . . ."

They turned into a narrower and more secluded road. The houses were smaller than the Matthews had expected, but in charming taste, with lovely gardens and lawns as smooth as bowling greens. Bright flowers showed dimly in the dark, and shady trees.

They stopped outside a little house in the Spanish style, with pink stucco walls and a roof of wavy, bright red tiles. There was an intriguing, rambling look about it, with wrought iron screens across the lower windows and a little Spanish balcony painted in bright colours and a long weird-shaped cactus on the lawn. "This is it," said Mr. Cogweiler. "It's nice inside. I guess you'll like it quite a lot."

A coloured woman answered the door—very clean and happy-looking, with wonderful white teeth when she smiled. "This is Elizabeth," said Mr. Cogweiler. "Elizabeth will take care of you."

After what they were accustomed to in Woodbank the simplicity and freshness of the little house were a revelation. At the Vicarage every room had a different design of wallpaper and a different kind of carpet. Here there was no wallpaper: the walls in every room and corridor were plain rough-cast and painted cream, and the powder-blue carpet went from room to room and across the hall and up the stairs with no apparent joins in it. It looked as if it had been put down in plastic form, and rolled out like dough to penetrate every corner. Even where the walls curved, the carpet curved with it—close up to it, like a calm blue sea against a cliff.

From the entrance hall the living-room lay straight ahead, through a broad archway. A small twilit garden lay beyond, and through another archway the dining-room was set for dinner. The stairs led up from the hall to an open landing from which four bedrooms opened—each with its own tiled bathroom and private balcony.

To Mr. Matthews—who had nerved himself for rooms in some vast grand hotel with wild Hollywood parties overhead and jazz bands below—the quietness and simplicity of it all was beyond belief. He went on to the balcony and looked around him. He saw white houses between the trees and a quiet road that might have belonged to the outskirts of an English country town. The setting sun still lit the hills that lay between them and the ocean, and far to the east the mountains were still capped in winter snow. "It's delightful," he said. "Quite delightful. . . ."

A van arrived with the trunks and baggage, and when everything was safely in Mr. Cogweiler said good night. "I'll be around in the morning to take Miss Matthews along to the Studio," he said. "If there's anything you need, just call me at Crestview 12693."

Elizabeth gave them sweet potatoes with their chicken dinner. The Matthews had not tasted them before: they were yellow and rather like parsnips, but stickier, with more fibre in them, and Ruth thought they would like them after a bit of practice. There was an apple-pie and ice-cream, and excellent coffee.

When dinner was over they went into the living-room where Elizabeth had lit a fire of eucalyptus wood that smelt like pine needles, and gave a bright gushing yellow flame because of the oil in it.

After she had washed up, Elizabeth went home saying she would be in at seven to see to breakfast. They sat round the fire for a while. It was hard to get accustomed to having no doors to the downstairs rooms, but the open archways gave a cheerful spacious feeling to the house. They were tired, and when they went to bed Mr. Matthews instinctively dropped back into the old home life again, going round locking the doors and turning out the lights.

For over a week they had slept with the rumble of engines beneath them and the thud of wheels, and they missed the rhythmic sounds and motions that had lulled them to sleep on the ship and train. "Perhaps we'll get an earthquake instead," said Ruth.

There was no earthquake that evening, but towards midnight a mocking bird began to sing in the trees at the bottom of the garden. It had notes like an English blackbird and some like a nightingale, but louder and more persistent. Mr. Matthews got up and looked out of the window to see if he could spot it. It was hidden away somewhere, but he saw the moon rising behind the trees.

The moon was on the wane now, but he remembered the young crescent of it over the Thames at Woodbank on the night before he came away. He thought of it behind the stern of the *Queen*

Mary—a fuller moon that swung about when the ship changed course: and above the skyscrapers of New York and over the Hudson river and the prairies. He thought of it over the desert, shining on the skeletons of cattle and turning the cactuses into witches. And here it was: the same old moon, looking down upon the roofs of Hollywood. No wonder it looked tarnished and a bit worn out.

A few hours ago it had shone on the boat-house by the Thames at home. It was morning in Woodbank now: the factory sirens were going, and as he drew the curtains to go back to bed he thought of Pete and the boys, going off to work.

Chapter Twenty Six

The sun was up and warm against the blinds at seven in the morning. Mr. Matthews took a cold bath and put on his light summer suit and went downstairs to see the garden.

The house was more attractive than ever in the morning sunshine. At home the sun had a disconcerting way of ferreting out the stains on the wallpaper and the threadbare patches in the carpet, but the fresh cream walls and spotless carpets in this little house had nothing to hide. The wrought iron glistened and the curtains shone, and the graceful Spanish archways framed the rooms and made delightful pictures of them.

He went out on to the red tiled patio that faced the garden. It was strange to come in a few days from the frozen slush of London to beds of summer flowers. A humming-bird was hovering round a shrub—pushing its little needle-sharp beak into the flowers and remaining motionless with its wings invisible in the quickness of their beat.

The garden was small but beautifully kept, with hedges of berberis to seclude it from the neighbouring gardens. The lawn was perfect, without a weed in sight, and the borders were full of bright petunias and marigolds and fleecy blue flowers that he had not seen before. There was a shady corner for a deck-chair in the afternoon, and as he stood there with the warm sunlight on his face he thought how vastly different everything was from what he had expected. He had never hoped for anything approaching a normal life in Hollywood. At the best he had imagined an ornate, unnatural hotel garden full of sickly tropical flowers, but this was almost like their country home in little Stanton.

While Rosemary made her picture Ruth and he could live very happily here. It would be a wonderful holiday. He would go back to Woodbank refreshed and strengthened; ready for anything that Mrs. Bannister Paget had in store for him.

He went round to the front of the house. There were no obscuring walls or railings between the garden and the footpath, and none between the gardens of each house. A broad strip of open lawn ran the whole length of Maple Drive as if the houses were sharing together in a private park.

There was nobody in sight except a boy on a bicycle. He was evidently a paper-boy, for he carried a canvas bag on his handle-bars, and as he drew level with each house he reached down into the bag, produced a paper fastened by an elastic band and threw it dexterously into the porch.

He pulled up when he saw Mr. Matthews and gave him a friendly smile. He was a tall fair-haired boy with a freckled nose and sunburnt arms. He wore a clean white cotton vest and a pair of thick brown corduroy trousers with one leg turned up to clear the bicycle chain, and a funny little cap of stiff white linen, shaped like a pork pie.

"You come to stay?" he asked.

"For a while," said Mr. Matthews—"about four months."

"Then I guess you'll want *The Examiner*."

He produced an order slip from the lining of his pork pie cap and explained to Mr. Matthews how to fill it in. "Here's two more," he added—"to pass on to your friends. I need a lot because I'm saving up for a surf board."

Mr. Matthews was not clear what a surf board was, but he promised to co-operate, and the boy said, "Swell!—my name's George. I'll be seeing you!"

There was another smile—a gleam of bright blue eyes that were almost too innocent to be true, and George was on his way again—whistling gaily and aiming the morning papers at the passing porches with redoubled vigour.

Mr. Matthews watched him go with interest. He had never spoken to an American boy before. He had an idea they were cheeky and precocious—unhealthily sophisticated and thoroughly impossible. But George was so genuinely boyish and instinctively courteous that all his old ideas went overboard.

He strolled down Maple Drive, content and happy. George was a symbol of California: he embodied all the freshness and honesty and genuine friendliness that bubbled out of it like a crystal spring. He was beginning to love the place and everybody in it, and it made him far happier about the future of his daughter. If Rosemary got a long contract with the Studio, they were sure to find nice people for her to live with in a place where everyone he had so far met was friendly and so genuine. He and Ruth might even come back every year and spend their holidays with her. The whole thing was a pleasant, unexpected surprise.

Elizabeth had arrived when he got back from his walk and set the breakfast on the patio. There was grape-fruit and toasted wheat flakes with abundant cream, and shirred eggs baked in small blue dishes. Ruth had asked for tea instead of coffee, but it was not so good as the tea at home. The tea was contained in a small muslin bag that dangled in the pot from a piece of string. It prevented the leaves from getting into the cups, but it gave the tea a flavour of the string and muslin and Ruth said they would explore the shops and see if they could find the ordinary English kind.

At ten o'clock Mr. Cogweiler turned up to take Rosemary to the Studio. "It'll just be tests and make-up and costume work to-day," he said—"and rehearsals all this week. But everything's set to start shooting next Monday, and then you folks can come along and watch."

He sprang a surprise by asking Mr. Matthews whether he would like a car to run around in.

"Distances are long out here," he said. "It's no good trying to walk. You'll need a little car to take you round the shops and down to the Ocean."

Years ago Mr. Matthews had owned a small Ford car, but it had gone when Rosemary had come. "I'd like it very much," he said. "It's very kind of you."

"Okay," said Mr. Cogweiler. "I'll have it round here some time this afternoon. Don't forget: just take it easy and relax, and I'll have your daughter back for dinner."

They were very happy in Maple Drive. Ruth took over the housekeeping, and after breakfast every morning they walked down to the shopping district of Beverly Hills. The big markets were all laid out alike, and provided nearly everything they needed. In every market the fruit and vegetables were displayed in front—attractively laid out and presided over by a lot of earnest little Japanese. Next came the meat, with the wine department opposite: then a delicatessen counter, and beyond that a turnstile where one took a basket and walked round the grocery shelves, helping oneself to tinned salmon and tinned fruit and cereals and cocoa, finishing up with a bottle of milk from a refrigerator with glass doors. You took the laden basket to the exit turnstile, where a man checked everything and took your money and packed the goods in paper bags. It was all so orderly and neat and quick that the Matthews wondered why nobody had ever tried that kind of thing in England. It was good to meet some old friends in the grocery department like Colman's mustard and Lea and Perrin's Worcester Sauce, and a great relief to find a plentiful supply of Lipton's tea without the linen bags around it. Everything was good except the fish, which had no taste to it. Grape-fruit the size of footballs were ten cents each, and oranges and lemons hardly any price at all.

They found a library, and every afternoon they took their books to the shady corner of the garden and sat in deck-chairs and read and dozed till tea-time—"taking it easy" as Mr. Cogweiler had advised. After tea, in the cool of the evening, they got the car out and went exploring. They confined themselves at first to the easy tree-lined avenues of Beverly Hills, but as the Vicar got more confidence they went farther afield and explored the canyons that led into the mountains. When he was sure of his brakes they even went into the foothills.

In a bookshop they found a *Guide to the Movie Homes*—with the houses of all the famous people marked. They searched out the homes of their own screen favourites and drove slowly by, gazing up the lovely drives and peering at the windows in the hope of seeing a star looking out. They saw where Mary Pickford lived, and Harold Lloyd's house in a splendid park, but the stars themselves were elusive, and they saw none in the flesh until one day they spotted Spencer Tracy, driving into the grounds of the Beverly Hills Hotel.

One day they took a picnic lunch and drove down to the Ocean at Santa Monica and sat on the beach and watched the ungainly pelicans flapping to and fro, and bronzed young people riding the big breakers on their surf boards. They were happy, golden days, but Mr. Matthews often had a pang of conscience about Woodbank. Those dismal streets and clammy fogs and smells of tannery and river rot seemed in a dark world of the past. But he wrote a long letter to Pete, sending him the *Queen Mary* ash-tray and telling him all about Hollywood and how they had seen Spencer Tracy, and somebody shutting a window in Hedy Lamarr's house.

In the evenings they were always home in time for Rosemary's return, and all through dinner she would pour out the news of what had happened at the Studio. She was thrilled and delighted with it all. Everybody was wonderful, she said: they treated her like a princess, and Norman Walter, who was to act with her, was awfully nice, and took her to lunch at the studio restaurant one day. But most of all she was thrilled about John Coburn, who was going to direct the picture. He was quite young, she said, and awfully good-looking. He spent hours with her, coaching her in her part, explaining the story and seeing that her make-up and costumes were right.

The picture was postponed for a week, but one day Mr. Cogweiler took the Vicar and his wife to see the first scenes being made.

Paragon Studios were in Westwood Village—a few miles out of Beverly Hills on the way down to the Ocean. From Sunset Boulevarde it looked like a World Fair with its long frontage of dazzling white buildings and mysterious Martian structures standing up behind. Mr. Cogweiler took them into a lofty entrance hall, decorated with large framed pictures of the stars who were under contract with Paragon Films. "They'll have your daughter up there one day," he whispered as they waited for their passes, but Mr. Matthews was too interested in the things around him, even to enjoy the prospect of Rosemary one day being on the wall.

They were taken through a door that only opened when a studio policeman touched a button on his desk, and found themselves in a miniature town, laid out with streets and gardens and restaurants and laboratories and wardrobes and small exclusive bungalows for the special use of stars. Dominating all else were the huge "stages": vast structures like the hangars they used to build for airships.

They were taken on to "Stage 14", and it was hard to accustom ones eyes to the darkness after the glaring sunlight of the streets. They went along a passage between some stacks of scenery, feeling their way gingerly across the thick power cables that lay across their path. They turned a corner, and saw beneath a cluster of dazzling arc lamps an amazingly realistic country cottage, with an old-world garden that contained real bushes and real trees and genuine flowers in bloom—and most startling of all, a big brown cow, grazing placidly on a piece of real authentic grass. Mr. Matthews had to look around him and up at the vast twilit roof before he could assure himself that the whole thing, cow and all, was actually indoors.

They were given seats in a secluded corner, and for a while they watched the crew around the camera, rehearsing a run along the rustic lane towards the cottage. They saw an alert young man in a dark blue jersey and flannel trousers, whom they guessed to be John Coburn the director. Presently he shouted—"Okay!—stand by!" and silence fell. There were some preliminary technical man(ce)uvres, and then they were thrilled to see Rosemary—their own daughter—come out of the cottage door into the blaze of artificial sunlight. She looked around her, smiled and waved her hand in the direction of the road, then ran down the pathway to the garden gate. Mr. Matthews strained forward in his chair, expecting to see Norman Walter, the star, come striding along to greet Rosemary, but to his surprise the director shouted, "Okay!—cut!"—and everybody relaxed and began to talk again.

"What happened?" he whispered to Mr. Cogweiler—"did it go wrong?"

"Wrong?" said Mr. Cogweiler. "No!—That was all of that shot. It's all made in bits like that. They'll do it again in a minute from a different angle, and later on they'll keep the best shot for the picture and throw the rest away."

Despite the novelty and the thrill of seeing Rosemary in her first picture, they began to get rather tired of it in a couple of hours. There were long intervals to change the lights and move the camera, and then they would do the same bit over again. There was nothing for the Vicar and Ruth to do in those long intervals but sit in their hard little chairs and talk in whispers and watch the cow, and they were rather glad when the company broke up for lunch.

In the restaurant Mr. Cogweiler pointed out some famous actors as they came in, and they caught a fleeting glimpse of Gary Cooper, in cowboy costume, sitting in a corner. He looked very handsome, and very tall when he got up to go. "He's a swell guy," said Mr. Cogweiler ... "a great fellow to work with. I wish they were all like him."

After lunch Mr. Cogweiler took them for a complete tour of the studio. They saw the sets of famous pictures they had seen in Woodbank—the ship that was used in "Westward Ho!" and the castle they had built for "Sir Galahad". There were whole streets and city squares: a complete mosque and half a cathedral—all astonishingly real and solid-looking until you peered behind and saw the canvas backs to them. There was an artificial lake with a machine to churn the water up for storms and a life-size ship that sank by the stern or the bow as necessary, and even came in two when a drama of the sea required it to. By the time the tour was over they hardly knew what was real and what wasn't.

A month passed by—full of interest—with new experiences every day. They went to the Studio twice a week to watch them making Rosemary's picture: for the rest they went out shopping and read their books and drove the car, probing deeper into the surrounding country until they were making long excursions to the orange groves and mountains.

One day Ruth got a letter from Mrs. Burgin enclosing a snowdrop that had come out on the border under the chestnut tree, and Mr. Matthews got a letter from Pete. It was strange to see Pete's big, scrawling hand on the envelope and pull out the cheap little sheet of writing paper, thumbed and soiled by Pete's laborious effort—

"Dear Mr. Matthews (it read),

Thanks for your long interesting letter which I was glad to get. I guess you're having a grand time out there. Everything's okay with the Club. I got those two new chaps down and took them out in the pair. One's okay but the other's rotten and gave it up. I'm trying to get some other chaps down. We have the club evenings on Wednesday and Dick brought a bango last week. But we miss you more than we thought. The weather's been bloody. All rain and fog for weeks, but there's some things coming up in that wood where you set a lot of stuff last year. I got the chaps to get their rowing things washed out because they were making the changing room smell bad. . . ."

He read the letter in the patio. It had come in the evening post, and the sun was setting in the same clear golden sky. He saw the blaze of flowers and the blossom on the trees and thought of Woodbank—"all rain and fog". "The things coming up in the wood" must be the primroses that he and Ruth had set in the autumn. They had wanted wild ones, and had taken a bus to some woods in Kent and dug the roots and brought them back in a basket. While they were planting them Ruth had said: "It'll be a great moment when we see the new leaves coming on them. It'll be about February ... the first sign of spring."

He went into the house and turned on the light in its dainty little pink shade and wrote—

"Dear Pete,

It was grand to get your letter and hear the news from home. We're ten hours behind your time in Woodbank. The sun is setting now but it's eight o'clock in the morning with you. When I go to bed at eleven, you'll just be finishing lunch.

When you say you miss me I expect you are just being polite, but it's good of you to say it, and I'm not just being polite when I say how much I miss you, and the other fellows at the club. I'm enjoying the fun of living here for a little while; the country is lovely and the sun shines all the time and the people are generous and friendly—but it isn't quite like home. I miss the river and the nip in the air on a frosty morning. Even though I used to curse it sometimes, I know I can't live without it really, because it's home and always will be. I could never get to know the people here in the way I know you and Tom and Dick and Tony. We've done so much together, and we'll do a great deal more, and while I'm happy here, the happiest day will be when I walk down to the Club again and help you get the boat out and start work on our plans to make that club the best in the world. So keep the flag flying, Pete. I'll soon be home again."

There was time before dinner to walk down to the Post Office and send the letter off. He sent it by Air Mail, partly so that Pete would get it quickly and partly because he thought that Pete would like to show the long blue Air Mail stamp to his friends.

He walked back in the twilight. In the public gardens a fountain played at night above a cluster of coloured lights that changed from blue to green and rose to amber. Away in the distance a white glow in the sky showed where a studio was preparing to shoot some night scenes out of doors. Eastward, in the city, searchlights were swinging in the sky to mark the première of a picture.

In the gardens of Beverly Hills it was quiet and peaceful. In later years he looked back on that evening walk as the last of his really happy ones in Hollywood—the last completely carefree evening of his life.

Chapter Twenty Seven

During the first weeks of the picture Rosemary had returned home each night in such a state of pent-up excitement that her parents had begun to worry about it. It was bad for her nerves, and they knew there would be a reaction. On that account they were more relieved than concerned when she returned one night with nothing to say about the work of that day. The reaction had apparently begun. The sooner it was over the sooner she would settle down to a more normal life.

Next evening she had come home tired and sullen, and when Mr. Matthews had suggested a run in the car on the following Sunday, with a picnic on the beach at Santa Monica, she had snubbed him and gone up to her room. "It was bound to happen," said Ruth. "She'll be much better when it's over. It's kinder just to leave her alone and let things straighten out in the normal way."

But they did not straighten out in quite the way that Ruth had hoped for. When Mr. Matthews came back from posting his letter to Pete, Rosemary had arrived home and gone up to her room. They called out that dinner was ready but there was no reply, and when they went up to her, she was lying on her bed, sobbing her heart out.

"Rosemary, darling!" said Ruth. "What is it?—what's happened?" But Rosemary lay there with her face buried in her pillow, sobbing and sobbing. "Go away!" she cried. "Leave me alone!"

Ruth sat beside her on the bed and took her hand. "Tell us what it is, dear . . . you've been working too hard and you're tired out.

It must be terribly exhausting sometimes. You must let them know and they must give you a rest for a few days."

"I don't need a rest!" sobbed Rosemary. "I'd be all right if they didn't nag!—it's nag—nag—nag all day! . . . I could do it all right if they'd leave me alone!—but they keep on stopping me and making me sick and tired . . . and then I forget . . . and then they start nagging again . . . they nag and nag till I can't think any more! . . ."

Ruth took some hot milk up to her, but she refused it, and lay there crying and moaning like a beaten child. They left her alone and had a silent, unhappy dinner by themselves.

"I can't understand it," said Mr. Matthews. "When we were there the other day she was getting on so well."

"They were doing the easy parts," Ruth answered—"just small bits with scarcely any lines for her to say. They're getting to the harder scenes now . . . and the thing I was always afraid of. . . I suppose, it's happening."

"We ought to tell the director," said Mr. Matthews—"he probably doesn't realise how inexperienced and highly strung she is. It isn't fair to her—or to him—if we don't let him know."

They talked it over for a long time and decided in the end to leave it for a day or two. "It may be just a passing thing," said Ruth—"they've all got to go through it, I suppose, and we don't want them to think at the Studio that we're fussy interfering parents."

Ruth seemed justified next day. Rosemary came home more like her old self—quieter and more cheerful. The director had been very nice to her, she said. He had given her lunch in his own room and talked to her for a long time, explaining the scenes. Then Norman Walter had come in and they had rehearsed a scene together, privately—just with the director—and everything had been all right. Ruth and Roger felt so much happier that they went to the Studio next day to watch them shoot the scene that the director had rehearsed in private.

They were working now on a smaller stage and the setting was the interior of the cottage.

The Matthews no longer watched as proud, admiring parents. They were anxious and critical, and it was soon very clear that things were far from well.

They were playing a long, difficult scene in which Norman Walter had to come in and quarrel with Rosemary about disturbing some papers on his desk, and after a stormy exchange of words, they made it up and kissed, and sat down to tea.

But they hardly ever got as far as tea. Time and again, half through the quarrel scene, Rosemary would falter, confuse her words and stop. The director was very quiet and patient. He did not nag. He would say—"All right, cut. Take it easy a minute and try again."

Mr. Matthews grew more and more unhappy as the morning wore on. It must be costing the Studio a small fortune, he thought, having all those expensive people there and getting nowhere with the picture. But his heart went out to Rosemary—standing there ashamed and humiliated, knowing that it was all her fault. It must have been torment for her, and he was powerless to help. His only comfort was that he and Ruth were hidden away in a dark corner where Rosemary could not see them. Had they been in her full view, he could not have endured it.

He was sorry too for John Coburn, the young director, and grateful to him for his patience and gentleness with Rosemary. He came over once and had a friendly word with them, but he was troubled and disturbed, and during the constant intervals he walked slowly up and down by himself, deep in thought.

It was during one of these intervals that the Vicar first became aware that John Coburn was looking at him. The young man was standing in the shadows outside the glare of arc light when Mr. Matthews turned his head and saw his eyes upon him—so intent that it was quite embarrassing. When he returned the gaze, Coburn continued to stare. It seemed as if he were so wrapped up in his scrutiny that he did not even realise that the Vicar had noticed it.

But when he did, he turned quickly away and called out to the actors "Okay!—let's try again!"

Several more times that morning the Vicar was aware of John Coburn's eyes upon him. He wondered whether the young director resented the parents being there to see his difficulties with their daughter, and when a break for lunch was called he decided to take the hint and not come back in the afternoon. He gave Rosemary what he hoped would look like a cheerful and encouraging smile, and left the stage with Ruth.

He was outside in the brilliant sunlight, walking down the street to where their car was parked, when he heard his name called and saw John Coburn coming after them.

"Were you lunching anywhere?" asked John.

"We were going home for lunch," said Mr. Matthews.

"Come and have a sandwich in my room."

They walked down a street between the stages, and the young man talked volubly in a forced, nervous way that puzzled the Vicar until the truth dawned on him. Before they reached John Coburn's bungalow he felt fairly certain what lay behind this unexpected invitation to lunch: Coburn had made up his mind about Rosemary: he wanted to break it quietly to her parents—in the privacy of his bungalow—that she had failed. . . .

"I owe you an apology," John was saying. "You've been in here to watch the shooting a dozen times and I've never had more than a "good morning" with you since you came. But when you're directing there's always something—all the time."

"It's good of you to let us come," said Mr. Matthews.

Coburn laughed. "As one Oxford man to another," he said, "I'm delighted!"

"You're an Oxford man?"

"Balliol."

"I didn't realise that. Are . . . are you English, then?"

"No," said John. "I'm an American—from down south . . . Houston, Texas. I was a Rhodes scholar . . . read History . . . had a swell time and went all British ... played English rugger and even had a go at cricket!"

They came to a neat bungalow with shrubs and trees around it, and "JOHN COBURN" painted on the door. John stopped in the outer office and told his secretary to order sandwiches and coffee, then took his guests into a pleasant room, tastefully furnished with well-filled bookshelves and comfortable arm-chairs. It was cool in there, shaded from the sun by closed venetian blinds.

They talked for a while about Oxford and London, and the Highlands that John knew well from a walk during one of the vacations, but all the time the Vicar knew that the young director was only trying to put off the unhappy subject of Rosemary until he could approach it in a gentle, painless way.

When the sandwiches arrived there was a lull in the conversation, and Mr. Matthews decided to help the tactful young man by taking the bull by the horns himself.

"I'm afraid you're having difficulty with Rosemary," he said.

John looked startled, as if he had not expected this.

"Yes," he said. "To tell you the truth, I am."

"She's very young and inexperienced," replied the Vicar. "But I'm sorry ... very sorry—I'm afraid it must have made things very difficult. ..."

John stood up and walked to the window and fumbled with the blind. He let a little sunlight in and shut it out again.

"It isn't fair to bring a nice kid like that straight out and throw her bang into a picture," he said. "Specially an English kid—because English kids are shyer than the ones out here. But that's the way of it: that's what they're always doing nowadays." He turned, and looked at Mr. Matthews in the same intent, appraising way as he had looked at him that morning on the stage.

"Ever done any acting yourself, Mr. Matthews" he enquired.

The Vicar laughed. "I was a butler once in a play my wife produced in Little Stanton, down in Dorset. But I'm afraid I wasn't a resounding success!"

There was a silence, and John busied himself pouring the coffee and handing round the sandwiches.

"There's a small part in this picture," he said—"of the girl's father. We haven't got to it yet and we haven't cast it. I'm wondering whether you would care to have a shot at playing it yourself?"

Mr. Matthews looked up so blankly that John laughed.

"I guess you've heard we do crazy things in Hollywood," he said—"now you know!"

He drank some coffee and began to talk in his quick, nervous way: "But it isn't quite so crazy as you think," he said—"there's two reasons—two very good reasons. One is that you happen to be dead right for the part. I mean that honestly . . . your personality . . . voice . . . appearance . . . they fit the part exactly. I was watching you on the stage this morning, and I'm certain of it. But the other reason is the one that matters most. I'm worried about Rosemary. She's lost her confidence . . . she's scared stiff of Norman Walter and those experienced, old-time actors she's playing with. There's a real danger of her breaking down. I've seen it happen. I know the signs, and between ourselves I had almost decided to drop her out and re-shoot her scenes with another girl when I saw you sitting there in that corner and got this sudden idea. The girl and the father have two good scenes together: she wouldn't be scared of you: she would play those scenes easily and naturally, and get her confidence back. We'd work like hell on those scenes—quietly, in my house or yours—until you played them together as if they were real life. Then there are two good scenes between the father, the girl and Norman Walter. We'd do those next . . . you see what I'm driving at? . . . we'd bring her quietly and easily back to play with Norman Walter without her being scared of him. It may sound crazy—but I've got a hunch it might come off. In any case, it's the *only* way—because I tell you honestly, she'd never finish that picture as things are going now. That would mean she'd be out of the "Children's Crusade" as well. So there's nothing to lose and everything to gain."

"I'd do anything, naturally, to help her," said the Vicar.—"anything in my power . . . but . . . but, you see, I've never acted in my life. . . . I'd be absolutely, utterly hopeless."

"You wouldn't have to act," returned the director. "You'd just have to be yourself, that's all—because that's the part." He poured the Vicar another cup of coffee. "As one Oxford man to another," he said—"come in and make a go of it!"

"I hardly know what my bishop would say," murmured Mr. Matthews, "if he saw me acting on the screen."

"I saw the Archbishop of Canterbury on the screen the other day," said John. "It was a news-reel, but it was the screen just the same. If an Archbishop can do it—why not a Vicar?"

There were plenty of answers to that, thought Mr. Matthews. The Archbishop wasn't acting, anyway. He tried to imagine what Mrs. Bannister Paget and the Church Council in Woodbank would have to say if they got wind of it. . . .

"I tell you what I'll do," said John. "I'll give you a promise. If your scenes turn out bad—(although I don't believe they will)—I guarantee to shoot them again with another actor and put yours in the ash can. Even if that happens, you'd still have done the job and given Rosemary the chance of acting with somebody she isn't scared of."

He looked at his watch and swallowed up his coffee. "I must get back on the set," he said. "Here's a copy of the script . . . and one for Mrs. Matthews. You won't be disturbed in here. Just sit down quietly and read it through. The part I want you to play is Dr. Hensen. When you've read it and thought about it, give me a ring on Stage 9 and let me know."

They knew the story well enough through reading Rosemary's script, but they read it again with careful attention to the lines of Dr. Hensen. It was about a girl with two men after her—one old and rich, the other young and poor. The girl's mother wanted her to marry the old, rich one, but the father put youth above wealth and plumped for the poor one, who romped home an easy winner in the end. It was not very original, but it was told in a pleasant, unpretentious way, and John was right when he had said that Dr. Hensen had some good scenes with his daughter. Mr. Matthews read these scenes aloud, with Ruth reading the girl's part to him. Dr. Hensen was a Professor of Literature at a small provincial University: the dialogue was natural and easy to speak: Mr. Matthews could quite imagine himself in the part and he felt happy and at home with it.

"It's perfect," said Ruth. "You absolutely *are* the part: I can hear you saying those words yourself if you were in the same position. If you do it exactly as you've read it, you can't go wrong."

"It's easy enough in here alone with you," he said—"but what about when the spotlights go on, and the camera starts turning and all those technical men stare at me, and the director says, 'Okay!—shoot!'—I'll die of fright!"

"Not if you take it in the right spirit," said Ruth—"after all, your life doesn't depend on it. If I were you I'd do it like a shot, Roger. It'll be quite an experience, and anyway, it's for Rosemary's sake . . . that's what really matters."

He took up the telephone and asked for Stage 9, and when John answered, he told him he would do it. "On condition you burn it all up if I make a fool of myself," he added.

"Swell!" said John. "I do appreciate it—and I promise you I'll re-shoot your scenes with another actor if they turn out a flop. Would you walk across and see Andy Cummings, the casting director?—He's in the Executive buildings—second floor. I've spoken to him and he knows all about it."

Andy Cummings was a heavy, bull-necked man with beetling brows and a big desk with three telephones and a bottle of Alka-Seltzer tablets on it.

"Coburn's told me the set-up," he said. "You're to play Dr. Hensen and we'll draw you a four-week contract."

"Do I need a contract?" asked the Vicar—"I'm really only doing it in a friendly way. Mr. Coburn thinks it might help my daughter if. . ."

"Yeah," broke in Mr. Cummings—"I know the set-up—but I got to have things straight. If you play a part, we draw a contract, and this one calls for a four-week deal with $500 a week marked up against it."

Something shot up out of the Vicar's stomach and knocked his heart into his throat. It had never dawned on him that he would be paid. He stared incredulously at the big man behind the telephones, who appeared to put the wrong interpretation on the Vicar's dumbfounded silence, for he stuck his chin out and looked truculent.

"That's $2000 for four weeks' work," he snapped—"and that ain't no chicken feed for a beginner. Still, if it ain't okay I guess I can fill that part in two minutes with plenty of . . ."

"No!" cried the Vicar in a strangled voice. "It's . . . it's okay! . . . absolutely okay!"

Ruth was waiting in the outer room. He looked so pale and strange when he came out of Mr. Cummings' office that she jumped up in alarm.

"What is it, Roger? What's happened? . . . are you all right?"

He took her arm and led her out into the passage.

"They've . . . they've offered me $2000 to play the part!" he whispered—"$2000!—that's—that's £500!—D'you realise what that means, Ruth? . . . the land!"

Chapter Twenty Eight

On the way back in the car they passed a Western Union Office, and Ruth suggested sending a cable to Mr. Jupp, the estate agent in Woodbank, telling him to go ahead and buy the land at once. "It'll take some time to settle," she said—"and you can send the money over each week as you get it."

Mr. Matthews thought it was rather premature, but he had not forgotten Mrs. Bannister Paget and her threats to turn him out. Now that the precious property was almost his it would be appalling if the evil old woman suddenly took it into her head to buy the land herself and beat him to it by a matter of hours. He stopped the car and went into the cable office, but before he had finished the message he laid the pencil down.

"I'd love to send it," he said—"but aren't we tempting providence too much? ... counting our chickens before they're hatched?—Supposing I'm ill and can't act? ... or supposing I'm such a hopeless flop that they turn me out? ... I couldn't honestly take the money then."

"You aren't going to be ill and you aren't going to be a flop," said Ruth. "Come on!—get it off and start things moving!"

He took another form and made a fair copy:—

MONEY NOW AVAILABLE TO BUY LAND BY RIVER. PLEASE SEE OWNER AND SETTLE AT £500 AS ARRANGED.

MATTHEWS

"Will he know what 'as arranged' means?" asked Ruth.

247

"He knows £500 was arranged," said Mr. Matthews. "He knows the old lady promised to sell at that price if I ever got the money."

They had tea in the garden and talked of all the splendid things they would do with the land when at last it was really theirs. "We'll plant some almond trees and flowering cherries and lilacs," said Ruth. "We'll have a blaze of colour down there in the spring next year." But even while they talked the Vicar kept his fingers crossed. It was all so unexpected and astonishing that he hardly dared believe that it was true. Things like this just did not happen in real life, and he steeled himself to face the news that they had thought it over and decided on another actor for the part. When the phone bell rang he went to answer it with a chill foreboding. He expected to hear the voice of Andy Cummings telling him that the whole thing was off, but to his relief a woman's voice asked whether he was the Phoenix Cake Shop.

Rosemary came home puzzled and resentful. John Coburn had told her that her own father was to play her "screen" father in the picture. He had concealed the true reason, and merely said that her father was playing the part because he was exactly like the character required. But Rosemary had come to Hollywood to act with famous stars. There was not much glamour in acting with her own father, and she let him know it. But she cheered up when John Coburn telephoned to say he would drop in after dinner for a chat. The young director had never been to the house before, and with the help of Elizabeth, Ruth mobilised some cakes and coffee and sandwiches and sherry.

When John arrived it was like the old days at Little Stanton, when they used to rehearse their annual play in the Vicarage drawing-room. He entered into the fun of it and set the furniture as it would be in the picture and rehearsed the scenes between the father and the daughter several times. Then he played Norman Walter's part himself and made Ruth read the lines of the maid, and when they finished at eleven o'clock he looked very happy and arranged to come again.

For a week the shooting programme of the picture was re-arranged to meet the new conditions. Each day John Coburn "shot around" Mr. Matthews and Rosemary, going ahead with exterior work and scenes in which they did not appear, and every evening he came to the house in Maple Drive and worked with the Vicar and his daughter on their scenes together.

In the easy atmosphere of home—away from the arc lamps and cameras and the strange faces of the camera crew, Rosemary improved beyond all recognition. She lost her nervousness and acted naturally, and as a consequence her dialogue flowed smoothly and her dread of forgetting her lines was over. As for Mr. Matthews, he did what John Coburn told him and simply "played himself". He did not attempt to act: partly because he knew that he couldn't act, even if he tried, but mainly because there was no need to, for the part of Doctor Hensen might easily have been written specially for him. In fact, as the days went by, he studied the part so thoroughly and grew into it so deeply that Ruth declared that she did not know whether she was married to Roger Matthews or Doctor Gustav Hensen. Doctor Hensen, in the picture, was supposed to be slightly lame, and more than once Ruth caught her husband limping round the garden.

He spent a day at the studio making tests, and another with the make-up people working on him. They whitened his hair a bit and gave him a small, trim moustache; otherwise they left him alone. On John's suggestion he even wore his own grey flannel suit because it suited the part and made him feel at ease.

One evening at the end of this week of home rehearsals Norman Walter himself dropped in at Maple Drive—ostensibly to see how things were getting on, but actually to join in the rehearsal as gently and as informally as possible to avoid a return of Rosemary's "star-fright". It was an anxious moment for the Vicar when he found himself acting with a famous star whom he had admired so often in pictures he had seen at home. He felt like a village cricketer bowling to an All England batsman. For a while he was stiff and artificial and muddled up his lines, but after knocking off for cakes and sherry, everything went splendidly and he acted as if he really was the father of the girl whom he wished the young man to marry.

"Swell!" said John. "We've had a grand week. Now we're going to knock off till Monday, then get back to the Studio and shoot the stuff. Just take it easy for a couple of days and forget all about it."

Mr. Matthews walked out with John Coburn to his car. He wanted a word with him alone.

"I've enjoyed this week enormously," he said—"but if you *do* feel you'd like me to stand down now for a more experienced actor . . ."

John looked round, surprised. "You don't want to do it?" he asked.

"Good gracious, yes!" said Mr. Matthews—"I'd *love* to do it . . . more than I can say. But Rosemary seems to have got over her nerves now, and I didn't want you to feel *obliged* to keep me—if you know what I mean."

"Look," said John. "You're doing fine—so don't let's have any more talk about dropping out. If you weren't good enough I'd say so. Now take an easy week-end and don't worry about a thing."

On Sunday they took a picnic lunch to Griffiths Park and spread the cloth out under the trees. Ruth had made a veal and ham pie as near to an English one as the shape of the dish allowed, and a trifle that she was renowned for. It was like a picnic in the Dorset woods at home, and after it was over they drove up to the Planetarium on the hill and went to an afternoon lecture about the planet Mars.

The sun was setting when they came out of the dark hall and sat on the terrace with the wondrous view of the great city on the plain beneath. They watched the lights come on along the boulevardes until the whole city was criss-crossed with golden chains that stretched for miles into the distant hills, and as the quick twilight fell the dark squares between the chains lit up until the whole plain glittered with a million lights—the breath-taking, unforgettable "star-dust of Hollywood".

All day they tried to carry out John Coburn's orders to "forget all about it". They talked about everything on earth except the picture, but in the small hours next morning Mr. Matthews woke up to the grim realisation that the day of trial had come at last. In a few short hours he would be before the cameras with the arc lights on him and a crowd of remorseless strangers watching and appraising him—waiting to see John Coburn's freak protégé make an arrant fool of himself. He lay awake for hours—listening to the mournful hooting of the night trains in the desert, praying that he would not disgrace himself when he walked on to the big stage and faced the cameras.

Long afterwards—in the days when he had time to reflect at leisure—he realised how well John Coburn had helped him in those hours of crisis. He had come over to the make-up room and sat with the nerve-wracked Vicar as the hairdresser had worked on him. He had made none of those heavy-handed efforts to "talk of other things"—well-meant but so torturing at such times. He talked quite casually about the scenes they were going to shoot that morning. "If you dry up once or twice," he said, 'you don't have to worry. I could give you the names of half a dozen top stars who dry up at least a dozen times a day."

He slipped his hand through Mr. Matthews' arm as they walked in the hot sunlight to the stage.
"You don't have to worry about a thing," he said.—"I tell you that honestly—although you won't believe it when you hear me say 'shoot'—because then you'll have a Godawful feeling that you've forgotten every word. You'll feel you can't even stand up because your legs have gone, too—and your head'll feel like a box of cotton wool at the bottom of the ocean. Everybody's like that at first—then you'll hear me say, 'Okay—action!' and you'll feel as if a switch goes on inside you and everything lights up again, and it all comes back as smooth as silk"
Fortified by the young director's parting words, the Vicar felt almost normal when he walked on to the set and took his place

in a chair before a desk on which were laid some papers he was supposed to be correcting. Had they started there and then, all would have been well—but there followed an agonising last-minute delay while the camera man fiddled about with a spotlight. It took about a minute, but it seemed an hour, and when at last John Coburn said: "Okay—stand by!" and the man with the clapper-board stepped forward and said: "Scene 5—Take 1" the Vicar felt a sickly perspiration on his brow and a numbing, paralysing panic, with all his carefully studied lines fading horribly away into a black void of frozen silence. Then John Coburn said: "Okay: take it easy now—action!" and Rosemary came down the cottage stairs, looking lovely in a pair of blue-and-white pyjamas. She called out—"What are you doing, daddy?—why don't you come to bed?" and Mr. Matthews heard a voice—remote and disembodied—yet vaguely like his own, that said: "I've got a few more of these papers to correct, Joan—and I'm half expecting a late visitor to-night."

Gradually the vast stage faded: the director and the camera crew and the script girl and the dresser dissolved into the shadows and Mr. Matthews was no longer a panic-stricken Vicar, struggling to help his daughter to become a star. He was Doctor Gustav Hensen, Professor of English at Burnside University in Carolina, gently persuading his daughter into a penniless but happy marriage. . . .

When the director said: "Okay!—that's swell!—cut!"—the Vicar felt as if he were awakened from a pleasant dream. He resented the awakening: he wanted to go on and on . . . he wanted to go with Doctor Gustav Hensen and his daughter—away into a realm of make-believe uncharted by the script.

Week by week and scene by scene the picture grew: forming itself into a cohesive, coherent narrative. The Vicar "played himself", but there was more than his superficial character in it: he put into it his very heart and soul in humble gratitude for its magnificent reward. When his first salary cheque was given him, he took it to the Bank of America and changed it into a sterling note of credit and sent it by Air Mail to his bank at home. In the same post he wrote to Mr. Jupp, the Estate Agent:

"Dear Mr. Jupr,

£125 is now available in Barclay's Bank, Woodbank, for immediate payment as deposit on the land. I trust by now you have seen Miss Ponsonby and advised her that I am prepared to purchase. The balance of the money will be air mailed to England in three weeks...."

It was a moonlight night, and he took a walk with Ruth that evening around the tree-lined roads of Beverly Hills. It reminded them of their walks in the Dorset lanes of long ago, when they had planned the work they would do one day in the London slums, and they talked about the first instalment of the money that would soon be safely in the bank at home. It would pay for a quarter of the land, and they decided to look upon the corner with the trees and primroses as the piece that his first salary cheque had gained for them. "Next week's money will buy the river front," he said—"the third will buy the long strip where we'll put the cherry trees, and the last will buy the boat-house."

"Do you remember I once said that £500 wasn't going to drop from heaven?" said Ruth. "How little we ever thought that one day it would drop from Hollywood!"

Chapter Twenty Nine

The picture was finished by the middle of April, three weeks before Mr. Matthews had promised to be back in Woodbank. He had received his $2000. The bank in England had acknowledged it, and his mind was at rest on that. It was at rest too about Rosemary, for they had made friends with a retired English Colonel and his American wife, who lived next door to them in Maple Drive. Their own children were married and living in New York, and they said they would be glad if Rosemary would make her home with them when her parents returned to England. They were nice people, and the Matthews were very happy about it.

On the advice of John Coburn Mr. Matthews had engaged an agent named Mike Goody to look after his daughter's contract with the Film Company. Mike Goody was well known in Hollywood: Rosemary's future engagements were safe in his hands, and all the Vicar now desired was to pack up and go home. They had had a wonderful holiday and a memorable experience, but he wanted to get back now to complete the purchase of his land and begin his plans for training the boys for the summer races.

But a matter concerning Rosemary's contract came up to delay them. The Film Company was not obliged to engage her for the "Children's Crusade" until her first picture had been previewed, and this had been arranged for the first week in May. Mike Goody urged the Vicar to stay until the thing was settled. "You'll have to countersign the option letter," he said. "The preview is on the 3rd. They'll fix up everything next day and you can leave for New York on the 5th. The *Queen Elizabeth* sails on the 10th, so you'll still be home by the time you promised."

It was cutting things fine, but after his exertions in the picture Mr. Matthews was glad of a quiet fortnight to relax and rest before he started home.

California was now at its loveliest. The days were warm but the nights were cool, and the summer sun had not yet dried the wild grass on the Canyon sides. The trees that fringed the boulevardes were bursting into huge blossoms of white and crimson and purple flowers and the banks behind were massed with pink geraniums. They planned a fortnight of farewell visits to the places they had discovered and enjoyed the most. They had a day among the orange groves in the San Fernando Valley, and one at Palm Springs to see the desert flowers. They drove along the coastal highway to Santa Barbara and went to a Rodeo and saw the cowboys being tossed off bucking horses. They went to see the rose gardens in Los Angeles and a Spanish Fiesta and a moonlight concert in the Hollywood Bowl.

As the day of their departure drew steadily nearer, the charm and romance of the country tugged harder at their heart strings. "We're going to miss California," said Ruth—and Mr. Matthews knew it. They would miss the freshness and comfort of the house in Maple Drive, and the palm trees and the mountains and the light-hearted, friendly people. They would miss the car that had given them so many happy hours, and the rose gardens and the clear blue skies and the juicy grape-fruit. But it was spring in England too, and the flowers they had set on the land round the boat-house would be in bloom by now.

The preview had been arranged at Pasadena—"the millionaires' suburb" at the foot of the mountains a few miles from Los Angeles. John Coburn called for them at six o'clock and took them for an early dinner at The Brown Derby in Hollywood and drove them out to Pasadena in his car.

"It's what we call a 'sneak preview'," he said. "We just slip the picture on to the screen without any warning. You get the reaction of an ordinary, average audience that way, and cut the bits you feel they didn't like. If we didn't keep it secret all the people in the trade would turn up for one reason or another. The place would be full of professionals and we wouldn't gain a thing."

Mr. Matthews would have stayed away from the preview if he could have found a reasonable excuse. He had seen most of the picture in bits and pieces in the projection room: he had gone through the eerie sensation of seeing himself on the screen, and the novelty was over. He was keen to see Rosemary because she had improved so much, but as for himself, he had the worst forebodings. John Coburn, he thought, had gone a bit too far in making him act naturally, and he had "played himself" to the point of being dull and humdrum. American audiences never minced matters when an actor bored them, and he dreaded the humiliation of hearing the boys whistling at him on the screen.

As they came near Pasadena he felt as if he were going to a dentist to have a tooth out: he wished they could forget the preview and drive right on into the desert, with the night birds and the croaking frogs and the starlit sky. It was pleasant and restful, driving along those broad smooth roads at night, and his heart fell when the lights of a big town glowed ahead, and John said—"Pasadena".

The preview was secret to Hollywood at large, but there was no secret about it for the big men of Paragon Pictures. Mr. Matthews saw Danny Bernstein the studio manager going in—and Andy Cummings the casting chief and Harry Loeb the First Vice-President, and he caught a fleeting glimpse of Tom Garner the Head of the Studio, the biggest man of all.

The two back rows of the stalls had been reserved for the people of Paragon Pictures. They entered unobtrusively and sat through the last five minutes of another film. Mr. Matthews had tried to persuade himself that there was nothing to worry about: he had done his best and earned his money . . . in any case his part was not big enough to hurt the picture. But as he waited he felt an intolerable suspense. His heart was beating so hard and loud against his ribs that he half expected the man in front of him to swing round and say: "Stop that damn thumping!"

At last the other picture ended. There was a short wait in the darkness, then the familiar Eagle of Paragon Pictures flashed on to the screen.

The audience knew at once that a "sneak preview" was ahead. Some people groaned, because they had come to see the picture that was advertised, but most of them sat up expectantly, and a round of applause greeted the name of Norman Walter. Opposite the name of Doctor Gustav Hensen appeared "Roger Desmond", because Mr. Matthews was afraid his Bishop might object to his displaying his real name on the screen. The Studio had left him to choose anything he liked, and Ruth had generously offered him her maiden name.

The titles ended, and the picture ran its course. There were a few scenes—exteriors and long shots—that Mr. Matthews had not seen before. There were even a few in which actors appeared whom he had never met—their work having been done on days when Mr. Matthews had not been needed at the Studio. With the incidental music and polished cutting the whole thing came out much better than he had expected. John was a good director and he had given charm and atmosphere to the simple story. Even Mr. Matthews' own scenes came out more favourably than he had hoped for. When he first appeared, walking into his house with a bundle of books under his arm, he was quite relieved when there was no derisive laughter. The audience accepted him quite normally: they even laughed at several of his lines that were intended to be funny, and he was quite startled when some scattered but spontaneous applause came after the fade-out from his best and longest scene. They did not seem to take much notice of Rosemary, but that was because she was playing with Norman Walter, an established star.

The picture ended. There was enough applause to prove that it was not an abject failure, and the Paragon people got up to go. What surprised the Vicar was a sudden noisy rush of the younger members of the audience to the entrance lobby, and when he got there himself, he was astonished to find it packed with a surging, excited crowd.

The reason for the rush was soon apparent. They were after Norman Walter's autograph. The handsome young star had been spotted in the back row of the stalls and he was now besieged by a frantic crowd of boys and girls, waving autograph books and pencils. Rosemary had been sitting separately from her parents with Mike Goody the agent, and the Vicar retired with Ruth to a quiet corner of the lobby to wait for her.

It was then that the most surprising part of the evening began for Mr. Matthews. It happened so suddenly and violently that it stunned him with astonishment. He heard a girl shout—"Look, there's the father!—the professor!—Dr. Hensen!"—and before he could collect himself, he was mobbed and overwhelmed by a crowd of struggling, laughing girls. He was mistily conscious of dozens of autograph books fluttering in his face—of writing "Roger Desmond—Roger Desmond" time and again in a shaky hand. He would have written "Roger Matthews" if "Desmond—Roger Desmond!" had not been dinning in his ears like an outlandish symphony. They jostled him: they pawed at his coat sleeves and patted his back: a pretty girl was pouring out a flood of questions that were taken up by those around her—"We haven't seen you before, Mr. Desmond—Are you a New York stage actor?—Is it your first movie?—You were awfully good!" "Best thing in the picture!" shouted a boy with a shock of yellow hair.

"Thank you—thank you!" blurted out the bewildered Vicar—"thank you very much." He wondered what they would think if they could see him going round the squalid streets of Woodbank, knocking at doors and having them slammed back in his face: if they could see him preaching to a frowsy little congregation that ignored him. . . .

"Hey!—make way there!" came a familiar, welcome voice, and Mr. Matthews saw John Coburn cleaving a passage through the struggling throng. John was wise to the antics of young film-fans: he elbowed them gently but firmly away, took Mr. Matthews by the arm and made a passage for him and Ruth to the street. But the fans pursued them to John Coburn's waiting car: an athletic youngster jumped on to the running-board as the car moved off and thrust a book and pencil through the window.

"Where's Rosemary?" gasped the Vicar—"we haven't got Rosemary!"

"She's okay," said John. "She's coming along with Mike Goody in his car."

Chapter Thirty

Next morning, after breakfast, the Matthews sat waiting for the telephone to ring at their house in Maple Drive.

Mike Goody the agent had gone to the Studio to arrange about Rosemary's contract. He had promised to ring up directly things were settled, and Mr. Matthews was then to drive over to the Studio with Rosemary to countersign the letters formally taking up the option. When that was done, everything was all right for Mr. and Mrs. Matthews to leave for England on the following day.

But there seemed to be a hitch somewhere. Mike Goody had assured them that everything would be settled directly the big men got to the Studio that morning. "I guess I'll have word for you to come around about ten-thirty." he said.

But nothing happened at ten-thirty. At eleven Mike called up to say the big men were still in conference and hadn't seen him yet.

At half-past eleven Mr. Matthews got restless. They were due to leave next day by the morning train and he hated a last-minute rush. He wanted a clear afternoon and evening to finish packing and see Rosemary safely installed at their neighbour's house, and he had promised Ruth a final, farewell run in the car before they left.

It was twelve o'clock before the phone bell rang again, and it was not Mike Goody even then. It was Danny Bernstein, the Studio Manager. Rosemary answered the call, but Danny asked for Mr. Matthews.

"We'd like you to come right over," he said. "Come straight to Mr. Garner's office."

"Shall I bring my daughter?" asked the Vicar.

"No," said Danny. "Just you—by yourself."

He drove out to the Studio, puzzled and disturbed. Why had they asked him to go alone when Rosemary was the person most concerned? It would be appalling if they had decided to turn her down. He could not believe they would do a thing like that. She had not, he knew, been a sensational success at the preview, but the big men of the Studio must have known it was her first attempt: they must have realised she was overshadowed by Norman Walter, an established star. They could not possibly go back on her like that. They were rich: they had millions to play with and Rosemary's salary was a mere drop in the ocean. But he was responsible, after all, for signing her contracts until she was of age. A mere signing matter would not require Rosemary to be there. He tried to reassure himself with that, but he still felt uneasy when he drew up in the car park at the Studio.

Mike Goody was waiting in the hall outside the Executive Offices, and he looked puzzled, too. They were still in conference, he said. They had been in conference for over an hour, and that was a long time for the top men to talk together. But he brightened up when the Vicar said he had been called straight to the offices of Mr. Garner, the Head of the Studio. "Gee!" said Mike—"that's swell!—that means it's okay! Tom Garner doesn't concern himself with routine stuff. If it was to say they didn't want her, then Danny Bernstein's office would have done that. Don't let 'em talk you into any changes in her contract, though. Leave all that to me!"

Tom Garner's office was at the far end of the north wing on the second floor: a holy of holies to which only a chosen few gained entrance. First came a spacious waiting-room, luxuriously furnished with deep leather arm-chairs and settees, and a fine carved table of Spanish workmanship displaying a wide assortment of magazines. Then came a secretary's office with ultra-modern furnishings and three smart, attractive secretaries, selected for their efficiency and looks.

There was no waiting for Mr. Matthews that morning. One of the girls smiled and pressed a button that automatically released the lock on Mr. Garner's private door. "They're waiting for you now, Mr. Matthews," she said. "Will you go right in?"

Tom Garner's private room did not accord with the legends of vulgarity and golden door-knobs that surround the big men in Hollywood. It was a simple, almost austere room, but very charming in its colour scheme of old ivory and pale green. The arm-chairs and settees were upholstered in a green unpolished leather, with window curtains of the same attractive shade. Walls and ceiling, even the telephones, were in old ivory: and the carpet was so thick and soft that one might have been walking on the Dorset Downs. The only splash of colour came from a bowl of roses on a table by the window, and the only picture was a framed photograph on Mr. Garner's desk—of a handsome woman with two sturdy, fair-headed boys.

There were four men in the room: what Mike Goody the agent would have called "a million-dollars-worth of executives". There was Danny Bernstein, the Studio Manager: Andy Cummings, the bull-necked Casting Director: John Coburn and Tom Garner himself.

Mr. Matthews had only met Tom Garner once: for a fleeting moment in the projection theatre when they were running some early scenes of the picture. He was a big broad man with a clear bronzed face and the blue eyes and fair hair of a Scandinavian. He rose and greeted Mr. Matthews very courteously, and indicated the arm-chair by his desk. The others nodded amiably—said: "How do, Mr. Matthews," but took little part in the proceedings. Big men though they were, they spoke when they were spoken to in Tom Garner's room.

Mr. Garner showed no anxiety to get down to whatever business he had in mind. He asked the Vicar whether he had been comfortable in the house on Maple Drive: whether he liked California, and what he thought of Hollywood. He noticed Mr. Matthews looking at the roses, and seemed quite pleased about it. "My hobby," he said. "I grow them all myself. It isn't easy, growing roses in California: the soil's too dry and sandy and the sun's too strong. You can get 'em as big as cabbages if you want 'em—with about the same smell, but for scent and form you need good loam with a bit of clay. I had a truckful of both sent down from Oregon: had a three-foot-deep garden made and put the clay at the bottom—"

The Vicar was interested in Mr. Garner's rose garden, but he wondered what it was really all about. It seemed an awful waste of money to have those expensive Executives sitting round, just listening. But the friendly reception had set his mind at rest about Rosemary. If they had decided against her they would not have wasted words about it. They would have said so at once and got it over ... in any case four big Executives weren't needed to tell him that.

The conversation about the roses tailed off: there was a lull, and Mr. Garner turned his eyes toward the window. The routine of the great Studio went on outside. From a big stage opposite some men were carrying the sections of a log cabin and loading it on a lorry: down the street a wind machine was humming on a truck—pumping air through a fat canvas tube into a studio that needed a breeze to blow through the hair of a star or flutter the curtains of a window. Over it all the clear hot sun beat down.

Then Mr. Garner brought his eyes back from the window. "I'm afraid I've got some bad news for you," he said.

He picked up a pencil and began to roll it between his fingers. "I was at the preview last night. We had a long talk afterwards—and another this morning—and we're all agreed about what I've got to say. Your daughter's a charming girl, Mr. Matthews. She's worked hard, and there's nothing we'd have liked more than to see her a success. But she just doesn't get across: she doesn't register with the audience. You've got a right to ask us why we didn't find that out before we engaged her and brought her out here and raised her hopes. The answer is we didn't know—nobody ever knows for certain—until the picture's made and put on the screen before an audience. There's a thing we call 'screen personality" for want of a better name. It's a mystery and I guess it always will be. Sometimes the most unlikely people have it—more often the most likely ones haven't. I'm sorry, Mr. Matthews. I know it's a disappointment for you and Mrs. Matthews and a cruel one for your daughter, but it's best to tell you straight out instead of beating around the bush."

Mr. Matthews listened with a heavy heart. His first impulse was to protest and argue the unfairness of judging his daughter on her first attempt, but when he looked round at the four experienced men whose judgment was unanimous, he knew that protests would be futile. He was shocked, but not very much surprised. In his heart he had known all along, as Ruth had known, that nothing short of a miracle could have made of Rosemary a screen star. . . .

There was a silence. The thing seemed over and he got up to go.

"I'm sorry," he said. "I'm afraid it's going to be a sad disappointment to my daughter, but I'm grateful to you for being frank about it—and for the kindness and generosity you've given us over here. There's only one thing I would ask you—and that's to see my daughter and explain it to her yourselves . . . breaking it as gently as you can. She would understand and accept it so much better if it came from you."

"Sure," said Mr. Garner. "Danny Bernstein will see her right away." He pressed a lever on his desk and said to his secretary—"Send a car for Miss Matthews and have her taken to Mr. Bernstein's office."

"Thank you," said Mr. Matthews. "My wife and I had arranged to start back for England to-morrow, and Rosemary was to stay in Hollywood with friends. I think—in the circumstances we'll . . ."

"Just a minute," broke in Mr. Garner—"won't you sit down?" He began to rub the pencil between his fingers again. He put it down and lit a cigar, and said: "What did you think about your own performance at the preview last night?"

It seemed a silly, tactless thing to ask at such a moment. Garner must have known that what he had just said would completely disorganise the Vicar's plans and leave a lot of urgent things to re-arrange about the journey home. He declined the offer to sit down again. "I did my best," he said as politely as he could. "You know I only took the part for special reasons. I'm not expert enough to give any opinion on it."

Mr. Garner was silent for a while. He studied the glowing end of his cigar.

"D'you realise you made a great personal success?" he said.

Mr. Matthews laughed. "I think it was pure chance they saw me there in the lobby," he replied. "I understand that kind of thing often happens after a preview."

"I don't mean that," said Mr. Garner. "I mean your reception on the screen. There was a mixed audience there last night—all kinds from millionaires to college girls and milk roundsmen. You got away with it with the whole lot of them. You rang the bell. You registered . . . did you know that?"

"If I did, then I'm glad," replied the Vicar, who had a feeling that these crude and clumsy compliments were a sop for the bad news about his daughter. He appreciated the thought behind it, but he didn't want it. He wanted to get home. "You paid me generously for the small part I took," he added. "I could only return it by doing my best."

Mr. Garner leant back in his chair. "I told you about "screen personality" just now," he said. "I told you that sometimes the people you least expected had it. There's no offence to you when I say I wouldn't have picked you out of a thousand, Mr. Matthews—but there it is: you've got it. You've got something people like, and you're a lucky man. We're just starting a picture based on the best-selling novel *City of Spires*. It would appeal to you because it's about Oxford—and there's a fine part in it that'll appeal to you, too. It's Robert Drake . . . Chaplain of a College. You're cut out for that part and we want you to play it. It's a big picture and it'll be worth your while. We've written $15,000 against the part: that's nearly £4000 in your money. It calls for two months' work and we want you to begin at once—in ten days' time."

Chapter Thirty One

Danny Bernstein the Studio Manager took Rosemary to lunch in the Studio restaurant and broke the sad news very gently to her. Youth and inexperience, he said, were the only things against her, and everything would come right in time.

He told her to go back to England and forget all about being a screen star till she was twenty-one. "Go to college," he said—"study art: learn to dance and sing and ride and swim: travel round a bit with the money you've earned and see the world. Then, in three years maybe, think about the screen again, and you'll be all the better for what you've seen and learnt."

He sent her home much happier than her parents had expected, but as the day wore on, and the charm of Danny's honeyed words wore off, poor Rosemary had glimpsed the cruel truth behind them. She was not to star in the "Children's Crusade": nobody would call for her and drive her to the Studio to-morrow: no more John Coburn and no more Norman Walter: no more thrills and no more glamour. She had broken down in a flood of hopeless tears, refused her dinner and said she wanted to die.

Mr. Matthews scarcely had a chance all day to talk to Ruth about what had happened to him in Mr. Garner's office. To discuss it in front of Rosemary was impossible, and he waited until he was alone with Ruth at dinner.

"You remember the night when those two men came to the Vicarage," he said, "and it all began to happen?—We agreed then that if Rosemary failed it would be our duty to do everything we could to help her to forget the cruel disappointment of it. The only way to do that is to take her right away from Hollywood—forget the place and help her to forget it. How can I possibly take this part and still be fair to Rosemary?—It would remind her every day of what she's lost—it would torture her and embitter her and make all our lives a misery."

"And yet," said Ruth "—£4000! . . . think what that would mean in Woodbank . . . think of the things you could do with it!"

"I know," he said—"I know. . . ."

"If I were you," suggested Ruth, "I'd go and see Mr. Garner in the morning. Tell him everything—exactly as you see it and feel it yourself. You say he's an understanding man with children of his own. He may have some suggestion that would help."

Knowing that Mr. Garner's time was worth about a shilling a second, the Vicar cut his story as short as possible next morning.

"There's the Bishop on the one hand," he said, "and my daughter on the other. The Bishop gave me four months' leave, but that was only to look after Rosemary in Hollywood. If I had asked leave to come and act in pictures I'm pretty certain he would have taken a different view. He *might* extend my leave, but I'm in his hands and would have to ask him."

"Sure," said Mr. Garner. "I see that."

"I'm sorry to waste your time on these personal things."

"That's okay," said Mr. Garner. "I want you in this picture and I'll fix it up for you. What sort of a guy *is* this Bishop?"

"He's a very nice man. He's broadminded and I know he doesn't object to pictures on any principle, but . . ."

"Okay," said Mr. Garner. "I'll cable our London office and tell 'em to see him for you and straighten it out."

"I think," said Mr. Matthews, "it's a thing I ought to do myself. I could explain certain matters that might influence him, and . . ."

"Okay," said Mr. Garner. "See him yourself. Fly home to-morrow. It'll take two days. Have a couple of days in London to fix up the Bishop and fly back on Friday. That'll have you back in a week and ready to start the picture comfortably in ten days' time."

"Even if he agreed," said Mr. Matthews, "there's still my daughter to consider."

"Sure," said Mr. Garner, "I've thought of that. I understand how you feel, and how she feels—and this is how we'll work it. We'll cable the London office telling them to make an appointment for you to see your Bishop some time Monday or Tuesday. As for Rosemary, you don't have to worry about a thing. You say she's interested in painting. You've heard of Monterey, no doubt—lovely place away up the coast of California. There's an artists' colony there and a fine teacher named Salvador. I'll fix up for your wife and daughter to go right up there the day you fly home. Salvador's a fine fellow. I guarantee Rosemary will like him and forget all about her Hollywood disappointment in a week. They can stay at the Del Monte Hotel—one of the best in the world . . . swimming, riding, painting . . . everything. If she *still* wants to act, then I promise you this, Mr. Matthews—I'll find her a part in some picture or other while you're working in 'City of Spires'. That's the last resource, mind you—because she's better out of pictures—but I want you to give a great performance, and you can't do that unless your own mind is at rest. So I give you my word, I'll see she's happy."

When the Vicar had gone Mr. Gamer touched a button on his desk that connected him with Pat Donnely—who dwelt in a room behind a door marked "PUBLIC RELATIONS".

"Fix up a suite at the Del Monte Hotel for this girl Matthews and her mother," said Mr. Garner, "and write to Salvador to give her painting lessons. See she gets everything. Give her the earth if she wants it. I'm leaving you to make her and the mother so happy they'll never want to go back to England again. And you might find out who the big shot is above this Bishop of his—the chap to go to if the Bishop gets tough and tries to stop him coming back. See what I mean?—I want that old guy and I'm going to have him."

Chapter Thirty Two

The Paragon Film people talked about flying to England as if it were of no more account than a team ride to the city. They called it "hopping on a plane", but Mr. Matthews said good-bye to Ruth at Burbank Air Field with little hope of ever seeing her again.

He had carried a dread of heights from childhood: to look over the cliffs of Dover made him sick and dizzy, and the prospect of flying miles high across deserts and mountains and lonely seas filled him with dismay.

All night he had dreamt of giant air liners crashing into mountain sides and plunging into shark-infested oceans, but to his surprise he found boredom more paramount than anxiety on the journey. Once the plane was in the air he lost all sense of height and the precarious thinness of the floor between his boot soles and disaster. He lost all sense of movement, for the plane appeared to be the only firmly established thing in the universe. It was the hub of the universe around which sun and moon and stars revolved, and the moon went chasing after the sun each night in its hurry to be up again in its proper place next evening. The world beneath became a cardboard panorama that swung about and dipped and rose as if it were controlled by strings beneath the plane. For the rest it was monotony, controlled with superb efficiency and interspersed with chicken sandwiches.

An official of Paragon Pictures met him at the London Airport and drove him to the Savoy Hotel, where a luxury suite and been reserved. Word had clearly come from Hollywood that he was now an important person with every attention to be lavished on him.

When he arrived at the Savoy there was a message to ring up Mr. Hamel the London Manager.

"I've been able to arrange for you to see the Bishop at eleven to-morrow morning," said Mr. Hamel. "Would you care to go to a theatre or show of any kind to-night?"

But Mr. Matthews was tired, and said he would rather spend the evening quietly. "Okay," said Mr. Hamel. "After you've seen the Bishop, come along and lunch with me at the Dorchester at one o'clock."

"Thank you," said Mr. Matthews—"and thanks for getting me such pleasant rooms."

He put on his slippers and lit his pipe and sat down by the window. He badly needed a quiet evening to think things out. He had not had time to think in a calm and lucid way for days.

It was pleasant to see the Thames again. A tug with a string of barges went by on the ebbing tide and he reckoned that in half an hour it would be going by his boat-house on the land at Woodbank. *His* boat-house! A week ago the ownership of that land and boat-house was all he wanted in the world, but now the wonder of it shrank to something almost commonplace in the light of his new success.

Mike Goody the agent had told him that when income tax was paid, he would still have a clear £3000 to do what he liked with.

A waiter came in with a tray of tea. He poured himself a cup and ate a sandwich and settled down to work out how he would spend the fortune. It was time Ruth had some reward: she had stinted herself enough in the past two years: he would give her £500 to spend in any way she liked—new clothes and theatres and a few nice things for her bedroom. Another £500 would buy a car for runs out in the country. The rest—£2000—would make his Boys' Club one of the best in London. He would enlarge it and have a gymnasium and electric light ... a new racing eight to row in at the Thames Regattas and a fine big Union Jack for the flagstaff. His problems, at first so unsurmountable, had resolved themselves miraculously in Tom Garner's hands. He was not over-anxious about the Bishop. It was only a matter of another two months' leave. If his deputy wanted to go they could find another one. The Bishop approved the Boys' Club and would hardly object to a further short period of leave when it would bring such a rich return for the Club's improvement. Above all, Rosemary would be all right. Tom Garner had promised it and Tom Garner could do anything. By now she would be in Monterey with Ruth—riding and swimming and beginning her painting lessons.

He jotted down a programme for the two brief days ahead of him in England—

Wednesday	11 o'clock	See Bishop.
	1 o'clock	Lunch at Dorchester with Hamel.
	afternoon	Woodbank: see Jupp about purchase of land.
		See deputy about staying on 2 months.
		See Mrs. Burgin and have look round.
		5 o'clock at boat-house for evening with boys.
Thursday	morning	Back in Woodbank if necessary.
	afternoon	Paragon Offices.
	evening	Free in London.
Friday	12 o'clock	Leave Savoy Hotel. Drive to Airport for plane back to Hollywood.

Hollywood!—how pleasant and exhilarating that name had become!

The sun was setting. He slipped the programme into his pocket and went for a stroll down the Strand and Pall Mall to St. James' Park. It was a lovely May evening and he found a quiet seat under the trees to admire the tulips and listen to the birds. The tulips were at their best, and he decided to have a fine big bed of them on his land at Wood-bank. He could buy 500 now and barely miss the £10 they would cost him. He thought of a day last autumn when he spent 5s. on a dozen and blamed himself for such extravagance. It was very pleasant to be free from those sordid, poverty-stricken days.

He walked back in the twilight and dined in a quiet corner of the grill room on a nice fried sole and a bottle of claret. He found a copy of *City of Spires* on the hotel bookstall and took it up to bed with him. He saw what a fine part Robert Drake the Chaplain was going to be for him to play. There was one splendid scene where the Chaplain saved a young man from disgrace. It was rather like the scene he nearly played with Pete when he had found Pete drunk outside the Vicarage, although Robert Drake did it much better than he could ever have done. He knew the words by heart before he went to sleep. It was a glorious part and he loved the thought of playing it.

Chapter Thirty Three

The Bishop stood with his back to the fireplace and Mr. Matthews sat in the arm-chair by the window. Everything was very much the same as when he had come for his first leave of absence, except that there had been snow in the garden on that occasion and now there were flowers.

Everything was the same, the Vicar kept on trying to assure himself, and yet from the moment he had entered the room he had felt a subtle difference in the atmosphere.

There was no question of the Bishop's friendliness and sympathy. He listened with interest: he asked questions about life in Hollywood and making pictures—and yet there was that indefinable something.

"If it were merely a question of acting in a film," said Mr. Matthews, "I would not give it a second thought. My work is in Woodbank and I'm not an actor."

"They seem to think you are!" said the Bishop with a laugh, but Mr. Matthews shook his head.

"It was a pure fluke," he said, "that I suited the part they gave me—and a fluke that this second part will possibly suit me, too. But flukes don't happen all the time. Directly I have finished 'City of Spire' I want to get back to my parish."

"Yes," said the Bishop—and he turned away and looked out of the window. That sudden turn and sudden silence reminded Mr. Matthews of something that disturbed him. It reminded him of Tom Garner turning his head to look out of his window just before he broke the news of Rosemary's failure . . .

The Bishop went over to his desk and picked up a letter.

"I want you to know, Matthews," he said, "that I support you entirely in all this. You've done good work for that club of yours. You deserve every penny you can get to develop it, and I see nothing wrong in you playing in a film when the part is obviously a dignified one. But there's a difficulty ..."

He glanced down at the letter. "It seems that you don't get on very well with the Church Council in Woodbank. I have something here ... I suppose one would call it a petition, because it's signed by the whole Council including the Churchwardens. It's a long rigmarole, but I'll read you a piece of it—

"It has come to our knowledge that The Reverend Roger Matthews has allowed himself to appear in a Hollywood Cinematograph Film.

In our view this is an undignified and degrading exhibition for a Priest and we cannot in the circumstances recognise him as a fit person to hold his present office at St. Peter's. It is our unanimous wish that Your Lordship should take the necessary steps to remove him from the office he now holds. The Reverend Walter Montagu, who has deputised during the above-mentioned's absence, has proved himself a sincere and devoted man. We understand that he is prepared to accept the living if it is offered to him, and we are united in expressing the hope that Your Lordship may see your way to making him the offer.

We feel sure that such a step would go far towards remedying the intolerable state of affairs now existing in the parish."

The Bishop dropped the letter on to his desk as if the smell of it had got into his nostrils.

"You see my difficulty?" he said. "I imagined that you would come back to your parish this week with Hollywood settled and done with. In that case I could have told these people that you took part in this picture to help your daughter, and I would have said that I entirely approved of what you did.

"But what can I say if you take another two months to make another picture?—this time without the reason of helping your daughter? I know this letter reeks of spite and prejudice, and I know a good deal about the people who concocted it, but unfortunately they represent a parish in my Diocese, and I have a duty to them as well as to you. I can even understand that a Church Council in no way prejudiced against their Vicar might have a reasonable and honest objection to him acting in the films—narrow-minded though I think it would be."

He looked out of the window again: he wandered up and down the room and straightened an almanack on the mantelpiece. He looked troubled and unhappy—and Mr. Matthews felt so sick with the shock of it that it hardly seemed worth while to say a word.

"Is there anything to be done, my lord?" he asked.

"The obvious thing," said the Bishop—"if these people were possible to argue with—would be for you to go and talk to them and make them realise that you're only doing it to help your club. . . ."

"They hate my club," said Mr. Matthews. "One of them at least would give everything she has to smash it. Unfortunately her word on this council is law and the others follow her like sheep."

"I rather gathered that," said the Bishop. "It makes it very difficult. It isn't easy to be a parish priest and a Hollywood film actor at the same time, is it?"

Chapter Thirty Four

Mr. Hamel, the London Manager of Paragon Pictures, was waiting at the Dorchester Hotel. He greeted the Vicar jovially and took him in to lunch.

He ordered sherry and suggested oysters: he even proposed champagne, but Mr. Matthews felt too miserable for anything more than a glass of lager.

"Well," said Mr. Hamel, raising his sherry—"here's to 'City of Spires' and your own success in it!—The Picture of the Year!—the Academy winner!—It's to be Tom Garner's own personal production, and that's the hall-mark. You're a lucky man, Mr. Matthews."

Mr. Matthews sipped his sherry and wondered how he could explain to his exuberant host that the whole thing had collapsed in dust. He couldn't face the long-winded argument that was certain to follow: he had almost decided to keep quiet about it during lunch' and explain the whole thing in a letter, when Mr. Hamel forced his hand.

"How was the old Bish?" he asked—"everything fine and dandy?"

"I'm afraid not," said Mr. Matthews. "I don't know how to tell you this . . . it's all so terribly disappointing."

Mr. Hamel listened incredulously to what had happened in the Bishop's study.

"But you aren't going to sit down under that!" he exclaimed.

"What else can I do?" said the dejected Vicar.

"You're not telling me you're going to give up the chance of a lifetime and throw a fortune down the drain because of a piddling little gang of nobodies in that church?"

"If it were simply on their account," said Mr. Matthews, "I

wouldn't . . . but there's something else. There's a Boys' Club down there that I started last year with one or two good youngsters. Woodbank's the kind of place that needs a Club like that. It was hard work getting it started, and I want to go on with it."

"But why shouldn't you?" asked Mr. Hamel.

"Because . . . if I go back to Hollywood to make another picture, these people will move heaven and earth to get me thrown out of my living."

Mr. Hamel stared. The whole thing seemed beyond him. Then he leaned across the table and laid his hand on the Vicar's arm and spoke to him slowly and distinctly, as though he were explaining something to a child.

"Look," he said. "Why can't you see what's happened to you? Tom Garner—Head of Paragon—has picked you out for a fine part in the biggest picture he's ever made. He's never done a thing like that before: he always sticks to established stars—but he's crazy about you. D'you suppose he would have gone to all this trouble if he wasn't? You're a new personality, and in Hollywood that's gold. Don't you see what it means? Millions of people all over the world will see you playing the chaplain in 'City of Spires'." You'll be world-famous . . . a made man . . . a famous star. All the producers in Hollywood will be scrambling to give you parts. You're sixty years old, they tell me. You've got at least ten good working years ahead. What do they pay you as Vicar of Woodbank?"

"£450 a year," said Mr. Matthews, and Mr. Hamel sat back and laughed.

"You'll make £450 a week in pictures!" he said—"well over £20,000 a year!—I'm not joking—I mean it!—They're bursting with money and they'll pay the earth for the men they want. When you've paid your living costs and taxes you'll have £10,000 a year. £10,000 a year for ten years is £100,000—and you're worrying your nut off about that £9 a week job in Woodbank!"

"But that would mean I would have to live in Hollywood."

"Naturally," said Mr. Hamel.

"But I couldn't go on being Vicar of Woodbank in that case. I would have to resign."

"But why in heaven's name be Vicar of Woodbank when you can make all that dough as an actor!"

"I've just told you," said Mr. Matthews. "Because of my Club down there. I like those boys and I think I've been able to help them. I want to go on helping them, and to do that I must be with them all the time."

"How many of them are there?"

"Six or eight at present ... but I'm hoping to get more."

"Look," said Mr. Hamel, trying to keep his patience. "Why don't you see this in the big way—like Baden-Powell did with his Boy Scouts?—Where would the Boy Scouts be to-day if Baden-Powell had been content to jog along with the first little gang of six or eight he started?—But he saw things big, and now there are thousands of Scouts all over the world!

"Don't you see what you could do with £100,000 for the kids in the London slums?—You could build twenty fine clubs in different parts of London and help *thousands* of boys all over the East End. Isn't that a bigger thing than just going on mucking about in Woodbank?"

Mr. Hamel was leaning forward, looking up into the Vicar's face with his piercing eyes, and Mr. Matthews turned his head away. He was tired: he did not know what to say. All these film executives had such bounding, overwhelming vitality: they thought and spoke so fast that they left you floundering along miles behind in a morass of uncertainty and bewilderment: they talked of boys' clubs in dozens as they "hopped on to planes" to fly the Atlantic ... and yet there was something in what Hamel said ... something that opened up wonderful, majestic possibilities that kindled the Vicar's imagination and thrilled him.

"If. .. if it *could* be done ..." he murmured.

"Why not?" demanded Mr. Hamel. "It *can* be done, and you know it!—We're not talking about ifs and buts—the things you *might* do if you found a gold mine. The gold mine's there—inside you, but you're the only man who can dig it up and use the gold to help those East End kids by thousands!"

Chapter Thirty Five

It was near three o'clock and the Dorchester dining-room was almost empty by the time the Vicar and Mr. Hamel got up to go.

Mr. Hamel had persuaded Mr. Matthews to change his mind and have a glass of champagne after all, but the champagne had only quickened his decision. From the moment the magnificent idea had been suggested to him, he had known that he would do it, and he knew that Ruth would be with him heart and soul. With her keen spirit of adventure he could almost hear her saying: "Of course you must do it, Roger. Of course it's a bigger thing to work for thousands than just for those few in Woodbank. It's a wonderful chance. You'd be mad to lose it—or even hesitate."

"I'll see the Bishop in the morning," he said to Mr. Hamel—"and tell him."

"Swell!" said Mr. Hamel.

"If I can delay my resignation until after 'City of Spires' is made, it'll be all the better. Then—if I'm a flop . . ."

"You won't be a flop," said Mr. Hamel. "I'm ready to lay a thousand to one against that right now!—Will you take it in fivers?"

Mr. Matthews laughed and said he wouldn't risk it, and Mr. Hamel laughed and slapped him on the back and took his arm and walked across the lounge with him.

"I'm going down to Woodbank now," said Mr. Matthews. "I'll walk up to Marble Arch and get a bus to Fenchurch Street." But Mr. Hamel laughed again and pushed him into a taxi. "Stars don't go about in buses!" he said. "A year from now you'll be recognised wherever you go, all over London—like Aubrey Smith and Ronnie

Colman. So you'd better get used to travelling in private right away!"

All the way to Woodbank he was thinking of the plans ahead. However much he earned in pictures: however many clubs he founded, he was resolved that the Woodbank Club, and the first boys who had rallied to him, would always be the nearest to his heart. He would make his headquarters in Woodbank: buy a house and work from there—or possibly build rooms over the old boat-house and live in them on his visits home.

It was strange how suddenly and completely Mrs. Bannister Paget had ceased to matter. If the new Vicar of St. Peter's was on his side, all to the good. If he wasn't, that also was of small account. He would be a free man on his own land: free to appoint whoever he chose to deputise in his absence. Three pictures a year, Mr. Hamel had said, would be the average: three at three months each would give ample time to work at home on all the things the money would allow him to do.

As the train approached Woodbank he set aside the plans of the future to concentrate on the business of the afternoon. He had to see Jupp the Estate Agent to settle about the land before he went down to the boat-house to give the boys the news that the place was now their own.

Woodbank High Street had the same old squalid look about it ... the same forlorn, uncared-for shops ... the same old rattling trams and ugly black lines overhead. He got the same old musty smell that used to haunt his nostrils on those endless, futile walks around his parish and he saw the same old line of nondescript topers propping up the walls outside the pubs—some swollen purple like ripe plums, some pale and wrinkled like dried peas. It was all as it used to be, but after four months of golden sunlight he seemed to see the town through a dusty shroud of gauze.

He caught Mr. Jupp on the point of going out to value some furniture for an auction. He was in a hurry, but the Vicar said their business would not take long. "I just want to pay over the

£500 for the land," he said. "I've got to go back to America, but you can go ahead with the Agreement and send it over to me."

Mr. Jupp stared. "But didn't you get my letter?" he asked.

"I got the acknowledgment of my cable," said Mr. Matthews. "I've had no letter since."

"But I wrote last week—by Air Mail!—It must have got there after you had left."

"Did you send the Agreement?"

"No," said Mr. Jupp. "I'm sorry you didn't get the letter because I'm afraid it's going to upset you quite a bit. The whole thing's off. You can't have the land. Old Miss Ponsonby died in April—nearly a month ago. She left the boat-house and the land to her nephew, John Hayes, and I'm afraid Mr. Hayes hasn't got any crackpot ideas about it. He gave me orders to find a buyer at its proper market value and I've sold it to the Claremont Wharf Company."

Mr. Matthews felt as if a thunderbolt had hit him.

"But why didn't you *tell* me!" he cried.

"I did—in my letter."

"What price is the Wharf paying?"

"£2500. It's worth every penny of that in the open market."

"Have the Agreements been signed?"

"They're just waiting for a Surveyor's report—that's all. Otherwise it's settled."

"At £2500?"

"That's the price."

"Then I'll pay you more!"

Mr. Jupp blinked. "You . . . what?" he said.

"I said I'll pay you more. I need that land. I can't go into the reasons now—but I *must* have it and I will!"

"But the price, Mr. Matthews!—it's far and away . . ."

"I will pay £3000," said the Vicar. "I will pay you £500 now and the balance in two months."

Mr. Jupp took up the telephone. He appeared to have forgotten about his other appointment, but he looked at the Vicar in grave doubt.

"You honestly mean this?—you've got the money?"

"I don't say a thing unless I mean it."

Mr. Jupp got through to John Hayes and told him what had happened. Mr. Hayes appeared to have a lot to say, and Mr. Jupp kept murmuring: "Yes—quite . . . yes, I see your point—absolutely." At last he hung the receiver up and turned to Mr. Matthews.

"Mr. Hayes agrees," he said. "He'll accept £3000—but he wants to feel that it's absolutely definite. The fact is the Claremont Wharf had another property in mind, further down the river. The moment we tell them they can't have the Woodbank land they'll swing round and buy the other. You see the point? We might not get another offer like theirs, you understand, and if . . . in the end . . . yours fell through . . . we'd be in the cart, good and proper."

"It won't fall through," retorted Mr. Matthews. "It's absolutely definite."

But Mr. Jupp sat there, fidgeting and suspicious.

"I'll write you my cheque for £500—payable at once. I'll write you another—dated in two months' time—for the balance."

The agent hesitated a fraction longer.

"Very well," he said—"a man in your position wouldn't write a cheque unless it could be met. Mr. Hayes left it to my discretion—and I'm sure I can trust you."

He unscrewed the top from a penny bottle of ink and the Vicar pulled out his cheque-book.

Chapter Thirty Six

Mr. Matthews walked out of the frowsy little office—angry at having to pay such a vastly increased price but devoutly thankful that he could now afford it. He thought how much worse it would have been if he had refused the part in "City of Spires" and come home with the bare £500, blissfully thinking the land was in his pocket. He had a feeling that he could get into trouble for writing a postdated cheque on money not yet earned, but desperate situations called for desperate measures. In a few days the Claremont Wharf would have got it: the last toe-hold of green land in Woodbank would have gone for ever, and his Club with it.

As he went down the High Street on his way to the boat-house he heard the flour mill hooter going. It was five o'clock. Pete and the others would soon be on their way for their usual Wednesday club night, and he hurried to get there first and give them a surprise. There had been no time to let them know he was coming and he guessed their astonishment when they saw him sitting calmly on the balcony.

Pete had not written for two months—but Pete was not a letter writer. He had mentioned in his one and only letter that new members were coming down, and Mr. Matthews was looking forward to seeing what they were like. As he turned down the road that led to the allotments he called in at the corner wine shop for a bottle of sherry to celebrate his fleeting visit. The boys had bought the last bottle with their own money on the night of their race against the Tigers and it was a good moment to return the compliment.

A glad sight met his eyes when the old boat-house came to view, for even at a distance he could see a bright spangle of golden heads in the grass around the trees. They were the daffodils that Ruth and he had planted in the autumn. Ruth would be glad to know they were in bloom. It was a feather in her cap, for he had argued that it was too late to plant daffodils in mid-November, and Ruth had said it wasn't. In garden matters Ruth wasn't often wrong.

When he came to the gate he noticed something that puzzled him. The grass was growing so strongly round it that he had to trample it down before the gate would open. The grass grew quickly in the spring, but not as thick as that in a week, or even a month. The gate had obviously not been used for a long time. He looked along the fence to see whether the boys, for some reason, had made another way in, but there was none.

He forced the gate open and went along the weed-grown path. The grass was growing up between the boat-house steps. The key was in the club-room lock, but when he opened the door there was a cold mustiness inside. The room was dusty and deserted: no rowing shorts or vests hung from the pegs above the lockers in the changing-room: the wash-basins and shower were dry and dirty, with dead leaves in them that had blown in through the window. A solitary, worn-out grey woollen sock lay on the floor, and it looked like something that had died.

He wandered round the silent, ghostly place, bewildered by it. He began to search for clues that might explain the mystery, and discovered a grubby half sheet of writing-paper under the table in the changing-room. There was a pin in it, and it had evidently fallen off the notice board. It was dated "Saturday, March 3rd"—two months ago, in Pete's handwriting, with a list of crews for tubbing practise. There were six names in all: Pete and Tony and Bill and Tom, with two new ones—Fred and Harry.

He found the Club Diary on the mantelpiece and sat down to examine it. The boys had been there every Saturday and Wednesday in the first month after he had gone, and things had clearly flourished. On February the 10th "Fred Gates and Billy Potter turned up and joined Club". On February 17th "Harry Douglas joined". On the 26th no less than nine boys were recorded as going for a training run and having supper, and on the 30th four pairs were out practising under Pete's direction.

Then came the final entry:

"Saturday 3rd March. Stormy, but three pairs out. Fred Gates coming on fine."

After that, nothing . . . like the log of the *Marie Celeste*. There was something uncanny and unreal about it—as if the boys had been wiped off the earth.

He stood by the window, looking out at the neglected weed-grown land, wondering what had happened, and what to do. The only thing he could think of was a quarrel of some kind between Pete and Tony. With Pete as Captain and Tony as Vice, a quarrel between those two would certainly disrupt the Club, and it troubled him that he only had one day to spare in Woodbank to put things right. To go back to Hollywood with the Club closed up would be disastrous. He would have to see Pete at once and find out what had happened. He locked up the bottle of sherry in the kitchen cupboard and set off for Harpers Mews, where Pete lived with his mother.

There was no answer when he rang the bell: the place looked empty and neglected. Pete had once said he was going to find better rooms for his mother to live in, and Mr. Matthews wondered how he could trace them if they had moved. Mrs. Burgin at the Vicarage might know, he thought, and he was about to leave when he saw a slight movement of the window curtains in the sitting-room, as if somebody were trying to see him without being seen. He rang again, and at last the door was opened, and Pete's mother stood there.

He remembered her as a nice, good-looking woman with a friendly smile, but the woman who stood there looked so pale and tired that he scarcely recognised her.

Nor did she recognise him at first: she stared at him in a frightened, defensive, hostile way.

"Good evening," he said. "It's Mr. Matthews. Don't you remember me?"

For a while she went on staring as if she could not believe it. Then her eyes lit up: she began to laugh—she gripped his hand, and then, to his dismay, she began to cry.

All kinds of horrid possibilities flashed through his mind: Pete was ill: he might have had an accident and was dead. It would explain his not writing, and the mystery of the Club, but when she took him into the twilit sitting-room he saw that tea was laid for two—and one of Pete's coats was hanging by the fire to dry.

She could not contain her joy at seeing him: she held his hand as if she dreaded he might escape, and went on laughing and smiling through her tears.

"I'm so glad," she said—"and so sorry I kept you standing out there! I saw it was a clergyman and thought it was that other man. They said you weren't ever coming back, and I couldn't believe it was you!"

He looked at her, astonished. "Who said I wasn't coming back?" he asked.

She didn't answer. She did not seem to care. All she cared about was that he was with her—in her home, and she was desperately anxious that he should stay.

"You'll have some tea, Mr. Matthews—won't you?—It's all ready ... the kettle's boiling ... it won't take a moment... take your coat off, please. .."

"I went down to the Club to see Pete," he said. "Is he well? ... will he be home to tea?"

"I don't think he'll be in now," she answered. "I always keep it for him ... but he won't be in now."

She made him sit down at the table. She brought a plate of hot scones from the fender, and made the tea and poured him some.

She came and sat opposite him at the table. He had never seen such a change in a woman: the pallor and the haggard lines were gone: her cheeks were flushed and her eyes were shining.

"It's wonderful," she said—"wonderful to see you home!—It's been a terrible time, Mr. Matthews . . . like a nightmare. But everything will come right again now. . . . I know it will!"

She told him the whole story since the evening he had left for America.

"Pete came back from the station after seeing you off," she said—"very proud about you leaving him in charge. Tony came back with him and they had tea together. They said you had told them to get some more boys for the Club and they sat here till supper time, going through the names of all the boys they knew, deciding which to ask. I remember that night so well. They were so keen about it they couldn't stop talking, and I went out and got some herrings and Tony stayed to supper and they went on talking by the fire till ten o'clock. They were going to try and get twenty boys to give you a surprise when you came back . . ."

Everything had gone splendidly, it seemed, for about a month. Pete and Tony worked like trojans. They got new boys and had training evenings twice a week instead of once. They planned to paint the boat-house and varnish all the lockers to give him an extra surprise on his return. "They just lived for the Club."

Then one Saturday afternoon in early March, Montagu the deputy Vicar had turned up at the boat-house.

"I don't want you to think too hardly of him," she said—" because I'm certain he wouldn't have done the things he did if he had been left alone. But that woman got after him . . . that woman in your church. She talked him into it . . . I know she did.

"He went down to the Club determined to make trouble. Pete had been taking the boys out rowing on Sunday afternoons because there was no light for rowing in the winter evenings, and Mr. Montagu said it was a disgrace to row on Sundays and they'd got to stop it. Pete argued, and said he was in charge, but Mr. Montagu said *he* was in charge because he was your deputy. Then there was the beer the boys took down to the Club on the evenings they had supper. It was only a few bottles and Pete only let them have a glass, but Mr. Montagu said it was against the law because they hadn't got a licence. Pete told him to get out and stop out—but he went on nagging and pinpricking until one day the boys threw a bucket of water over him. They shouldn't have done a thing like that to a clergyman, but honestly, Mr. Matthews—he asked for it and deserved it.

"I hoped he would say nothing about it because of the scandal. I hoped he would take the hint and keep away from the boys after that—but I'm certain it was that woman that made him go and report it to the police

"One night a sergeant came here to see Pete about it. They had a black mark against him for a silly, reckless thing he had done in the days before you met him, and they brought it all up again and threatened to have him in the courts for assaulting Mr. Montagu. And the sergeant talked about that old four-oared boat they use as well.

"He said it had been reported to him that it was not their property, and they must show proof it was theirs before they could use it any more. And he talked about them having beer down there without a licence. It was all so unfair and undeserved. Pete stuck to his guns as long as he could. He kept saying he would hang on till you came back—but somebody put it round that you weren't even coming back to Woodbank any more—because the Church Council had petitioned, or something, to have you removed.

I know that was a lie now—but Pete had nobody to advise him and naturally he believed it when the Church people were saying it themselves. I think that was the end of it. He came back one night with his rowing clothes and threw them in the cupboard and said: 'Good riddance to them'. He was just lost, and bewildered, and after supper that night he called for Tony and they went back to 'The Fighting Cocks'."

Joe Briggs, of course, had greeted them in triumph. That same night he had set Pete up against a broken-down old boxer and Pete had knocked him out and won £5. He had come home drunk and exultant, saying he wondered why he had wasted all that time fooling at the boat-house when he could pick up £5 in ten minutes.

"He was drinking again," she said—"And when Pete's like that you can't reason with him. Then one night Joe Briggs put him up to fight a great giant of a black man from the Tilbury Docks, and it was terrible. He came home with his lips cut to pieces and the old place on his forehead open again and his eyes all bruised and horrible. He said he had fought the black man for nearly an hour and only lost because of the blood in his eyes. But there was something worse that night. He was hurt inside—somewhere in his stomach, because he kept retching, and blood came up. I wanted to call the doctor but I think he was crazy with the pain, and he swore he'd walk out and never come back if I did. All night I heard him groaning and retching in his room, and there was nothing I could do but make him a little tea.

"But you know what Pete is. He was up and at work next morning, and although he couldn't eat properly he seemed to get better and started fighting again. He came home with the old wounds torn open and I prayed he wouldn't be hit in the stomach where he was so badly hurt."

But even Pete, with all his courage and endurance, went under in the end. One night there was rain and a cold east wind and Pete lay drunk, somewhere out on a piece of waste land near the station. He came home at dawn, and when his mother took him tea he was lying on his bed, drenched to the skin and delirious with fever. The doctor came and said it was pneumonia. They took him to hospital and he was there three weeks, very ill. He only came home, his mother said, a fortnight ago, but he was so pigheaded and defiant and ashamed of his illness that he went down to "The Fighting Cocks" that same night to show his friends he was strong enough to fight again. Even Joe Briggs, it seemed, realised that the boy was beyond fighting now, and made him a "steward" instead. A "steward" at "The Fighting Cocks" had to qualify each night by drinking off three pints of beer while the clock struck nine. If he brought it up within half an hour he lost his half-crown fee.

Pete's injured stomach had let him down. He drank the beer and lost it again within three minutes to the merriment of the assembled throng, but he tried again each night—and vowed, no matter what they said, he was going to fight again.

"Is he there now?" asked Mr. Matthews.

"Yes," she said. "He's down there now."

"Why didn't you write and tell me this?"

"How could I?" she replied. "How could I worry you when they said you had left Woodbank and weren't ever coming back? That's why I couldn't believe it when I saw you standing at the door. And that's why I behaved so silly ... laughing and crying like I did. You're the only man Pete's ever believed in, Mr. Matthews—the only one he respects—and the only one who can save him."

She looked up, and saw a hesitancy in his face that terrified her.

"It isn't true what they say?" she cried—"It isn't true!—You aren't going away any more, Mr. Matthews?"

"No," he said. "I'm not going away any more."

THE END

Lightning Source UK Ltd.
Milton Keynes UK
UKHW01f0033040718
325198UK00004B/102/P